T3-BHD-803

THE CHALLENGES

Living with Humility

Further Adventures of the Hollow Folks

Paul H. Jones

© 2007 Paul H. Jones

All rights reserved. No portion of this book may be reproduced, stored in a retrieval system, or transmitted in any form or by any means, electronic, mechanical, photocopying, recording, or otherwise without written permission of the author.

All scripture quotations, unless otherwise indicated, are taken from the HOLY BIBLE, NEW INTERNATIONAL VERSION®. NIV®. Copyright ©1973, 1978, 1984 by International Bible Society. Used by permission of Zondervan. All rights reserved.

Contact:
Paul H. Jones
1685 Oak Level Road
Bassett, Virginia 24055

phjones@sitestar.net

Printed in the United States of America by:
Video Publishing and Printing, Inc.
3102 Schadd Road
Knoxville, TN 37902

ISBN 10 digit: 0-89826-135-X
ISBN 13 digit: 978-0-89826-135-6

Acknowledgments

The quiet environment for writing that continued for my fifth novel was no accident either as my wife, Margaret, provided time and space in our country home free of interruptions. Also, she again doubled as an encourager and sounding board while doing the job of chief editor and proofreader.

My daughter, Bonnie, as always, provided my computer wherewithal as she formatted the manuscript for printing. Her involvement went beyond on site to lengthy telephone calls to remove electronic snags.

Certainly, further adventures about the Hollow folks would not have been written, if it were not for the special encouragement by many of you who read my four other novels: The Hollow, Life in the Shadows, The Missions, Living by Faith, The Hijacking, Living Beyond Fear *and* The Rescue, Living on the Edge. *Your kind words added much to my enthusiasm to complete this fifth novel.*

Jokingly, my comment to you has been, "If I'm going to write these books, it's your responsibility to read them." Thank you for being faithful readers.

About the Author

Born on September 20, 1933, in Henry County, Virginia, my youthful days were spent on Grassy Creek where home was a four room framed house nestled against a steep, wooded hill. The branch in front provided many experiences recounted over and over again during the later years.

School was very special at Spencer-Penn High School where I spent all my public school years with a dedicated, serious, caring and enthusiastic staff of teachers. Graduating in 1951, I entered Bluefield Junior College and later High Point College, receiving a Bachelor's Degree in business administration. A career in education began in 1955 with an outstanding large class of eager seventh grade students who provided enough successful days to plan a continuation of teaching. The assignment of principal came at age twenty-five, following a two-year stint in the military service. A career interrupted intermittently was enhanced by fulfilling requirements of a Master's Degree and later a Doctor of Education Degree in the early seventies from the University of Virginia.

We were genuinely blessed to have four children. Bonnie Annette was born in 1960, Mark Russell in 1962, Sidney Amos in 1963 and Paul Stanley in 1968.

Genuine excitement ran through my family of wife and four children in 1973 when I was appointed superintendent of schools in my home community. This was followed by nineteen years as chief school officer in school districts in Virginia and Kentucky.

During the past few years we have enjoyed our seven grandchildren who live in Danville and Richmond, Virginia, Minneapolis, Minnesota and Buford, Georgia. It has been a genuine joy to watch them grow and develop as the years pass. Margaret and I are just like all the other parents as we are so very proud of our children, and now as grandparents, we are genuinely blessed to have ***the opportunity*** *to watch their offspring as they develop.*

FOREWORD

As more and more people become acquainted with the Hollow folks in my first novel, The Hollow, Living in the Shadows, *they probe their own existence to determine whether or not their relationship with others could match that of these special folks. With meager wherewithal the Hollow folks continued to present their armor of humility in such a way that it seemed so easy, yet, when we try to emulate their behavioral characteristics, most of us fall considerably short of the standard displayed by them.*

Writing The Hollow, Life in the Shadows, *during my initial fleeting retirement years was truly an exciting adventure, and with the positive public response to my first novel, a second novel was printed.*

In my second book, The Missions, Living by Faith, *these same humble folks found themselves continuing to undertake a mercy mission activity much more difficult and complex than any of the other benevolent activities in which they were engaged in the past. With their selfless attitude they extraordinarily fulfilled a perilous mission in such a manner that it left all totally aghast.*

Also, a career missionary family emerges with a young daughter who delights soccer spectators in the jungle area of south Costa Rica, the home base of their mission activities. While following the Hollow parents and the exploits of this new mission family, the Hollow girls show the basketball world their playing ability on the college level.

Having served with my wife, Margaret, as International Service Corps volunteers in Costa Rica on two occasions for more than one and one-half years on two similar assignments and having completed a year of service in Mali in West Africa, I used these countries as settings for narrative generated in The Missions, Living by Faith. *The events by the characters in my novel in both countries were described in an environment in which I was familiar.*

Fulfilling all of the initial obligatory requirements stipulated when the first huge anonymous gift of money was received, the Bacon College president found himself faced with another similar challenge. This challenge was made even more difficult amidst the growing curiosity of the various media to discover the source of the benevolent money that so mysteriously was donated to the small college in southwest Virginia.

The Hijacking, Living Beyond Fear, *showcased the courage, wisdom and strength of the young Hollow college students, and the trials of their parents. Their obedience to follow the leadership of their coach without hesitation paid great dividends as they foiled a terrorist plot, thereby saving the aircraft occupants and their crew. Playing basketball took on an entirely different meaning on this morning in Roanoke, Virginia when three Mid-Easterners joined the team on a flight to the southwest.*

Having deep roots that were truly from the Hollow, they possessed an armor plate of protection from a secular world about which they knew but a little. Cohesive love was maintained all the while as they abundantly displayed the Hollow spirit in all aspects of their lives.

Loving their neighbor as they loved themselves again took on an entirely different meaning when the Hollow girls discovered that three missionaries had been captured, held and possibly tortured by a terrorist group. In my fourth novel, The Rescue, Living on the Edge, *they put themselves in harm's way to remove these young ladies from the grips of notorious terrorists bent on doing evil.*

A brilliant, young and very talented young man is introduced in my fifth book, The Challenges, Living with Humility. *His running prowess defies tradition. On the home front Bacon College is met with unusual jealousy such that their excellent record in basketball and soccer is challenged by the other competitors throughout the college community. Right trumps wrong in this episode, also, as they follow closely Jesus' two additional commandments found in Matthew 22:* [37] *Love the Lord your God with all your heart and with all your soul and with all your mind* [39] *And. . . Love your neighbor as yourself.*

INTRODUCTION

In the mountains of southwest Virginia snow was commonplace in the winter, and this one was no exception. On the snow covered slopes at the end of the Hollow one could see the men busily constructing an addition to the wood frame church which was long overdue. The congregation for services on Sunday morning had exceeded the limits of the original construction completed several years ago by Josh, the pastor, and Charlene, his wife, so to accommodate increased attendance, the men of the church were completing an addition. Merriment filled the air as one could hear hammers pounding and the planks from abandoned buildings being sawed and nailed on the sides. Matching the other part of the roof, metal strips were utilized to cover the structure. Songs rang out as happy workers joined to sing their favorite hymns with their special neighbors in this coal mining region of years ago.

The men and women of the Hollow had really worked hard on their mission trip to Wasi to distribute food supplies to the starving people in that West African country, such that they often thought of their many friends they had made there. While they had hoped that some day in the future they would be able to invite some of the Wasians to the Hollow for a visit, nothing had been done to this point to effect such a visit. But this still did not preclude their regularly including it in their conversation.

Excitement was always evident at this most special time of year when all of the families would gather for the celebration of the birth of Jesus with an ever growing group of friends. The additional space would provide room for their very large extended family to join them in the church as they joyfully met together for Christmas.

"Who all are going to be here this Christmas?" Tom asked Josh, as they nailed the last metal strip on the roof.

"You know, Tom," Josh said. "I don't really know for sure. I believe Bob Waters and his wife will come."

"They are very special people who have done so much for us in the Hollow," Tom noted. "The Hollow team bus he bought for us several years ago is still running well, and he never fails to deliver the food to us each week from his distribution company, Tiger Foods, and from another distributor. Many times Jim and his wife join us on other occasions."

A newcomer was present on this day to help on construction as the superintendent of schools had come, having been inspired by his own church to do local mission activities. Josh knew the superintendent was carrying a heavy burden, because he had resigned only a few days ago under severe pressure from the school board, parents and teachers, because the achievement scores of students were less than satisfactory. Josh was very impressed as to how he had voluntarily given up his excellent position of educational leadership, yielding to another to lead a reform movement. At another time soon Josh wanted to talk to him about his resignation, and especially his thoughts on how best to establish a wholesome and productive teaching-learning environment for children in school. Today was not the time, because the superintendent was totally engrossed in his work on the church.

"I want to remind you of our Christmas celebration on the twenty-fourth," Josh yelled to him, as he nailed another board to the side. "Please bring your wife."

"We wouldn't miss it for anything," he replied, as he continued to hammer the nail. "We have been talking about it for several days and wouldn't miss it for the world."

"Be sure to invite Mrs. Joy Brown and the elementary principal, Mrs. Sally Dunden, and the high school principal, Raymond Forrester, also" Josh requested. Mrs. Brown had really been helpful to Charlene and him when the two decided to teach the children in the Hollow. It reminded Josh of the cool reception they received at the elementary school when the children were made fun of, because they were from the Hollow and wore poor clothing. The derision had always been so terrible that no one from the Hollow had ever graduated from high school. Mrs. Brown was the supervisor from the county office over the little private school in the Hollow, and became good friends of Josh and Charlene.

Josh continued his thoughts about the Hollow's extended family, which included a special senior citizen, who was the maid of the Bacon College athletic dormitory where the girls' basketball team lived. Maudie Graves was someone very special to all of the girls and really had become their most special friend. Josh and Charlene had talked many times about her uniqueness and wondered how she wound up as the maid for the college. In fact, she was somewhat of a mystery woman, because little was known about her except what she was doing at present.

In a few days Josh was going to remind the girls to invite Dr. John Damond, the president of Bacon College, and his wife to join them this Christmas. He was such a brilliant leader dispensing his wisdom all the while on campus.

Although it was very cold in the area, their conversation as they worked tended to provide warmth for the entire group. Robert contrasted the climate in the Hollow with that in Wasi of West Africa where they spent several weeks distributing rice to the starving, drought stricken people, when he stated, "I wonder what Konatone, Tanko and Pierre would think of our weather here when compared to their hot climate all the year around. You know the president of Wasi insisted that we agree to invite a girls' team of basketball players to the Hollow for our girls to teach them how to play."

"Our Bacon College girls really impressed the president, such that he didn't want them to forget to permit the Wasian girls to come here to learn how to play," Josh responded.

"Did you hear Coach Anna say when she was going to invite the group to come to the Hollow to learn more about playing basketball?" James asked.

"She didn't indicate a specific date, but she was very committed about inviting them," Josh responded.

"Esther told me that Coach Anna had a meeting with the girls a few days ago to talk about Wasi," James related. "In the session with the entire team of girls, including the soccer players, she indicated that in a few days she was going to contact the president to begin to establish a suggested itinerary for the Wasian girls when they come here for basketball training. In their discussion it was decided that several young high school players from our country would join the Wasian group in a basketball camp here in the Hollow."

"That really sounds exciting, doesn't it?" Josh said.

"It really does," James responded. "Esther didn't talk too much about it, but she did say that Coach Anna was thinking about inviting twenty girls from that country for an extended visit, so if that's the case, they would have to come during the summer when the girls are out of college."

"We'll need to prepare for the group to come to the Hollow," Josh indicated. "It will be a special time for all of us here."

Meanwhile, the girls at Bacon were preparing to leave to play their final two games before Christmas in a four-team tournament in Hawaii. All the students were very excited about their team, especially their perfect record again this year, and the fact that they were atop every poll.

excited about their team, especially their perfect record again this year, and the fact that they were atop every poll.

The Powerful Talk

In a couple of days Josh attended the regular ministerial association meeting in the nearby town. Being a most special time for him each month, he always was elated to see his many counterparts in the area as they met to discuss timely contemporary issues affecting the lives of the people. Josh had always been faced with disparaging remarks from one or two of the other ministers every time they met, and this one was no exception.

"Did you get up early today to slop all the hogs in the Hollow?" one yelled across the room to Josh.

"Didn't you know that we killed all of them at Thanksgiving?" Josh replied quickly.

"Has the congregation in the Hollow bought you a new car yet?" another asked, as he looked out the window at Josh's old dilapidated van in the parking lot.

"Not yet," Josh responded, "because they know how much I have gotten attached to my current vehicle."

As Josh made his rounds speaking to everyone and shaking everybody's hand, he introduced himself to an older man he had not seen before.

"My name is Josh, and I am the pastor of the Hollow Church," Josh said. "I am Chester Gravely, a doctor in the area who has been invited to speak to your group today," he stated in a serious tone, which seemed to reveal that what he was planning to say to the group was going to be very important.

Josh completed his greetings and took a seat with the others as the leader announced the beginning of the session. Following prayer, he stated that he was turning the meeting over to the program chairman so that he could introduce the speaker for today.

"Gentlemen," the program chairman stated, "the program committee was delighted to get our speaker today to break away from his work to come to be with us and shed some light on a most important issue facing the Christian community today. As you all know, he has been a doctor in the adjoining community for nearly forty years and has delivered most of the children there. One of the things he will tell us will be a shock to our tranquil community."

Following a few preliminary remarks, Dr. Gravely stated the purpose of his presence on this day. "I am a devout Christian, having accepted Jesus Christ as my personal Savior when I was a teenager, and have tried to follow the precepts of His teaching ever since," he indicated. "I wish I could say that I have faithfully adhered to all of the guidelines set forth in the scriptures, but that would not be true.

"My reason for coming today is not to talk about myself but to advise you of a most devastating issue that plagues our world today. In one way or the other it affects all of us, and as Christians, it is our responsibility to alter the course of events surrounding this scourge on our common decency. The battle lines have been drawn between righteous behavior and secular conduct with our political culture carrying it along. What I am talking about is abortion.

"How on earth did we get to where we are regarding killing of our little babies, wherein one of our political parties embraces abortion with a rationale that it's a woman's choice to kill or not to kill her baby before it's born? Can you believe that? I have spent much time thinking about what would motivate one to believe that murdering one's child in the womb was acceptable behavior, and nothing I conjure up in my mind seems to explain such a rationale.

"If a new mother discards her new born child in a trash dump, she is legally bound to face the consequences, but a doctor dressed in a white jacket could have killed this same baby before actual birth, and it would be totally acceptable. What has gotten into our people?

"We all will suffer from our transgressions at the time of judgment, I know, but it seems that without some kind of deterrent, babies will continue to be slaughtered each year, because of the decisions of the warped minds of our legislative and judicial bodies made up almost entirely of lawyers. It doesn't take a rocket scientist to understand that an abortion is murder. And I might add, murder of the worst kind.

"But I have thought this for years, yet the practice continues unabated as women young and old kill their defenseless little babies day after day in our most blessed country on the planet. We all think of this as a problem in the metropolitan areas and other parts of our country, but we are just fooling ourselves to harbor those thoughts. Plans have been developed and construction is underway for an abortion clinic right here in our back yard so you see the grievous error of our society is now permeating our own serene community that we love so dearly. I am sure that the propinquity of this most abominable edifice in our area will send a message to our people that our culture has given a green light to aborting children, thus passing on a seal of approval.

"What do you think? I know I am talking to the spiritual leaders of the area, but even you need to revisit this horrid subject from time to time to remind you just how far our society has thwarted following the commandments that God set forth many years ago. Those same guidelines were effective years ago, and in today's modern world they should have the same impact. The target of holiness does not move.

"Let me further get your attention by refreshing your memory about data and statistics regarding the abortion controversy. We are always concerned about casualties when we are involved in a war as we should be, so let me give you approximate numbers from some of our conflicts: Revolutionary War, 4,500; Civil War, 500,000; World War I, 115,000; World War II, 400,000; Korean War, 25,000; and the Vietnam War, 58,000.

Regarding abortions, it is believed that there have been as many as 40,000,000 since 1973 with almost all being for the purpose of birth control. Does this cause us just a little to be concerned?

"There are all kinds of reasons given for aborting a child, but the bottom line is that it is murder, no more and no less. A bumper sticker I saw the other day sums up my belief very well: 'My mother did not abort.' Your mother could have just as easily aborted you as so many others have done with more than 25,000 in Virginia each year. Now to add to statistics of our country, we are going to have our own personal abortion clinic right here in our own neighborhood so transportation to and from will not be a hindrance. Just the fact that abortions can now be blatantly done right here in our own neighborhood is very offensive to me.

"The information that I have just provided to you pales in comparison to the details of partial birth abortion. It's horrible!

"The most appalling of the whole situation is that many of our church people either support abortion concepts or just acquiesce and do nothing to prevent these babies to be killed each day. How can we call ourselves Christians, if we subscribe to such a primitive notion of birth control?"

For nearly an hour the local doctor continued his compassionate and informative talk to the very attentive ministers. Facts and descriptions he conveyed would be long remembered by the group and would generate many messages at the worship services of the various churches in the area.

Of course, Josh was overwhelmed with all he had heard, such that he wondered to himself about the surrogate decision makers of the unborn children who were aborted each year. The numbers were so astounding that he couldn't get them out of his mind, so as usual, he decided to visit his good friend, Bob Waters, at Tiger Foods.

Bob seemed to be in a pensive mood as Josh was invited into his office by his efficient secretary. Turning around in his executive chair, he immediately greeted Josh and asked, "What brings you here to Tiger Foods today?"

"As you know, when I am concerned about something, many times I come to talk to you about it," Josh replied.

"Well, what do you have on your mind for this visit?" Bob said with a warm smile.

"I am burdened by something this morning that has plagued me for years, and it was reinforced in my mind at our ministerial meeting earlier," Josh responded, as he leaned toward the desk. "At our meeting today a local doctor made a talk about abortions, giving us many statistics regarding that atrocious act. Even though I knew that there were countless numbers of unborn children aborted each year, it seems today's data and statistics somehow put meaning to the numbers he divulged. I am just appalled that our country has stooped to this depth as a leader of the world community."

"During the last several months, I have worked hard politically to change our stance on abortions," Bob hastily replied, as though he was waiting for someone to discuss the issues of abortion with him. "I have never been very political about anything until recently, when I realized that not only did we need to pray for our leadership in government, we must not just sit on our hands and permit things to happen that we truly oppose, either."

"I felt somewhat the same way this morning as Dr. Gravely spoke to us," Josh stated.

"When you came into my office just now, I was thinking about a meeting that has been scheduled in Richmond in a few days for a group of Christian businessmen around the state who are concerned about the direction we are going in the name of progress," Bob indicated with a more serious tone than was usually detected. "This is an initial meeting to brainstorm about many issues, and one of them is abortion. As I have more carefully pondered abortion, I realize that many people believe as I do but seem to repress their thoughts not daring to let our liberal media know. Obviously, it makes it very difficult for us to get our conservative message to the public except in what appears to be a negative manner."

"I am glad you are working on a solution," Josh said.

"I wouldn't call it a plan for an immediate solution to abortion, but it does give members of the group a way to express themselves in a positive forum," Bob stated. "Why don't you come with me to the meeting?"

"I would be much out of place," Josh said. "You will do an outstanding job representing our area, because you are so highly respected by those near and far."

Josh always enjoyed visiting Bob at Tiger Foods, and today was no exception. They were such good friends, and Bob had done so much for the Hollow folks, including buying them a bus, and delivering surplus items from Tiger Foods and another food distributor in the area and much more.

Josh left Tiger Foods with a heavy heart, but just talking to Bob had eased his mind somewhat, because he knew that Bob had much influence in the region and in the state. The fact that he was meeting with other citizens later to discuss the issues facing the people of the Commonwealth was very satisfying to Josh. "It's very interesting that on the day the talk on abortion is delivered to the ministers, Bob advises me of his being actively involved in attempting to change our laws," Josh thought, as he turned into the

Hollow. Upon arrival at his house, he told Charlene all about the talk and the meeting with Bob, indicating that soon he was going to present a message to the Hollow congregation about abortion.

Paul H. Jones

DISCOVERIES

Marsha was really elated not only because of the trip to Hawaii, but, also, the fact that her mom now was able to walk without any support, thanks to a special cure made possible by the benevolent person. In their small community in northwest New Mexico neighbors had donated enough money for Marsha's parents and the parents of Lota Minota, and Vanona Massat, also, from the same neighborhood who had accepted scholarships to play soccer at Bacon College, to make periodic telephone calls to their children. Now that her parents were much better, Coach Anna could see Marsha react as though her heart was overflowing with joy.

The telephone call Mit received provided elation on the one hand and some concern on the other. Neither did Mit nor her friends know that in the jungle of south Costa Rica in Central America where Dan and Pat, Mit's parents, were assigned as missionaries, the Traverses were faced with a very difficult decision. Only recently they had been approached by the regional director who presented an unusual request. "Dan and Pat," he said, "you have done an extremely commendable job here in the entire jungle area, and everyone wants to emulate your endeavor here."

"We just try to present God's word one day at a time among these wonderful friends," Dan said. "To tell you the truth, the real leader for us here in spreading the salvation message of Jesus was Mit, as she used her skill God gave her in soccer to win the people to Christ."

"I know you miss her very much," the director said. "You know, I watch her participate in basketball with the

Bacon College team, and she displays excellent prowess in basketball, also. To play with the Bacon team, you have to be very skillful, and Mit really is a good addition to the team."

"They start soccer in the near futurc," Pat stated, "and Mit tells us that the basketball players are joining her on the team. She is so excited to be able to play with them in soccer, too."

"According to the news earlier, Mit participated in the dangerous mission to rescue the three missionaries who had been captured in Abedistan," the director indicated. "Our Missionary Magazine is going to follow-up on this news and do a complete story about Mit's participation in the jungle mission program, her attendance at Bacon College and her involvement in the rescue of the three female missionaries. It is my understanding that all of our missionaries can't wait until the story is printed in our magazine so that they will be able to read it."

"We have talked to Mit about the rescue several times on the telephone, and we both cry when she tells of her experience and especially when her parachute failed to deploy, while they were parachuting into the country," Pat related. "She was shot in the leg by the terrorists but recovered excellently."

"They were really brave to have undertaken such a mission in the first place," the director pointed out.

"Mit tells us that their coach, Anna Bosley, is an extremely special human being who loves her team members very much and is a very devout Christian," Pat stated. "She has an unusual arsenal of wherewithal in ability that only a few understand, and when the need arises, she utilizes wisdom beyond her years to effect solutions to difficult problems. Dan and I can't believe how God has intervened to provide such a wonderful higher educational environment for Mit."

"I could talk to you all day about Mit," the director said, "but now I want to talk about you all. As I indicated, you all have done such an outstanding job here with the people such that hundreds have accepted Jesus Christ and are faithfully following His precepts. That being said, I want to turn our attention to another part of the world wherein God's message has not been accepted by the native people. In east Africa there is a vast land made up of various tribal people who align themselves to several different kinds of religion. Christianity is extremely limited, because it has been so difficult for our mission personnel who are assigned to that area, because they quickly succumb to the unfavorable environment. Not a single missionary has remained on task in the area to establish a beachhead of Christianity such that a movement of any kind can take hold.

"Year after year we face the same problem of replacement, only to have to replicate our actions a few months later. Our officials have been searching for an answer to this serious problem, but until recently didn't know how to resolve it. In our last meeting at the main office in Richmond, Virginia, we settled on a plan that would be a genuine solution to our problem. Specifically, they want you and Pat to transfer to east Africa and begin a ministry similar to that which you so expertly have done here in the jungle area."

"This is really a shock," Dan responded, while holding Pat's hand. "We have thought all along that we would continue to minister here until we get too old to do a satisfactory job."

"The Mission Board understands your feelings well, and wants to reward you all for your sacrifice here in this area, where other missionaries would not dare to tread," the director related.

"We have so many dreams for this area including the return of Mit to help us here after she graduates from college and the seminary," Dan pointed out.

"If you move to the new setting, the Mission Board will provide two opportunities each year for Mit to come to visit you, and one round trip per year for you all to visit her at Bacon College," the director cited, now adding enticements to this very dedicated pair of missionaries. "Your program here will be continued by a new family graduating from the Language Study School in a few days, and guess what, they have two female soccer players. They are not as good as Mit, but I am told that what they lack in skill they make up in desire."

"That is really good news," Dan said. "This will go a long way in establishing them here, because the chief of this village calls the soccer players his team."

Their conversation continued into the night and resumed the next morning around the open fire in front of their bamboo house. Late in the morning after much discussion, the director asked, "Would you two agree to accept a new assignment in east Africa, starting almost immediately?"

"We prayed hard about this last night and this morning early, and the two of us believe it's in God's will for us to accept this challenging new role, but always hoping we can return again to be with these special people here," Dan said.

"The Mission Board is so grateful to you both for accepting this new role," the director stated. "I'll begin to work through on the details immediately. You will be going to Richmond, Virginia for an orientation program, but before you do that I will see that you all go by Bacon College to stay a few days with Mit."

The telephone call to Mit came as a shock that her parents were going to leave the Corbri village to assume an assignment in east Africa, but the decision was softened somewhat when her mother told her that they would be visiting her at Bacon College for a few days. All of the basketball and soccer team members were really excited for

Mit, because they loved her so much and knew how much she missed her parents.

HAWAII

There was much ado around the campus as the girls prepared to leave for Hawaii to participate in a tournament that had been reserved for the best teams for the last two decades. Bacon College had been invited, and the girls were very excited about going to the beautiful state in the Pacific. What a thrill for them!

The merriment on the van included the singing of numerous Christmas carols as they headed east toward Roanoke to catch their plane to California and then on to Hawaii. Mit and Marsha took turns telling their stories to the group with both revealing their emotion by the tears that welled up in their eyes. "Ever since I can remember my mother has been bedridden," Marsha said, "but now for the first time she is mobile and can maneuver by herself. It's truly a miracle!"

Mit told the others that her mom and dad would be visiting the Bacon campus shortly on their way to a new assignment in east Africa where they will continue their mission work with the people there. "I am so excited that they are going to visit on the one hand," she said, "but I grieve with them as they prepare to leave Corbri where they have lived with the wonderful native people for nearly ten years. The jungle has been their home so to move I know will be really traumatic for them. They are being asked to conduct the same kind of ministry in their new setting as they did in Costa Rica."

The other girls had many questions for both of them, as they flew through the "spacious skies" and over the "purple mountains" they could see as they looked out the window on this clear day on God's good earth. It was a loving scene as the two newcomers to the team this year were sharing with the group.

Following this lengthy period of sharing, Coach Anna advised the group that she had something that she wanted to share with the girls. "I know you all remember President Kantitore of Wasi who invited the Hollow families for the visit to his country last summer," Coach Anna said to them, as they leaned over their seats and as she unfolded a lengthy letter that appeared to be official. "Yesterday, I received a letter from the president wanting to know whether or not the invitation for the Wasian girls was still open so they could come to learn more about basketball. Let me read the letter to you."

Dear Coach Bosley:

The memories of your visit last summer are vivid in the minds of all of us who had an opportunity to meet you and your excellent basketball players. Best regards are extended to the entire group, especially the parents of the girls who did that brave and glorious humanitarian act in providing food for our starving people under extremely adverse conditions.

Since your visit, which included those excellent basketball demonstrations for our young people, much interest has been generated to elevate the participation in basketball in our country. It seems now that all of our girls want to play.

All of them remember that you invited them to come to your country for basketball training and have been asking about it in recent days. All of us do hope that you would be able to teach them some of the skills you all do so well.

Your Wasian ambassador and I met a few days ago to begin planning for a trip for our girls to be with you. At this time it is agreed that we shall select twenty girls to be on our national team so at this juncture we want to send the whole group, if you can handle that many. As you indicated, this will take place in early June through the whole month.

By the way I have another proposition to present to you later about our girls' basketball. I'll let you know later through further correspondence.

Thank you again for the invitation. I await your reply.

Sincerely,

Madu Kantitore
President, Republic of Wasi

"Can you believe you got a letter from the president?" Dorothy said very excitedly. "I didn't think he was serious about the Wasian girls coming here to learn basketball, bur apparently he was, as the letter indicates."

"Look at the presidential seal at the bottom of the letter and the embossed gold letterhead that really looks impressive," Diane noted.

"You know, when he mentioned that he wanted us to work with the Wasian girls on their basketball skills, I didn't think that he would remember it either," Coach Anna said, "but he has and apparently has developed some plans already."

"When will they be coming, and how will we handle the program when they come?" Tonisha asked.

"We'll need to talk about that later," Coach Anna replied.

Looking down from overhead, the girls could see the beauty of this gorgeous state as the aircraft descended to land. They always wore the same on road trips, the blue and gold warm-up suit including the monogram jacket. As they entered the terminal, two classes of school children converged on them, having used one of their field trips to see the basketball team as they arrived for this most popular tournament. To accommodate the large group of young people, the team just sat down in the middle of the floor to sign numerous autographs and posed for dozens of pictures with the students and their teachers. Coach Anna just joined in with the others, too, as she sat among the charming young people who provided such a special welcome.

Arriving at their hotel later in the afternoon, they had a brief rest before their scheduled time for practice in the large basketball arena. Several hundred basketball fans were on hand when the team entered for practice, utilizing the entire floor. As they were practicing, Coach Anna noticed that Esther seemed to be distracted somewhat such that she continued to look into the bleachers several rows up. Seated in that area was a pale, young fellow with a bald head, displaying a wide smile while waving an American flag and watching every movement of the team.

Stopping practice, Esther came over to where Coach Anna was standing and asked, "Who is that young fellow waving the flag so enthusiastically sitting up there?"

"I don't know," Coach Anna answered in a perplexed tone.

"For some reason I can't concentrate on our practice session, because I am just overcome by his animated gestures," Esther said to Coach Anna, as the other girls came nearby to hear the conversation.

"I'll go up to where he is sitting and ask his parents," Coach Anna stated.

Leaving the group of girls standing on the floor looking up toward the seat where the young fellow was sitting while still waving his flag, Coach Anna made her way to visit the mystery person. All the others in the coliseum, including the reporters, wondered what was taking place, because the Bacon team had stopped practice altogether. All eyes were focused on Coach Anna as she came near the young man.

"How are you all doing this afternoon?" Coach Anna asked, now standing beside the flag waving young man.

"We are fine," the young lady stated quickly. "Are you Coach Bosley?"

"I am," Coach Anna said. "and who are you?"

"My name is Patsy Liggon and this is my son, Casey," she said. "My son is ten years old and has kept up with the Bacon team faithfully all of last year and thus far this year on television. He watches every game and reads all about the team in magazines and the newspapers. Several pictures of the team are in his room on the wall."

"He seems very excited to be here today," Coach Anna said.

"He certainly is," Patsy said. "Three months ago he was diagnosed with a rare form of cancer, and he presently is being treated, leaving him with a bald head. He has not wanted to go anywhere outside the house, because of the way he looks until today when he wanted to come here to see his favorite team."

Patsy stood up and walked with Coach Anna to the side aisle away from Casey, and said, "He is a very sick child, and the doctors give him little hope of survival. He has talked very little since the start of his illness and didn't appear to have the will to live until today, coming here to be with your team. It's like a miracle to see him glowing with enthusiasm just like old times."

By this time tears rolled down Patsy's cheeks and soon Coach Anna joined her. "Would you mind if Casey would come down on the floor where we are practicing?" Coach Anna asked.

"Would you all let him be with the team?" she asked excitedly.

"That's what we want him to do," Coach Anna said, "and you may come also."

Holding onto his mother's hand on one side and that of Coach Anna's on the other, the pale and weak young man headed to the floor area, albeit ever so slowly and cautiously. Sports' reporters watched from several selected points, as now he was meeting his very special team. His smile could not have been wider as each of the girls hugged him more than once. Soon they continued their practice session as Casey and his mom sat on the sidelines watching all the while.

Practice was over too soon for Casey, but not before several reporters got much information from the family. Casey's dad was serving in the army reserves before being called to active duty and was currently stationed in Iraq as a tank commander on the front lines near Baghdad. Patsy explained, "Casey's dad and I are devout Christians and try to serve the Lord with all of our hearts. When Casey got sick, he had already been in Kuwait for several months and was advised that, because of family illness he could come home. He and I agreed that he should stay and help his unit win this war to give the people in Iraq some semblance of the freedom that we take for granted each day. I talk to him regularly on the telephone, and we both cry, but we believe that we are doing the best thing by his staying with his unit. An imbedded reporter knows our son's condition so he permits Casey's dad to use his electronic equipment to talk to us regularly.

"The doctors have advised that Casey will need a bone marrow transplant, and there is a match in the eastern area where there is a hospital specializing in that kind of procedure in upper New York. The expense of this medical treatment, including other attention, however, is prohibitive."

"Don't you have insurance?" Coach Anna asked.

"We do," she said, "but because he had a flare up several months ago our new policy did not cover what they have described as a preexisting disease. What Casey has now they say started several months ago."

"I am very sorry," Coach Anna stated.

"You know though," Patsy said, "his only wish was to see the Bacon team in person, and he is getting to do this today. He is the happiest child alive. His special wish has come true. For the first time in many, many days he is happy. It is as though his life is complete now."

The wide smile sported by Casey was accented by his very frail body that vividly displayed his weakness as he struggled with the debilitating cancer controlling his youthful body. The basketball autographed by the entire team boosted his will to live to a higher level, and when Coach Anna draped her warm-up jacket around his frail shoulders as a gift to their new special friend, he was overcome by crying simultaneously with the several others standing nearby. It was a very touching scene.

That evening in their hotel room they heard a startling news account of a sergeant of the l05th Tank Battalion who undertook a bold and dangerous rescue of three young Iraqi lads. While showing a video of the daring rescue, the imbedded reporter told the viewing audience, "For more than three hours now, we have remained in place outside this large city of Basra, south of Baghdad, watching as the Iraqi officials use human shields to protect themselves from the onslaught of the American fire power. This has been going on all the while, but only recently have they decided to use young children for this endeavor. As I speak, three young boys are being forced to stand beyond the burning oil that was placed in the trenches to impede the advance of our forces. Something is going to have to be done soon, because too much delay will cause considerable harm to the overall mission. Yet, the boys stand fearfully between our forces and the enemy.

"As the afternoon wore on I overheard a tank operator talking to his battalion commander about a rescue attempt of the children involved. I couldn't believe anyone would even consider such a daring move, but there they were talking about it. The tank operator said that he had a son about the age of the three boys, and he was really concerned about their welfare, knowing that if they didn't do something soon, the boys would either be killed by the enemy or by shelling as the American soldiers captured the city.

"As I watched, suddenly one of our tanks pulled out from its position and moved swiftly across the desert sand at top speed, without regard that there might be land mines along the way. Reaching the burning trenches, the tank dipped down in the fire and smoke, and all of us watching knew it was not going to make it through the obstacle. In what I thought was a long while, the tank emerged on the other side of the smoke headed directly toward the three young boys who seemed to be frightened to death. 'Would they run,' we thought, and if they did, we knew they would be killed.

"Huge billows of dust were generated by the tank as it sped even faster toward its destination as the enemy fired at will toward it. Our forces responded with a barrage of fire toward the enemy to attempt to protect the tank now proceeding on course to rescue the three young human shields. The tank was fully exposed as it sped straight ahead to the left of the boys, and then abruptly turned to the right directly toward them. Stopping behind the boys with the tank now acting as a shield, the sergeant jumped out of the tank and seized two of the lads and beckoned the third to follow as they scaled the side of the tank with the other members of the tank brigade watching and praying for their safety. Inside the Abram tank the sergeant revved up the engine and turned toward his group when a small missile struck the side of the vehicle with a glancing strike.

"This did not seem to slow the sergeant down with his special cargo as he soon was back in place in his brigade receiving plaudits from those all along the firing line.

"I want you all to meet our hero who pulled off this unique and dangerous mission. This is Sergeant Liggon," the imbedded reporter stated, as the two stood beside the tank that was used to rescue the three young men. "Would you tell us about the rescue of the lads?"

"First of all I want to say hello to my wife, Patsy, and my son, Casey, who is a very sick young man now," Sergeant Greg Liggon stated, as he looked directly toward the camera. "Casey, I want you to get well, and you know how much I miss you all. I am torn between being here fighting for the freedom of the Iraqi people and being at home with you. Remember how God has blessed us all.

"Regarding the rescue of the young boys about my son's age, I thought of them as being my children and realized that they needed assistance, or they would be killed. As I watched the boys standing there in fear, I could only think of my ailing son at home and wondered if my son were in the same position as these boys, would anyone come to his rescue? More and more I began to think that I was the person who should remove these handsome young men from a sure death. With approval from the battalion commander that is what I did."

The girls and Coach Anna couldn't believe what they were hearing, such that Coach Anna called Patsy Liggon to ask her whether or not she saw the news on television.

"I did see the news," Patsy said immediately. "Casey and I are still crying for joy after witnessing Greg's heroic feat. Casey got so very excited while the reporter was interviewing Greg."

"We are so happy that you got to see the television report," Coach Anna stated. "We want Casey to be our special assistant for tomorrow's game at two o'clock. We shall arrive at the coliseum at one o'clock so you all come any time after that."

"Casey is so excited that he won't sleep a wink tonight," Patsy said. "Thank you all so very much for being a special part of his life that has been so difficult during the last several days."

The tournament was a popular annual event so it was no surprise to see a big article on the front page of the local newspaper about the games. A large picture was displayed showing the Bacon team hovered around the bald headed young man, Casey. It was a touching human interest story.

> "A young man suffering from cancer had one special wish and that was to meet his most favorite team, the Bacon College girls' basketball team. Yesterday, that dream came true for the lad as he was on hand at the practice session of the team. Observing an American flag waving continuously, practice was temporarily halted as the coach went up into the seats to speak to the young mother and her son. It was love at first sight as the lad and his mother were invited to sit on the bench as the girls on the team hovered around. It was truly a sight to behold, a time to remember and an event to hold onto the remainder of your life as reciprocated love exuded in abundance from all participants.
>
> "An autographed basketball and a 'way-to-large' warm-up jacket given by the coach became the capstone for this meeting. It was a special day for this young man and his mother who are living now without the third member of their little family who is now a soldier fighting to free the Iraqi people. The young man's wish will continue to be fulfilled today when he will be honorary assistant coach on the bench when Bacon College meets Dorcas University in the first game of the tournament."

It was a well written article that covered a large portion of the front page and continued on another. Being an associated media article, it was carried in most of the newspapers throughout the country with two papers in Virginia carrying it on the sports' page.

By game time the overflow crowd of basketball fans was in place in the huge arena, the story of the seriously ill child had stirred the emotion of everybody. Shortly after one o'clock, the Bacon team came out of their locker room and headed to the floor area being led by Casey with his mother pushing him in a wheelchair. Having lost his hair because of the treatment he was receiving, everyone knew who he was as he looked around with his American flag waving from side to side. Tears of joy were running down the cheeks of both as Patsy pushed her son around the floor just ahead of the girls' team. Soon tears were commonplace as all were watching this wish of the sick young lad unfold before their eyes.

Spontaneously, someone began to play "God Bless America," as everyone joined to sing to celebrate the many blessings God had given so freely to all of those in attendance. After several minutes Esther and the others began their practice session, delighting those present with their astute ball handling and shooting. It was a good practice that was concluded with Casey being hoisted on the shoulders of Dorothy and Jennifer to make a basket.

Electricity of emotion filled the arena as the referee tossed the ball in the air that was tipped out of bounds. Without hesitation the head referee retrieved the ball and quickly headed to the Bacon bench to give the game ball to Casey. Everyone applauded for several minutes as the darling of the arena and the whole country was recognized for this special moment that he would remember the rest of his life.

With the score six to six Coach Anna inserted Mit, Maggie and Marsha to team up with Esther and Dorothy for an all-guard team to the surprise of everybody. The whole complexion of the game suddenly changed, as Dorcas couldn't get the ball down court, because of the fierce defense. Mit had really developed into a star player herself, now displaying before the basketball world her blazing speed on the court. Playing all of the girls before the half, Bacon had pushed ahead for a commanding lead that continued through the second half. Casey was the most excited of them all.

The team arrived early the next day to spend some more time with young Casey and his mom, but they were not present. "I wonder what happened to them," Coach Anna said to Hanna.

"Something must have happened, because he would not have wanted to miss this game," Hanna responded.

A solemn group of girls prepared for the game with E. G. Darden University, a perennially powerful team that had won its first game, also. When they arrived on the floor, several reporters came over to inquire about Casey. About half way through their practice, a young man came over with a portable telephone and told Coach Anna that someone wanted to speak to her.

"This is Coach Bosley," she said somewhat perplexed that someone would call at this time.

"This is Patsy Liggon, Casey's mother," she stated. "I am sorry to call you now when you are busy preparing for your big game, but I wanted to tell you about Casey. He had s seizure this morning and was admitted to the hospital where he now lies in a coma. His condition is serious."

"We all are so very sorry," Coach Anna responded. "We all love him very much."

"I know you all do," Patsy said. "His wish came true yesterday as he got to meet his favorite team, Bacon College, and as an added bonus he saw his dad on the news clip on television. Thank you all so very much for your special love."

Coach Anna immediately called the girls off the floor to the surprise of everyone. Advising them about little Casey's condition, they all held hands with several praying on behalf of their sick friend. It was a touching scene, as the girls seemed to be totally impervious to the surroundings as they prayed to God.

Following prayer, Coach Anna left her bench area to speak to a television commentator to get him to make a video of the game so they could give it to Patsy so that Casey could watch it later. The commentator was elated and assured Coach Anna that one would be available at the conclusion of the game.

With the girls playing with their usual intensity, the score was lopsided in favor of Bacon by half time. Following a brief respite in their locker room, the girls proceeded to the floor for loosening up exercises before the start of the second half, when the announcer got everyone's attention. "At yesterday's game we were all treated to a rare display of courage on the one hand, and a show of abundant love on the other as a young man had his wish come true. Our young Casey Liggon, who is suffering from cancer, got to meet his favorite team, Bacon College, and was the happiest young man one would ever want to see. With the game ball in yesterday's game, a ball autographed by the Bacon team and the special warm-up jacket from the team, his wish had really come true.

"Casey is not with us today, because he now is in the hospital in a coma with the prognosis of recovery not looking good until just now. We just received a telephone call from a medical center in New York advising all of us that money for a bone marrow transplant was now available to effect this procedure as soon as possible. An anonymous donor from the Bacon area called the hospital to advise of this huge gift of money. So now, our little Casey has a fighting chance to overcome this dreaded disease, thanks to someone special who is providing this wherewithal."

The huge crowd stood and applauded loudly for a very long time, and again spontaneously, they began to sing "God Bless America," that was carried via television to all parts of the country, including Bacon College, where several hundred people were on hand to see the game on the large television screen in the campus coliseum. It was an emotional time for everyone.

As the team walked on the floor to start the second half of the championship game, Esther thought, "Maudie never misses a chance to give to those who need financial help."

E. G. Darden University was a formidable opponent but couldn't match the powerful Bacon team. With all players participating from the small mountain college, the final score was seventy-eight to forty-three in favor of Bacon.

Early the next morning before flying home, the team went to the hospital to visit young Casey who just lay in a coma with his mother holding his hand. Coach Anna gave her the video of the game, and the two nets that they cut down from the goals.

"We want to pray for Casey so let's all hold hands around his bed," Coach Anna instructed. Each was asked to say a sentence prayer, as the tearful group encircled the bed of their special friend.

The prayers were so beautifully and eloquently stated as they surrounded Casey with their love on this morning in Hawaii. Following this special time, Patsy said to them, "Did you all hear that money has been given for Casey's bone marrow transplant?"

"We certainly did," Coach Anna replied excitedly.

"Not only that," Patsy continued, "I received a call this morning to indicate that they had a match for him. God is so wonderful!"

"May God continue to bless you, Casey and your husband who is fighting in a land far away so that we can pray and speak freely," Coach Anna said.

CHRISTMAS

The enlargement of the church was going to come in handy for this Christmas, because the list of those attending had swollen beyond one's imagination. Josh and Charlene were so delighted that so many were coming to celebrate the birth of Jesus with them in their church in the Hollow.

Joy and excitement extended throughout the Hollow as the orphan children couldn't wait to eat the refreshments that everyone had mentioned to them. Madu, the Abedistany young man, was the most excited of them all, because he was going to celebrate his first Christmas with his new Christian friends. He had really adjusted well since his arrival, having assisted in the rescue of the three missionaries from the terrorists in his own country. Because of this assistance and his being converted to Christianity by the missionaries, he fled the country and all the while helped the rescue team of Coach Anna and some of the Hollow girls to escape without harm.

In the modern orphan house three of the parents were helping the children make cookies for the festivities later in the day. They were not the best cookie makers, but they were surely the happiest of them all. Madu had not grown up with a "sweet tooth" but was acquiring one very fast. Much had been written in the newspaper about the activities of the children in the orphan home so everyone in the area was aware that the children without parents were progressing very nicely under the leadership of the Hollow folks.

All of the churches in the area participated in the angel tree program each year, and this one was no exception.

But something very unusual was taking place quietly in the community. When the orphanage burned in the community, many voiced their opinions publicly at two of the town meetings that they surely didn't want an orphan home in their neighborhood. Both meetings were almost like a mob scene with yelling and ugly, demeaning comments about the children, such that the Hollow folks agreed to care for the orphans. The receipt of a large sum of money followed that was donated by the benevolent person to build a home. The home was the only modern building in the entire Hollow, and all were very proud of it.

A few weeks ago a seven-year old lad was left homeless when his parents were killed in an automobile accident. A distant relative in the area was named as his temporary guardian, but because of illness, he knew that he was unable to care for the boy. "What can I do?" Ben Walker thought. After a while he realized that his only answer was to send him to the orphan home.

Speaking to his wife, Ben pointed out, "The orphan home would receive the young fellow with open arms, but I can't make the request, because of what I said at the town meeting when there was discussion about building an orphan home in the area. With the several others at the loud meeting, I shouted derogatory comments to our governmental leaders."

"You can't ask the orphanage to take him after having been so terrible at that meeting," his wife said in agreement. "No one at the meeting had one good thing to say about the children who are left to live without parents."

"Now that we need help ourselves, the whole idea of orphans takes on an entirely different meaning," Ben said. "As we talk now, I am embarrassed about the whole affair."

Ben wasn't the only one who was feeling guilty about the orphan situation, but he was the only one who was making an effort to apologize for his behavior. At the local governmental meeting Ben requested to be put on the agenda, and all the supervisors cringed when they saw his name, because they remembered all too well the meetings wherein he and so many others vociferously verbalized their negative opinions about the orphan children. The local reporters couldn't wait to hear Ben's comments.

"Mr. Walker, we are ready to hear from you at this time," the chairman stated.

Ben rose slowly while looking around at some of his earlier like-minded group seated in the audience. All eyes were focused on him as he stood behind the speaker's stand, placing a hand on each side with a more peaceful expression than the governmental officials had observed earlier. Ben began to speak.

"For several days now I have given much thought to my position regarding the orphanage question you all handled so masterfully. As you remember, I joined many others who spoke out against any kind of orphan home being constructed in our neighborhood, particularly near our homes. The emotions ran high at these two meetings, but you helped us all get through this dark time for everybody. My ugly comments, just like the others, are indelibly preserved in your minutes of the meeting.

"My reasons for being here for your meeting tonight are not because I find myself needing the services of an orphan home, but mainly because of what was said many days ago about all of us Christians. It seems that we all want to do Christian things as long as it doesn't really impact on our comfortable lives. The chairman of this group stated something to the effect that the orphan children were the same young people for whom we bought Christmas presents each year, getting their names off the angel tree in our churches in the area. Again this year the orphan children's names are hanging on our angel trees in our various churches so most of us will buy them a gift of some kind. But they are not good enough to live with us in our wonderful neighborhoods. We all told you that when you were trying to locate another site following the orphanage burning down.

"Not too long after our infamous meetings, I realized that I had made a bad choice by siding with the vocal community folks and not supporting the lovely young people who now had nothing. But it wasn't until Josh Morrow, the pastor of the Hollow Church, agreed to take the orphan children did I fully understand what Jesus spoke about hundreds of years ago about loving our neighbors. Without electricity, running water, indoor plumbing, or telephones, these good souls volunteered to take care of these homeless children, while the rest of us vehemently balked at any constructive action to assist the youngsters even with our ultimate comfort.

"With the money from the benevolent person a beautiful house with all the modern conveniences is now provided for the orphan children as they are cared for each day by the pastor and his flock. But wait! You see, these folks still live in two-room houses without any modern conveniences, yet these homeless children live in splendor measured by the Hollow standards.

"Our Bible is replete with guidelines for us to follow, but it seems that we have a different interpretation from that of the Hollow folks. Starting now, I'm going to pursue a route much different from the past. I ask for your forgiveness in my earlier debacle with you all, and trust that there will not be a recurrence or a relapse to revive my poor judgment during this period in my life. When I leave here today, I'm going to take my angel tree gift to the Hollow and thank those there for caring for our much less fortunate children whom we now call orphans."

The meeting chamber was very quiet as Ben made his way to where his wife was seated. Just as he sat down those in attendance stood and applauded, followed immediately by the board of supervisors. The touching scene was described by the media in different ways, but each expressed that possibly this was a start to heal the divisiveness in the community as a result of the tumultuous meetings earlier regarding the orphan question.

Ben received many telephone calls that day, and when the newspapers were distributed the next morning, he was swamped with many more calls. Because his behavior at the previous day's meeting was so different from his demeanor of the past gatherings, there was much discussion about the reversal of his position. Two of those people who had joined him in the two hostile meetings, called and wanted to talk to him further about his new thoughts about the orphan question. Inviting them to breakfast, they, too, expressed their heartfelt remorse for their demeaning comments and wanted to join with Ben to redeem themselves from their transgressions.

One could readily understand that there was not an avalanche of apologies being uttered by those who had so vehemently voiced their negative thoughts about the orphanage several weeks ago, but it was a start. Ben was taking the lead, and now with two more in his camp, he realized that more could be done for them to discover a greater peace in their hearts. Knowing that it would be impossible to eradicate what had transpired in the past, he was elated at the response of the people in the area.

"I feel like a new person," Ben said to his two companions now harboring the same expressions of joy, having made at least a start in removing what Ben had called a "thorn in his flesh."

"I have felt so guilty about what I said at the public meeting," one of the men stated. "Let's go out to the orphanage and talk to the young pastor there, and we might discover a special need for the group."

Although the three men had lived all their years in the area, neither had ever been in the Hollow. "I have heard about this place for several years, but I have never been here before," one of the men said as they drove carefully up the

Hollow, looking at the two-room houses constructed on the steep slopes.

"Do the people live in these houses?" the third man asked.

"I guess they do," Ben responded. "I have heard that all the houses are the same in the area except the orphan home which is a very modern building."

"I can't believe that the orphan children live in much better quarters than the folks who take care of them," the first man stated.

"It is my understanding that this is the way they live," Ben quickly replied. "They always put their neighbor first in all of their decisions, so for the orphan children, they want them to be comfortable first."

"I am really feeling terribly guilty every second as we continue up the hill," the second man indicated. "Although I haven't seen the orphans or people yet, I sense a deep spiritual feeling here, such that I have never experienced before."

"It is as though we are entering another world altogether," Ben said, as they crossed the narrow, precarious bridge where there was a greater incline in the road.

"Have you seen the Bacon College basketball team play?" the first man asked.

"I have been to all of their home games, and they are really good players," Ben responded. "They have won all of their games so far."

"Do they live in these houses?" the second man asked.

"I am told that they all live in the same kind of houses with no running water, indoor plumbing, electricity or telephones," Ben noted. "But in all of this that we would obviously judge as poverty, these people are rich in the spirit of our Lord. They live beyond treasures for themselves or the judgment of others about them, never responding to derogatory comments at all. The parents of the children were made fun of in school such that they failed to graduate, and the children were headed in the same direction, if it had not been for the young preacher and his wife who taught the children in the little church for several years."

"I remember the first time I knew the Hollow existed," the first man said. "There was this large newspaper article about the men who cleaned up a small town ravaged by a flood, and they did it free of charge for the people. And another time this same bunch became expert firefighters to extinguish a fire that was burning out of control over pristine hardwood timber."

"There have been such marvelous stories about these people that when one begins to relate them, it's difficult to cut them off," the second man indicated. "My favorite is the story about the lost child that was found after they searched for several days even after the sheriff had called off the hunt. They just seem to know when 'to hold and when to fold.'"

"When I heard that they had undertaken the job of distributing foodstuff to the starving people in Africa after the president of that country had strongly and repeatedly warned those outside the country not to interfere in their internal affairs, I knew they had overstepped their bounds of benevolence," Ben stated. "But look what happened. When they were discovered making these distributions of food, the president not only concurred, but had his military personnel to assist them. They have truly been part of many miracles."

"The president was so delighted over the leadership of the pastor, he invited them to return for a visit," the first man stated. "It is my understanding that the girls will be helping the Wasian girls train for the Olympics."

"Can you all believe that the best female basketball player in the country comes from the Hollow?" the second man exclaimed, as they observed the beautiful brick home to their left which they perceived to be the orphanage.

"What a lovely building!" Ben stated excitedly, as they parked near the entrance.

Getting out, they were greeted by Betty, Patsy and Nettie who were on duty on this day. Inside the house they were asked to sit in the commons area where the children congregated when not in their room.

"This is certainly a beautiful house for the children," Ben said.

"The children really like it here," Nettie said. "From the start they seemed to have fallen in love with the Hollow. When they have free time they run all over these hills exploring for all kinds of things."

"You all seem to enjoy your work here with these young people," Ben indicated.

"We surely do," Betty said, showing a wide smile on her face.

"Where are the children today?" Ben asked.

"They are at the church with Josh," Patsy stated. "They just dearly love to be with him so whenever they get a chance they go to his house which is near the church."

"Are they excited about Christmas?" Ben asked.

"This is their first Christmas in the Hollow," Betty said, "so this year we shall have a larger group. The men just constructed an addition to our church so it will accommodate a growing number who participate in our services."

"There is much interest in your program here," Ben stated. "You all seem to have a very serene community with all of you enjoying every minute together."

"That's true," Patsy quickly reacted. "The pastor and his wife are genuine spiritual leaders for all of us here, and they go about it in such an unassuming way."

"Obviously, there is much love here in the Hollow," Ben said.

"You really can't help showing love to one another around Josh," Betty responded. "He knows no other way to live."

"Is everybody at the church now?" Ben asked.

"Our children will be coming from college this afternoon to join us for Christmas in the church," Patsy stated. "Many others will come this evening as we celebrate the birth of our Lord together again this year."

Soon, bidding farewell, the trio of men headed farther up the narrow road to meet the pastor and the orphans at the small church.

Josh didn't recognize the men as they entered the church where all of the orphan children were seated on the floor at the conclusion of the morning Bible study. Taking a seat to the rear of the children, the men watched Josh as he interacted with the very obedient young people as they discussed the story of the birth of Jesus two thousand years ago.

"Why did God select the shepherds to advise of the coming of the Messiah?" Josh asked the attentive group.

An older young man raised his hand and after being recognized by Josh, answered, "I believe God wanted to use ordinary people to announce that His son was born in Bethlehem."

A young lady indicated, "God even today wants us all to tell others of His son who came on earth, later died and was resurrected from the dead and now lives with God in heaven."

After several more comments Josh praised the group for their intelligent answers to his questions and noted the schedule for their next meeting. Following a prayer by Josh, the children were dismissed to return to their home that they loved so very much.

After the children had departed Ben and his two companions introduced themselves to Josh, and asked to speak to him. Ben related the lengthy story about their misguided early thoughts about the orphans, and in truth they were on a mission of redemption not knowing what direction it was going to take. The simplest of their undertaking was to ask for forgiveness of the children and the Hollow folks, and then pursue farther reaching long term activities to provide for the orphan children.

"You know we have been angel tree participants for years, always selecting many years the names of several children to buy Christmas gifts," Ben stated. "While I believe in this program conducted by most churches in our area, it doesn't fully meet the Biblical description of loving our neighbor. We have seriously transgressed when we led a hostile group of people against the retention of the orphan home in its original community following the fire that destroyed everything. We come today bearing our shame for what we did and want to reveal our new beginning by not only expressing our forgiveness in words but follow-up with strong, long lasting and steadfast attempts to provide a better environment for the orphan children."

"You certainly have a wonderful story to tell," Josh responded. "There are many ways you all can help us with these delightful children. Almost anything you would suggest would be acceptable.

"I have been thinking about one thing that I thought might be of some assistance," Ben said. "Would it be possible to buy clothes for them from time to time during the year?"

"We always need clothing," Josh quickly responded. "They are really happy campers when they have something new to wear. As you probably don't know, we have twenty-one young people with us now, and three couples each day from the Hollow provide their meals and generally their full care, acting as their parents. The participation of our girls from Bacon College has elevated their joy and happiness to a much higher level. Even with everyone participating, you still should know that there is much room for additional services for the orphan children."

"As a starter, would it be possible for us to take the orphan children shopping on some kind of acceptable schedule making purchases of items that you all believe they could use?" Ben asked.

"That sounds like a wonderful idea," Josh said. "We can work out a plan for you all to follow."

"When could we have this plan?" Ben asked, wanting to get started as soon as possible.

"I will get James to develop a plan today, and it will be ready by this evening," Josh said. "By the way this is our special Christmas celebration, and you and your families are invited to come to eat and share in the celebration of the birth of our Lord and Savior Jesus Christ. Please come and join with us."

Without any reluctance Ben and his friends did not hesitate to accept the invitation rendered by Josh. The extended family of the Hollow folks was getting larger and larger as time passed.

The Celebration

The girls were so very excited when the black and gold bus pulled up on the campus following their final basketball practice until after the Christmas holiday period. Maudie and Hanna were joining the group of girls in the Hollow to celebrate Christmas. Coach Anna was delighted that the team had a perfect record in basketball, now ranked number one in the nation by all polls. Hanna's mom and dad were driving up from the east coast so her little family would be sharing this time with the Hollow folks, also. Coach Anna was going to meet her parents and arrive later in the afternoon to join her team.

The girls who joined the team selected by the other students really had gotten attached to the Hollow girls, such that they, too, were invited to come to the Hollow to participate in the festivities. Bob Waters, who delivered the unsaleable foods and much more to the Hollow from two giant food distribution centers, knew that this year's crowd in the Hollow was going to be very large so he increased the volume greatly to accommodate the anticipated group. He had received so very much joy from bringing this food to his special and unique friends in this remote section of the area.

The Hollow folks and the orphans headed to the little church on this Christmas Eve to start a gala affair that extended beyond the imagination of anyone in this part of the country. The whole scenario unfolded slowly after the girls arrived from Bacon College.

"I am so very excited to join in this wonderful celebration with all of you," Maudie said to Josh.

"You know," Josh said, "a Christmas celebration would not be complete without you. You are dearly loved by everyone."

"It was going to be a different kind of Christmas," Charlene thought, as Josh was putting the finishing touches on the duty roster for the evening. "It's the first year that Josh and I have not had money to buy candy and fruit sacks for everyone, because we have used all of our extra money to buy things for the orphans."

Seeing Charlene looking sad, Josh put his arm around her shoulders and whispered in her ear, "Jesus taught us all that love is the greatest thing we all should display. Love abounds this afternoon among our friends so that is sufficient to sustain us."

"I know you are right, Josh," Charlene responded, "but it's difficult not to have something to give everyone. Christmas is the time for giving as Jesus gave His life for all of us."

"God's abounding love always is with us," Josh stated. "Our love to all of our friends on this day will be in spirit and not in things."

"I know Josh," Charlene said, "but I have really enjoyed giving everybody the Christmas bag of goodies each year."

"This is going to be a very different Christmas," Josh said. "The angel tree gifts will be for the orphan children this year and not for our Hollow families. What a wonderful time we are going to have!"

"Josh has always been so positive and so much filled with faith," Charlene thought, as he kissed her lightly on the cheek, which indicated to her that everything was going to be just fine.

About the time Josh was getting ready to assign different duties and responsibilities, Ben came with thirteen other men and their wives to join in the celebration. Josh included their names in the box before the drawing to see who would be on the Christmas tree, cooking, dessert, ornament, and clean-up teams. Maudie was surprised when she was selected again this year to join six others to be on the tree selection group. This was the second reason for her to shed some tears of joy, because she was overcome when they arrived, and this would not be the last.

As soon as the lovely tree was in place, many made comments about its beauty. The decorating committee began to place the ornaments on the tree that they had made, and finally placed the well-worn angel right on the top. When the last string of popcorn was put around the tree, Ben and his group moved forward and placed twenty-one envelopes under the tree without saying a word. Charlene shortly brought out a large box and put it under the tree, also.

Charlene was leading the group in another wonderful Christmas carol when Hanna's mom and dad arrived. They were so excited to see their daughter and others, such that tears were flowing freely from the eyes of many on this night. "Hanna," her dad said, "would you mind getting the girls and others to help unload the van and a trailer?"

"I would love to do that," Hanna said. "Did you and mom bring Christmas gifts for the team?"

"We certainly did," her mom said, "and we brought gifts for all the others, also."

"This is my best Christmas ever," Hanna said, as she cried, too, while her mom and dad joined her in this wonderful moment of joy.

There was an overflow of gifts under the tree now, such that Charlene revisited her earlier concern that she and Josh were unable to purchase the usual sacks of goodies this year, because they had spent their extra money for different things for the orphan children.

Bob, Janie, Jim and Susan arrived with a huge load of additional foodstuff. They were joined by Dr. Damond, his wife and grandson, Bobby, who was very delighted to see his very special friend, Jim Baldwin, again. Jim had made giant strides in his life, having gotten a job as an engineer with a local construction company. He was still somewhat unsure of himself at times, because alcohol had been used so heavily during several years of his life. But because of Bobby's special love for him, he now had been free of alcohol for over a year. For several months now he had sent money anonymously to his wife, but at no time revealing the source or the location of the sender.

Having made many friends among the Hollow folks, especially that of Josh, Jim felt very much like he had conquered alcoholism with God's help all the way. He really enjoyed being in the company of these special people, but his greatest yearning was to be reunited with his wife and daughters so they could become a family again. "I really made a mess of my life," Jim thought, as he sat on the floor with the others celebrating the birth of the Lord.

Devin, the newspaper owner, and his wife showed up, wanting to be a part of this unusual group of folks from a most remote area of the region. "What a Christmas story that is unfolding here in the Hollow!" he thought.

"You have really overdone it this time with all of the food," Josh said to Bob.

"I felt like you would have many more guests than for last year so I brought several gallons of prepared food that were so generously donated by several of our restaurants," Bob replied. "The manager of the large restaurant where the Hollow men ate after cleaning the little town following the flood gave a huge part of what we brought. He told me he was coming later with his most delicious desserts for his good friends."

"Tony is our very good friend, but he didn't have to donate all of this food," Josh pointed out.

"You know how he is," Bob noted, "because he wouldn't miss being with you all for all the treasures in the world."

"It's going to be good seeing him again," Josh said, as he turned to find out what was the commotion at the door.

"Look who is here," Tom yelled, while shaking the hands of Glenn Colson, the superintendent, Joy Brown, the school supervisor, the elementary principal, Sally Dunden and high school principal, Raymond Forrester. They all had brought gifts that they placed under the tree.

Following a most bountiful and delicious meal, Josh was headed up front to speak to the group when he was interrupted by Tony, the restaurant owner who, with the help of several others, brought in many different kinds of dessert for the group.

Two large United Express trucks came up the Hollow to deliver Christmas gifts. The drivers entered the little church now filled with guests and handed Josh a letter, which stated:

> To Josh and His Flock,
>
> It is my prayer that God will bless you and the Hollow folks for all that you do for others in the area and other places. This small gift for each of you is only a small gesture during this season of celebration of the birth of our Lord and Savior Jesus Christ.
>
> Merry Christmas to you all and your enormous group of friends!
>
> May God continue to bless you all mightily!
>
> With much love,
> An Admirer

Helping the drivers, the Hollow folks brought in exactly one hundred boxes that looked like pirate treasure chests, with ornate gold colored trimming and painted a glossy black. "They are simply beautiful," Josh said, as he stopped the group long enough to open one. Looking up and straight toward Charlene, he said excitedly, "They are filled with all kinds of goodies, including a large assortment of cookies, various kinds of fruit, popcorn, and an abundance of different kinds of candy. What a special gift!" Josh continued, as he walked over to hug Charlene who had broken down and couldn't hold back the tears.

With much attention now on the beautiful boxes, Esther slipped over and hugged so warmly her special friend, Maudie, who was responsible for the gifts that were just received. "You don't miss a thing, do you?" Esther whispered in her ear, while holding her around the shoulders.

"Do you think they like them?" she whispered to Esther.

"They absolutely love them," Esther responded. "Someone overheard Charlene and Josh talking about not having sacks of goodies this year so this is a miracle for them."

Coach Anna and her parents arrived just in time for dessert only after she had hugged everyone at least once. On the strip mine marked with a large white "X" a helicopter from Mateland Air Force Base was descending with General Rootle, Captains Molton and Tolbot bearing gifts from the personnel on the base.

Every available space was utilized to house the group overnight, because the program did not end until the early hours of the morning. Many remained in the church while others found a place in the orphan home to stay.

The numerous and beautifully wrapped Christmas gifts inundated the floor all around the tree as breakfast was being served to everybody. Following the meal together, it was announced that the presents would be opened. Everyone agreed that this was the best Christmas ever!

THE STRANGER

The miracles were not over yet. Descending in an aircraft to the landing strip in Roanoke, Virginia, was a middle age woman headed on a journey guided by an anonymous letter received several days earlier. "Why did someone send me this information about my husband, Jim?" Sally Baldwin thought, as she examined the letter again that bore the postmark of Bacon on the envelope. "I have received anonymously money regularly over the past several months that I believed was from Jim, but I have been unable to trace the source," she continued to think. The letter added a new dimension to her thoughts, because it provided her directions to where Jim was located, and too, a round trip airline ticket was enclosed in addition to six hundred dollars to pay expenses on the trip.

Sally's mind was racing with thoughts of her courting days with Jim when he was the best athlete in their large high school and later performed in college equally as well. She had noticed that alcohol in college was taking its toll on Jim, but she believed that when they were married, she would help him get rid of the bad habit. With an excellent job Jim provided all of their wherewithal and more for several years. Being regular church members, they participated in many of the functions of the congregation before and especially after the two girls were born. The strain of his engineering job and his weakness for alcohol did not make good bedfellows, as he turned more and more to this crutch such that Sally had to make a choice.

Going to work herself, she could see that it was very important for her to become less dependent on his providing for the family, and this was a wise decision, because he soon lost his job. Taking their two beautiful young girls, Sally moved out and soon Jim disappeared, and no one had heard from him since. "I can't believe that after all of these years I get this anonymous letter telling me where Jim is located," Sally thought, as she folded up the letter and put it in her purse.

Much ran through her mind as she drove her rented car west toward the mountains. "Had Jim tried to get in touch with her, or had Jim written the anonymous letter himself?" she further thought. She wondered why the writer indicated that she should arrive in a place called the Hollow not any later than one o'clock. Stopping near Bluefield to ask for directions to the Hollow, one person told her that the only Hollow he knew was where the most outstanding girls' basketball team lived.

"Do you think that is the place you want to go?" he said.

"According to my direction, there is no road number leading to this area," Sally said.

Continuing to drive west through the mountains in this remote part of the beautiful state of Virginia, she made regular stops to refine her route. She knew that she was getting closer and closer, because of the eyes of those being asked when they heard the word Hollow. Each would want to tell about the best girls' team in the country coming from this area and would divulge how proud everyone was of the team.

"How on earth could Jim have gotten involved with this community being an alcoholic?" she continued to think, as her heart was beginning to pound in her chest.

Turning up the road she believed was the Hollow, she noticed several vehicle tracks that were visible. "A lot of cars have gone in and out of this place during the last several hours," she thought, as she carefully maneuvered her rented vehicle up the narrow roadway. Further, she asked herself, "Could this letter I received be just a hoax or is it genuine?"

Soon she noticed a two-room frame house to her left up the steep slope and wondered whether or not someone lived in it. "I have longed to see Jim so much since he disappeared with that dreadful alcohol problem, and to think I may be within minutes of seeing him again is almost overwhelming," she thought. She had always loved him since they met each other in high school, and because of this strong love, she tolerated his drinking problem until it became unbearable. Having withstood much during this bleak period in her life, she wondered whether or not Jim would have the same understanding.

Creeping up the Hollow, she saw several more houses of similar construction, but there was no sign of life in any of the buildings so she continued. "I'll just follow the other vehicle tracks," she thought, as her excitement continued to escalate. To her left she saw a beautiful brick structure and wondered about it, because it was different from the other buildings in the Hollow. Because there were no cars nearby, she continued her dangerous trip up the slippery roadway, with a steep bank to her right and a swiftly moving mountain stream.

She saw the tops of several basketball goals on the hill at the same time she saw several vehicles parked above a building made of wood boards that appeared to be a quaint little church. Very nervously, she parked and got out of the car, put on her coat, pulled on a cape and headed toward this building that had smoke coming from the chimney. "I have to be strong," she thought, as she walked through the slick snow toward the entrance.

Turning the doorknob, she opened the door and stepped inside to witness first hand much merriment, but she did not see Jim. Josh saw her immediately, and always being a special host, went to her and said, "We are so glad you could come to join us in our continuing celebration of the birth of our Lord." By this time Charlene was headed that way, also, but as she moved toward the door, everyone became very quiet. The newcomer had generated much curiosity so everybody became noiseless, wanting to discover who the new person was on this Christmas day.

With a shaky voice she said to Josh, "Could you please tell me whether or not Jim Baldwin is here?"

"He certainly is," Josh answered. "He is in the house nearby helping to prepare lunch for us. We believe he is the best cook we have."

"Where is this house?" she asked.

"I'll take you to him," Josh replied, as he and Charlene grabbed her hands to direct her toward their house.

It seemed that everyone followed outside in the cold to watch this stranger being led by Josh and Charlene. When they got to the door of their house only about fifty feet away, Josh went inside to get Jim. With a wide smile Jim followed Josh outside, and when he looked up and saw Sally, his smile disappeared and he momentarily became pale. Suspended in time, both stood looking at one another while the other folks waited quietly.

No one knew too much about Jim so this lady added to the mystery.

Josh just stood there with Jim, and Charlene was standing beside Sally as they looked at each other. They both presented such piercing stares at each other it appeared that everyone else was holding his breath.

Jim made the first move, a short step toward Sally and then Sally reciprocated. The pace quickened as both opened their arms and received the other, hugging so warmly in the midst of a large crowd on this Christmas morning as they stood in the snow.

Soon Josh and Charlene were leading them both back into the church while they held onto each other, never indicating that they would ever let go. Seated on one of the homemade pews, looking Jim right in the eye, Sally said, "Oh Jim! You look so good."

"You look so very good, too, as you always have, and you haven't changed a bit," Jim responded. "How did you know I was here?"

"I didn't until several days ago when I received an anonymous letter with airline tickets and directions to the Hollow," Sally said.

"This is an unusual place," Jim said. "The whole group, led by their pastor, just spend all their time and energy helping others. I could spend hours talking about them, but I'll hold that until later. I believe God provided me with an angel to help me overcome alcoholism. For over a year now I have had no alcohol of any kind so I believe I am cured of my dreaded habit that totally ruined my life and made it so miserable for you. Because I was not quite sure that I had truly conquered my drinking problem, I was waiting until later to try to contact you."

"I am so proud of you," Sally said. "I have always prayed that one day you would be delivered from that ugly addiction."

"How are the girls?" Jim asked.

"They are fine," she replied, "and they really wanted to come with me, but I didn't know what might be in store for me responding to an anonymous letter. I am so glad I came."

"Thank you for coming," Jim said. "I am so very glad that someone wrote you that letter."

The conversation continued for a very long period of time as everyone else scurried around getting ready for lunch. Later, Sally asked, "How on earth did you get to this remote area called the Hollow?"

"Being totally dependent on alcohol to get me through each day, I had a dream one night that led me to the Bacon community where the college is located that has the most outstanding girls' basketball team in the country," Jim related. "No one really wanted to have anything to do with me until a young man stopped by one day where I was begging for money to support my disastrous habit. He was a genuine encourager. His innocent love for me made me realize that I could overcome my terrible problem. You see, because he had an alcoholic friend, his peers at school and church, including most adults, ostracized him unmercifully, but he maintained his belief in me, looking beyond the terrible harassment he was getting from everyone. That young man is here today so I want you to meet him. Again, I believe God used him as my angel."

"He must be a special young man," Sally said, as she reached over and held Jim's hand.

"I really don't know what Bobby saw in me that caused him to do what others would have never done," Jim said. "It was somewhat love at first sight, as this young lad befriended a terrible alcoholic while the whole community watched and criticized him all the while. When I was deathly sick he took me to his home and nursed me back to health, and when I was hungry he fed me. Where have you heard that before?"

"I believe God was involved in your recovery," Sally said.

"I know He was," Jim quickly responded.

Sally leaned over on Jim's shoulder and said in a soft voice, "I have been waiting for this day for so many years, and now we are together again. God has intervened in your life to lift you up beyond your terrible addiction. The Hollow folks have provided for you a wholesome environment so that your recovery could be complete."

Jim and Sally just sat all morning on the wooden pew conversing with one another, almost being impervious to their surroundings. Esther slipped over and sat beside Maudie, who was enjoying every minute of these Christmas festivities. "You have been at it again on this Christmas, haven't you?" Esther whispered to Maudie.

Not responding to that question, Maudie looked up at Esther with a wide and warm smile and said, “Isn’t God wonderful?”

“He certainly is,” Esther responded, “and He uses some of His people to act on His behalf.”

Josh’s concern about Christmas gifts and bags of goodies had been alleviated yesterday such that under the tree now were numerous beautifully wrapped packages for everybody. Several had pitched in to prepare the special noon time meal of food brought again so generously by Bob. Now, even Sally and Jim were assisting in getting everything ready, as the children waited anxiously, realizing that soon the gifts would be handed out.

Everybody got a special craft gift from the Hollow folks. Maudie received a beautiful quilt that was put under the tree in the big box by Charlene that caused her to cry again for joy. Another laptop computer was given to Josh and the others and a year’s paid contract to send e-mail to their children, using the first laptop given by the elementary principal. Bringing many kinds of wearing apparel from their factory, Hanna’s mom and dad were noticeably very happy as they distributed their many gifts with the help of their only daughter. Also, each of the orphan children received an envelope from Ben’s group containing one hundred dollars each to be used to buy clothing. Included in each envelope was a note that indicated that the group would continue to provide financial assistance for the children on a regular basis.

As tranquility finally filled the small church, Hanna was the first to break the silence when she said, “I want all of you to know how special this Christmas has been for me to be here celebrating the birth of Jesus with my loving friends from college. Speaking on behalf of my whole family, I want to thank you all, and especially the basketball team, for permitting us to discover from you all how to express our love to one another.”

Then Jim stood up and spoke to the group. "I want you all to meet my wife who came today, because she received an anonymous letter with money and airline tickets to travel to the Hollow. I don't know who sent the letter, but whoever did it, I do want to thank that person very much. My story is long and parts of it are very ugly, but because of you all, especially Bobby Damond, I believe I am cured of my dreaded alcohol problem that ruined much of my life. With you all I saw hope and a life that was God centered and not one that focused on oneself. In the Hollow you all reach out with humility and deny yourselves as you go about each day as though God's grace is fully wrapped around your entire beings. Thank you all for permitting me to join with you inside that special loop."

With the two still holding hands, Sally said between sobs, "God showed us a way to return to each other in a unique way as He always does by using people as His couriers. I do not know the secret one who sent me the letter, but today I would like to use this forum to thank the one or ones who were responsible to reunite us."

After many had spoken, Josh said some words and then read this scripture found in Luke 2:

1 In those days a decree went out from Emperor Augustus that all the world should be registered.
2 This was the first registration and was taken while Quirinius was governor of Syria.
3 All went to their own towns to be registered.
4 Joseph also went from the town of Nazareth in Galilee to Judea, to the city of David called Bethlehem, because he was descended from the house and family of David.
5 He went to be registered with Mary, to whom he was engaged and who was expecting a child.
6 While they were there, the time came for her to deliver her child.

7 *And she gave birth to her firstborn son and wrapped him in*
bands of cloth, and laid him in a manger, because there was
no place for them in the inn.
8 *In that region there were shepherds living in the fields,*
keeping watch over their flock by night.
9 *Then an angel of the Lord stood before them, and the glory*
of the Lord shone around them, and they were terrified.
10 *But the angel said to them, "Do not be afraid; for see—I*
am bringing you good news of great joy for all the people:
11 *to you is born this day in the city of David a Savior, who is*
the Messiah, the Lord.
12 *This will be a sign for you: you will find a child wrapped in*
bands of cloth and lying in a manger."
13 *And suddenly there was with the angel a multitude of the*
heavenly host, praising God and saying,
14 *"Glory to God in the highest heaven, and on earth peace*
among those whom he favors!"
15 *When the angels had left them and gone into heaven, the*
shepherds said to one another, "Let us go now to Bethlehem
and see this thing that has taken place, which the Lord has
made known to us."
16 *So they went with haste and found Mary and Joseph, and*
the child lying in the manger.
17 *When they saw this, they made known what had been told*
them about this child;
18 *and all who heard it were amazed at what the shepherds*
told them.
19 *But Mary treasured all these words and pondered them in*
her heart.
20 *The shepherds returned, glorifying and praising God for*
all they had heard and seen, as it had been told them.

Concluding the wonderful and joyous celebration, Charlene led the group in singing several beautiful Christmas songs.

"What a spirit filled event!" Josh said to Charlene, as they both sat on the front pew after having hugged all of the guests at least once before they left to return to their homes.

MIT AND MAUDIE

One evening following basketball practice, Mit wanted to talk to Maudie about her parents who had been transferred from Costa Rica to Tanzania in East Africa so she went to her very modest apartment at the edge of the small campus. "What brings you here?" Maudie asked, as she opened the door.

"We haven't had a long talk in a few days so while the other girls are studying, I thought it would be a good time to come over for a visit," Mit said.

"I'm so glad you came," Maudie responded. "I'll make us some hot chocolate."

"That would be great," Mit replied.

"I have told you many times how proud I am of you and your mom and dad," Maudie said, as she was preparing the hot chocolate. "It's as though I am living in a dream world to have you here at Bacon College where I work, and can be with you each day."

"You know, Aunt Maudie," Mit said, "I feel the same way living with you and these special girls from the Hollow. I really can't believe that I have this opportunity, and the bonus is that I have the opportunity to play basketball with them all the while. And of course, a giant second bonus is that I'll be playing soccer with these same girls on the college team starting in a week or two."

"You just fit right in with the Hollow girls," Maudie indicated. "They all love you very much, and are so happy that you agreed to come to Bacon to receive your education with this precious group."

"God works in mysterious ways, doesn't He?" Mit stated. "It was just a plain miracle that the Bacon College team came to the jungle in south Costa Rica to where we were living with the Corbri village people."

"It certainly was," Maudie said. "When Coach Anna saw you play soccer, she became so excited that she could hardly utter her sentences coherently. She couldn't wait to ask you about coming to Bacon to play, and finally got the opportunity to speak to you. She was so very happy that you agreed to accept the full scholarship."

"Mom, Dad and I had spent much time talking about my college education, but each time we knew that the cost would be prohibitive. I am so appreciative of the athletic scholarship," Mit replied.

"Are you aware that you and several of the other athletes could have gotten an academic scholarship, because of your excellent secondary school achievement, if you had not gotten athletic scholarships?" Maudie said. "I understand that you and Esther have the highest academic record of any of the students ever enrolled at Bacon."

"I was really concerned that I would not have the proper clothing to wear in college," Mit pointed out, "but I learned very soon that the basketball players had very little, also. They don't seem to mind that the other students on campus wear stylish garments while they are seen with old clothes that they brought from the Hollow. Esther told me that Josh had really helped them by going to the Good Deed Store to get their clothing. You know, Aunt Maudie, I have been ashamed of myself for even thinking about what I wear, when compared to clothing of the other girls."

"Don't feel ashamed," Maudie said, "All of us learn each day from this humble and gracious group of young ladies who make up the basketball team. I used to try to save some money to buy some item of apparel that was in style, but since knowing the girls from the Hollow, it's now not a meaningful activity at all."

"You know how I got to Bacon," Mit said, "but how did you become a part of this institution?"

"About two years ago I moved to my apartment, and because I was nearby, I decided to apply for a job," Maudie said. "I didn't dream that they would receive a mysterious donation of a large sum of money to start a basketball team, but that's what happened. My first job was to clean the old gymnasium and some other areas, which I thoroughly enjoyed. As soon as the athletic dormitory was completed, I was transferred to this building where I have worked ever since."

"Do you like to work here?" Mit asked.

"Mit, it's the most fulfilling job that I ever had," Maudie said. "I love every minute and many times spend my evenings there. When you all are traveling, I remain in the building twenty-four hours a day. God is so good to me."

"Isn't it wonderful that we are together here?" Mit said, as she leaned over and hugged her Aunt Maudie.

"Do you have some time now that I can talk to you about something else?" Mit asked.

"I have all the time in the world," Maudie answered. "Thank you for wanting to talk to me."

"As you know about the time I enrolled here in college, Mom and Dad were shocked to discover that they were being asked to transfer from Costa Rica to Tanzania in East Africa," Mit stated. "They had done such a wonderful job in the jungle area bringing the native people to Jesus Christ such that it appeared that this was going to be their life long undertaking. The people loved them very much, and Mom and Dad loved the villagers so very much. Truly, their love for one another was unmistakable. Now they no longer are with these lovely and precious people, but in a land very new to them."

"I know that you have received several letters from them," Maudie said. "Are they settled down in their setting yet?"

"You know how they are," Mit said. "Following a brief period of homesickness followed by some discouragement, they are becoming God's messengers on that continent. They are making good progress, but I am really concerned about them."

"I know you are, Mit," Maudie said, while hugging her grandniece so warmly.

Following a lengthy conversation and several more hugs, Mit returned to the dormitory feeling much better to join her special counterparts in preparing their lessons for the next day.

A CONTINENT AWAY

It had really not been a smooth journey from the jungle area of Costa Rica to the East African country of Tanzania, but Dan and Pat Travers prayed for guidance as they searched for a place to live. Previous missionaries seemed to have let the environment direct their thinking such that all gave up and requested softer assignments in the capital city where life was filled with more comfort. The missionary leadership was putting great faith in the Traverses to buck the trend and remain steadfast to their mission even in a most difficult environment.

The couple hired a man with a dilapidated truck to carry them from the large airport city to the west where their assignment in the villages was located. They knew that they would get the best results by living among the people so they loaded their three trunks of personal belongings, three more of school supplies and settled back with the driver to find their new home. Far into the bush country the next day, they came to an area where there were seven villages located in a radius of twenty-five miles or so. On the edge of the village near the center they stopped, unloaded their mere belongings, paid the driver and began to unpack their tent.

Dan and Pat both had become strong warriors in delivering the Good News message, but they both realized that this was going to be a challenge. As they prepared their site under the large mango tree, several children from the village came but stood a good distance away watching their new guests. The on-the-field language study left much to be desired, but Dan and Pat knew that because of the urgent request, they would have to forego the usual study that preceded going on the field.

Early the next morning they decided to visit the village nearby to introduce themselves to the chief. "We don't have Mit this time to pave the way for us," Dan said to Pat, as they held hands to start their journey of about one-half mile.

"It's going to be difficult to make any kind of an inroad, because the native people are so suspicious of us," Pat responded.

"God has something in mind, I'm sure," Dan said, as they walked along with several children following behind, keeping a safe distance.

As they entered the village, they noticed several mud brick houses in a cluster that were vacant surrounded by a wall about four feet high. "This appears to have been constructed for a particular purpose," Pat said to Dan, as they walked by.

Their meeting with the chief was most interesting as he told of other missionaries of the past who had come to this area, and how they all left after spending just a little time with them. "You see the area with the wall and the several houses inside," the chief said in his village language, as he pointed to the area in which they had just walked, and making all kinds of gestures and signs to convey his message.

Soon they realized that he was telling them that people like them had constructed the buildings several years ago, but they left, never really using them for their purpose.

When he made that statement that finally they understood, Dan suddenly could see an opportunity presenting itself that could advance their cause immensely. "Could we use that area now?" Dan asked the chief, making all kinds of gestures and signs to get his message across.

"No one else is using it so just go ahead," the chief said, using hand motions.

"Thank you so very much," Dan responded, now both bowing to the chief and stepping back with heads bowed.

What a productive meeting! It was their first of many meetings with the chief, but none would surpass the gracious manner in which they were received on this day. Neither Dan nor Pat could believe that they would be moving into permanent quarters so soon after their arrival. Later that morning, they moved into the compound and started cleaning up the area while the children peered over the wall at their new neighbors.

It was early evening when they started their supper of rice with a magi cube which was so very delicious. After the meal was prepared Dan kept the fire burning while he and Pat sat to discuss their first day in this new country. "I can't believe how much progress we made today, can you?" Pat said to Dan.

"It's almost unbelievable," Dan replied. "We can start our school immediately, and from what I observe, there are many children around the area, so let's hope we can get them to attend our school. You know, we don't have Mit here as an enticement for them to enroll so it probably will be very slow for a while."

"I miss Mit so very much," Pat said. "She has been such a joy for us over the years, and has never complained about not having things like other children, but appreciates what she does have. She really is enjoying Bacon College very much. She says that it's such a bonus for her to be able to play basketball as well as soccer. She has difficulty in finding words to describe her feeling about the Hollow girls."

"I wish we were nearby so we could watch her play this year," Dan said.

"That would be a treasure," Pat indicated, as they turned in for the night in their new quarters in the bush country of Tanzania.

Waking early the next morning, Dan and Pat were greeted by village children peering over the compound wall, watching every movement they made. After a little while, Pat suggested that they get their school supplies to see how the children would respond. Seating themselves on the ground, Pat beckoned for the children to join them. Following the unique invitation, some of the children laughed as all of them disappeared behind the mud brick wall surrounding the property.

Soon they looked over again so Pat repeated her gesture, and they responded as they did before. After several replications of gesturing, two of the beautiful young girls came over to where Dan and Pat were sitting. It was a start, albeit very meager, but a genuine beginning that they would remember for a long time. Soon the school grew in number, but nearly not like what was going to take place in the future, as a result of their advertising in other villages.

Not too far away in a village called Trenka, there was young man named Galu whose daily routine included gathering food to help feed his parents, the other twelve children, and him. Being the oldest, he was expected to hunt for food just as his father so most of his time was utilized in this manner.

Galu was a very intelligent young man who could find much more food than his father, because he would run from place to place at such a fast pace that he could cover much more ground than any of the other food hunters. The repetition of the same effort each day consumed much of his early life so education for him had to be "placed on the back burner" until other members of his family became of age. As each child matured, Galu and his father would teach him or her how to secure food for the family, and as time passed several of the children were involved in the food search so it became easier and required less time to fulfill.

With more "free" time to pursue other interests, Galu heard about the Traverses' school several miles away that taught young people to read, write, and compute. Following approval from his parents, one day he left home to go to see what it was that was being taught in this school in the village to the east. Running all the way, nationals along the way were amazed at the stamina and speed of this young lad who had run so far yet seemed not to be winded at all. Arriving at the little school inside the compound, where Dan had placed hewn benches of wood and two more that he made with bamboo, Galu introduced himself to Dan and Pat who greeted him with open arms. The reciprocal bear hugs made them feel as though they had been friends all the while.

It was during the bear hug that Galu saw a strange thing on the front of one of the small rooms. It was a large pole that had a small pole across it one-third down the larger pole that was perpendicular to the ground. In response to the inquiry by Galu, Dan related the story of Jesus Christ who was crucified, buried and was resurrected, all to save us from our sins. Of course, all of this was very perplexing to him, but the main thing he wanted to find out was about the school for young people.

After meeting the other students that had grown to eleven, Dan showed him the material being utilized and had several of the children to read aloud to him. Galu's heart pounded as he heard the other children his age reading their textbook, and the wide smile on his face gave Dan the genuine answer that he, too, wanted to be a part of this special learning process. The run of twenty miles back to his thatched roof home was done with ease and with a special glow on his face that was responding to a childhood song that he sang all the way.

Seated on the side of his bamboo bed, Galu drew lines on the dirt floor as he told of his trip to the school, and as he explained what he saw. His parents and brothers and sisters were all "ears" as he related his experience. When he told about the cross, a quizzical look was observed on their faces, because they had never heard of this Jesus, but they told Galu to let them know more about this Man as he studied in the school. It was obvious that he had the support of the family, and now that the other children were older, they could assist with the gathering of food, which would give Galu ample time to go to school and do his part after school and on days when the school was not in session.

At eleven Galu was older than the other children when they entered school for the first time; however, it was soon discovered that with his ambitious approach to learning, he was advancing at a rapid pace. In fact it wasn't too long before he was at the top of the class, and Dan utilized his expertise to teach other children in school.

“May I take some of my education materials home to teach my brothers and sisters in the way I’m being taught?” Galu asked one day just as he was getting ready to leave.

“Certainly you may,” Dan responded, as they loaded a bag of materials, including textbooks, that was thrown over Galu's shoulder as he left the school campus headed for home. On the way to pass the time, Galu took a book from the bag called the "Holy Bible," and read it during his delightful journey home, as he couldn't wait to see the eyes of his brothers and sisters when he opened the bag.

As he perused the "Holy Bible" walking along on this day, he noticed on the inside page that this book was donated by the Gideons, and further it stated that the Gideons were from the U. S. A. He had never heard of the Gideons or the U. S. A. so he continued reading the contents starting with Genesis. While he did not understand all that he was reading, he did have a better understanding of this textbook. because his master teacher spent a lot of time each day using it. Walking, reading, and humming, Galu was a conversation piece as fellow villagers saw him as he trudged home with his heavily laden bag draped over his shoulder. In fact, there was some murmuring about his glowing countenance, as he seemed to be at peace with all people, and seemed to emit love with his every action as he went about his activities each day.

"Galu, you are invited to come to church on Sunday to join with other villagers at ten o'clock," Pat said to Galu, their prize student. "There are thirty-three who usually attend the Sunday morning worship service, and there is room for more to attend so you and your family are cordially invited to be a part of the program."

After talking it over with his parents at home, Galu was permitted to attend this "church" thing, because his parents thought that it was part of the school program, and it was very important for Galu not to get behind in his schoolwork. His parents could see the immense progress that he had made to this point, and they wanted him to continue to build on what he had already learned.

Because there was no school on Saturday and Sunday, Galu was a vital part of food gathering on the weekends, but on this Sunday he was being permitted to go to church instead of working with the other members of the family as he usually did. Barefooted, as usual, and wearing his best clothes that would be considered by many in the world as simple rags, Galu headed toward his school village to attend church for the first time. Upon arrival, he was greeted by everyone, and a special greeting was extended by Dan and Pat who were so fond of Galu, and who knew the potential in this young man.

As Dan stood before the group, everyone sat very still on the benches awaiting instructions. They sang several songs, a few in the congregation went to the front and told of their weekly blessings, and others spoke of their problems. Galu felt a sense of family among the group, especially as they gave their heartfelt talk before the group, so he became very attentive as Dan read Luke 10:

> 25 *Just then a lawyer stood up to test Jesus. "Teacher," he said, "what must I do to inherit eternal life?"*

26 He said to him, "What is written in the law? What do you
read there?"
27 He answered, "You shall love the Lord your God with all
your heart, and with all your soul, and with all your
strength, and with all your mind; and your neighbor as
yourself."
28 And he said to him, "You have given the right answer; do
this, and you will live."
29 But wanting to justify himself, he asked Jesus, "And who is
my neighbor?"
30 Jesus replied, "A man was going down from Jerusalem to
Jericho, and fell into the hands of robbers, who stripped him,
beat him, and went away, leaving him half dead.
31 Now by chance a priest was going down that road; and
when he saw him, he passed by on the other side.
32 So likewise a Levite, when he came to the place and saw
him, passed by on the other side.
33 But a Samaritan while traveling came near him; and when
he saw him, he was moved with pity.
34 He went to him and bandaged his wounds, having poured
oil and wine on them. Then he put him on his own animal,
brought him to an inn, and took care of him.
35 The next day he took out two denarii, gave them to the
innkeeper, and said, 'Take care of him; and when I come
back, I will repay you whatever more you spend.'
36 Which of these three, do you think, was a neighbor to the
man who fell into the hands of the robbers?"
37 He said, "The one who showed him mercy." Jesus said to
him, "Go and do likewise."

Then Dan spoke to the group about his interpretation of what he had read. It was a very inspiring message as he related the story of the good Samaritan, and compared it to a similar circumstance that had occurred in the village just last week. At the conclusion of the talk Dan went over what he called a plan of salvation wherein those who believed in their heart that Jesus was the Son of God, died for our sins, was buried, and in three days was raised from the dead, could confess that they were sinners by coming to the front of the congregation. It was a new activity for Galu, but he knew that something was tugging strongly at him to go to the front and confess of his sins. But being a deliberate and cautious individual who thought through on things of life before plunging into them with no understanding, he decided to delay any decision of this kind on his part until another day after he had time to think more about it and discuss it with the master teacher.

As he walked pensively back home, Galu thought about the plan of salvation and what it would take for him to be a brother in Christ with all of the other members of the small church. There was no doubt in his heart that this decision needed to be made so it was only a matter of time before it would be done. His achievement in school was advancing at a very fast pace, and all of those associated with the school marveled at the way in which he learned so quickly with what appeared to be such a little effort.

VILLAGE MARATHON

Now approaching his twelfth birthday, Galu's thoughts were divided between school, which he loved so much, and the big marathon race in the area that covered twenty-six miles across difficult terrain. As a twelve-year old young man, he could participate in this widely publicized event held each year in the neighborhood. In fact all of the villagers became spectators on this day, because all attention was on the village marathon that included all of the best runners in the neighborhood. Several of the previous winners each year continued in their pursuit to be the top runner, because they realized that the champion each year became the "darling" of the local people who seemed to generate a serious bond of love with that individual.

No youngster had ever entered this race which began more than one hundred years ago so it was extremely rare that any teenager would think of doing it now. Galu had thought about the race for years and had fantasized how he would compete in this event, but he knew that it did not appear to be for young people so, although he was going to be eligible to participate, he believed that he would wait several years until he was older.

Putting aside the thought about the marathon, Galu began to think about becoming a Christian so in a few Sundays he found himself walking to the front of the church, giving his life to Christ. Not knowing what God had in store for him, he said that he would do what was asked of him. It was the special day of his life, and he felt he could talk to God now being a part of the family. On the day of the baptism his parents, brothers and sisters were on hand to congratulate him for something they did not understand, but they had much support for their very obedient and faithful cldest son and brother. Little did they all know what was ahead for Galu and them in the years to come.

There being several days before the close of registration for entering the marathon, Galu marveled over the interest of the village people and wondered who would be the winner this year. He could hear the elders talking about the entrants and their anticipating how they would fare in this big event, the grandest community event of the year.

Sometime later, not sleeping too well that night, Galu was up early the next morning and before too long, he was telling his parents about his thinking about entering the marathon.

"This marathon race is for older men and not for a lad who has just reached his twelfth birthday," his father said to him, when the subject was brought up. Galu could see that the whole family was accepting this idea very coolly, because he could hear his brothers and sisters in the background sniggling and laughing about such a ridiculous notion. Galu's spirits plummeted to a low level. Not receiving the blessing of his family, the whole idea took on a new meaning, and inside Galu felt that that he was in a severe storm being twisted back and forth.

It was the final day for registering for the big race, and from what he could understand all of the major runners were already included so the village talk was that it was the strongest field of runners that they had ever had. With a churning in his stomach and a feeling of loneliness, he wrestled with the big decision that he knew he had to make. Furtively, Galu made his way toward the registration area, and with all of the strength he could muster, he stepped up to the registrar to become a runner in the neighborhood's prestigious marathon. The registrar and those in earshot tried to convince Galu that this race was for adults and not for children even though he qualified, because he was twelve, but they contended that no one under twenty years of age had ever entered the race to their knowledge. Stubbornly, he held on dearly to his commitment, and he was finally registered, albeit their urging him to do otherwise.

The news of his entry was not widely circulated, because for the most part the leaders felt embarrassed that a local youth had upset a tradition that had been prevalent since the inception of the race. Not to cause any more disruption of village life, Galu used a different route from home to his school so he would not have to pass where people could see him run. However, he increased the length of his running to coincide with the marathon distance of twenty-six miles. Having run very long distances all of his life, the marathon would be just another day for this young lad who had become a favorite at the school.

In a few days Galu told his parents that he had entered the race, and that he didn't want his actions to be an embarrassment to them. He went on to say that they did not have to come to the event; yet, he would be so very much honored, if they would be present. While his parents did not scold him, their quiet manner indicated to Galu that they were not all that enamored about his breaking a long standing tradition by being the first youth to participate in this local marathon. Still, they did not say that they would not be present at the event, which was scheduled to take place in two weeks.

The other students at the school took a different view about the entry of Galu in the race, because they supported him fully, and encouraged him each day as they patted him on the back, wished him well and even made up songs to sing to him. In fact the students would line up at the school each morning to watch Galu run his last five hundred yards to the school grounds, and when he would come into sight, they would break out into a chant saying, "Ga-luuuuuuuu, Ga-luuuuuuuu, Ga-luuuuuuuu, Ga-luuuuuuuu, . . ." Each day would start with this very emotional time as each child seemed totally to be engrossed in this activity on behalf of Galu. But Galu did not let all this "go to his head," because he continued to put his school work first just as he had always done, so to all of those who knew him, he was the same popular, easy going, excellent student he had always been.

Two days before the race Dan and Pat took Galu to the side, hugged him, and said, “We are so proud of you to pursue your dream of running in the big marathon even though many do not want you to enter, because of your age.”

Having not wavered in his school work during this very emotional time, Galu had earned even deeper respect from his two master teachers who were using him more and more to be the beacon of the school. The school was growing in number all the while, because of the contribution being made by Galu, and now that he was doing something that the village fathers did not approve, Dan and Pat wanted to assure him that they believed he was doing the right thing.

The day of the big race came all too soon, and the night before was almost sleepless for Galu, because he was so excited, and the morning meal at home was almost untouched. A brief and almost inaudible statement made by his mother after he hugged all of the family before he departed was a big boost to him. “You should eat a big meal so you will have strength to run the race,” she said. This brought a big smile, because this was the first time that either of his parents had even mentioned the race to him.

Knowing that he was going to arrive at the starting point too early, Galu stopped under a spreading mango tree just on the outskirts of the little village where he prayed, thanking God for his many blessings and for His will to be done in the race on this day. In a while upon seeing several of the other runners, Galu made his way to the starting area almost unnoticed. It was an eerie feeling, because all the people didn't seem to want to notice that he was even present, and they looked away as he got his number, 123, the highest in the race.

As he lined up with the others and looked around, Galu couldn't believe how many people had come to see the start of the race, and he knew, too, that there would be many people along the running trail who would be cheering the participants all the while. One thing that he did notice as he waited for the race to start was that some of the runners had on pretty shirts and shorts and most were even wearing shoes. Galu was so proud of what he was wearing, an old ragged pair of pants that were cut off just below his knees and no shoes. "A shirt and shoes would only be extra weight along the way," he thought.

The marathon officials gave the leading runners low numbers and placed them in the front, a good distance ahead of Galu who was in the back with the slower group. As he scanned the group of runners, he could readily see that he was the youngest by far, and because of that, the other runners did not talk to him. As the starting official was preparing to get the race underway, Galu began to think what a lonely time this would be, because the other runners were not speaking to him, and to his knowledge at this point there were certainly no spectators who were going to be pulling for him to win. Anyway, with the race beginning he would have to concentrate on his running and forget about these other things.

On the starter's signal to begin, it was a while before those on the back could move, waiting for those in front, but soon they began to spread out a little. Having no professional assistance and having not run a race like this before, Galu thought, "I will manage to run about two hundred yards behind the leaders for the first half of the race so I won't get in the way of those who are thought to be the best runners."

Before too long into the race, the pack of runners seemed to spread out with the fastest ones remaining in a group up front and the slower ones in the back. Not knowing exactly where he would fit in, Galu decided, " For the time being, I'll run in the middle all alone." With this strategy in place he settled in for what was going to be an interesting afternoon. The sun was boiling down, as usual, and the terrain was undulating so he kept his mind on the business of running, except from time to time he thought about his family and his mom's coded best wish message which brought a warm smile to his face.

Everything was going well for Galu, but it was a lonely adventure, because no one near the road said anything to him, as he ran along at an easy pace just maintaining his distance with the top runners up front. As they began to reach the ten-mile marker, Galu noticed that a few of the runners up front were beginning to drop back just a little so now there were two groups being formed to the front. "We are beginning to make our way through another village so I don't want to change any strategy until I am beyond the area where there are so many spectators, because I still feel somewhat out of place," he thought, as he pressed on.

The twenty-five runners leading the pack seemed physically fit to maintain a rapid pace to the finish line, but the thirty or so runners now forming the second group appeared to be struggling somewhat. During the next three miles before they turned toward the school village, several of the runners in the second group began to fall back, so far that Galu had to pass them. As they turned toward the school area, Galu felt more comfortable as he thought, "My school friends will be there to boost my spirits somewhat, because to this point it has been a very lonely race."

It was at the eighteen-mile marker that the school village came into sight. The second group had totally dissolved, and Galu was running alone as the second group. As he approached the little school village still maintaining that two-hundred-yard distance behind the leaders, he noticed that the people on the sidelines were leaning and whispering into the ear of their neighbor. They were amazed that a young lad could still be running near the front after eighteen grueling miles in the heat and over such rough terrain, competing so well with the expected champions. No one was there to greet Galu, or they were afraid to say anything.

At this point the marathon route took a sharp turn to head back west toward the finish line which was fairly close to the starting area village. Galu knew that during the next five miles he would have to adjust to the leaders, if they did anything to try "to shake" the other runners so he was very attentive to what was happening. One thing he noticed was that the lead group had spread out somewhat, and there appeared to be jockeying up front to see who was going to run the point. One thing Galu had heard about running a race of this length was that during the last few miles a runner feels like he is running into a wall and that has to be overcome with all the courage that could be mustered.

These five miles took their toll on the runners as runner after runner fell back trying to get a "second wind" to finish the race, but Galu trudged on, and as they came to the twenty-three mile marker, Galu knew he could make it the rest of the way. More people were along the road, and then there was more and more disbelief that a twelve-year-old lad would be running within striking distance of the lead group at this juncture of the race.

The last three miles were run in an "S-shape" route leading to the finish line so the hills were packed with spectators, and the roadway was lined with people all along the way. There were thirteen runners ahead of Galu as he entered the "S" route, and he could tell that some of the runners ahead of him were struggling to keep pace. Galu's constant vigil was on the lead runner so he continued to maintain about two hundred yards behind until he reached the one-mile marker where the marathon route circled the hill filled with adults and children alike.

With one mile to go and only six runners ahead of him, he entered the last stretch when he heard a group yelling, "Ga-luuuuuuuu, Ga-luuuuuuuu, Ga-luuuuuuuu, Ga-luuuuuuuu, Ga-luuuuuuuu, . . . " He could not determine where the chants were coming, but that was not important now, because he knew they were there to support and encourage him along, and yes, he now had some friends in the large crowd. Hearing every chant, he knew that he had to get his mind back on the race, because it was nearing the close with only one-half mile to go now. It was a good thing that he was paying attention, because the three lead runners began to increase the pace immensely, so it was now time for him to do likewise and try to run up front.

Making a last turn with one-fourth of a mile remaining in the race, Galu had caught up with the three lead runners to the amazement of all of the spectators. With three hundred yards remaining Galu could hear the chants louder and louder, and as he was beginning to boost his pace to a higher level, he caught a glimpse of his father, mother, and his brothers and sisters cheering on the side. With renewed energy that gave him a sudden burst of speed, Galu pulled alongside the three-time champion and with the world that he knew watching, he made his move to the front. As he continued to increase his lead, he could hear the loud chant of his classmates, but the other spectators fell silent, as this young, unsuspecting lad now was the marathon winner, having crossed the finish line several yards ahead of his nearest pursuer, the three-time champion.

With classmates surrounding Galu they joyfully celebrated, but it was short lived as Galu broke free to join his jubilant parents. With his parents, Galu said, “Please follow me.” They went a short way beyond the crowd that trained their eyes on him, watching his every movement. Reaching a clear spot, they knelt down, and Galu prayed, thanking God for his many blessings of the day, with the bystanders not really realizing what they were doing.

Galu was given a big trophy during a solemn ceremony, because a boy had won what the favorites were supposed to have won. Never in the history of the marathon had a youngster of twelve competed much less have won.

Running to school on Monday, Galu went a different route trying not to be seen, because it appeared that everyone was upset except his family and school friends, because he had won the marathon.

Galu had a full "plate" as he juggled his time to practice his running, gathering food for his family, going to school and church, helping to teach other students in the school, and teaching Sunday school. He did all of this and for each he did it well. Everyone was amazed at the stamina, perseverance, attentiveness, and faithfulness of this very young man, whom all admired, especially the other children in the neighborhood who simply adored him. Because of this adoration, the Christian school began to grow rapidly and his Sunday school class overflowed with the old and young alike. Everyone with whom he touched in the neighborhood dearly loved him and wanted to be a part of his small world in this East African community.

REGIONAL MARATHON

One day after much strenuous activity, Galu began to run home, and he noticed a piece of paper in a ditch so he slowed sufficiently to pick it up. Reading while running, he became aware of an annual regional twenty-six mile marathon race which was scheduled in nearly three weeks in a large city more than four hundred miles away. Upon reading the advertisement, he folded it carefully and placed it in his pocket where it would remain so that his parents would not be concerned about another race until he had a chance to talk to his master teachers.

Each evening upon his arrival at home, he would run to gather food for the family, helping the other male members while the females worked with their mother preparing the evening meal. It was always a lot of fun to be at home with his parents and his many brothers and sisters. With the work came a little teasing of one another so Galu learned the "give and take" of having fun with others, and in fact from time to time the other children would get together and yell, "Ga-luuuuuuuu, Ga-luuuuuuuu, Ga-luuuuuuuu, Ga-luuuuuuuu, Ga-luuuuuuuu, . . . " to make him feel self-conscious. Theirs was a happy family with loving and caring parents who wanted to bring them up so that they would be a credit to the community.

Arriving at school a little earlier than usual the next day, Galu went straight to see one of his master teachers about the marathon race in the large eastern city.

"I found this piece of paper advertising a marathon run in a large city to the east," Galu said, handing it to Dan.

After examining its contents, Dan commented, "It really appears to be a prestigious race drawing a large number of runners from several countries."

"Have you ever heard of this race?" Galu asked.

"No, I haven't," Dan replied.

They talked about it until the other children came to school, and at that point discontinued their conversation until lunch time. Teaching and assisting the teachers and at the same time advancing his studies at his own pace, Galu covered a lot of "academic territory" each day, and this one was no exception. Nothing stood in the way of his school work, and the prospect of entering the prestigious regional marathon was not going to interfere with his program of studies.

At lunch when the conversation about the race was renewed, Dan stated, "I believe that it would be very helpful for you to enter such a race, because the neighborhood has not really accepted your local marathon championship, so you would be running in an event outside the area and would be representing the village citizens many miles away."

"To enter the race, I'll need to get approval from my parents," Galu indicated to Dan not showing any emotion now that he was going to pursue entering the prestigious race.

"Following your parents' approval, to bring this idea to full fruition, I'll work to get you registered," Dan pointed out.

"How will we get to the race?" Galu asked.

"We'll have to work on that part of the plan," Dan quickly responded. "For the necessary financial support, at this time I'm not sure, but God works in mysterious ways,"

"I want you always to go with me," Galu stated, now realizing that the bond between Dan and him was strengthened each day.

It was agreed that Galu would get the approval of his parents, and when that was done, Dan would find out how one registered for the race and see that the registration was completed so he would be eligible to run.

After Galu completed his chores that evening, did his homework, helped his brothers and sisters with their homework, and finished the family Bible study, he stated, "There is another marathon race being conducted in a large eastern city, and I am asking for your approval to participate in it."

His parents really were excited when Galu, their oldest son, won the neighborhood marathon, but they had not shown any signs of emotion that he recognized. In their hearts they knew that they would approve his participation in this race, but they didn't want to appear that they were overly anxious in making such a big decision. For nearly an hour they discussed the pros and cons of participating in such an event, and finally and somewhat unexpectedly, they agreed for him to run with the stipulation that the master teacher would handle all of the details, because they, as parents, did not know what to do.

Running to school the next morning following a loving bear hug to his parents, Galu arrived early to announce to his master teacher that his parents had concurred on his participating in the race. The "ball was in Dan's court" now.

"How are you going to raise the money for this huge undertaking?" Pat asked. "It does mean so much to Galu to be a part of this race, because the people have obviously responded very negatively about his winning the village race."

"Let me share a tentative plan of how we might secure the wherewithal for such an activity. "First of all, let's take the trophy that Galu won in the neighborhood to the local governmental office and ask them to put it on display for several days in the window adjacent to the street. In addition we can make a large poster that will read: 'Ga-luuuuuuuu, Our Regional Entry in Regional Marathon,

November 21, Urga City, Eastern Tanzania. Assistance Needed!'"

Dan headed to the Christian Association headquarters in the district and sent a fax to the address on the marathon advertisement. Shortly, via returned fax, he received an application with a deadline for entry only two days away. Following the completion of the application form, Dan sent the application to the marathon officials.

Upon his arrival back home Dan asked, “Have you heard any talk in the neighborhood about Galu?”

“This morning I did overhear two men discussing something, and one mentioned Galu’s name when I passed,” Pat replied.

For his practice every day for the big event, Dan instructed Galu, “I want you to run through the neighborhoods and not around them as you have done lately to avoid coming into contact with the citizens.”

As the date of the race grew near, Galu noticed that the citizens would not turn their heads when he passed but would actually appear to recognize him. Upon arrival at school one morning being greeted by: "Ga-luuuuuuuu, Ga-luuuuuuuu, Ga-luuuuuuuu, . . ." by the other students, he was overwhelmed when Dan told him that a villager was going to drive his old van to the race carrying Galu and as many of the students, as possible. Suddenly, Galu could feel that this event was more than just one being run by an individual, because now it was that of a neighborhood.

Not known by Galu and Dan, the marathon officials in the eastern city discovered that Galu was only twelve years of age, much too young to run in the adult marathon of twenty-six miles, they mused. After scrubbing his name, one of the officials casually indicated that they should look at the guidelines so that they could cite the age rule when they sent him a letter, which would apprise Galu that his name had been removed. To their knowledge, no one under twenty had ever entered this race so they did not want to include a child who might disrupt the whole event. Looking through the rule book hurriedly, one official indicated that he could not find an age limit so he invited several of the others to do likewise. After a full afternoon the four officials agreed that there was no age limitation so this young man would be permitted to run. But they would have the final word by giving him the last number in a field of more than two thousand runners.

It was after school on Friday that the old van jalopy pulled up to the school yard to load up the students and Galu for the big race. There were only fifteen who could go, so the others wished them well many times as the van belched and coughed balls of blue smoke as they left the premises. It was more than a ten-hour drive so it was calculated that with no mechanical failure they would arrive at three in the morning and have five hours before the race. Each student had four meals packed from home so that the only known expenses would be that for gasoline for the van.

Singing and all kinds of merriment filled the walls of the vehicle as they headed beyond the boundaries of the known world of the children. Everyone was concerned about the comfort of Galu as they shifted from side to side traversing the rough terrain. As darkness spread over the landscape, silence became more commonplace, and the thoughts of the children put them in a pensive mood, so there was a quietude that was eerie where young people are involved.

Stopping to eat and to check the map more carefully, they all disembarked and went to the side of the road to be seated. Dan carefully watched Galu open his bag of food, because he wanted to be sure that he was strong for the race. As he pulled from his bag a baked sweet potato, he noticed that he reached in again to retrieve a note which he read and grinned widely, displaying a countenance of supreme peace on his face. Then Dan asked Galu, “Would you thank God for our food?”

Among many things he included a petition for God to have all things to happen within the framework of His will. Not wanting to eat too much of his food before the big race, because he knew that he would be hungry after running twenty-six miles, in addition to the sweet potato, which was very good, he ate a large ear of roasted corn on the cob.

Loading back into the van, they became genuine young people as they teased each other about everything imaginable before giving way to a quiet time that captured most of them, and one by one they fell asleep. It wasn't until about two o'clock that they were awakened by a loud thumping sound that they did not understand. “I believe we have a flat tire,” said the driver. “It will be necessary for everyone to get out for a few minutes until I can replace the punctured tire with one of our two spares.” They all watched him as he changed the tire with some wanting desperately to help.

As they came into the outskirts of the city with dark streets at four in the morning, the youth were awakened so they could experience the excitement of entering a city of this size. Of course, they were all eyes with head movement so swift that Dan thought that they would get a crick in their neck. Driving on the empty streets for a while, they finally discovered the starting point of the race and the check-in station for all participants so at this time they parked the van and told the young people to sleep until seven o'clock.

At six o'clock Dan noticed that runners were getting their numbers at the check-in station, so he slipped quietly out of the van and went to get Galu's number for him. When he arrived at the table, the officials looked up his number, and they realized that this was the young "upstart" kid who was entering this prestigious race relegated always for adults. They gave Dan a good lecture and told him that if they saw anything in the race that he did that would be disruptive, he not only would be removed from this race but would be declared ineligible for any marathon in the future. After this strong "tongue lashing" they gave the master teacher, the number 2143, the last number of a runner in the marathon. As he walked back to the van, he was almost applauding himself for not saying anything derogatorily, because he had not slept all night, and his temperament was not at its usual high point without sufficient rest. Of course, he was glad that Galu did not hear all that was said, because he was so sensitive about the feelings of others.

In the small brochure it was indicated that the terrain and running area were very similar to that of the neighborhood marathon, which Galu should like. All runners were expected to be in place at least fifteen minutes before the starting time so Dan awakened them for their morning meal. Following the blessing given by Dan in which he included asking for strength for Galu, the young people began to eat their meal. The van driver had gotten them a container of water to drink. Watching again very closely to see that Galu ate well before the race of his life and the race of his community's life, Dan noticed that he first got out the piece of paper from his bag which he read, and it produced another wide smile again. He proceeded to eat a small bread log, an orange, a piece of dried meat, and then drank some water.

Following breakfast, Galu went to the van and put on his "running britches" which were the same pair that he wore in the previous race. After they spent some time together with small talk, Dan escorted the young twelve-year old to the starting point to join more than two thousand other runners, more people than in his whole community by far. The numerous spectators had arrived early to see the runners as they started this event that had been staged for more than a hundred years. There were several reasons why the spectators examined Galu very closely: that he was very much younger than the others, that he was not dressed appropriately for the race, and that his countenance was so peaceful and calm. Of course his very presence brought on some laughter, and in fact, some of the spectators chided Galu, telling him to go home to his mother, asking him how long he had been out of diapers and don't cry along the way.

The other children heard all of the derogatory comments being said about their friend, and some of them broke down and cried as they watched Galu standing there awaiting the start of the race, taking all that abuse and not even saying a word. It seemed that the officials had spread the word that a young whippersnapper had entered the race, and that it was embarrassing to the race officials, but they couldn't do anything about it. The officials thought that with continuous and harsh heckling at the start and along the race route that Galu would withdraw under the pressure being brought to bear on him. Observing all of the outrageous verbal abuse and knowing the extreme sensitivity of Galu, Dan eased over to the back of the runners where Galu was positioned for the start of the race and gave him a strong and loving bear hug. He whispered in his ear to forgive them for their behavior and be prepared to endure it for the first five to eight miles, and it will end.

Following the starter's signal, the runners with the low numbers in the front moved out, and in a little while Galu and those around him did likewise. There were so many runners that it was hard for Galu to maneuver during the inception of the race, so he patiently jogged along awaiting their coming upon a wider running area to pass some of those in the front of him. As he made his pass, he could hear loudly and clearly the hecklers on the side that made him feel sad, so he remembered what the master teacher told him that it would be over in a while. With that renewed strength, he began to look over the mass of runners to see the front group so he could pick up that pace, but for the first five to eight miles he was going to hide among the runners that were in the pack just behind the leading group of several hundred.

The strategy seemed to be paying off as the vociferous crowd of hecklers sometimes didn't even recognize him, because he was surrounded by several hundred other runners pounding the roadway. As in the previous race in his neighborhood, no one had spoken to him except for the hecklers with whom he could do without, so he just established a comfortable pace for a long marathon race.

To pass the time, he would hum a few gospel tunes, occasionally coming through with some lyrics that on one occasion caused another runner to sneer at him. For the most part he thought of his family and the friends at the race and back at home. When he saw the eight-mile marker, he knew he could go to his usual strategy, so he moved to his right just a little and passed the members of his group to form his own group of one about three hundred yards behind the leaders. This is where he ran for a long time.

The race was somewhat uneventful until they entered a village nearly twelve miles east of the large city wherein there was considerable clamoring in the makeshift bleachers as he made his way through the area.

"I can't believe that this lad is running so well," one man in the bleachers said loudly, which caused others to look.

"He doesn't seem to be tired at all," another pointed out, as they all examined this very young, unknown runner in their regional marathon.

The spectators continued pointing toward him and talking about him as he comfortably and easily passed through their neighborhood. A young lad of fifteen or so noticed that Galu had not gotten any water that was placed along the way, and thinking that he had missed it, ran hurriedly with a container for him to drink. Galu was so thankful as the young man continued to run with him for a while only to give out and give up at the same time wishing Galu well all the while.

"I hope that you do well in the race," the young man yelled, as Galu continued his rapid pace.

As he passed the fifteen-mile sign, Galu checked his position carefully, because he knew that if the runners did the same as in the neighborhood race, he would need to watch the front runners, because some would be dropping back. The best he could determine there were still two to three hundred ahead of him, and he was only a short distance back. Following this assessment, he thought about the magnitude of this race, and what a blessing God had given him to permit his participation and to have the approval of his loving parents.

The racers were going through their final village before the conclusion with an estimated crowd of more than three thousand on hand to wish the runners well. Several of the lead runners began to drop back, and Galu was placed in more of a conspicuous position as they turned to make the stretch drive of six miles. The village people could not believe what they were seeing, a young twelve-year old only two hundred yards behind the best runners in the region. Via telephone, the word spread to the finish line that the youngster was near the lead pack running smoothly and with a tranquil countenance that none had seen before.

As Dan, the van driver and Galu's classmates waited anxiously at the finish line, it was noticed that several of the officials were on the telephone. One of the officials went to the public address announcer who had kept all of the spectators apprised of the leaders of the race and whispered something in his ear. In a while the announcer said, "There is something unusual occurring in this race today that has never happened in the more than one hundred-year history of the marathon. A young lad of twelve entered the race, and he is only about three hundred yards behind the leaders as they raced through the last village with six miles to go."

Galu knew now that he had to count off the miles carefully so he could use the same strategy as before. As they reached the twenty-one mile marker several more of the lead runners began to fade so between that marker and the twenty-third, there were only about fifty runners ahead of him. As they passed each mile marker, the excited announcer would tell the spectators who was leading, and as they recognized all of them, because of their prowess in previous events, they applauded for them. Each time the announcer would conclude saying, “The young lad is still only three hundred yards behind.”

Galu's classmates moved down the racing route for about a mile so they could run with him during the last mile with their usual encouragement. But that time had not come yet, as Galu watched as the pace quickened with some of the favorites dropping back, and as they approached the twenty-four mile marker, Galu picked up the pace himself, getting to only two hundred yards from the front. With this the public address announcer indicated that three of the previous champions were still in the lead, but that there was other maneuvering among the leading runners. He stated that the kid was now only two hundred yards off the pace, still running comfortably and with that unusual appearance. The announcer indicated that they had spotters every half mile for the remainder of the race except for the last quarter of a mile where they were stationed every few yards.

There were only seven runners ahead of Galu when he observed the twenty-five mile marker, and in the distance he could hear the chant, “Ga-luuuuuuuu, Ga-luuuuuuuu, Ga-luuuuuuuu, Ga-luuuuuuuu, Ga-luuuuuuuu, . . . " He knew it was time now to get within striking distance so he moved on up, passing five of the favorites to run very closely with the two leaders. When this happened, the announcer was beside himself to tell the spectators that the young lad was running neck and neck with two previous champions who both had previously broken the marathon time record.

Dan, standing on top of the van with the driver at this time, began to hear the chant, and he could see his young

Christian running so comfortably and confidently about a half mile away. Everyone was standing and the announcer was trying to describe something he had never seen before as young Galu, responding to the chant, moved ahead of the second runner, and with ease went around the lead runner and for nearly a quarter of a mile, he continued to stretch his lead. As Galu crossed the finish line, there appeared to be total silence, and then everyone knew that a special thing had happened in this marathon so they applauded for such a very long time.

Galu hugged his classmates, Dan, and the van driver and asked them to go over to the grassy area to have prayer. Following this event, which puzzled the onlookers, they got into the van, although many people, including the animated announcer, wanted to speak to Galu. It was Galu's style not to linger at these events so Dan got his trophy, loaded the van which reluctantly cranked, and began their westward trek through beautiful Tanzania just ahead of the puff of smoke that had the smell of oil. Not too far down the road they were singing school type songs and teasing each other as before. It was not like Galu to make any fuss over a little race such as this, so the racing subject was not entertained during the long ride home.

They went through village after village unnoticed except for the noises emitted from the van and the occasional ball of smoke that floated through the air. Arriving at the school in late evening, Galu led a prayer in a shady area, thanking God that they had a safe trip and giving somewhat of an apology for spending time on such a frivolous matter as a marathon race, instead of doing more directly His work in the community.

Pat met them at the school and was elated that Galu had won the regional marathon run. “I can’t believe you won the race,” Pat said, while hugging Galu and embarrassing him greatly.

“He ran such a marvelous race,” Dan said to Pat.

Following the beautiful prayer, a warm hug and bidding everyone farewell, Galu began his run home to be with his family before they went to bed. Of course, he didn't take the huge trophy, and in fact, Dan didn't think that he had even looked at it all the way home.

It was good that Galu was back in school learning all that was taught and helping the younger ones along in their achievement. In a few days though the villagers learned that Galu had won the regional marathon in the large eastern city, and they began to use this as a major topic of conversation in the various neighborhoods. The young "whippersnapper" had defied community tradition by entering the local race and ultimately winning it, and had gone to another area and had won that prestigious race, also. Many villagers had difficulty believing that he had actually won this marathon so they checked it out with others, including the van driver, who told them the whole story using numerous gestures that punctuated this animated story. The story soon circulated among the several areas until it reached the parents of Galu who did not know about the race result except for a faint response by Galu that he had won.

Because of Galu, the school had grown to a very large membership, and Dan and Pat were requesting help from the regional Christian associational office for financial assistance for some capital improvements to enlarge the present facilities to accommodate the expanded enrollment. It wasn't too long before the officials scheduled a visit to assess the situation at this school site, because this one was the only school in the whole region that was growing. Upon arrival the officials discovered a very large number of young people holding on to every word spoken by Dan and Pat. It was truly a model teaching-learning environment. But they realized that there was something very special about this group, because it had a young man only twelve years of age, who was the student leader who all respected and seemed to emulate his every move. They soon found out that his name was Galu, an extremely intelligent young man who was the genuine "hero" but who behaved in such an unassuming manner one would never suspect it.

At the exit interview all of the officials commended Dan and Pat for an excellent program that had enlarged the membership much beyond any of the other schools in the association wherein the enrollment figures had remained constant during the past several months. They all wanted to encourage further growth, but they wanted to be realistic with Dan to indicate that all capital outlay funds had been frozen since last year, and they did not know when additional funding would be available for new construction and for improvements to present structures. But they would place their request in a position of high priority, because of what they had observed today and the large increase in membership, so several forms would be left to be completed for this purpose.

The church service at the school on Sundays was growing at a very impressive rate, also, and to accommodate additional persons attending both Sunday school and morning worship, it took all of the ingenuity Dan and Pat could muster. They used all of the chairs, benches, logs, and everything else that would be in any way suitable for sitting, knowing that as the numbers increased each Sunday, the seating would have to be increased likewise. For Galu's Sunday school class the young people came from miles around to hear him teach the others his age and many older, and they sat on the ground holding on to every word spoken by their "hero" who had not changed one bit following his two marathon victories. Church associational officials were looking into expanding the sanctuary and school classroom space as soon as funds were available, also.

BASKETBALL RESUMES

Meanwhile, back at Bacon excitement was in the air as the girls scurried around getting ready to depart on their first basketball trip following the most delightful and worshipful Christmas season. Marsha, Lota and Vanona were back from a short visit to their home in New Mexico, and Mit was filled with joy, having received three lengthy letters from her mom and dad in Tanzania telling about their work, particularly about Galu. Each of Mit's young friends at Bacon from Costa Rica had received a long telephone call from her parents that was arranged by the business manager of the Baptist mission. What a special group that was unaffected by the world around them!

Renting a van in Roanoke, they traveled through the piedmont section of southern Virginia, passing Bassett High School where Mit advised the group where she used to live and attend church. Coach Anna had read the story of Mit in the mission magazine that Maudie cherished so she was aware of Mit having saved the life of a young two-year old years ago, and in the process almost losing her own.

"Mit, we have scheduled a preseason game of soccer in your beautiful high school stadium," Coach Anna stated.

"I can't believe you have done that!" Mit responded excitedly. "I can get to see all my friends here at that time."

"Renovations are being made on Grant Baptist Church so the pastor there asked another church group to host our team," Coach said. "I believe the name is Fort Trial Baptist Church. Do you know of a church by that name in Bassett?"

"It is a wonderful church much like Grant Baptist that involves young people in all kinds of activities," Mit excitedly replied. "We used to go there and participate in all kinds of programs when I was really young."

"We are scheduled to play a practice game following a soccer demonstration program, and then go to the Fort Trial Baptist Church for dinner," Coach Anna indicated. "After dinner the youth from the area will join us in an informal session in the fellowship hall."

"I can't wait to go back to my hometown," Mit said. "It's been a very long time since I lived there, but I really have fond memories of the wonderful people in the area."

"It had been such a special Christmas time for everybody," Coach Anna thought, as they entered North Carolina, having passed through the town of Ridgeway, the last little town in Virginia.

"Welcome to North Carolina," the sign stated, as the van proceeded south toward Webster University in the triad section. What was once a sprawling countryside of tobacco, corn and dairy farms had given away to an expanded metropolitan area covering many miles in all directions. The old south was becoming the new south with international airports, and modern four-lane roads filled with eighteen wheelers carrying products everywhere, having almost totally replaced the trains, but a few still traversed the railroads that could still be seen along the way.

The girls were really excited as they gathered for a meeting after they had gotten situated in their motel on the outskirts of the capital city. "During the Christmas season I talked to you all about visiting a hospital on each of our trips, and you seemed to be overjoyed to add this to our regular itinerary," Coach Anna said. "Let me read to you a portion of scripture that has been on my mind for a while." Turning in her small Bible, she read from Matthew 23:

31 "When the Son of Man comes in his glory, and all the angels with him, then he will sit on the throne of his glory.

32All the nations will be gathered before him, and he will separate people one from another as a shepherd separates the sheep from the goats,

33and he will put the sheep at his right hand and the goats at the left.

34Then the king will say to those at his right hand, 'Come, you that are blessed by my Father, inherit the kingdom prepared for you from the foundation of the world;

35for I was hungry and you gave me food, I was thirsty and you gave me something to drink, I was a stranger and you welcomed me,

36I was naked and you gave me clothing, I was sick and you took care of me, I was in prison and you visited me.'

37Then the righteous will answer him, 'Lord, when was it that we saw you hungry and gave you food, or thirsty and gave you something to drink?

38And when was it that we saw you a stranger and welcomed you, or naked and gave you clothing?

39And when was it that we saw you sick or in prison and visited you?'

40And the king will answer them, 'Truly I tell you, just as you did it to one of the least of these who are members of my family, you did it to me.'

"Those with much; much is expected.

"God has really blessed you and me to be able to go all over the country and play basketball and later soccer, so because of this I believe we should do more to spread kindness, compassion and love as God provides kindness, compassion and His special and continuous love to all of us. To do this, we will forego our practice session this afternoon and visit patients in the local hospital. All of you brought some item from the Hollow that you will be passing onto some sick person."

Their eating in the Rural Eatery where many of the local people dined created quite a stir, such that the girls could hardly serve themselves from the huge buffet of vegetables, because of those who wanted an autograph or just to speak to the team members. Several were soccer fans and had read about Mit and Marsha so they sought them out to get their signature on a restaurant napkin.

Wondering whether or not she had made an appropriate schedule for the team, because of the unusual disturbance caused by their presence in the restaurant and later in the hospital when they entered, Coach Anna still maintained her steadfast resolve to follow the plan bringing what she believed would be good tidings to the young patients in the hospital, some of whom were terminal cases. Moving to the different beds, the team members conversed with all of them. Pictures were made by the staff and parents of the children, especially when the girls passed on their gifts which included items made personally by the Hollow folks. Esther took time to read a couple of her short stories, and afterward gave her young patient a copy of the story signed by her and the other team members.

"What an exciting time!" Coach Anna thought, but it wasn't over yet, because surprisingly the hospital staff approved for several of the young people to attend the night's game with Webster.

"We are so grateful to you for permitting these young people to come to our game this evening," Coach Anna told the head nurse. "The Bacon team will dearly love their presence."

Arriving somewhat earlier than usual so the team could have an informal practice session, Bacon took the floor to the delight of those fans, who had been waiting to see the best team in the country. Upon completion of the preliminary session the team headed back to the bench to be greeted by the group from the hospital who were provided seats just behind the team. There was much commotion near their bench as they hugged their special guests for the evening, accompanied by their parents and several from the hospital staff. Returning to the floor, the rest of the pregame activity was normal until Esther suddenly ran over to the bench area and swooped up a young, bald oncology patient in her arms. Galloping across the floor with the capacity crowd watching with the young lady expressing her pleasure with a radiant smile, Esther grabbed a basketball in one hand, gave it to the excited child, whose name was Tabatha, and said, “Shoot it into the basket.”

With maximum encouragement from the crowd the young lady bounced it off the backboard into the net on her second try. With loud cheers Esther gave her the ball and immediately went to return her to her parents now tearfully watching their precious, afflicted young daughter.

With everybody ready, the game soon started, and as soon as the ball was tipped into the hands of a Webster player, the referee called time out and then ran quickly to give the game ball to the special hospital patients. It was a touching scene as most wiped their eyes, including the referee, as he blew his whistle to resume play.

Bacon, as usual, looked very sharp as Esther and Dorothy led the team to a large lead early. Soon Coach Anna had inserted Mit, so the fans got to see an exceptionally fast young lady moving up and down the floor, seemingly never being windless but always strong. “I can’t believe how fast Mit is,” Coach Anna thought, as she whizzed by the Bacon bench to retrieve a loose ball, and then swiftly moved down the floor to lay it in the basket without being contested.

Following the triumph in the game with a wide score differential, the team bade farewell to their special new friends as they swapped addresses, telephone numbers and e-mail addresses. Ineradicable memories were etched in the minds of all as the sad farewell was concluded.

Up the coast they flew early the next morning, arriving in Connecticut to play the University of Gordon on the campus of the main higher educational institution in the state. The hospital nearby was waiting anxiously for their visit, having been apprised of their very successful stopover in the triad in North Carolina.

The team replicated its activities of the previous hospital visit, and everyone enjoyed every minute. One young lad of seven literally stole the hearts of the entire group. Everyone just loved him as he kept all the others laughing and not thinking of their own physical condition. The crippling cancer had reduced his mobility somewhat, but his awkwardness in walking didn't deter his expressing his love for his peers, who had serious health problems, also. Mike was his name, and one could readily determine his popularity by just listening at the times his name was called during their visit.

At the game that evening Mike was still the center of attention, giving encouragement to his friends. He had learned numerous Bible verses and used them when speaking to others all the while. During the warm-up period, the team took the whole group of young patients on the floor with them, and then asked whom would they like to shoot the basketball. Of course, everyone said loudly, "We want Mike!"

With that wide, pleasant smile he stepped forward to get the ball with his frail little body barely supporting his own weight. Clutching the ball with all the energy he could muster, he moved closer to the basket, so wobbly and yet so determined. With the arena totally quiet, Esther and Dorothy lifted up the little hero for this moment to dunk the ball in front of a national audience throughout the country. When the ball was stuffed into the basket by Mike, the crowd cheered continuously until he was carried back to the sidelines still sporting that very contagious and loving smile.

Although the University of Gordon was a powerful team, it was no match for the small southwest Virginia Bacon College, as the team continued to add to its perfect record. Coach Anna could tell that the team's appearance of happiness was overshadowed by its deep concern for Mike, who was a very sick young man.

Arriving at Horban University in New Jersey the next afternoon, the group duplicated its activities for the previous two days by visiting a hospital and inviting the youngsters to the game. Everyone was so kind all the while, but there was difficulty at the game when numerous people had to be turned away after all of the tickets were sold. Advancing to a wide margin in the score at the inception of the game, Coach Anna used the other girls mainly in the contest.

It was really an excellent trip, but it was always good to get back home to the college.

BOB WATERS' MEETING

Knowing all along that there would be several people at the meeting to discuss the direction the state was headed, Bob was still surprised at the large number of people who showed enough interest to be present in the capital city. He had only been made aware of a portion of the topics to be discussed, but soon it was obvious what the main thrust of the meeting would be. It seemed that speaker after speaker noted the powerful role lawyers were playing in the lives of the people each day, certainly too much for this group that was for sure.

While Bob was much concerned himself about these issues that were being considered, he dared not say anything until he had more information or until a different forum was present. There were several pieces of paper handed out with numerous statistics supporting the group's claims. "Some people have done much work in preparation for this meeting," Bob thought, as he perused another document while seated about half way to the front of the large conference room filled to capacity.

The setting seemed to be informal as one speaker after another would stand and go to the front where the microphones were located so there was no fixed agenda. Having like interests, the whole scene was very cordial and tranquil. From time to time the group would burst out in spontaneous applause when someone would say something of special importance.

From the notes that Bob had taken, he could see succinctly that there was grave concern about how our legal and judicial systems had in many ways hamstrung the populace over the years so gradually that it almost went unnoticed. Instead of the law institution being one of help, it was paving the way in making it more difficult for business, industry and the average citizen to function without becoming more and more dependent on the services of that institution.

The growth of the number of lawyers in the state was greater than even Bob realized, and when there was the revelation of the volume of lawsuits between and among people, business and industry, he was shocked. The multitude of trial lawyers kept the settlements high according to a report of one of the speakers, providing inordinate incomes that in some way were being paid by the general population. Another pointed out how that the wording of our statutes had become so complex that interpretations were absolutely necessary by other lawyers, thereby making the average citizen even more dependent.

After more than a two-hour session, a middle-age gentleman stood up to speak. “We have not even scratched the surface today, but we have developed commonality of interest which should provide us with direction as we continue. From all of the discussion today we can be assured that we all agree on two subjects. Most of our energy today provided a time to speak about our legal system, which we believe has possibly outlived its usefulness in the present form. This whole issue will be addressed in writing during our next meeting. Secondly, we shall examine more closely the dismal failure of our affluent society to correct the posture regarding the practice of aborting live little babies in the name of mother’s choice. These two areas and others will be addressed in written form and will be mailed to all of you within two weeks.”

Many of the individuals at the meeting remained in the conference room so Bob discovered much from his informal discussion with several of the people in attendance. He overheard the leader say that today’s meeting was really only to see whether or not there was sufficient interest to continue to attempt to effect some changes in the way the state is operated. "Obviously," he said, "just putting and explaining things on paper would not get the group too much closer to its goal. But keep in mind, if we can get the right candidates who are not lawyers but are intelligent, hard working lay people, we can become effective change agents."

Bob was really not a political person, but his concern regarding decisions that had been made during the last few years had increased such that when he received his invitation to attend this meeting, he was very interested. During his long ride back to the mountains in southwest Virginia from the capital, he thought about the meeting and how informative it had really been. It was obvious that those in attendance had the same concerns as he had, if he interpreted correctly what they were saying. One of the things he had observed during his lifetime was the tremendous increase in lawsuits, and his concern was compounded when thinking about the huge settlements of many. He remembered what one man said at the meeting, "It's difficult for me to have a peaceful day around my home, realizing that with one lawsuit, and I could lose all that I have."

Another pointed out, "Years ago there were only a couple lawyers in my small town situated in old offices, and now there are dozens operating out of numerous, large and beautifully adorned buildings lining both sides of our main street." Bob had really not thought of this, but it was true of his own neighborhood in the mountains.

One older man pointed out that years ago it was an unwritten rule for lawyers not to advertise their business, but in recent times all the media carry advertisements trying to lure clients. He went on to say that the advertisements themselves somewhat depicted the situation, as it is today by telling us that with a good lawyer we can be saved from each other

A recent college graduate told the group that he grew up after lawyers had begun to play such a prominent role in our society. Then he said, "It wasn't until after the huge tobacco settlements that I began to think about our system of justice very much. When I was young my parents told me not to smoke, because it was not good for my health, and even my grandfather told me that his mother had warned him about the dangers of smoking. Now even with warnings everywhere, people who smoke and contract cancer can hire the right lawyers and receive huge, and I mean huge, settlements as a reward for doing something that was considered and known all the while was detrimental to one's health. I can only attribute this direction of our courts to the lawyers. And by the way, expect much more of the same, particularly regarding fast foods with grease, automobile accidents, alcohol, and much more. Everywhere there is money to be made there will be lawsuits."

Bob's mind was swirling as he rehashed the comments by the people at the meeting. "It was as though the ones who spoke were saying what I believe," Bob thought, as he drove through scenic Virginia's south side through Halifax County.

Not being able to get the meeting off his mind, Bob decided that he would go to the Hollow to speak to Josh about what he had heard. Josh was a very wise gentleman, one that Bob respected highly. "I really like to discuss things with Josh," Bob thought, as he drove up the Hollow. "He never gives one the appearance that he is a leader, but beneath the veneer of kindness, compassion, trust and love, there is even a stronger being that is manifested in his actions and his verbal expressions."

Following greetings and some small talk, Bob asked Josh to sit down with him to talk about the citizens' meeting he just attended. With both sitting on the front pew in the wood frame church, Bob rendered a lengthy dissertation concerning the meeting in Richmond. Just telling Josh seemed to provide relief for Bob, but he was surprised when Josh reacted with a couple of unusual and wise thoughts.

"You know Bob," Josh said, "I believe you could be describing in a way the period when Jesus walked on earth with the Scribes and Pharisees involving themselves with how we should interpret the law. Jesus was trying to tell the people that there was a new law, but the strength of tradition was overwhelming, and it slowed their acceptance of Jesus' teaching."

"That is interesting," Bob said.

"During recent years there have been more and more translations of the Bible," Josh stated. "The idea is to make the Bible readable and understandable by everybody, which is an admirable goal."

"In your own way you are saying that our laws are very complex, and only lawyers can interpret them properly," Bob reacted. "Are you saying that if our laws were written differently, we all could read and understand them without the assistance of lawyers?"

"I believe that they could be written that way, don't you?" Josh said.

"I think they could," Bob said. "That would be a tremendous step in empowering the individual citizen."

"I hadn't really thought of it that way," Josh said, "but it would certainly help."

"What a powerful meeting with Josh," Bob thought, as he departed the Hollow after spending more than an hour with his special friend. "He has such wise thoughts that are not clouded by a world beyond the Hollow, which makes him as pure as wind blown snow. He could be a guiding force to people beyond these mountain ranges framing in the Hollow."

CONTINENTAL MARATHON

In the bush country of Tanzania once every three months, Dan and Pat went to the associational headquarters where the teachers and other Christian leaders held their quarterly business meeting. These were very intense and informative meetings that kept everyone abreast with the latest activities, and gave them an opportunity to share what they were doing at the various centers. Much attention was being given to the Traverses' program wherein their membership was growing very much, so the others in attendance at the meeting asked them to explain what they were doing that might be replicated in the other learning centers.

"Would you all mind telling us what it is that you are doing that causes your program to grow so rapidly?" the associational director asked.

"I wish I could say that we had a lot to do with the growth directly, but we didn't," Dan explained. "As all of you may not know our background in mission work, let me tell you that we spent more than ten years in the jungle of southern Costa Rica. We experienced considerable growth there, also, over a period of time, but we had our daughter, who was really the reason for our advancing the message of our Savior, Jesus Christ. When we were assigned to Tanzania, Pat and I both realized that for us we would be operating with a considerable handicap without Mit. But we learned long ago to trust in the Lord and not to labor only on our understanding.

"God really blessed us mightily as he sent a young man named Galu to our school to be enrolled. Galu ran twenty miles to and from school each day, because he yearned for learning so much. At the time he was eleven years of age, but because this was the first time that he had been involved in any kind of school, I thought that he would be handicapped for getting such a late start. But to the contrary, he has achieved much beyond where he would be expected. In fact he has done so well, we have him teaching younger children and many his age and older. They all respect this young man who is so mature and wise way beyond his chronological age. The respect that the other children and adults in the church and school have for him seems to grow with each day."

Dan continued, "You may not know it, but this young man has won two twenty-six-mile marathons, the local and regional, during the last several weeks. For anyone to win such a prestigious event, it would somehow impact on his actions, attitude, or personality in some way, but for Galu he is exactly the same, not ever mentioning anything about either of the races, as it is as though he had not participated in them much less won the events."

It was at break time that one of the teachers from another area in the association half jokingly mentioned, "You know there is a twenty-six-mile marathon for the continent of Africa to be held in Johannesburg in a few weeks. I believe you should register this young runner in that race."

Slipping over to where Pat was standing, Dan whispered, "Are you aware that there is an African marathon being staged in South Africa sometime soon?"

"No, I didn't know that," Pat stated in a low voice. "Do you think it would be possible for Galu to compete in this race?"

"When we first discussed about his participating in the regional event, I thought it would be impossible, but look what happened," Dan said. "It would be a shame for him not to be able to continue something that he loves so very much.

In all of my years I have never seen a young man who behaves the way he does. You and I are the ones who try to teach the young and old alike to be godly in all of their dealings in life, and here we are learning from this young man. God has sent us a genuine treasure to replace our Mit."

"I agree with you that Galu ought to continue to run in these events, if that is what he wants to do," Pat responded.

"After the meeting I shall attempt to get him registered," Dan stated, as the couple walked back to the conference room.

Through the rest of the meeting, Dan and Pat had much difficulty in keeping their minds focused on the conference, because their thoughts would always return to the African national marathon. "Surely it would contain all of the world class runners from all over this continent and even other parts of the world, who would be superior to any runners in the previous races," Dan thought. It was difficult to put his thoughts into perspective, as the whole idea seemed to be beyond reach, and in fact overwhelming. The whole thing consumed all of their energy so they decided to put it on the "back burner" for awhile, or at least until the conference was over, when they would get back on the subject, hopefully, with somewhat clearer vision.

Following the last session in the associational conference, Dan asked a headquarters' official to permit him to use the telephone to call Johannesburg to get Galu registered for the marathon that was to be held in the near future. It took a while, but before too long Dan got one of the marathon officials on the telephone, and was surprised to discover that runners could be registered via the telephone during the next six days, if they were native Africans and had run in at least two marathons before. As Dan supplied the necessary data, the marathon official completed the form including the full name of Galu, which Dan indicated was Young Christian Galu, because as far as he knew, Galu had no other name except Galu. Although the registrar was surprised that Galu was only twelve, and they had never had an entry under twenty before, it was indicated that the age cut off was twelve, just as it was in the two previous races. Upon conclusion Dan was advised to come to one of the registration booths at least one hour before the start of the marathon to confirm the entry and to receive his number.

Dan and Pat were really excited about getting Galu registered for this huge race, but they both suddenly were shocked when the director told them that they could use the telephone to call their daughter Mit in the United States.

"You mean we can call our daughter at Bacon College," Pat repeated with a high pitched voice.

"You certainly may," he responded.

Nervously, Dan retrieved the telephone number from his billfold, and Pat carefully dialed the number.

"Hello, this is Anna Bosley of the Bacon athletic dormitory," Coach Anna said. "How may I help you?"

"This is Pat Travers calling from Tanzania," Pat stated with an emotional voice.

"How are you all doing?" Coach Anna excitedly said.

"We are fine," Pat indicated. "How is Mit doing?"

"She is doing extremely well," Coach Anna noted. "Let me get her to the telephone so she can tell you herself."

"Mom, how are you and Dad doing?" Mit said immediately.

"We are fine and how are you?" Pat replied.

"I am so happy here at Bacon with all the other girls," Mit said, "but I miss you and Dad so very much."

"We surely miss you, too," Pat stated.

"Have you received my letters that I wrote?" Mit asked.

"We received one last week," Pat responded. "Mail service to our area here is not very strong, but do keep on writing to us."

"We played in Hawaii a couple of days ago and met a ten-year old boy who was suffering from cancer," Mit related. "He needed a bone marrow transplant, but the family didn't have money to have the procedure performed. After a story was written about him in the newspaper, an anonymous donor from the Bacon area gave sufficient money to pay all the medical costs and other expenses. We all cried with joy."

"God is so wonderful," Pat responded. "How are Maria and Monita getting along?"

"They really have adjusted well, and they can't wait until our soccer season starts shortly," Mit answered. "Coach Anna is making arrangements for us to play a practice game at Bassett High School, your and Dad's alma mater."

"I know you all will have a good time when you go there to play," Pat said. "All of our friends will be there."

"Coach Anna read us a letter she received from the president of Wasi in which he indicated that he was taking her up on the invitation for the Wasian girls to come to the Hollow to learn more about playing basketball," Mit stated. "Won't that be a lot of fun?"

"It certainly will," Pat said. "All of you are very excited about their coming, I am sure."

"We certainly are," Mit quickly responded. "In the letter he mentioned something else that he would divulge to her at a later date. We don't know what else he is planning."

"Let me tell you more about our mission activities here that I mentioned in our letters to you," Pat stated. "We knew we would have difficulty here establishing a school and planting a church, because you are not with us. You did such a marvelous job of spreading the good news of Jesus Christ in the jungle of Costa Rica, such that our program grew beyond our greatest imagination. Without you we were at a loss just how to start. But isn't God wonderful?

"One day a young man came to our fledgling school and shortly was enrolled. He is the most charming twelve-year-old young man one would ever want to meet. Soon he was at the head of the class such that he began to help the others with their school work, and later started teaching Sunday school. In the school the number of students has grown tremendously, and likewise, the Sunday school class is bursting at the seams.

"The other children love him to death. Recently, he entered the local marathon race and won to the surprise and disbelief of the village folks. You see he was by far the youngest runner ever to participate. Your dad entered his name in the regional marathon in eastern Tanzania, and he won that race, also. Now he is entered in the African marathon held in Johannesburg, South Africa, where there will be thousands of runners. He is our little unassuming hero here now, not showing expressions that might reveal to others that he is a local hero."

"What is his name?" Mit asked.

"It is Galu," Pat answered. "We have not discovered any other name. He is such a precious Christian young man who is truly a God send to us here."

In the telephone conversation Pat made her round in asking about everybody, but soon they closed as each expressed her love for the other.

Upon arriving back at the village Dan knew that he had a monumental task to get Galu involved in another marathon, but he would begin the next morning at the start of the school day. Arriving at school the following morning, Galu made his same entrance to school as in the past days while the other children waited, as usual, to yell in unison: "Galuuuuuuuu, Galuuuuuuuu, Galuuuuuuuu, . . . " as they had done for so many days, seemingly not tiring of expressing their adoration of a most special peer.

Prior to the start of the first class, Dan broached the subject of the Johannesburg marathon with Galu, and he just listened without showing any emotion as he had done so many times before. The start of the first class brought a halt to their discussion that Dan said would be resumed later in the day, if they had time. It was such a full day that they were not able to return to the subject so at the end of school, Dan told Galu that they would discuss the marathon the next morning.

As Galu ran to and from school each day, the villagers became more and more accepting of him, yet they were reluctant to express their feelings to him. As he gracefully moved along while usually singing one of the church hymns, he thought about how much his teachers had meant to him over the most recent period of his short life. Soon his thoughts were on the big African national marathon that would be such a huge decision to be a part of this celebrated race that had a rich tradition and drew the world class runners. In the previous two races he never questioned his ability to compete, and when he thought of this powerful and most prestigious marathon, he never doubted himself at all. He was a very confident but extremely humble young man.

During this day on the trip home, Galu thought about the Johannesburg race and how his parents would react when they were told that he was entered. His teaching of the other students was very important to him so he did not want to do anything that would interfere with that effort, and also, his Sunday school teaching was done with a great deal of zeal so this, too, should not be slighted in the least. Pondering the various ramifications of the continental trip to run in a marathon with world class runners, Galu knew that financial assistance would be needed, and he didn't want anything in which he was involved to cause problems for any of the programs.

Arriving at home, Galu went about his business, as usual, gathering food and doing his chores with the same fervor. It was after the evening meal with all of the family that he thought that it would be in the best interest to ask his parents about registering for the big marathon in South Africa. Getting them alone, Galu requested their approval of the event that he thought he was expected to participate. Many times his parents would not immediately give him an answer to his requests, and in fact, some responses came even days later. This one was one of those delayed answers that he had come to tolerate without even a hint of discontent, or any kind of a facial expression that would indicate he was upset with anything his parents did. They were the ones to provide the answer, and he would be the gracious recipient.

Arriving at school early the next morning, Galu went directly to work on his teaching assignments for the day, and he took just a little time to adjust a piece of work that was to be turned in to Dan and Pat. Dan really was anxious to talk to Galu, but knowing that teaching and learning took precedent over anything else, including marathons, he did not approach Galu about registering for the Johannesburg competition. However, when they took their lunch break, the whole atmosphere changed as Galu found a note from his parents in his lunch bag that gave their approval for him to participate in the marathon. Hearing of the good news, Dan took Galu aside and said, "I'll begin making plans for the long journey, and make all preparations for your entering this race."

"Thank you very much for doing that," Galu responded.

Included in their conversation was the fact that there would be numerous world class runners, and just to enter and especially to finish this race was a goal of many of the entrants, because it was so prestigious. "This will be a huge race, drawing runners from all over Africa and elsewhere," Dan stated. "Are you concerned about participating with all of these runners that we only read about in the sports' magazine?"

"My main concern is always the decisions that are made by my parents," he said so humbly. "I am really at peace with this race, having received the blessing of my parents."

Dan knew that he would have a lot of difficulty in getting sufficient financial help to get them to the race, because they would have to travel for several days, and funds would be scarce for gasoline and food. As the days wore on, he talked with more and more of the villagers, but each time there was a negative response. He could discern from the way they were responding to his inquiry that they had not forgiven Galu for running in their local race, and they were not going to contribute toward his welfare as he prepared for another event. Furthermore, Dan could detect, also, that the villagers thought that Galu would be "biting off more than he could chew" if he ran in the celebrated Johannesburg race. In other words they didn't want any part of this situation.

Within two weeks of the racing date, the van driver came to Dan and told him that he didn't know whether or not his old dilapidated vehicle could make such a long trip to Johannesburg, but because no one else had offered any alternative, he would be willing to attempt to make the trip. It was estimated that one hundred fifty gallons of gasoline would be needed for the van along with several quarts of oil, so now the "wick would have to be turned up" to raise the money for the fuel. Dan believed that they had enough saved to pay one-half of the expenses, the van driver contributed enough for a few gallons, so they were still in need of a little less than half of the fuel expense.

In a few days Dan indicated, "Galu, we'll have to leave for Johannesburg tomorrow, if we expect to arrive in time for the race, because it would take them three days, at least, to get there." They still did not have enough money to make the trip.

On the eve of their departure when Galu arrived at home, his mother told him to do the work of his father, also, because he would not be home until late that night. This was perplexing to Galu, because this was the first time he could remember that his father was not at home in the evening, but he put the concern aside for the time being to concentrate on his chores and assisting the other children in doing their work. It was late in the evening when his father did come home, and upon his arrival he and Galu's mother went to one side to talk to each other very quietly. Soon, they returned and with all of the children, they gathered to eat their evening meal at this late hour, because they always waited for their parents to be present before they ate. Following a prayer to God thanking Him for their many blessings and the special love He had given to the entire family, they ate with just a minimum of talking, but there was no mention of the marathon that Galu would leave tomorrow to run in Johannesburg.

Galu got ready for school on this morning by getting his woven bag that had been used to carry onions and put on his running pants, rope belt, and the big handkerchief his mother had given him to take. In addition he took two bags of food including sweet potatoes, dried meat, bread logs, and oranges. As he got ready to depart, all of his brothers and sisters, mother and father hugged him, and they all wished him well. While they were all together, Galu asked them to bow their heads, and he prayed to God that his family would be safe until his return, and he asked God to bless them, because of the great love they had shown to him.

When the van driver pulled up to Dan's and Pat's house which was very near the school, he saw that Dan was sporting a wide smile. Before he could get out of the van, Dan said, "Let me tell you what happened early last evening. We heard a thump at our door, and when we went to see what it was, we discovered an old bag lying on the floor. Taking the bag inside, we opened it and found exactly enough money to complete the financing of the trip. In addition to the money of coins of small denominations in the bag, there was an accompanying note which read: 'May your God be pleased and best wishes in marathon.' It was unsigned; however, we think that it is likely contributions from many villagers that were collected by a brave person who wanted to see that the trip was financed."

A ten-year-old student was permitted to go along as a representative voted on by the school, so Galu had a schoolmate to provide some youthful company for the very long trip. With a couple of hours into the journey, Dan told Galu about the money he had received anonymously to help defray the fuel expense for the trip, and he showed him the note that was in the bag. Upon seeing the note, Galu knew that he had seen the handwriting before, because it was his father's, but he knew that he must not betray his father who wanted to do this benevolent act secretly. Now he understood why his father was not at home the previous evening when he got home, because his father was collecting contributions from his village friends so that Galu and his group could get to Johannesburg to enter the national marathon. Quietly handing the note back to the master teacher, Galu rendered a silent prayer, thanking God for working through his father and others to make this trip possible. Galu had such a good feeling now about the whole affair dealing with this trip.

The scenery was very beautiful as they traveled through Tanzania and the other countries to the south. Stopping every several hours for all of them to rest, the early stages of their journey were uneventful, and they were right on schedule. All of them would sleep in the van in different corners, because they believed that it would be safer in the van than sleeping under the stars where they might be attacked by wild animals roaming in the night. For each meal they would each go to his bag of food, sharing items from time to time. Each had some kind of fresh fruit, bread, some kind of dried meat, and at least one type of vegetables, which was very nourishing.

On their last travel day before entering Johannesburg, it was noon and the master teacher knew that they had about nine hours of driving to do to get to the outskirts of the city, and it would take them at least an hour to find the starting point of the race. If this schedule held up, Galu would be able to rest from about ten o'clock that evening until five-thirty the next morning, which would be sufficient.

All of them became "all eyes" as they got closer and closer to this large metropolitan center. About six miles from the city, they began to hear a clanging sound near the right rear of the van so the van driver pulled to the side of the road and examined the right rear wheel to discover that it was nearly off the axle. Checking his watch, Dan knew that they had time to get the vehicle repaired, but there was no one available at this time of night so they used all of the tools available in the van to try to make the repairs themselves. After about two hours and with little progress, it was agreed that they needed mechanical assistance to have the broken part repaired. At this time the van driver thought that it would be best for Galu, the other student and Dan to go on ahead so they could be in place for the start of the race the next morning.

It was much after midnight when they found the starting point of the race. A short distance from the bleachers that had been erected for this celebrated event, Galu crawled under a small tree surrounded by green grass to get some sleep during the remainder of the night. With the marathon beginning at eight o'clock, Dan awakened Galu at six-thirty so he could go through his morning routine before the start. Dan went to register his little runner and upon receiving his number of 10364, the registrar warned that he would be disqualified if he interfered with the other runners. Furthermore, he was advised that there had been much discussion about permitting such a young runner in their prestigious race, because no one under twenty years of age had ever entered the race before.

By this time many spectators were already in place, and when the master teacher began to put on Galu's number, there was disbelief among those in the stands that could see them. In fact disbelief turned to laughter after a while as more and more of the spectators witnessed the scene. But, as usual, it didn't seem to phase Galu in the least, because he always appeared focused on what his goal was whether it was in his school work, church activities, or marathon events. When he ate his pre-race meal of a sweet potato, dried meat, log of bread, and orange, there was considerable discussion generated among the spectators. They were still looking at the odd group with the poorly clad diminutive child runner as the time approached seven-thirty, and Galu asked that they all go to the grassy area for their prayer of thanksgiving. All bowing before numerous and curious onlookers, Galu prayed that God's will would be done for all during the day, and that the Holy Spirit would guide the actions of him and all others in attendance and observing the event.

Galu took his place at the back of more than ten thousand runners and was soon swallowed up by the large number of runners surrounding him. The start came exactly at eight o'clock, but because of the thousands of runners in front of him, he didn't start running for a while until the front runners got out of the way. There were no hecklers at this race so he just ran smoothly to try to get up closer to the front, because he was now very far behind. The crowded running area precluded his passing others very early, but soon after four or five miles they began to spread out, and he began to make his early move. Between six and nine miles into the race he was working himself into a position to be close to the lead groups as he had done in the previous two events. He seemed to have an unusual instinct to know where to position himself on the race course even though he had never seen the route before.

By this time in the race the people lined up beside the road to give best wishes to their favorite runners, and they began to notice this very youthful lad keeping pace with the leaders just a few hundred yards behind the lead groups. It was during this part of the race that the children and youth along the road started to become acquainted with Galu, and as he would pass them, they would yell some kind words of encouragement. One group in unison yelled: "Keep it up; doing a great job!" Galu was very much touched that his peers would want to give him a boost even though he knew none of them.

As Galu approached the twelve-mile marker, he read a sign, which indicated that there would be no more water for the next several hundred yards. Soon he realized that for this part of the route spectators were not permitted to stand along the road, because there was no room on either side. It reminded Galu of his previous two races wherein there were long parts of the course where there were no spectators at all, but here, it was unusual to be running without those on the side cheering.

Being about one hundred yards into the isolated area, Galu could see a person on the rough roadway that appeared to be unconscious and bleeding profusely near the temple area. Galu stopped and realized that it was a fallen runner who was seriously hurt and needed attention immediately, so he carefully dragged him beyond harm's way to a shady area on the right side of the course. There he took his large, red handkerchief and wiped the blood from the face of the injured runner. He knew that the downed runner needed water so with no hesitation he turned and ran back to the water table that was near the entrance to the "no spectator" area. Many of the onlookers saw Galu return to get three plastic containers of water, and then head back toward where the injured runner was lying.

A spotter saw his actions and mentioned it to the main commentator when he called in his report. The main commentator, who was at the starting area, kept the spectators apprised of what was taking place on the race course by telling them who was leading at various points along the way. When the main commentator heard about a runner 10364 helping an injured comrade, he told the spectators about the event and that he would keep them posted. Dan, the van driver and the student were all proud of Galu for what he was doing, but they were astute enough about marathon racing to know that he had given up any hope of winning.

Upon Galu's return to the injured runner he could hear the crunching of broken underbrush in the wooded area just beyond where he was kneeling down, but he gave his complete attention to the victim. Very patiently, he poured water on his large handkerchief and again cleaned the injured's head wound. “Please drink some water,” Galu stated.

His regaining consciousness gave Galu a big boost, and as he turned to see what was making the noise in the wooded area, he saw a photographer who made several pictures as Galu bound the wound of the injured man and of Galu's bleeding bare feet as he knelt down. Seeing the photographer, Galu motioned and said, “Please come and help the downed runner.”

At this point Galu bade farewell to the fallen runner and the photographer and proceeded to continue the race, being now very far behind the others, having been passed by runner after runner during the several minutes he was giving the needed assistance. Soon he exited the "no spectator" area now seeing the route filled with bystanders.

It was after he had completed thirteen miles that a spotter noticed Galu and reported back to the main commentator that the "benevolent boy" was now running again after helping the fallen runner. The spotter went on to say that he was running well even though his feet were bleeding on the bottom, but he had lost so much time that it was impossible for him to be a top finisher.

The pace of Galu had quickened, and when he approached a spotter at about the eighteen-mile mark, the main commentator related to those at the finish line that the "benevolent boy," number 10364, was making his way through the pack of runners and had remarkably closed the distance to the front.

Everyone marveled at the peaceful countenance expressed on the youthful face as his blood stained bare feet pounded the pavement as he passed the thousands of onlookers on both sides of the marathon route. When the main commentator announced the leaders again and then gave an account of "BB," as he called Galu, everyone along the way seemed to know who this young man was. He had stolen the hearts of all of those present and the radio listening audience as well. The question on everyone's mind was how a marathon runner could lose all this time and still continue to make up the distance.

At this point the van driver, Dan and the student made their way over several blocks where they could see the runners as they came by the twenty-first-mile point. They eased themselves through the record crowd until they were positioned right on the side of the road, and they saw the lead runner and then a small group of about seven other runners and then a larger group just behind them. All of them had low numbers, which meant they were either champions or former champions. Suddenly, the van driver, Dan and the student heard shouting of "BB, BB, BB, BB, ..." as Galu came by almost not seeing his friends on the side who yelled "Galuuuuuuuu" as loudly as they could as he sped by.

They all agreed that Galu did not understand what the spectators were yelling when they called out "BB." Very quickly Dan told the student to run as fast as he could to the sharp turn at the twenty-third mile marker where the runners turned to run the long straight in the homeward stretch, and tell Galu that "BB" was a loving name he had been given, and all the onlookers were pulling for him.

In the meantime the main commentator told the thousands of spectators at the finish line, “There is something I have not told you and that is that the young ‘BB’ is only twelve years old.”

Everyone was shocked to hear this. Further, the main commentator stated that the young runner was continuing his catch-up pace, and as they approached the twenty-third-mile marker, he was only three hundred yards behind, even after spending several minutes nursing a fallen runner.

The other student barely made it to the sharp turn just ahead of Galu, who was running very fast now. As Galu started to make the turn and with everyone yelling "BB," the student got Galu's attention and told him that "BB" meant that they loved him and were pulling for him. The booming sound of "BB" being yelled by the thousands of onlookers nearly drowned out what the young student told Galu, but he did hear and gave him just a little smile. The smile was enough, because he knew Galu was not one to show much emotion.

The long straight away made it possible for those in the bleachers all along the side of the road to see much of the end of the race, because it was up a slight incline for half the way before it leveled off for the last one and one-half miles. The van driver, and Dan had made their way back to the finish line, being reminded now that their young Christian runner was very unique.

As they got in position, the main commentator indicated, “There are two former champions leading the eleven other front runners who will be coming into view in a short while. ‘BB’ has pulled up to within one hundred yards of the leader and is now continuing his move, being boosted by the loud chant: ‘BB, BB, BB, BB, . . .’ all the while.”

The main commentator further stated to the crowd. “I have been doing the announcing for this marathon for more that thirty years, and I have never seen anything like what is happening today. First of all there is an entrant who was only twelve years of age who ran barefooted, and he then stoppcd and spent several minutes helping a runner who was injured in a fall. With all of that I now stand here to tell everyone that the youthful runner would be in the fourth position when they appear over the crest to start their long, level stretch toward the finish line."

Several with binoculars could see the lead runner coming over the crest and in a short while there came the second, and then they heard him yell that the youth was now in third, running at a very fast pace. The main commentator had binoculars, and many of his associates were assisting him so he could keep everyone informed about what was taking place. The whole scene was one of cheering and jubilation for a young marathon runner that they had never seen, but one who had done on this day that which they would always remember.

By this time the van driver, Dan and the student had worked themselves in position to see about one-half mile down the road, but the runners were not yet in view. Suddenly, the main commentator indicated excitedly, "'BB' has just passed the third runner and is only about fifty yards behind the leader." Following this statement, everyone applauded loudly.

As Galu passed the second runner, the main commentator told the spectators that "BB's" feet were bleeding badly, and the last spotter had noticed drops on the pavement. Everyone got very quiet realizing that their little hero who had given so much was now in pain himself, and each wanted to go out and help him. But they knew they couldn't, so they continued their vociferous cheering as each announcement was made.

Within full view now only one-half mile away, the main commentator said, "I am going to turn my microphone off and let all of you witness along with me what might be the greatest marathon run in the history of the sport."

When Galu could be seen by the van driver, Dan and the student, he was only about twenty yards behind the leader who wore number 1. The spectators couldn't believe what they were seeing that a child with the large number 10364 gaining with every stride on their last year's champion. Furthermore, how he could run with many cuts on his feet no one knew. Yet, Galu continued to quicken the pace still possessing that serene look on his face, still running with confidence and still instinctively knowing just how fast to run to overtake the leader.

The crowd had gone wild watching their hero run the last quarter of a mile to the finish as he passed the leader with nearly one hundred yards remaining and gracefully broke the finish line tape. There was complete bedlam when he came across the line as everyone applauded, cried and continued to shout "BB" long after the race was over.

Meanwhile, Galu, as usual, made his way to the side, and the van driver, Dan and the student joined him for prayer. Following this, Dan went back to get his trophy and caught up with them as they got to the van. Dan knew that Galu was very independent, but he looked at his feet anyway, and he took some of their water and cleaned them well and wrapped them in his shirt so that they would not get infected. Within a very short time they were on their way home in the dilapidated old van sporting the most prestigious trophy, but no one talked about it, because Galu didn't want to discuss anything about himself. Soon they were singing some hymns, rejoicing before God, as the old van belched its blue balls of smoke and chugged north to their home country.

The news of Galu's marathon victory spread throughout the continent, and Tanzania was no exception. It seemed that all knew about it, and they wanted to claim him as their hero, so when they entered the border of Tanzania, people came from everywhere to see the twelve-year old who had turned the continent upside down. The villagers, old and young alike, came from everywhere to speak to their little marathon runner. Sometimes the van would have to stop, because so many people were in the roadway it was difficult to drive passed them. During one stretch of road, it was so crowded that the people refused to get out of the way, so in order to appease them, Galu was asked to sit on top of the van. Of course, he was very reluctant, but after the other student was permitted to sit on the top, also, he agreed. It was very embarrassing for him so as soon as he could, they both got back into the van.

News had gotten to Galu's home village, and the leaders were planning a big feast to celebrate their favorite son's marathon victory. One could readily see that Galu was now fully accepted as a marathon runner, and now the village people were going to lay claim that he was one of theirs. As the van drove into the school village, following days of being on the road, they could hear the students yelling: "Galuuuuuuuu, Galuuuuuuuu, Galuuuuuuuu, Galuuuuuuuu, . . . " just as they had chanted on every school morning. The van driver was so excited about all of the fanfare, he insisted that he would drive the van to Galu's home.

As usual, Galu was his same serene self, not getting caught up in the victorious movement, so when he arrived at home everyone greeted him in the usual manner, without talking about the race. As soon as the van departed, one would have thought that this was just another day in the life of Galu's family. It was nightfall so the evening meal was being served. Following the blessing rendered by Galu, they all ate a hearty meal together, talking about school and family things with all of the children and parents joining the conversation. It was obvious that Galu was very happy to be home with his loving family.

There was secretiveness about the feast that was being planned for Galu, honoring him as the current national hero. Several village officials in the area had decided that it would be scheduled on Saturday so that it would not interfere with the educational program. They had planned to cook a couple of fat sheep and a young cow, with the village folks furnishing all of the other foods, such as vegetables, bread and sweets.

Feast day came, and Galu was lured to the site by his parents, brothers and sisters, as they pretended to be going to the village to see some friends. Of all the people in the community Galu was the least to want anybody to praise him for anything, especially for his running. It was a big day for the community, because everyone was together focusing on their little hero, who seemed to be bonding them together like no one had seen before.

The children romped and played all kinds of games, and in fact there was a mini marathon, and all the children dressed just like Galu when he ran his marathons with the shin-length ragged pants, a rope belt and a large handkerchief in his pocket. Galu positioned himself inconspicuously so he could avoid the limelight. At the close of the special feast that was the first for the community, Galu was hoisted on the shoulders of two of the community's forefathers and marched around while everyone chanted: "Galuuuuuuuu, Galuuuuuuuu, Galuuuuuuuu, Galuuuuuuuu, Galuuuuuuuu, Galuuuuuuuu, . . . " on into the evening.

A Sad Day

Back in southwest Virginia with the basketball season winding down, the Bacon girls were preparing for their last trip before the ACUWAA tournament. Merriment filled the athletic dormitory as the group prepared to depart for their two games in the southeast with singing and humorous talk, when the telephone rang.

"This is the athletic dormitory," Maudie said, when she answered the telephone.

"My name is Oscar Northy," a man stated. "Several days ago the Bacon College team played a game with the University of Gordon in Connecticut, and when they were here, they visited the local hospital where my son was a patient. It was his dream to see the Bacon team play, obviously his favorite team. Mike died yesterday, and before he died he asked his mother and me to invite the Bacon team to be at his funeral. The funeral is scheduled for two o'clock tomorrow. We do hope the team can honor our son's final wish. He told us that he wanted his friends to have the opportunity to meet his special friends on his most favorite basketball team ever, the Bacon College team, so he wanted us to invite the team to his funeral."

"I know that they can," Maudie answered for the team. "Give me your number, and I shall have Coach Bosley to call you right back."

Shortly, Coach Anna called to talk to the grieving father to gather all of the details. When she hung up, she asked the team to assemble for a prayer spoken so eloquently by her. It was a very sad time for the girls who quietly completed their packing in a still environment.

"Maudie," Coach Anna stated, "because we are going to have to alter our schedule so very much, would you be able to go to assist us?"

"I would love to go and do whatever I can," Maudie responded, "but I would have to get approval from Dr. Damond."

"I'll call him while you go quickly to pack," Coach Anna suggested.

By the time Maudie was back from her apartment with her luggage, Coach Anna had received approval from Dr. Damond, and by this time everyone was ready to go.

Arriving late in the afternoon in New Orleans, Coach Anna had the team to rest before they ate their pregame meal together. After she explained the situation, the airline agent was very courteous in attempting to help her get tickets to Connecticut early the next morning, and then another flight to Atlanta for the second game the next evening. With the funeral set for two o'clock in the afternoon, it was going to be a tight schedule for sure.

Later, just when they were headed to the game, Coach Anna received a telephone call from the airline agent who informed her that at this time she only had seats for five people leaving Hartford at three-thirty o'clock in the afternoon and arriving in Atlanta at six-thirty in the evening. "I'll continue to work on this request and will advise you later in the evening following your game," the very friendly and helpful agent indicated.

Fralon State University was a formidable opponent and was well supported by a standing room only crowd that filled the arena. Coach Anna knew that the next twenty-four hours were going to be painfully tiring for the team so she decided to play the whole group liberally in the game. Fralon had been known for its quickness and speed, but as the Bacon team whizzed up and down the floor, one could readily ascertain that it was no match for this mountain team from Virginia.

Because Coach Anna could not get Mike Northy off her mind during the game, she called a time out, and she prayed for the grieving family of this beloved son who had been such a wonderful encourager for those around him. As the team returned to the floor, Maudie hugged Coach Anna so warmly, and said, "You are truly a special person."

Winning the game handily, they headed back to the hotel to be greeted by a telephone call from the airline agent. "I still have not gotten tickets except for five of your group," she sadly related. "I have a call in to several airlines leaving Hartford in the afternoon so I feel comfortable that I can get you all placed on some kind of flight to get you to Atlanta before seven-thirty tomorrow evening, the time of your game."

"I know you are having a difficult time with this, but please know that we appreciate your efforts," Coach Anna responded.

"Could only part of your team go to Connecticut?" she agent inquired.

"It's so very important that the whole team participate in this funeral service," Coach Anna stated. "The young man requested that we all come to his funeral service so that his friends could meet the Bacon team members."

"That brings tears to my eyes," the agent replied. "Please know that I will have you all tickets of some kind by tomorrow afternoon.

"Thank you so very much," Coach Anna said, as they discontinued their conversation.

Very early the next morning the team headed to the airport to board a plane to Atlanta where they would take another plane to the northeast. In Atlanta Coach Anna called the athletic department of the University of Allenton to advise that the team would not arrive for the game scheduled for seven-thirty until about the time of the game. Explaining their situation, the coach of Allenton wished her well and wanted Coach Anna to pass on her condolences to the family of the young man.

The husband of the coach of Allenton was a free lance news reporter, and because the story related by Coach Anna was so intriguing, the coach called him. "This is a most interesting situation wherein Bacon College is presently in flight to a funeral of a young man they met some time ago," she said. "The young man's last wish was to invite the Bacon team to his funeral so all of his friends would have a chance to meet his most favorite team."

"Where did you find this out?" her husband asked.

"I just received a telephone call from Coach Bosley of Bacon College who related the story to me just a few minutes ago," she answered.

"The story is very heart warming," he responded, "but they can't go to Hartford, Connecticut, attend a funeral and return in time to play you all tonight, can they?"

"I don't see how they can do that either, but she was committed to do just that," she stated.

"What if they don't get back in time?" her husband asked.

"Of course they would have to forfeit the game to us," she replied. "I wish we could do something here to help the situation, but we can't, because all tickets have been sold, and the officials indicate that the game is to be played at seven-thirty. To make any changes would be impossible."

"You know this is not a regular team but the best women's team in the country," he said. "To cap that off, the players have never lost a game, and here they are jeopardizing that perfect record, because they are attending a funeral of a young lad. Obviously, it's a tremendous human interest story."

"It is something very special," she said, "as they are fulfilling a dying wish of this child without regard for their own situation."

"Do you think I could write about this?" he asked.

"I think it would be good, if you did," she responded.

Renting a van, the team headed to the address of Nile Baptist Church where the family and friends of Mike Northy were located. As they approached the church, which had a towering spire on its roof, they could see a large crowd of people standing in the parking lot and on the huge lawn. "The church must already be full," Coach Anna said to Maudie, as they maneuvered the van between cars parked on both sides of the street.

A policeman motioned for them to move forward, and when they came up to him, Coach Anna asked, "Where can we park?"

"The best place is at the end of the street," he said, as he pointed his arm down the street. Just then he turned back to look at Coach Anna and then saw the girls in the van. "Are you the Bacon College team?"

"We are," Coach Anna said.

"Everyone is waiting for you all to arrive," he said excitedly. "We have a special place for you all to park near the church. Everybody is so appreciative that you all could come."

As the van pulled through the crowd to the reserved parking space, the people moved nearby to get a glimpse of the best basketball team in America. On the lengthy sidewalk children formed two lines, acting as greeters at this sad occasion. Coach Anna got out of the van, followed by Maudie and then the girls. With all the others in sight wearing new and fashionable clothes on this day, the Bacon girls seemed to be outwardly much out of place. They had never let earthly things get in their way to express their love for the Lord, and on this day to fulfill a dying wish of a special young man. Obviously, some were a little shocked as they judged the Bacon girls based on their clothing.

The mystique of the girls permeated the entire group waiting outside for their arrival and the funeral service.

Several reporters were present wanting to expand the story that was carried by the various media that was written by the husband of the coach of Allenton. His article entitled, "Keeping the Main Thing, the Main Thing," had been discussed since noon on the various channels on the radio and television, so the people present at the funeral service knew what a supreme sacrifice the team was making to fulfill a dying wish of a precious young man.

Trying to be impervious to the large crowd of people, Coach Anna assembled the group at the end of the sidewalk and had prayer. Among other things she asked that God's will be done regarding Mike, and further asked for God to have mercy on him and forgive him of any transgressions he might have committed during his short life. Following the conclusion of the prayer, Coach Anna turned to head up the walk to enter the sanctuary when she saw Mrs. Northy and her husband moving swiftly down the walk.

With tears streaming down their cheeks, there were numerous hugs and embraces as they greeted each other. Soon somewhat more composed, Mr. Northy said, "Thank you so very much for coming today. It was Mike's final wish that brought closure to his short life. He loved you all so very much. He couldn't play too much with the other children, so he staked out his claim early on the Bacon College team about two years ago. Meeting you all several days ago was the crowning touch in his life. He never stopped talking about you from that day."

With Mr. Northy having paused just for a moment to wipe the tears away, Coach Anna said, "Thank you so very much for letting us know of the service, and Mike's final wish. We are so very much honored to be here today."

"I know what I am going to ask you to do will be unusual, but Mike was an unusual little boy," Mrs. Northy said, crying all the while. "All of Mike's numerous friends were asked to come today as honorary pall bearers, and he wanted you all to sign autographs for them so they, too, would have what he had. So you can see the children lined on both sides of the sidewalk waiting for you all to give your signatures to them. I hope you don't mind doing it. Mike was so excited when he talked to us about this."

"We would be pleased to do whatever you wish," Coach Anna said. Signing they did for over an hour to the delight of the all of those in attendance.

Following this activity, the group was escorted down the center aisle to the front with everybody watching every step they made. Lying in the small casket was the corpse of young Mike, wearing his Bacon warm-up jacket, holding the autographed basketball, and numerous clippings from the newspaper and magazines of his favorite college team. In his hands was his last note written to the team which read, "Thank you for being my friends. Win all your games for me." It was signed, "Your special friend, Mike."

The whole team stood in front of the large crowd and cried as those in attendance joined in this very emotional moment. Leaning over toward Coach Anna, Mrs. Northy said, "Mike told us the other day that if you all brought another autographed basketball to his funeral, he wanted me to have it so I would always remember his special team."

Coach Anna and Esther had been asked to speak following the warm remarks by two pastors participating in the service. Coach Anna told those present how the team had met Mike, and how much of an encourager he was to everyone around him. "It was love at first sight for all of us on that day, and during the period hence we have kept him in our minds and our prayers. The shock came yesterday morning when we got the news of his death. Needless to say we have grieved much. We are not privy to God's plans and the reasons for His actions, but we all can be assured that Mike is with our Lord and even on this day continuing to be the giant he always was in encouraging those around him.

"It's difficult for all of us today to say good-bye to this special young man. His productivity far exceeds that of many of us who have outlived him, because he was such a dynamic individual possessing all of those personality traits we all gloat about. Did any of you ever hear him mention his thorn in the flesh? He put that aside and rose beyond his difficulties to assist those who usually were more fortunate, but that didn't make any difference to him. He truly showed special and continuous love to his multitude of friends. When I picked him up after our game with the University of Gordon several days ago, his heart was just pounding he was so excited. That's when I knew he was a genuine 'blue blood' Bacon College fan. Those fleeting moments with him have changed our lives, and I'm sure that he has had that same kind of impact on your lives."

Following Coach Anna's comments, the pastor stood up again and said, "The Bacon College team has meant so very much to Mike during his last days on earth with us. Please know that this team is jeopardizing their perfect record by coming to pay the last respects to Mike. They have to travel back to Atlanta for a game tonight at seven-thirty. Mike would want me to tell you to watch his favorite team tonight. From the team itself that has never lost a single college game or a high school game or even any games over the years, it's a fabulous record, and from this group their captain wants to make some remarks."

Esther stood and walked to the podium wearing her out of style pleated dark blue skirt, her well worn white blouse, her secondhand patent leather shoes and her always present pony tail. "My name is Esther Minold, a member of the Bacon College basketball team," she said succinctly, articulately and eloquently. "Much has been said today about our close and special friend, Mike Northy. Words don't seem to shape and mold the character of this lovely being God placed in the paths of all of us. Exuding an environment fraught with love, he became a master teacher not only in showing us how to live life abundantly, but he showed how to die with grace, passing into the arms of God with seemingly great delight.

"Yes, we all will genuinely miss this courageous young fellow who was such a deceptive thief as he stole all of our hearts, but on the flip side he filled our beings with plenary joy so freely given. His joy was free; he asked for nothing in exchange.

"There were no demands; there were no expectations of reciprocity; there was no time for grief; and there was no reluctance of showing love. A heart that overflows with joy, humility, compassion, kindness and love is a contagious heart.

"Never walking in the shadows but always in the sunlight, casting his beam that permeated all existence, in his very fleeting time with us, he revealed his treasures that he shared so gracefully with all of us. A minute in his presence was enough to last a lifetime. A hug from him was indelible. Oh, how envious are we who watched as others lived their lives with him!

"Mike was a scriptural template as his little light always was shining. never growing dim but always bright and never hidden under a bushel.

"Remember, we are all children of our Lord. Mike, through the words of Jesus, taught us all so well regarding this most scriptural concept. We all will miss our special little lover, our special little encourager, and our most ardent and dedicated Bacon College girls' team fan. The permanence of our relationship will always manifest itself with numerous fond memories as we continue our lives on this earth that God created years ago. We all have been humbled by the presence of the little one, God's messenger to us all."

With all in attendance crying by this time, Esther walked back to sit on the front pew with the other team members and Mike's family. After the pastor made some final remarks, his young friends acting as pall bearers carried his small casket down the aisle to the hearse to be carried to the nearby church grave site. The Bacon team walked behind the family as all observed their every movement.

Following a brief grave side service, the team members hugged Mr. and Mrs. Northy and other family members and headed to the van to go quickly to the airport to catch their flight to Atlanta. It was 3:15 p.m.

As Coach Anna pulled the van from the parking space, a policeman ran up and said he would escort them to the airport. "Thank you so very much," Coach Anna said out the window.

With the blue lights flashing and the siren sounding, the policeman threaded the traffic with the van carrying the team on his bumper. Upon arrival at the Hartford airport, the team thanked the policeman who said he would be watching the game on television that night. Turning in the rental van, they rushed to the ticket agent to get their tickets to Atlanta.

"Our department worked all day on this, but we finally had to split your team," the agent said. "One aircraft that is going directly to Atlanta has six seats available, and another that will be traveling through Pittsburgh has room for the remainder of you."

Realizing that they would have to accept whatever was available, because they were at the mercy of the airline officials, Coach Anna said, "Maudie, would you mind going with Dorothy, Jonsie, Cindy, Diane and Hanna on the direct flight?"

"I would be happy to do that," Maudie responded.

"When you get to Atlanta, go ahead to the arena, if the rest of us are not there at that time," Coach Anna instructed. "We'll come immediately upon our arrival."

In Atlanta the arena was filled to watch the biggest game of the year for Allenton, the last game for both teams before the ACUWAA tournament. The story about the Bacon team had been widely reported all day so as the fans watched Allenton's team warm-up on the floor alone, they knew there was a problem. The announcer advised the fans that it was reported that six of the team had arrived at the airport and would be entering the arena shortly. "We understand that the others were routed through Pittsburgh and should arrive soon," he told the anxious crowd.

Maudie was always considered to be very wise by Coach Anna so during the flight to Atlanta, she made a very wise decision. "I want you girls one at a time to go into the aircraft bathroom and change in your playing uniforms in case we don't have time for you to dress," Maudie said to the girls.

The announcer at the game read the ACUWAA rule to everybody, which indicated that at least five players must be present at game time, or the team would have to forfeit the game. "It is now 7:20 p.m.," he said.

Just before 7:30 p.m. a guard hastily brought the remnant of the Bacon team to its bench area as the crowd burst into applause. Quickly, taking off their warm-up suits, the girls went on the floor to start a game with a most unusual line up of team members.

Allenton got the tipped ball and immediately scored. Maudie signaled for a time out so she could talk to the girls and get better organized. Hanna had not played very much all year, because of her crippled knee so Maudie said, "Hanna, don't run any more than you have to run, because of your knee problems. Dorothy, I want you to play a forward position, if they do not press you on defense. If they do, I want you to move back to your usual point guard position."

The announcer had related the story several times of the team having gone to a young man's funeral to fulfill a death bed wish. Also, he related that the team had never lost a game. As the game continued, everyone knew that the undefeated Bacon team might have given up its perfect record to fulfill a young man's dying wish.

The makeshift team coached by Maudie was holding its own against Allenton until Hanna fell and hurt her knee, such that she could barely hobble on the floor. At half time after Maudie had used all of her times out to delay the game, the score was forty-three to twenty-three. There was no sign of the other team members.

All across the country everyone was shocked to hear the score of the number one women's team; yet everybody knew why the team was losing. Then there came this announcement it the arena, "The remainder of the team has arrived at the airport and are being escorted by two state troopers to the arena."

In Connecticut Mr. and Mrs. Northy hugged each other as she said, "I don't want them to lose, because of fulfilling Mike's wish."

Maudie called two times out immediately at the start of the second half, thinking that the others would arrive soon. As the team headed to the floor after the second time out, there was a thunderous applause as the other girls entered the arena and headed for the bench area. Upon arrival Coach Anna hugged Maudie, as the other girls prepared to enter the game. "We are down by twenty points, and we all know why, but let's not ever have to use as our excuse that we were fulfilling a very precious and brave young man's final wish," Coach Anna told the team.

Back at Bacon where hundreds were watching on wide screen television, there was not a dry eye in the coliseum. "I never cease to discover something new to enhance the quality of these young people," Dr. Damond said to Josh.

Coach Anna had never directed Esther in any way during her coaching tenure. She wanted to remind her of the score and the short time left in the game, but she didn't in deference to the magnificent leadership she had always displayed without direction before. "How would Esther lead the team this time?" Coach Anna thought, as Esther, Dorothy, Jonsie, Diane and Mit went on the floor.

It was Allenton's ball for only a short while as the player was smothered, and Dorothy stripped the ball away into the hands of Esther who laid it in for two points. On the next two possessions a double team caused errant passes by Allenton that were converted into points for Bacon. As the game wound down, excitement was still being generated throughout the basketball world, because the best team in the country was behind by four points.

Dorothy brought the ball deliberately up the floor and penetrated inside the foul line, faked a jump shot, pivoted and bounced a pass to Esther for a three-pointer. Behind only by one point now seventy-six to seventy-five, Allenton called a time out. There were five seconds showing on the clock.

"I want Esther and Dorothy to guard the player bringing the ball in," Coach Anna told the players as they all huddled on the side of the floor. "Remember that we have enough time, if we get the ball, to attempt at least one shot so the one who snares it should move swiftly toward the basket. The clock will not start until a player touches the ball."

The sports' reporters were frantically describing the scene wherein the perfect record of Bacon College was in serious jeopardy. "There are only five ticks of the clock remaining so it's almost impossible for Bacon, if Allenton throws the ball down court," a reporter explained. "Even if Bacon does get an errant pass down court, they will not have time to get into shooting range."

All present on this night in the arena were standing, clapping and yelling mainly for Allenton, because it was about to do the impossible. Just as the players were in place on the floor, Allenton called another time out to talk over the situation by establishing an offensive plan to overcome the defense their coach had just observed. "We are going to remain with our original defense," Coach Anna said to the girls, even though she knew that the Allenton coach had seen what kind of defense they had planned.

As they were waiting for the resumption of the game, an older man dressed in a dark three-piece suit walked briskly over to Coach Anna and said, "Thank you all for playing this game tonight in spite of your serious schedule conflicts. Do you know who lined up your state-trooper escort from the airport? She would never tell you, but it was Denia Norvel, our Allenton basketball coach."

"Thank you so very much for telling me this," Coach Anna replied to the gentleman.

The tallest girl on the Allenton team took the ball out of bounds under the Bacon goal to throw it in. Dorothy and Esther did a masterful job such that the young lady finally threw a hard pass toward the foul line of Allenton that was picked off by Mit. Not breaking stride, Mit dribbled toward Bacon's goal, and seeing this, Esther set herself in position to screen the tall girl who was the only Allenton player on their end of the court. With blinding speed Mit dashed toward her goal, putting in a soft lay up just as the buzzer sounded. Bacon had done the improbable, if not the impossible. Bacon had won!

After the fans had caught their breath, they knew that they had witnessed something special on this evening, a game that would fill their minds for many years to come. Coach Anna and the girls headed to congratulate Allenton. Hugging the coach so warmly, Coach Anna thanked her over and over again for having the escort provided at the airport. "We would not have gotten to the game on time, if you had not done this," Coach Anna related.

"I would not have been able to live with myself, if I had done otherwise," she said, as the two popular coaches continued to embrace each other. All in all the day had been filled with compassion, integrity, love and plenary sportsmanship. Mike's parents were so relieved now knowing that Bacon's perfect record remained, the special team of a most ardent fan. What a warm telephone call that was made to the Northy home! All the girls had an opportunity to speak to the family members and some of Mike's closest friends, who now had Bacon College as their favorite team, also.

Bob Waters' Determination

Following a short meeting with Josh, Bob was more determined than ever to attempt to effect some changes that would give regular folks an opportunity to express themselves in ways that would be meaningful. It was a surprise awakening for him to discover what Josh had on his mind in that brief meeting with him. "Would other people who were outside the decision making loop be just as expressive as his good friend?" he thought, as he dialed a committee member to discuss the status of the newly formed team of apolitical individuals forging ahead in a political arena.

Bob was really amazed how cohesive the group was and the progress they were making in developing strategies to fulfill their mission. It seemed that each of the several ad hoc committee members was saying, "Enough is enough." Following conversations with about a half dozen persons on the team, the next day Bob headed for the Hollow to speak again with Josh about the issues confronting the group to get his refreshing perspective.

When he arrived at the church, Josh was conducting a meeting of the entire group regarding several areas concerning the Hollow so he just took a seat on a pew in the rear observing the group in its discussion. Soon though the meeting was concluded, and Josh went back to hug Bob, and as always, extend a warm welcome.

"What brings you to the Hollow today?" Josh asked, while still shaking Bob's hand.

"I have been thinking a lot about the citizens' group that is concerned about the direction our government is headed," he responded.

"I know you have a lot on your mind," Josh replied.

"Would you have time just to discuss with me several issues I believe are important for all of us, if we are going to prosper as a state?" Bob asked.

"I would be happy to talk to you about anything, but remember that I am not one who has much experience outside the Hollow," Josh noted. "Do you want to do this privately, or would you like to include the entire group?"

"Why don't we include everybody in our discussion?" Bob happily responded.

Some had already made their way to the door when Josh beckoned for them to return to hear what Bob had to say.

After they were seated, Josh indicated that Bob wanted to talk to the group about something and get their reaction. Instead of standing up at the front, Bob sat down before he addressed the group.

"For several years now I have been concerned about the way our state has been governed, particularly as it relates to the individual," he began. "More and more of us are becoming dependent on attorneys to indicate to us how it is we are supposed to relate to one another as we live each day. You see, our laws are written by lawyers, our laws are interpreted by lawyers, and lawyers become judges who decide whether or not we have acted in accordance with the law. It's similar to what has happened in our public schools, wherein teachers determine what to teach, when to teach and how to teach.

"What is happening did not occur overnight as it's been creeping into our environment very slowly, just as an erosion renders a piece of land useless. One might think that this movement of legal dependence is cyclical and will be phased out in the near future to be replaced by more palatable behavior, but that will never happen. The vine is getting tighter and tighter around the bush.

"I was talking with Josh a few weeks ago about the complexities in our present society caused by our myriad of present laws to control our behavior. It's not that we don't need laws, but it's that the laws we have are written in such a way that most of us have a difficult time understanding them. Simply stated, these laws written by lawyers that are difficult to understand now become, in a sense, the property of lawyers as they now place themselves in a position to be the interpreters. Of course, this perpetuates the problem.

"Josh and I talked about this problem several weeks ago and today I would like to continue the discussion with him and the rest of you. Josh, have you given much thought to what we were talking about earlier?"

"From time to time I have thought about it such that I have raised many questions in my own mind about the situation," Josh replied. "After talking with you I have continued to think that what you consider a problem will never be corrected until our elected officials become a good cross section of the people. A most politically correct term we now use is diversity, which in the case of legislators is certainly absent as most of our representatives are lawyers. To change the course in this area is going to be slow, but those who are concerned should support lay candidates in political races."

"Certainly, that is one area that is being considered by the ad hoc group," Bob responded. "How would you think that other areas of our present system could be adjusted to provide a fair and equitable society for all people based on our Christian principles?"

"I remember my discussions with Glenn Colson, the superintendent, and he told me that the main culprit in the schools today was that the children and parents did not know what the students were expected to learn," Josh said. "When only the teacher knows what it is he or she wants to teach, the parents and students just follow blindly, and in the end many times the students fail to respond adequately. In other words not holding students accountable to fulfill a specific curriculum appears to be the school's downfall. Glenn told me that it was very difficult for the teachers to see the importance of the development of a curriculum for the different study areas, because it had never been done in the past. Tradition was almost impossible to overcome."

"I believe this is going to be our most difficult challenge to get people to recognize that change will effect a different kind of citizenry," Bob said. "The individual is the most important ingredient of a strong society, so if the people can be more and more empowered such that they become independent, there can be hope. Presently though, our training institutions continue to graduate students who ascribe to the same philosophy, which perpetuates the problem."

"But if the first step could be to rewrite the laws in understandable terms for the individuals, each citizen could become a plenary participant in the community, and not have to depend on others to interpret and advise regarding day to day activities," Josh responded. "A book of laws could be in every household, and the use of case law could be phased out which might break the lock grip examining the past to solve the present conflicts"

"What would happen when conflicts emerge in your system that you advocate?" Bob asked, realizing how very dependent our society had become in recent years.

"In continuing with the individual empowerment concept, I believe that lay people should be used to solve most problems of individuals," Josh indicated. "A pool of rotating lay citizens could be utilized to act as judges in these cases, and if the individuals involved in the conflict wanted assistance, another group of citizens would be available to help. Courts and cases would be simplified and the costs to the individual would be minimal. All individuals would have equal access to justice with the assistance of fellow citizens so there would not be preferential treatment based on how much an individual was willing to pay for lawyers."

"Yours is an interesting concept," Bob noted. "In other words individuals with grievances would represent themselves in court before a judge who is a citizen temporarily assigned that duty, very similar to the way jurors are called for duty. Depending on the number of conflicts, there could be several lay judges handling cases at one time thereby keeping pace and not having a backlog of cases."

"Of course, those cases dealing with capital crimes would be handled by a specific pool of citizen judges," Josh said. "But they would be handled expeditiously in trials that dealt with witnesses being examined by lay people and not lawyers who are being paid huge sums to attempt to free many times guilty parties. Money should never be a deciding force regarding guilt or innocence."

"I remember in our discussion earlier you mentioned review panels," Bob stated. "Would you explain your views on the use of these panels?"

"In a way my whole scenario reflects my concern about one's wealth and his or her willingness to buy services," Josh replied. "If all had equal access to receiving justice in disagreements, there should only be a minimal cost, such that all people could participate equally. It seems now that there is a price tag on justice, and the individual is asked about how much justice for which he is willing to pay. Should individuals be able to buy justice?"

"I really agree with you and stated another way, greed has moved us in the direction we are going now," Bob said.

"About the review panels," Josh continued, "I think a story that Glenn Colson told me would adequately describe what I have in mind. When Glenn first became superintendent in our county, many of the nightly school board meetings lasted until the morning hours so he began to think about it. Soon he came up with the plan of having review panels preceding each meeting to review all of the personnel cases on the agenda to come before the school board. They were very informal in a relaxed atmosphere wherein the panel of three would judge the grievance or conflict and make its recommendation to the school board at its next meeting."

"How did this help?" Bob asked.

"Glenn told me that at the next meeting when the review panel made its recommendation to the board, there was very little discussion," Josh answered. "School board meetings from that day were not bogged down with lengthy personnel concerns but with substantive items."

"In other words you are saying that following the lead of the school superintendent, review panels could be established to hear all kinds of issues, thereby, precluding full blown cases in the court," Bob stated.

Their discussion was very fruitful and continued for more than two hours. Now Bob was slowly building a platform for the infant political group wanting to change the present landscape and climate of the legal system.

STORY OF GALU

Meanwhile, Dan and Pat Travers were continuing their work in Tanzania, making progress every day as more and more young people were following the lead of Galu in the village to become a part of the Christian school located in the bush country. They sorely missed their many friends from the Corbri tribe in the southern jungle area of Costa Rica, but they knew their new calling was important for the global mission group. Having to establish their mission activities in this new country without their daughter, Mit, was going to be very difficult. But with Galu becoming a part of their program, they now had another young person to lead the charge in getting others to join with them in spreading the Good News of Jesus Christ.

Dan and Pat were so grateful to Galu for his leadership in the small mission school and their church activities. Now that he had become not only a local and regional hero, because of his marathon competition, he was known all over Africa for his prowess, because he was so young and such a delightful person. Soon he was going to be known in other parts of the world that he hardly knew existed.

Recently, there had been a reporter who was covering the political situation in Johannesburg and attended the marathon being held in that city. Upon his reporting to a leading newspaper in the United States, he mentioned to the editor that he had witnessed a most unusual marathon race wherein a young lad had won, and had truly elevated himself to be the darling of the entire city even though no one seemed to know him. In a few days the editor called the reporter in Johannesburg to tell him that there was a slow period for news and with the Boston marathon coming within a short time, the editor wanted the reporter to follow up on the story about the little runner. After several days on the road he submitted his story to the world.

> "All of us become interested in activities along the way in life. Some like to fish while others like to play golf, and there are those who become spectators at different events. Over the years in covering political news for my stories, I have become more and more interested in marathon races where participants stretch their endurance to the limit. Runners in this activity are probably the most physically fit of all athletes in the world today so it's a joy to watch them as they compete on a long and meandering course to attempt to finish first. Some who enter the race just want to complete the event.
>
> "Over time I have been an observer at all of the larger marathon events throughout our country and have been present to witness several in foreign countries. Recently, I was privileged to be a spectator in the African Continental Marathon in Johannesburg, South Africa. On the surface it was a marathon, as usual, with hundreds and even thousands of entrants vying for the grand prize. Having been sent there to cover a political story, as I sat there early in the morning, my thoughts were elsewhere trying to conjure expressions to use in my article on that subject.
>
> "Seated purposefully from the crowd at the starting point that was growing by the minute, my attention was drawn to an American sitting with two African lads somewhat removed from the others. They seemed to be totally impervious to what was going on around them as they ate some food that they

took from a net like bag. After they had finished eating and had sat for a while just talking to each other, they bowed as though having prayer. Following this, they stood up, and the American man reached in his bag and removed a number that he placed over the head of the lad. 'He is a participant in this race,' I thought. 'That can't be, because he is just a mere child.'

"There he was with that very large number of 10364 hanging loosely around his neck wearing trousers held up by a rope belt and barefoot. 'Why would a child be running in this most prestigious event?' I asked myself.

"As the time approached to start the marathon, I had forgotten about the earlier scene and was concentrating on the runners with the low numbers who had done well in these events before. This was truly a championship field of participants on this beautiful day in South Africa. Not being one to sit too long in any one place when I attend a marathon event, I moved to about the half-way point to see how the various competitors were faring.

"I always go up ahead to see the runners coming so I can check their numbers. On this day there were no surprises as the expected leaders were clustered close to the front of the pack followed by others who were making a gallant effort to keep up. It was during this part of any race that the contenders knew would be a critical period for the race. It's always fun to watch the faces of the runners as they pass, and for many, I try to take a picture of them to put into my photo album at home.

"Suddenly, I looked up and not too far from the front runners came this lad with the number 10364 in his bare feet running so gracefully and peacefully. What a shock! 'How could this be,' I thought, as I stood with other spectators who appeared to be just as bewildered as I was.

"One person standing near me said, 'I can't believe that the young man is running so well at this stage of the race.'

"Another pointed out that he had never seen a young person his age ever running in such a race much less be running so well.

"A marathon official got the attention of everyone when he stated, 'This is the young man that the marathon officials wanted to remove from the list, because he was so young, but realized in their deliberation that the rules did not preclude his participation.'

"An older gentleman asked, 'Where is the young man from?'

"Scratching his head, the official indicated that he thought the young man was from the northern part of Africa.

"This part of the marathon course was different, because there was a long section that was rough and without spectators on the side of the roadway. In fact there was a sign for the runners to see that advised them that there would be no water for the next several hundred yards. I stood with the other observers watching the runners disappear into the wooded area.

"As I turned to leave for another location, I heard a spectator say in a loud voice, 'The little runner is coming back this way.'

"I immediately focused on the course to see other runners passing by, and there up ahead was the lad headed the wrong way. With that serene countenance he headed directly to the water tables, picked up three bottles of water and quickly returned to the wooded area, soon disappearing from sight.

"'What a strange turn of events,' I thought, as I instinctively ran down a path among the trees to determine what caused this young man to return to get water. Panting all the while, I finally moved toward the course where I could see him leaning over another runner who had apparently fallen. Obviously, he was hurt so the young lad was giving first aid to stop the bleeding and water to drink. 'What sportsmanship!' I thought, as I moved closer to the two as other runners raced by. I made several pictures of this young and very kind lad as he assisted one of his competitors on this day.

"Then he noticed that I was present and said in a calm voice, 'Would you mind helping this runner who fell on the rough terrain?'

"Of course I did help the fallen runner, but I knew that the lad had given up any chance of finishing high in the race, not only because he lost several precious minutes helping a comrade, but his feet were showing signs of cuts and abrasions which would hamper his running.

"I returned to the entrance of the isolated area to get help for the injured runner, and also, reported to the official what had transpired to cause the lad to reverse his course to get water. Of course, this was conveyed via telephone to the main commentator who advised many thousands of spectators what had transpired.

"When I got to my next point about three-fourths of the distance, many people were talking about the benevolent gesture of the young lad who was running so well, yet he gave of himself such that he was no longer a contender to be a top finisher. It was heart-warning to hear these comments when competition in recent years had become so aggressive that such an act of kindness was very refreshing for this popular sport. As I stood there listening to the acclamatory comments, I began to wonder who this lad was and what on earth would posses a mere lad to compete in such a grueling sport in the first place.

"Just then the lead runners came into view so I prepared my camera to get several shots of them as they passed. As usual, the runners were bunched together such that a second group came into view, and following them there were several running individually. Preparing my camera to move to another spot on the course, I heard loud noises sounding like chants coming from the course area several hundred yards away. As the seconds passed, the sound became louder, such that it reminded me of a herd of cattle loping along.

"The whole scene changed when I looked down the course, and there in the middle of the roadway running all alone was the lad with hundreds of children running by his side chanting all kinds of encouraging statements. 'That can't be the lad who lost so much valuable time helping the fallen runner," I thought, as I watched this touching scene unfold before my eyes. Making picture after picture as the lad went by, I tried to focus on the serene countenance displayed on his face that seemed to reflect no emotion whatsoever. I did notice that his feet were bleeding more now, because I could see spots on the roadway.

"Like the others standing there on this day, I couldn't believe what I was seeing. 'I believe I am witnessing the greatest feat ever in sports,' I continued to think as the young man disappeared around the next sharp turn on the course.

"The whole race had taken on an entirely different meaning with the act of benevolence of the lad weighing heavily on the minds of the thousands and thousands of spectators at this annual event. Being very familiar to the race course, I headed for a good spot on the route where visibility was extensive near the twenty-three-mile marker to get more pictures and to observe the mysterious young runner, who, I was sure, would be far behind the lead group. In fact, I would not have been surprised, if he had withdrawn from the race.

"Just as I got situated in a good place to see down the running route with thousands of spectators on both sides, the lead group of runners sporting low numbers gracefully passed through the crowd. At this time I noticed a young man a little younger than the young marathon runner, pushing his way to the very edge of the course, and when the young runner came by, he yelled as loudly as he could, 'When they yell BB they mean they love you.' When the young runner heard this, without turning his head he grinned just a little.

"Although I needed to reload my camera, I didn't want the friend of the young runner to get away before I had a chance to talk with him, so I quickly ran to catch him as he proceeded up the running course to watch the race. 'What is the name of the young runner?' I asked, as we both were walking at a very fast pace.

"'His name is Galu,' the young fellow politely responded, as he quickened his pace.

"'Where is he from?' I continued to probe.

"'He is from Trenka in Tanzania,' the young man replied.

"The young man ran on ahead of me, when I paused to reload my camera to get ready to get shots of those behind the leading contenders at the next course location. Suddenly, a loud shout was heard down the way, and then I heard a man with a very loud voice yell, ‘The lad is coming into view; I can see him now.’

“‘My goodness!’ I thought, the young man couldn’t be this close to the front runners after losing all that time helping the fallen runner. Yet, in a couple of minutes here he was running just in front of me with a wonderful facial expression that again showed no emotion whatsoever.

“‘You know,’ I continued to think, ‘this young man is now near the front with only three miles to go. It could be that he will get himself nearer to the leaders before the race was over.’ Even at this time wherein he had made so much progress since the assistance was given to the injured runner, I knew that making further improvement in his standing was just asking too much.

“Having hastily changed my location to another site farther down the course, I wound up on the twenty-five-mile marker where I could observe the runners at this point and only have to move about one hundred yards to be among those still present at the finish line. From where I was standing, I could hear the commentator’s voice as he described to the crowd what was taking place all along the route. I could tell he was excited about something, and then I discovered it when he said, ‘I have been involved in this event for all of my adult life, and what is happening today is unmatched in the annals of this or any other event. Our spotters choke up when they try to inform me about the progress being made by our benevolent boy, BB, who continues to move toward the front even though each one advises me that his feet are bleeding more, such that blood can be seen on the pavement when he passes.’

“As the leader made his final turn for the stretch drive, I saw the young marathoner’s friend on the side of the pavement waiting for his friend who had really picked up speed. Running as fast as he could beside the young runner, he yelled, 'Galuuuuuuuu, Galuuuuuuuu, Galuuuuuuuu, Galuuuuuuuu, Galuuuuuuuu, Galuuuuuuuu.' It was a touching scene as the comrade of the unknown benevolent youngster was encouraging him onward. Others picked up the chant so that when he turned directly toward the home stretch only a short distance from the front runners, there was a continuous chant of those caught up in the special moment in their lives.

"'There is no way that a mere child could be a winner of this prestigious continental marathon only reserved for genuine adult champions of great renown,' I continued to think, as I moved near the finish line where I could hear with more clarity what the main commentator was saying to the crowd.

"'I have been associated with this most popular world class marathon for many, many years now and never has there been a situation to emerge that is unfolding as I speak to you,' the commentator said. 'I choke up each time I try to tell you about our benevolent runner, but there is one thing that I have not told and that this young runner is only twelve years old.

"A hush fell over the crowd as the commentator told the record number of people present that the runners could be observed as they made their turn down the way. Just behind the three runners with small numbers was our lad wearing the number 10364 reducing the distance with each graceful stride. When Galu came into view, I could see the crowd starting to stand, and one after the other with tears in their eyes began to applaud louder and louder. When Galu passed the second runner, a loud yell accompanied the applause as the spectators watched this poorly clad young Tanzanian with badly injured feet continue to pound the pavement catching up with the lead runner all the while.

"I stood in disbelief and when two men and the friend I had spoken to earlier started to yell, 'Galuuuuuuuu, Galuuuuuuuu, Galuuuuuuuu, Galuuuuuuuu, Galuuuuuuuu, Galuuuuuuuu,' I found myself doing likewise, joining all the others present who were learning the little hero's name for the first time.

"Then the impossible happened. Young Galu passed the final runner to the delight of his many new fans, winning the most prestigious race on the continent of Africa. He didn't behave as I have seen other marathon winners as he just walked over to his friends where the two adults and other lad kneeled down and prayed. When they stood up, they loaded the old dilapidated van and just disappeared down the street while all the spectators continued to celebrate a most unusual marathon without being able to toast their genuine hero.

"The whole continent seemed to have been mesmerized by the behavior of this young man whose name was Galu, such that I, too, could not get him off my mind. With the nagging thoughts of the race, in a few days I headed for Trenka, a small village to the west of Tanzania to visit this community and talk to this young man in person.

"Right off my flight was delayed, and as soon as I was in the air, the flight was rerouted into eastern Zaire where I contracted with a private transportation group to continue my travel by land. It was a long a grueling trip, only made more interesting at the border where 'we jumped through several immigration hoops' to satisfy the officials at the check point. The long trip through the bush country measured from hours into days, but finally I arrived at a village where I was told that Galu came every day. Worn completely out, I was greeted by Dan and Pat Travers, who are Baptist missionaries, and the teachers of Galu in their quaint little school.

"'I am Dan Travers and this is my wife, Pat,' the man said, whom I had seen earlier in Johannesburg.

"'It's good to meet you,' I said. 'Aren't you the man who was with the young man who won the Continental Marathon?'

"'I certainly am,' Dan replied. 'I remember seeing you there making a lot of pictures.'

"The three of us spent the afternoon and up into the evening talking about Galu and how it was that he was involved in their mission program. Words seemed to fall short in describing this brilliant young man who had turned Africa upside down, because of his running prowess. Being advised that he would be present the next day at school, I hardly slept that night thinking about how such an outstanding young man came from such a very remote area of Tanzania.

"The next morning I came out of my thatched roof, mud brick hut early to the smell of something cooking on the open fire. A breakfast of rice and beans served by Pat Travers really did taste good. When we continued our talking at breakfast time, I discovered a most interesting thing about the Traverses. Their daughter, Mit, was attending Bacon College on scholarship to play soccer, and was on that brave and courageous team of girls who rescued the three missionaries in Abedistan.

"The time swiftly passed as I visited with this delightful couple who were very reluctant to talk about themselves. It was by accident that I discovered who their daughter was and that she played basketball and soccer for Bacon. Young Galu seemed to be emulating their style of conduct. Our quiet was broken when I heard the other children who had arrived early for school yelling in a loud voice, 'Galuuuuuuuu, Galuuuuuuuu, Galuuuuuuuu, Galuuuuuuuu, Galuuuuuuuu........................' as Galu arrived at the school.

"I stood somewhat in awe of this young man, still barefoot and wearing ragged clothing and carrying a woven orange bag that appeared to be holding his lunch. Everybody started to work on school activities, including Galu, so I knew he didn't want to be bothered until after class time, so I waited until lunch to attempt to talk to him for a while.

"At noon with Dan sitting with us, I managed to get him to answer a few questions, but he was extremely reticent about bringing any attention at all to himself. Here was a mere lad who had won the only three marathons he had ever entered not wanting to talk about it at all. Of course, I honored that request realizing that I had gotten acquainted with the most unusual young man whom I had ever met. No wonder all the other children in the area wanted to share in his environment."

BOSTON MARATHON

The article about this young runner was less of a task than the reporter thought, as he included pictures of Galu running and two showing him helping the fallen runner. When the newspaper hit the streets containing the story about Galu, the circulation exceeded any other publication as the people just became instantly enamored over this young lad about whom they knew nothing. The telephone in the editor's office "rang off the hook" as well wisher after well wisher called to try to find out whether or not this young runner of twelve had registered for the Boston marathon. At the Boston marathon headquarters, two additional telephone operators had to be employed to handle all of the inquiries about this young Galu.

Several days later Dan received a message from the associational office requesting that he come to headquarters for a brief meeting as soon as he could get there. Leaving the next morning, he arrived for the meeting in the late afternoon

"I hope that you have had a good trip to the associational office," the director stated, as the two sat down. "Would you like to have a cup of coffee?"

"That would be really nice," Dan responded, still not knowing why it was so urgent for him to come for the meeting.

With both having coffee each leaned back in his chair, as the director began to talk about the mission progress in that part of the world. "You know I am delighted to have you and Pat in my region to be a part of our mission team," he said. "After discovering that your daughter was very instrumental in enlarging your mission activities in southern Costa Rica, I wondered how you all would fare here in this part of the world without her."

"It really has been difficult for us here not to have her as part of the team," Dan said. "Ever since she was just a little girl, we made home a team effort, but it wasn't until when she was struck by a car that our whole lives began to change."

"How was that?" he asked.

"Pat and I had really gotten ourselves comfortable with much wherewithal in life, because I had a good, well-paying job, and she was staying at home caring for our only child, Mit," Dan indicated. "At this point in time we had no worries whatsoever, and then the bottom started dropping out."

"You never told me about that period of your life," he stated. "Would you tell me what happened then?"

"You might say that God was getting our attention, because we had quietly and defiantly told God that we could handle our own situation," Dan noted. "In a brief period of time I lost my job, and Mit was struck by a car, leaving her comatose for a long period of time."

"I guess you all were devastated," the director stated.

"We really were," Dan replied. "Soon though our whole existence changes such that I was taking seminary classes, we were active in our church and later Mit began to make progress toward full recovery."

"I remember reading about Mit in the mission magazine telling about her near death experience," the director indicated.

At this time the director pulled his chair closer to Dan and again told Dan how proud he was of them and their new ministry in the bush country. "Almost daily I am contacted by other missionaries who ask me about your program, because they do not have growth as you are having," he stated. "I try to tell them that in both your mission locations, you and Pat have utilized a young person as your catalyst to initiate a program. In Costa Rica it was your daughter and here it is Galu, who plays the point. Many want to know how it is you can develop such a strong and meaningful relationship with a young person such that it impacts on the entire program."

"Galu has been such a treasure of both of us, and each day he seems more and more to enrich our lives," Dan said excitedly. "He is a bright young man wanting to fulfill the lofty goals he has for himself in life. All the other children follow him all the while, and each wants to emulate his demeanor."

"Has the marathon running caused him to change?" the director asked.

"If we didn't know that he had won these races already, we wouldn't know it ourselves, because he never mentions them to me or to the others," Dan indicated.

Finally, after a lengthy conversation with Dan, the director advised him why he wanted to meet with him. "Are you aware of the article written by the reporter about the African Continental Marathon and Galu's participation?" the director asked.

"I remember the reporter well," Dan replied. "Galu was very reticent about the whole situation, when the reporter talked to him."

"It is my understanding that the article was circulated widely, such that everyone in the United States who read the story has become very enamored over Galu and want him to participate in the Boston marathon," the director told Dan. "I just received the official invitation by fax a couple of days ago."

"I didn't think anyone in the U. S. knew that Galu existed," Dan said.

"They certainly do now," the director quickly indicated. "From what I gather there is considerable excitement about his running prowess, particularly about his helping the fallen runner in Johannesburg, and yet still winning the race. They really want him to participate."

"I really don't know what to say in response to their invitation," Dan stated, as the director poured another cup of coffee.

"There is a lot to think about, I know," the director indicated.

"Yes, there is," Dan replied. "The whole marathon running has really advanced much beyond any of our wildest dreams. In all of the excitement the only part of this whole scenario that has remained absolutely constant is Galu, who never lets his success in winning these prestigious marathons alter his beautiful personality one iota."

"How did he get involved in marathon running in the first place?" the director asked.

"He apparently had dreamed of being in the village race for a number of years," Dan stated, "and when he entered he upset the entire community. In spite of all of the derision, he remained steadfast to his goal, and you know the outcome."

"But how did he continue in the regional event?" the director asked.

"Pat and I encouraged him to participate in this event, which he won, also, as you know," Dan stated. "Of course, one event led to another, but even now we don't know just how good a runner he really is. I thought that he would have met his match and reached the limit of his mastery in this competition, but you see what happened. In South Africa where the competition was outstanding, he just forged ahead after his most unusual benevolent act regarding a fallen runner. But with all of this said, he comes to our little school each day so humbly that no one could ever detect that he had won the most prestigious sporting event in all of Africa. He is just amazing."

"We could all learn from this young man," the director stated.

"We certainly could do that, and Pat and I are so dearly blessed that we can be around him each day," Dan said. "What is the deadline on the invitation?"

"It states that the cutoff for all applications is in exactly seven days so that doesn't give you much time," the director pointed out.

"Let me have the application, and if everything can be worked out, I'll return the completed form to you so it can be faxed to Boston," Dan said. "This marathon is much different, because of the distance and the expense."

"It would be good for Tanzania, if you could work out the details so he can go," the director indicated. "No other Tanzanian has ever competed in a transcontinental marathon before so it would boost the morale of the people, especially that Galu is going to be involved, and he is so very young."

Dan returned to the village, realizing that for Galu to enter in the Boston marathon was going to be a genuine challenge. When he arrived, Pat immediately asked, "Why did you have a meeting with the director?"

"You won't believe this, but he advised me that Galu has been invited to run in the Boston marathon," Dan replied, as he continued to hug Pat.

"What are you planning to do about the invitation?" Pat continued.

"It's really something that we had not anticipated, so at the present time the whole idea seems to be too overwhelming even to think about it," Dan reacted.

"I wonder how the Boston officials discovered Galu in the first place," Pat said.

"Do you remember the reporter who came here and interviewed Galu?" Dan asked. "Evidently, the article he wrote was disseminated widely such that there were thousands of readers, and many of them got acquainted with

Galu this way. Of course, the response then to the marathon officials was intense such that they want Galu to participate to satisfy the numerous people who have become so enamored over a young man of which they have only read."

"I know that you can work out all of the details which at this point seem to be insuperable," Pat said. "It's as though God's hand is in everything we do here just as it was when we were in Costa Rica."

"That seems to be case," Dan said. "I remember what Henry Blackaby said some years ago when we were training for the mission field that we needed to go where God was working. With that concept in mind, God must really be working here."

"You and I are following God's will," Pat indicated, "but God is using young people to pave the way in getting the Good News of Jesus Christ to the people. Mit did such a good job in the jungle, and now in the bush country in Africa here comes another young person to attract others to our mission."

"It's just amazing," Dan responded.

"Do you think that after you have worked out all of the details to enter Galu in the Boston marathon that we could call Mit from the associational office?" Pat asked. "We were advised that we could call her from time to time, so this might be a good time to bring her up to date on what we are doing, and let her know that Galu would be running in the marathon race. The girls might be able to watch it on television, and they might be able to see Galu. Mit has been so much concerned about us and has recently inquired about the welfare of Galu."

"I think that would be a good idea," Dan replied. "I'll begin immediately to attempt to get him in the event."

In the meantime in the village Galu was going about doing what he loved and that was school and church. Each was growing so rapidly that special meetings were being held to devise plans to handle the large numbers in attendance. He paid little attention to Dan when he came to him one day carrying a package addressed to Galu, Northern Tanzania. Expressionless, Galu opened it and discovered a beautiful pair of running shoes just like the champions wore, and he noticed that the sender was the reporter from Johannesburg, who wrote the long article about Galu that was so widely read. Placing the box on a table, Galu returned to his schoolwork, but he carried the shoes home that evening.

The deadline for registering for the Boston marathon was drawing near so Dan figured the exact cost of such a trip. It was a large sum, which would include going by plane from a large eastern city of Tanzania, to Addis Ababa, to Cairo, to Amsterdam, and on to Boston, with the cost of a taxi to the site. The sum was much too much for them even to consider any more so Dan put the subject aside. Furthermore, he thought that it would be impossible to get Galu to agree anyway.

Meanwhile, it was discovered in the village that Galu had been invited to participate in the Boston marathon, and hearing this, there were some secret meetings being held in the village wherein the community leaders were attempting to determine how funds could be raised to send their favorite son to the Boston marathon. One of these meetings had numerous village leaders from many parts of Tanzania in attendance, and it was decided that that they would tell Dan that they would finance the trip for Galu and him by accepting contributions from the nationals.

Hearing this, Dan and Pat met with Galu. “In the next several days a marathon is scheduled in Boston for runners all over the world,” Dan said, “and they want you to participate in this event.”

As usual, Galu showed no emotion and didn’t say anything.

“I’ll register you for this marathon, if you would like to participate,” Dan said.

"I'll need to talk to my parents about this marathon," Galu told Dan, as he responded in the same manner as for other events.

That evening Galu went about doing his chores, as usual, ate the evening meal with his family, and then he talked to his parents about the Boston marathon. His parents seemed to be overwhelmed with the whole thing, because they couldn't imagine their young son going to the United States to run in a marathon. They would let Galu know the next day their answer after the evening meal.

It was during the evening after a meal of bread, sweet potatoes, and beans the next day, that his parents talked to him about the big race. Both parents agreed that it was too much to ask of a young man only twelve years old to go such a long distance in a strange land to run a marathon. They didn't understand the magnitude of the event, but knew that whatever was required their Galu would do what was right.

With all of the other children listening, his father asked, "What is it you would want to do?"

"I want to honor the decision that you make," Galu responded.

Following a long discussion of the matter, his parents told Galu that they gave him approval to participate, and they knew he would represent the community well.

It was good news for Dan who began immediately to complete the registration to enter Galu in the prestigious marathon in the United States. To do this, he had to go to the associational headquarters where they faxed all of the information that was needed for Galu to run. When the fax was received in the Boston marathon office, there was a loud yell by the clerk. The marathon office had been bombarded with telephone calls to find out whether or not the twelve-year old lad was going to run in the marathon. The staff immediately prepared a press release to apprise all of the media that Galu was going to participate.

There was almost pandemonium when the news media discovered that the Boston marathon would have the twelve-year old African champion, the one so adored in the United States following the human interest article that the reporter wrote in the newspaper concerning Galu. Everyone wanted to get involved as there were T-shirts with Galu's picture splashed across the front, marathon magazines with his picture on the cover, food named after him to be sold by vendors at the race, and all types of trinkets with his name and picture. In fact, the adoration for a runner that none of them had ever seen in the United States extended much beyond anything anyone could ever remember.

Galu was told that the registration had been completed so he was a legitimate runner in the best of the world's marathon. Telling him changed his demeanor none, as he was always the same, the pleasant young man who possessed much wisdom way beyond his years. A few days before they were to depart for the big event, the village fathers invited Dan to a meeting wherein they gave him sufficient money for three people to make the trip to the United States. They knew that the funds would only cover the barest of the basics, but they wanted to reward the van driver who had given so much to assist Dan when other village people refused to accept Galu's unusual talent at first. His providing transportation was the difference between Galu's running and not running in the African marathons, and without these events he would not be going to the best marathon of them all, the Boston marathon. The village people indicated that there would be a big Galu send-off.

In Boston the world champion runners and even many of the hopefuls had been on location for some time preparing for the big race by practicing everyday, thereby getting used to the environment, especially the climate. As the date of the marathon approached, thousands of the runners were already present, many of whom were recognized by the interested group of early spectators who came to see their favorites before the race. Of course, the main topic of conversation was about the young lad about whom no one knew anything except the one newspaper article, which caused all of the sudden interest. Reporters hung around the marathon headquarters all the time inquiring about Galu to see whether or not they had heard anything, and whether or not he truly was going to run in the marathon.

On the morning of departure it was an interesting site as the van driver, Dan and Galu got in the old dilapidated van. They placed their orange webbed "onion" sacks containing all of their belongings that they were going to carry in the van. Because Galu carried his items of ragged running pants, rope, handkerchief, running shoes, and his food for the trip in this manner, Dan and the van driver, who was advised to do likewise, used the same so that Galu's "suitcase" would not be embarrassing to him. The van driver was so excited about getting to go, because he had never been anywhere except in the village until he began to drive his van to take Galu to the marathons, and now he was going to travel all the way to the United States. Galu, of course, did not show any of this kind of emotion even though all the traveling he had ever done outside his home community was on the marathon trips, and now that he was going to the Boston marathon, his same pleasant and calm countenance spread all over his face. Before they embarked on this long journey, Galu asked that all present hold hands as he prayed for God's guidance for the day and forever more.

The send-off was vociferous with hundreds of well wishers surrounding the van. All the children were present to say farewell to their genuine hero, and as the van pulled away with the blue balls of smoke, they began to chant: "Galuuuuuuuu, Galuuuuuuuu, Galuuuuuuuu, Galuuuuuuuu, Galuuuuuuuu, . . . " running alongside the van as long as they could keep up. There were numerous people along the roadway waving at them as they made their way to the large eastern city to catch a small plane to Addis Ababa where they would get another plane to Cairo. It was going to be a long journey, but the send-off of well wishers all of the way, and including the large eastern city, made the initial leg of the long journey very pleasant.

Hundreds of people were at the small airport when they arrived, shouting and holding banners of all kinds. Parking the van, the crowd made them a path, and the supporters patted them on the back as they walked to the small terminal. As they approached the entrance, the official stated that everything had been taken care of and that they could board the plane. Dan had flown many times before, but this was the first time for the van driver and Galu. The van driver was very nervous, and as the plane left the ground and continued to make its ascent, he held on to the seat and appeared not to take a breath for a long period. For Galu, he sat calmly in his seat looking as peaceful as he would if he were sitting in school, occasionally looking out the window at the beautiful scenery below.

The van driver had settled down a little as the commuter plane taxied into the Addis Ababa airport. Soon their only luggage that they had was being carried in their hands so it was easy to get in place for the next segment of their trip to Cairo. With only a short wait, they were off again with the van driver looking a little more at ease this time, and by the time they reached Cairo, his complexion was normal. Everything seemed to be going smoothly until there was a message delivered over the intercom at the Cairo airport that there was a storm overhead and the flight would be delayed.

In Boston the news media had discovered that the twelve-year old runner was on the way and would be arriving on the eve of the marathon on American Airlines, flight 4078. Of course, everyone who could read or hear in the Boston area and other parts of the United States would get the information as the media broadcasted and published the report. Talk shows gave the news of Galu's arrival as the hosts carried on a debate with their audience regarding whether or not a youngster should be permitted to run in the Boston marathon. Many indicated that there would be so much concern for the child's welfare that it would interfere with the others. Some stated that the marathons that he ran before were nothing like the Boston marathon which took all the energy even for the best of the world class runners.

As the large contingent of people watched the flight chart board in the Boston Airport, Galu, the van driver and Dan waited patiently in Cairo to continue their long journey. No one, who saw the three of them, looking more like vagrants with their "Samsonite" onion bags as they sat in the Cairo Airport, knew who they were. Soon though, after a three-hour delay they were on their way to Amsterdam. They were flying in a larger plane so the flight attendants began to serve them some food, and then one of them looked at the three of them, and said, “Is this young man the marathon runner everyone is talking about?”

“This young man’s name is Galu who has entered the marathon,” Dan responded to the attendant whose eyes just lit up when she was told this information.

Discovering that Galu was on board, soon everyone on the plane turned to look or came back to speak to all three of them. All of the attention embarrassed Galu.

The captain called ahead to Amsterdam to tell them that he had the young marathon runner and his two companions on board, which probably would cause a big scene at the airport so he asked the airport staff to make special arrangements for them so the three would not be trampled by well wishers. The captain told the airport official, “I can’t believe what they were carrying as luggage, orange onion sacks. Furthermore, Galu does not eat the food provided in flight, because he has brought his own food in his bag. A flight attendant saw Galu eat a baked sweet potato, a piece of what she believed was a dried meat, a piece of bread and a mango.”

At the Amsterdam Airport several hundred people, including numerous reporters, had gathered to see this young runner.

"Do you know where he lives?" one man asked another.

"I'm really not sure but I believe it's in Africa somewhere," the other replied.

"He seems to be a very young man running in a marathon," the first man said. "I don't believe that I have ever heard of a youngster running in such events."

"That's what makes this whole situation so bizarre," the second stated.

Before too long a reporter overheard airport staff personnel discussing what was occurring on Galu's flight, and the reporter immediately called it in to Boston where it was reported as breaking news over one of the local television channels. Everyone who heard the report could not believe what he was eating in preparation for the race, and furthermore, could not understand how he thought he could run well in the Boston marathon when he would be traveling until the last minute for the race. The world class champions of marathons always came to Boston several days and even weeks for training, and during the last hours they would relax, not be on a plane thousands of miles from the race course.

All the cities were so beautiful, including Amsterdam, where there was a layover of six hours. The crowd was immense and the airport staff shuttled the van driver, Dan and Galu through the airport as onlookers wished him well. Reporters were kept at "arms length" so there were no direct interviews permitted, but they made up for the shortfall by talking to everyone who even got close to Galu, including the whole flight crew. The news of Galu's arrival in Amsterdam hit the radio and television wires in Boston, and the whole community got very excited to think that in a short while the young lad would be arriving in their fair city.

As the time for departure drew near, a message came over the public address system that the flight to Boston would be delayed, because of a terrible storm in the area and the accompanying high winds. Shielded from the onslaught of the people who just wanted to get a glimpse of the little runner, the van driver, Dan and Galu sat quietly and patiently awaiting their flight. Dan calculated the time of arrival in Boston, if they left at a certain time from Amsterdam so he knew the latest they must depart to arrive in time for Galu to participate in the marathon.

"We'll have to leave soon to get there for the marathon," Dan said to the van driver. "We won't have any time to spare."

"It will be a long trip to Boston over the big ocean," the van driver stated, still not at ease when flying.

After a very long wait there was a public address announcement indicating that the flight to Boston would leave in thirty minutes and the passengers should make their way to the Gate E for the American Airline flight. After all of the other passengers were on board, the staff brought Galu, Dan and the van driver to the boarding area. Everybody hovered around the area that had been cordoned off wishing Galu well in the marathon. Some wanted to pass on gifts to him, including jackets, sweaters, shoes, etc., but he would not take them. The onlookers couldn't believe that he was carrying his belongings in an orange onion sack so many offered their beautiful luggage.

When they were on their way, the captain came on to welcome Galu and his friends, and he told them he would fly as fast as he could so Galu would not miss the marathon. The captain talked to the Boston airport personnel and told them that he had their little runner on board and would be delivering him on schedule, but much later than that which was expected. On board Dan knew that they would not have but very little time upon their arrival in Boston to register for the race, much less for Galu to get his rest caused by jet lag.

The attendants watched every move Galu made and reported it to the captain who was becoming somewhat of a reporter as he talked to the Boston airport. In Boston the report of Galu's being on the flight from Amsterdam caused all of the media to scurry to find a telephone to call in their breaking news. Everyone wondered how a runner could compete effectively arriving on the scene at such a late date and time. Most seemed to speculate that Galu would not fare well at all in the event, because he would not be physically able, following the flying experience since he left Tanzania. None of these thoughts would dampen the enthusiasm of the anticipated crowd that was expected to line the running route, and the record number that would be viewing on television the scenes captured by the many cameras.

As the other passengers ate the food provided by the airlines, Galu, Dan and the van driver dug into their orange onion sacks and got out their food. For Galu his food was the usual, a baked sweet potato, a piece of dried meat, bread log, and an orange or mango. He and the others requested water to drink with their meal. Those in earshot in the Boston airport got really excited when the captain reported what the little twelve-year old runner was eating for his dinner on the plane.

With the lights of Boston seen in the distance, the chief attendant said to Dan, “It will be so late when you all arrive at the airport, the officials will furnish a vehicle for you to drive to the marathon starting point. Further, they will provide special security so that you will not have to go the usual way when you leave the airplane, thereby avoiding the large crowd of well wishers in and around the airport terminal.”

“That is very kind of the officials,” Dan stated with a warm smile to the attendant.

“Galu is quite a world celebrity, isn’t he?” she responded.

“He just loves to run in marathon races,” Dan replied.

"But he is so very young," she said.

"Although he is very young, he has been running long distances for several years," Dan noted.

It was nearly two o'clock in the morning Boston time so they would have to drive to the marathon starting point and let Galu get as much rest as he could before the biggest event of his life.

It was a nice, new van well equipped so as Dan drove through the city, it was very comfortable. Following the route directions given by a staff member of the airport, they made it to the starting area without making too many unnecessary turns. It took a little while but within five blocks of the starting area, they found a good parking space. At this time the van driver and Galu slept while Dan stayed awake to be sure that they did not oversleep the next morning. During his hours before he awoke Galu for the race, Dan gave much thought as to how he could get Galu from the van to the starting area without being swarmed by interested people.

As he watched the area fill with spectators and early arriving runners, Dan went to the officials' table to be sure that Galu was included on the many sheets listing more than thirty thousand runners. Looking in the alphabetical list, there his name was with the number 30788, one of the highest numbers in the race. Finding the 30788 on a large rack near the main area, Dan got the number and proceeded to return to the van. As he walked briskly along, he could hear many people wanting to know whether or not the little Tanzanian was going to run in the event. There were television cameras everywhere that were going to capture every move of the adored runner, but no one had seen him yet, but according to the airport officials he had arrived after midnight. Dan knew that he had to get Galu into the starting group of runners without being observed by the large crowd that had gathered in the area. Seeing many vendors as he walked back to the van, the master teacher decided to buy

Galu a running shirt that would help provide a disguise along with his new running shoes. All knew that he ran without a shirt and did not wear shoes, so they would not recognize Galu with his new shoes and shirt.

Back at the van he awoke Galu and the van driver. "It's time to wake up and prepare for the race," Dan said.

"Thank you," Galu replied, as he raised up from the floor of the new van.

"I think we should remain in the van until closer to the time of the start of the race, don't you believe?" Dan said to them.

"I think that would be an excellent idea," the van driver responded. "It seems that everyone wants to talk to Galu."

"Let's eat now and with Galu wearing a shirt and his running shoes, he may get in the pack of runners without being noticed," Dan said.

Following prayer by Galu, they opened their orange onion sacks again to eat the last meal before the race. After the meal Dan gave Galu the shirt and told him to wear it for a while in the race, and then he could take it off, if he didn't want to wear it for the entire event. At seven thirty, one-half hour before the race, Galu, Dan and the van driver, discreetly departed the van through the back door. Galu walked between the other two as they walked hastily across the wooded lots to the starting place, as thousands of people seemed to be preoccupied with being the first to see the diminutive, adored runner. None expected, however, that he would be wearing a shirt and shoes.

Unnoticed, Galu slipped among the very large throng of runners and just disappeared among the many running hopefuls who were joined on the morning for a single purpose, to run the most prestigious marathon in the world. Just before the race was started, the public address announcer indicated that the mysterious little twelve-year old was somewhere in the group and had the number of 30788.

The front runners pulled away from the starting line very quickly after the marathon began, but those in the rear had a long wait, especially those whose numbers were higher than 30000. It was like a loud shriek after the whole group had started when a lady in the large set of bleachers saw the number 30788, and with this eerie announcement the loose television cameras began to converge on the entire area to get a glimpse of their hero so they could broadcast it back to their viewing audience. Even the helicopters overhead from the major networks began to scurry around to get Galu in view.

Nothing seemed to phase Galu, and this is what made him so different from others. As usual, he wanted to get up close to the front very quickly, but because of the large number of runners, he would have to be more patient. Within a mile or two he had passed hundreds and hundreds of runners only to see many more in front. Not to change his method of running in these events, he just kept on passing the slower runners for nearly five miles, then settled down in a little groove where he would run for a while. The helicopter cameras would zoom in on the diminutive twelve-year old, and all along the way there were spotter announcers and television cameras and reporters. Hearing about all of the attention given to his young runner, Dan knew that Galu would have to reach down and get all of the strength that he could muster to get through this colossal marathon, which far exceeded the other three he had run. Dan thought about how much he had learned from Galu, and it was not supposed to be this way, because he was the teacher and Galu the student. It was just turned around, because Galu had taught him and the others so much about living a life for God by always putting self second, and not taking secular activities seriously.

Meanwhile, back in Tanzania a large television with a satellite dish had been brought in from the associational office to the school so that local people, including students, could see Galu run in the Boston marathon. It was believed that everyone in the surrounding villages was present to see the race and to cheer Galu during the event. Each time that they could see Galu running, they would chant: "Galuuuuuuuu, Galuuuuuuuu, Galuuuuuuuu, Galuuuuuuuu, . . .

The story of Galu's mysterious arrival to the starting site began to circulate among the media and crowd. How a young man could run at all after the long ordeal on the airplane which caused him to arrive only a couple of hours before the start of the race, was more than anyone could understand. The major networks brought former marathon runners who were retired champions to talk to the reporters on television and radio, and each of them just knew that the little runner would not last long and would withdraw from the event or would continue and finish far from the front group. Everyone within earshot seemed to concur.

As the news spread that Galu could not possibly finish well in the race, it seemed that attention for just a while centered around covering some of the favorites. Meanwhile, Galu was making another smooth surge quietly toward the front runners with little fanfare. As he reached the ten-mile marker, he was only about three hundred yards away from the leaders, a comfortable position that he liked. Because he wanted to be even more comfortable in the race, he suddenly stopped and sat down on the curb and took off his shoes and his shirt. With the whole world viewing with some announcers explaining that he had gotten tired and needed the rest, Galu suddenly ran back about one hundred yards. Reaching a young lad in a wheel chair, Galu gave him his shoes and his shirt, with a big hug.

“Thank you for coming to the race today,” Galu said, as he handed his shirt and shoes to the young man.

“Thank you!” the young man yelled in a loud voice, as Galu joined the others in the race.

Then he proceeded the race, very comfortably in his regular attire, ragged, shin length pants, rope belt, and big handkerchief that was given by his mother.

There was a clamor to evaluate Galu's behavior, but all agreed that it was unusual, and he had lost a lot of time stopping and then running back to give his shoes and shirt to a young lad in a wheel chair. A couple of the reporters interviewed the recipient of Galu's racing shoes and shirt, and the young fellow was thrilled to death and hoped that Galu won the marathon.

"Do you know the name of the runner who gave you these items?" one asked.

"My mom told me his name was Galu," he replied, still sporting a wide and warm smile.

"What did he say to you?" another reporter asked.

"He just looked at me and asked me if I would like to have his shirt and his running shoes," the young man in the wheel chair responded.

"What did you say to him?" the first reporter asked.

"I didn't have time to say anything except to thank him for the items," the young man answered.

By twelve miles into the race the runners were thinning out, and Galu from time to time could run alone. Being barefoot and shirtless, he felt very good, so he continued his patient pace to get within three hundred yards of the front runner. There were television camera operators on backs of trucks, and it seemed that one always stayed with Galu. Dan and the van driver could almost follow their little runner all the while as they scanned the television monitors at the official station. Even they could not believe the serene countenance on Galu's face under these adverse conditions. They both smiled when they saw him running barefoot and without a shirt.

At about the seventeen-mile marker many of the runners in the lead group became exhausted and fell back, leaving Galu an open path even closer to the front, so during the next four miles he closed in on the leaders. When an update was made regarding the leaders after twenty-one miles, there were only about fifty runners within three hundred yards of the leader. Galu maintained a quick pace for the next three miles and during this stretch about forty of the lead runners dropped back beyond Galu. Now with two miles to go, there were only nine runners ahead of him, all within two hundred yards of the lead runner.

All of the media around the world were witnessing something spectacular, a twelve-year-old only two hundred yards off the pace of the most prestigious marathon in the world. It was hard for everybody quite to conceive of what was happening on this day. Thousands of spectators lined the streets to watch, to wave, and to wish the diminutive lad well as he pounded the streets, cutting into his feet that were showing signs of bleeding. Many of the onlookers cried with emotion when he so gracefully ran by wearing his ragged running pants held up with his rope. He was truly their darling little runner that all had laid claim, and just before their eyes, he was in position to win the whole affair.

Commentator after commentator tried to describe the last two miles of the race only to be overwhelmed. Reaching the start of the last mile, there were only five runners, including Galu, and as the whole world watched, the little twelve-year old, who grew up in a small village in Tanzania, began to quicken his pace so that as he reached the one-half mile marker, he was gaining on the leader. At this point several young people along the street that was packed with a record crowd of spectators began loudly to cheer by yelling: "Galuuuuuuuu, Galuuuuuuuu, Galuuuuuuuu, Galuuuuuuuu, . . . " and soon thousands of people were chanting the same until it was almost ear shattering.

With each step Galu was making his move to the front, the Boston marathon that was reserved for champions, and with every word all who could see it tried to describe it to themselves only to fall short of words. It was a phenomenal site, as Galu's little bleeding feet pulled up alongside the leader as the onlookers went completely wild, cheering him all the way. With every final step Galu extended his lead, breaking the tape in record time. Pandemonium broke out with hand clapping, cheering, yelling and even drum beats. Anyway, everyone was preoccupied trying to be a part of the remarkable finish of the best marathon ever.

Dan and the van driver went to where Galu was, and they walked quickly and discreetly to the van. In the van Galu rendered a prayer thanking God for the strength and wisdom that was given to all of them, because of God's grace. As usual, Dan went back and brought back the trophy to the van as the many thousands of spectators celebrated the twelve-year-old's victory. They were on their way to the airport before the marathon officials began to look for Galu, following the demand of the crowd for him to speak to the large gathering.

In the small village in Tanzania and all over the country, there were shouts of joy being uttered by the thousands of people who had just witnessed their favorite son win the most prestigious marathon on earth. They, too, wanted to see Galu on television, but they knew that he did not wait at the end of his races for anyone to praise him on his efforts. Some of the leaders in the group were beginning to plan a big homecoming for Galu so all the country could show him how much they loved him, how much they thanked him for his winning the many marathon events, and above all for his leadership for the young and old alike in the locality.

Returning their new van, an airport official took care of all of the details for their boarding the American Airlines flight number 3211, so they just followed along almost unnoticed. The flight was scheduled to depart in about forty-five minutes, and to shelter them from the well wishers, Dan, the van driver and Galu were permitted to board the airplane early and await departure. All were very nice to them as they wanted to bring food and other things to make them comfortable as they sat on the plane, but as usual, they did not eat any food except what they brought in their orange onion sacks. Of course, several of the flight staff got autographs from Galu, and on one occasion a stewardess came and requested an autograph for the pilot and co-pilot. All in all it was a restful time for the trio.

Leaving Boston on schedule, they settled back for a long flight to Amsterdam. The captain couldn't contain himself any longer so he divulged that the staff was honored to have the twelve-year-old winner of the Boston marathon on board. Following this announcement, there was almost bedlam as everyone wanted to see this young celebrity with many wanting to get his autograph.

By this time the media in Boston had discovered that Galu was on an airplane headed for Amsterdam so they tried their best to get one of the flight staff to interview the magnificent young runner, and pass the information on to them. No one agreed to interview the young man, because each could see how private he was about his thoughts and feelings. No one wanted to disturb that special calmness that shone all over his face.

A very large crowd had gathered at the airport terminal in Amsterdam, as the plane made its descent to land. Many were curious to see the little hero, having watched the Boston marathon on television while others had gotten caught up in the media hype of the local commentators. Of course, there were hundreds of media on site to get an interview from Galu, inasmuch as he departed the marathon area before the media in Boston could get to him. The flight staff knew of the large crowd of people in and around the terminal and the difficulty that Galu and his two friends would have getting to the boarding area for their flight to Cairo. To assist them, two members of the terminal staff took them through the lower level beyond the view of the onlookers and proceeded to carry them via a terminal cart to a secluded waiting area to wait for their flight.

An airport terminal official made an announcement that Galu would not be available to speak to the group, but that two of the stewardesses assigned to his flight from Boston would be available to answer questions that they might have. Of course, everyone was upset that Galu would not be available, but was thankful for any kind of information about the special hero even if it were second hand.

Boarding early for Cairo, Galu, Dan and van driver sat quietly reflecting on the many activities of the last twenty-four hours. In the air right on schedule the flight attendants advised the other passengers that the Boston marathon winner was on board, and in a little while the captain congratulated Galu for the victory in the prestigious marathon. Everyone on the flight was so very cordial to Galu and wished him well in other marathons. They all watched when he reached into his webbed orange onion sack and got his food, baked potato, dried meat, a bread log, and an orange. An attendant brought him some water.

With no staff assistance in Cairo, Galu, Dan and the van driver were swarmed in the airport terminal, but following Galu's signing numerous autographs, it settled down a little until the media reporters converged on the scene. Dan and the van driver protected Galu as they answered all of the questions for him. One question that puzzled them was what was Galu going to do with the money he got for winning the race. Because this was the first time that they knew there was money given to the winner in the race, they acknowledged that Galu and they were not aware that the victorious runner received any money. Of course, the whole mystique surrounding this diminutive twelve-year-old runner was growing by the hour, because now the news of his not knowing about the victory money would make the news all over the world.

The flight to Addis Ababa, too, was on time so they were still on schedule to get to Tanzania at the prescribed time. There was an hour layover in Addis Ababa and the president sent his limousine and guards to bring Galu, Dan and the van driver to visit his palace staff and to meet his family and the young people in the area. It was a most impressive visit as they were greeted at the steps by the president and several of his immediate staff. Following a brief visit to the council chambers, they went to the rear courtyard of the palace where there were more than a hundred young people waiting to see Galu. For the first time on the whole trip Galu volunteered to speak to a group, and he told them of winning the Boston marathon only by the grace of Jesus Christ who died for all of our sins. He went on to tell his young audience that all of God's people have special talents, and we should use them to the fullest each day of our lives.

The children gave Galu many gifts, so many in fact he had to get help from Dan and the van driver to carry all of them. It was a most cordial gesture by the president, and the visit seemed to be so short, but it was now time to get back to the airport for their final leg before getting to their home country. It was the final take off as they were headed for their country, Tanzania. The flight was short and uneventful except for the passengers wanting to talk to Galu or to touch him with most wanting his autograph. Landing in the large eastern city of Tanzania, they could see the large number of people near the airport terminal, and they realized that their trip to their home village would be longer than expected.

As Dan, the van driver and Galu disembarked from the airplane, the crowd burst out in the chant: "Galuuuuuuu, Galuuuuuuu, Galuuuuuuu, Galuuuuuuu, Galuuuuuuu, . ." It was a joyous scene as the country's favorite son had arrived from Boston after having won the world's most prestigious marathon, and they wanted to let Galu know how much they appreciated his victory. Among the group were thousands of young people who wanted to see their idol, one whom they emulated his every action. All three with their webbed orange onion bags were carried on the shoulders of the well wishers to the old dilapidated van so they could begin their trip westward to their home village.

The scene at the airport was duplicated many times over as the old van loaded with the country's hero puttered through the various villages along the way. All the young people wanted to see their hero who was their peer so many of them ran beside the van to get a longer and better look at Galu. Finally making it home, Galu was greeted warmly and lovingly by his parents and brothers who had watched him win the Boston marathon on the television that was brought to the village.

Within a short period of his arrival at home, Galu began doing his chores, because it was almost time for their evening meal. No one discussed the marathon, as usual, because Galu kept all of the marathon success in proper perspective, as he always put his relationship with his parents, brothers and sisters, along with school and his church before all else. Even though this was the pinnacle of success for any person, Galu took the victory in stride and went about his responsibilities in his home and community.

During the next few days plans for the feast were beginning to take shape. It was going to be the most elaborate and festive occasion that the area had ever known, because never in the history of the country had they had such a popular hero, one that everyone adored. Each village was participating so it was decided that the location for the event would be on the school grounds.

.Meanwhile, in the United States since the race the media were trying to piece together any shreds of information that they could publish or broadcast. The mystique of the twelve-year-old runner caused the search for bits and pieces of facts and hearsay to consume much of the time. The photographer who made the picture of Galu giving the shoes and shirt to the crippled young man in the wheel chair, let it be known that he had this picture of Galu. After he sold it to the highest bidder, it was published on the front page of the most popular Boston newspaper. This brought about thousands of calls to the editor wanting to know who the crippled young man was in the picture.

As the mother of the crippled child made her way home, which was a small, ill furnished room in a run down tenement house in a poor neighborhood, she saw a picture of Galu and her child on the front page. Arriving at home, she showed her son the picture, and they talked about it together before she started dinner, which would be potato soup and a few crackers. Working two jobs following the death of her husband in a car accident, it was impossible for her to make ends meet, because of the large hospital bills that kept piling up. She loved her son so much, and she wanted so much to provide for him the things that other children had, although he seemed to be content with what he had. Each Sunday she would go to the altar and pray that God would take care of them, and she asked for His guidance, because she knew that she could not make it alone.

The media continued to publish and broadcast all the while about the young runner who had "turned Boston upside down" during his stay of only a few hours. Everyone was getting in the act as talk shows after talk shows used their time talking about Galu. A most popular morning talk show invited Jamie, the wheel-chair lad, and his mother as guests to the delight of a wide viewing audience.

"If you had one wish," the host asked, "what would it be?"

Without hesitation, Jamie said, "I would wish that I could visit my good friend, Galu."

"Why do you call him your good friend?" the popular host asked.

"In the big race, the race of his life, he took time to come back and speak to me, and also, to give me his shirt and shoes that he didn't need any more," Jamie quickly noted.

"It's amazing," his mom said, "how much my son has adored this young man who can do something that my son will never be able to do. Ever since information about Galu has been put out, Jamie has clipped all the articles and put them in a scrapbook. I believe he has got every article that has been written about this little runner."

"It seems that Galu knew that your son was a big fan of his, doesn't it?" the host added.

"It certainly does," Jamie's mom responded, "but we all know that it was just a most unusual coincidence."

The interview that was going so well was interrupted by a telephone call. A station aide handed the telephone to the host of the popular morning show. "Hello, this is Morton Augsberry of LBN," he cordially stated, being very perplexed that he would be asked to answer a telephone while the program was in progress. "How may I help you?"

"I want to donate money for airline tickets and other expenses for Jamie and his mom to go to visit Galu in Trenka, Tanzania," a woman in a garbled voice indicated. "Just have Jamie's mom to give her address on the air, and I will see that she gets the money tomorrow."

"Who are you?" the surprised host asked, as the caller hung up.

"Mrs. McMaster, sometimes things happen on this show that I don't fully understand," the host stated. "I have never been interrupted by a telephone call before while on the air with a show so the call today was a first. Now let me tell you what the caller said to me. A garbled voice of a person indicated that enough money would be sent so that the both of you could go to visit Galu in Trenka, Tanzania. The caller seemed to know exactly where Galu lived in Tanzania which makes the call even more interesting."

"I can't believe that someone would give us money for such a long trip," Mrs. McMaster said, as she burst into tears. Sobbing all the while, she told the host what a special day it was for them.

"Are you excited now about being able to go to see your special friend?" the host asked Jamie, while his mom was continuing to cry.

"Oh! It will be a dream come true for me and my mom!" he excitedly responded.

Dressed in well worn clothing that appeared to have been out of style, Mrs. McMaster said, "I am better composed now. This is such a wonderful and special day for both of us."

"I am so happy for you," the host indicated.

"May I tell you something," Mrs. McMaster said. "My whole life is centered around Jamie. I love him so very much. He is such a wonderful and good young man who can't do the things other children can do, so when we have time, I take him to the park and to other places. Working two jobs so we can be debt free, I am following the wishes of my husband who died in a car crash when he was discharged from the military after our Middle East war. He wrote me many letters, and in one he told me that if anything happened to him in the war, he wanted me to promise him that I would always take care of Jamie and not send him to a school somewhere. You see, his pride and joy was his only child, Jamie, whom he loved so very much."

Mrs. McMaster broke down again, and the host tried to console her, but she continued to cry. Wanting to hear the rest of this most touching story, the host finally helped her so that she could continue this heart warming tale of her family.

"Several months after he died, I found a letter in the bottom of a drawer written to Jamie that told how much he loved him and not to let his handicap stand in the way of anything he wanted to do in life," she continued. "In the letter he wrote, 'God gives us all special wherewithal to live on this special earth He has created for us. It is only through the grace of God that we have this life so we all are special in the eyes of our Father in heaven.'"

"What a wonderful story!" the host stated. "Would you give the aide your address so we can flash it on the screen so the person who called can send you the money for the trip to see Galu?"

The scheduled visit of the crippled young man coincided with the big feast celebrating Galu's victory. It was a joyous occasion with Dan and Pat relishing every moment of the event, as did all of their students

The reuniting of Galu and the crippled young man was a special event as they hugged each other, and Galu took him all over the countryside so that he could get acquainted with Galu's environment. In fact he stayed at Galu's house for several days while they were visiting in Tanzania, enjoying the same love by Galu's parents as Galu experienced each day. What a special visit as a result of a wish and a response by the benevolent person!

THE SECOND SPORT

The Bacon girls were sporting a perfect record in basketball and ranked number one in the ACUWAA while at the same time practicing to get prepared for the soccer season. Excitement filled the athletic dormitory as they teased each other while getting ready to participate in their inaugural game, albeit a practice game. Mit was beside herself, because they were headed for her small town to the east where she lived during her formative years. She remembered that her mother was a teacher in the Henry County Public Schools with so many other dedicated and professional persons, and her father worked as an engineer in a large construction company in the area.

"I hope you all enjoy going to my hometown of Bassett," Mit stated to the group, as they began to assemble in the commons area.

"We are so happy for you, Mit," Dorothy said, as she walked over and hugged her ever so tightly.

Dr. Damond and the other students were on hand to see the group off for their first soccer match. Following an eloquent prayer by the president, they loaded the van and headed east on Route 460 to I77 going through the long tunnel. As they passed Carroll County High School in Hillsville, Virginia, they saw a team of girls playing soccer on a field near the school. Needing to have a rest stop, Coach Anna pulled over, and the girls got out and proceeded to watch the team practice. Someone recognized the Bacon girls so immediately the practice session ceased, and the girls were coaxed into giving an impromptu session as the high school girls watched.

After a very brief display of their soccer prowess, Coach Anna requested that the high school coach get a team ready, and Bacon would play a short period of time. It was an obvious mismatch from the start, and when Mit speedily moved up and down the field for three goals in succession, everyone present realized why she was pictured on the Sports Ramble Magazine even though she had not played one minute of college competition. Obviously, it was a time of great fun for all concerned, especially the high school students who saw first hand an outstanding college soccer team.

"There will be no more interruptions until we get to Bassett," Coach Anna told the group, as they piled back into the van with the several high school students and their parents wishing them well.

"We had a good time with the group," Dorothy said, speaking for the team.

Down the beautiful mountain they went through Patrick County before entering Henry County near Fairy Stone State Park. Although having not been to Bassett in many years, Mit still remembered much about this little furniture town to act as tour guide. She pointed out the furniture factories down Smith River and advised them when they got near the entrance of Bassett High School, which was constructed on a seventy-eight-acre tract of land in the late seventies. A huge banner was hanging at the entrance of the school driveway that read: "Welcome Home, Mit."

Coach Anna pulled on past the crowded soccer stadium toward the school where the team would dress for the afternoon practice session and demonstration. The school that was nearly twenty-five years old was immaculately clean and extremely well maintained. As soon as the girls were dressed, Coach Anna spoke an eloquent prayer, thanking God for safe travel and that the participants in the afternoon's session would be free from injury.

Opening the door to head for the field about three hundred yards away, the team was surprised to see two rows of students and spectators forming a lane all the way to the field. The girls jogged all the way with Mit leading the group with her blond pony tail bouncing from side to side with each stride.

A second surprise came when they entered the field where there was a temporary platform constructed now holding many dignitaries in the area. Among those privileged to be seated as distinguished leaders of the community were the county administrator, chairman of the board of supervisors, supervisors, superintendent of Henry County Public Schools, school board chairman, board members, Henry County sheriff and several deputies, and many elected officials of state and national bodies.

A key to the county was presented to Coach Anna after many of the dignitaries made some most flattering remarks about the Bacon team. The color guard of the high school's JROTC program under the direction of Colonel Richard Foster, presented the colors at which time distinguished awards and meritorious medals were presented to all of the girls for their efforts in foiling the hijacking attempt, and their brave and dangerous rescue of the three missionaries from the terrorists in Abedistan. What a colorful and professionally done program highlighted by the playing of several songs by the perennially award winning high school bengal band known throughout the area for its excellence!

The hundred or more high school soccer players from several of the local high schools were going to see an unusual demonstration of soccer skills. With each of the twenty girls with a soccer ball, including Hanna, each dribbled the ball to the far end, and coming back down each alternated the dribble with another still keeping the various balls moving in control all the way to the other end. Next, one behind the other, they dribbled directly toward the goal and when about fifty feet from the net let go a strong and blistering kick into the goal. No one missed.

While Mit was the darling of the group as attested by many yells to her, an equal number of people present wanted to get the attention of Esther when they finally knew she was present.

One spectator leaned over to another and said, "Can you believe that in our Ed Bassett Stadium here today we have the best soccer player in college and the best basketball player in the country?"

"It's just amazing that they would agree to be with us today which will be a big financial boost to our athletic program at the school," the first said.

Included in the demonstration were side corner kicks back to the front of the goal where a player would strike a header from a diving position. The culminating activity was a penalty kick in front of the net with seven goalies as defenders. Mit led the charge by striking a strong kick into the corner of the net, following by the other kickers to the delight of those in attendance. Before the scrimmage, Coach Anna was requested to permit various pictures to be made of the team by a local professional photographer, thus giving the local athletic boosters another means of making money during the event of this day.

"This is such a special day for Mit to return to her hometown in such a warm and joyous celebratory atmosphere at the high school she would have attended, if her parents had remained in the area and not having gone to Costa Rica as missionaries," Coach Anna thought. Mit was so much like Esther such that she was very businesslike on the soccer field not to be distracted by the events surrounding her, but suddenly something in the crowd caught her eye. Stopping her practice, she looked toward the stands about half way up where a young lady, a man and a woman were waving a huge bright red flag with the words, “Thank you, Mit!” printed in large white letters.

Mit broke away from her group and ran toward the restraining fence as the young lady left the stands and headed her way. Meeting at the gate, they hugged each other for a very long time as the crowd honored this mysterious meeting by remaining deftly silent until Mit invited Sarah Dudley to the center of the field to meet the other team.

“You have grown so much,” Mit said to Sarah, as they ran across the field to meet the other team members.

“Coach Anna, this is Sarah Dudley, a very dear friend of mine from Bassett,” Mit stated to her coach.

“I am glad to meet you, Sarah,” Coach Anna responded to this very strong looking fourteen-year-old girl. “Do you play soccer?”

“Yes, I do,” Sarah replied. “I play on two teams each year.”

Coach Anna didn’t realize who Sarah was until she remembered reading the story about Mit in the mission magazine that Maudie let her read one day. “I can’t believe that I am meeting the young lady whose life Mit saved while almost losing her own. What a special meeting of these two!”

Sarah was invited to sit with the team as the scrimmage activities were about to be gotten underway. The announcer, who was perplexed about Sarah’s presence on the field, was going to get another surprise. While he was trying to discover the relationship of Sarah to Mit, a man dressed in a wide, short yellow tie, and way-too-short pants with his white socks showing carrying something nearly six-feet high wrapped in a white cloth was trying to push his way through the crowd at the far end of the field. He was very determined such that it was causing a disturbance, and the deputies were moving in that direction to quell the situation.

As two deputies seized both his arms to take him away, Mit looked as he clutched onto the fence not wanting to be moved from the position he had struggled so hard to obtain during the last hour or so. With his hands now giving away by the pull of the strong deputies, his last hope was to call Mit's name so he yelled, "Mit, I'm down here!"

With all others in attendance turning to see the disturbance this man was making, Mit looked and immediately started running at blazing speed to the area yelling to the man, "Harris, is that you?"

The deputies turned then to see Mit running to the fence beyond which they were escorting this strange man to the exit. "I have come to see you," Harris replied.

"Oh! What a special day this is to have you here to see us play!" Mit responded.

"You know this man, Mit?" one deputy asked, as they turned toward Mit.

"I certainly do," she answered. "He is my good friend from Rondon."

With all of the spectators looking their way, Mit escorted Harris Day to the bench area as he held firmly his wrapped, mysterious item. Those in attendance were going to get a good lesson in not judging one by his appearance, because several years ago those in another city had had this same teacher.

With these two impromptu events one after the other, the soccer activity seemed to be taking a back seat, but the events were not over. Coach Anna slipped over to where Mit's new friend was standing as he met all of the team, and realized that what he had wrapped up might be a similar carving he did of Mit many years ago when she won a big race in Rondon. Mit had it on display in her room in college. "If that were the case," she thought, "he should unveil it in the middle of the field for all to see."

Not fully understanding all that was happening on the field, the public address announcer queried everybody in the booth high above the field regarding the mysterious newcomer now with the Bacon team.

"What do you know about the oddly dressed, small man now on the field with the girls from Bacon?" the announcer asked an individual nearby.

"I really don't know," he said. "I first saw him when I arrived earlier today so he must have been the first one in the stadium."

"Did you say anything to him?" the announcer asked, still trying to discover anything about the mysterious man.

"I spoke to him and he responded to me with an excited, high pitched voice with a strong colloquial tenor," he replied. "Actually, I didn't think he was too swift, if you know what I mean."

"Was he holding that thing wrapped in white cloth?" the announcer asked, realizing that this person was his only source for information regarding the stranger.

"He not only held the odd item, but he clutched it as though he was protecting it from the rest of us," the man said. "The thing was taller that he was so he had to wrestle with it just a little as I stood near him. I was near him for about five minutes, and he held it all the while never letting it touch the ground. It seemed to be very heavy, because I could hear him grunt just a little when he would shift it in his arms."

"What on earth do you think he has under that cloth anyway?" the announcer asked, realizing that he still did not discover anything about the mystery that by this time filled the entire stadium.

Coach Anna could sense that everyone in the stands seemed to be focused on the diminutive, ill clad man as he stood among the girls on the field, mainly because of his dress, how it was that he was an acquaintance of Mit and thirdly, that he was carrying an unusual item covered totally by a white cloth. Standing beside Mit and the strange man, Coach Anna thought, "Everybody is wondering about the little man, and what's in his wrapped cloth such that the delay of the soccer program doesn't seem to matter."

As she stood among her girls, Coach Anna continued to resurrect in her mind what part this mysterious figure played in the story of Mit. Soon she whispered in Mit's ear who was so preoccupied with her friend that time seemed to stand still for them as they continued to talk to each other. "Mit, everyone here is so enamored over your friend, Harris Day, why don't you take him to the middle of the field to show everyone what he has wrapped up in the cloth?" Coach Anna inquired.

"Oh! That is a splendid idea!" Mit replied, as she grabbed Harris by the hand and ran to the middle of the field with everyone watching. She turned to the crowd on both sides and said in a voice that no one could hear, "I want all of you to meet my good and special friend, Harris Day, who has come today all the way from Rondon to watch us play soccer."

A hush came over the capacity crowd of several thousand as Harris set the wrapped item on the ground for the first time since he arrived. Not having a microphone, he turned to the group on one side and then the other and said standing on center stage with his short, wide yellow tie and his pants hiked above his ankles, "Mit is me good friend; she talks to me. She is best runner in whole wide world. I ain't got no friends. Mit is me best friend ever. I made something for me Mit."

Harris reached over and held the top of the white cloth and unveiled it, and immediately there was a unified voice coming from the crowd, "Oh! How beautiful!"

Sitting now at midfield was a wood carved replica of Mit, the exact size, a perfect likeness of her. Mit spontaneously gave Harris a strong and lengthy bear hug as the spectators reacted with a loud and continuous applause. Some had binoculars, and they could not believe how much like Mit the carving really was. In fact, it was just like the picture of Mit that was on the Sports Ramble Magazine a few weeks ago.

The Bacon girls ran over and hugged Mit and Harris and carried the carved figure over their head to the sideline to the supreme delight of Harris. “Now you have two carvings of yourself,” Coach Anna said, now hugging Mit again. “This one is exactly like you now, and the other one is just like you when you were much younger.”

“Harris is such a special friend,” Mit replied. “I have invited Sarah and him for the afternoon and evening activities, if that’s all right?”

“Oh! That’s wonderful!” Coach Anna said. “They will add much to the whole celebration. “I know you are having such a good time on this trip, and because I read the story about you in the mission magazine, I understand better than most who these people are who have come to honor you today.”

“It’s such a special day to be back here in Basset where I lived several years ago,” she related with a wide smile coming through her serene countenance.

Being scrimmage time, the announcer indicated that he wanted to introduce the Bacon team to the spectators as the young high school players lined up in front of their bench on the opposite side of the field. My first introduction is Pattie Augburn, a student on the campus at Bacon selected by her peers to come with the team for this scrimmage today. For each game, just as the basketball team does, a student will participate. Now I want you to meet the basketball team from Bacon, the best in the country having not lost a game all year, and now participating in both soccer and basketball for the college. The members are Mabel Armbruster, Leslie Brewster, Jonsie Brown, Dorothy Buford, Jennifer Gaines, Hanna Green, Tonisha Hairston, Diane McCoy, Vivian Mason, Esther Minold, Cindy Love, and Maggie Morrow.

All of those in attendance were standing and cheering as they applauded this special group of athletes. After some semblance of quiet was restored, he introduced the players from New Mexico, Marsha Gavanto, Vanona Massat, and

Lota Minota, and the crowd continued its yells and loud applause. Now I want you to meet the remainder of this soccer team that has been assembled at Bacon by their coach, Annna Bosley. As Coach Anna ran to the middle of the field, the clapping and loud yells started all over again.

"Now from the jungle of Costa Rica come Nonita Arias, Monina Lada, Maria Salitada, and our own Mit Travers," the announcer said in a loud voice.

The high school players were divided into twelve teams with each playing against Bacon about ten minutes before another team would be rotated into the game. The whole affair was a true mismatch as the Bacon team scored at will with Mit and Marsha paving the way. Mit would from time to time turn on a burst of speed and the spectators would break into a loud cheer as they recognized the superior skill of this young lady. As the game wore on, Marsha picked up her pace such that many of the fans noticed her superior skill, also. Of course, any time Esther would get involved, they saw what they all had seen when she played basketball, a fierce competitive spirit with unusual talent.

The whole afternoon was a marvelous activity that everyone enjoyed, and as it wound down, an athletic boosters' club leader of the program came over to Coach Anna and said, "Thank you all so very much for coming to our community and presenting such a splendid soccer clinic for our athletes. Because the number of spectators grew beyond our control, the remainder of the program will not be at the church, but it will be held in the high school auditorium with the dinner in the cafeteria. Even the auditorium will not seat everybody so the spill over will have to sit in the large lobby area, and in the cafeteria itself where speakers will be set up for the overflow crowd.

"I want to tell you that we have made much money for our athletic program here at Bassett High School, because of your presence, and we are so very grateful," she continued. "Our initial plan was to conclude the event on the soccer field, but there was such a loud outcry for the area people to get to see and hear the team in person, it was decided that we would have you all to meet with the folks in the school. Please know that we sold tickets for this affair and the dinner, also, thus making the total of several thousands of dollars to boost our athletic program."

"We are so glad to be here with you all, and as you know, Mit just loves every minute of this time to be with her childhood friends," Coach Anna replied.

"The people here have been so very excited about your visit with us that they have asked me to request that you all tell us about your many adventures that have national notoriety," she related. "Hoping that you all would agree to do this, as soon as you all have showered, you are asked to go to the auditorium where the majority of the people will be located."

"You probably already know that the girls do not like to talk about themselves so I'll have to talk to them first," Coach Anna replied. "They are very private young people and are really humble except when on the basketball court and the soccer field."

"I do hope they will consent to do this for us this afternoon," she said, as they separated.

Not being able to move anywhere without a large group with them, they managed finally to make their way to the auditorium led by an athletic boosters' club leader. As they entered the door of the spacious auditorium, she said, "We have set chairs up for you on the flat part of the floor to the front and put seats for more people on the stage. I thought you would be more comfortable in this area instead of talking to us from the stage area."

"This arrangement will be excellent," Coach Anna said, not really wanting to be in front of anyone, but because the hosts were so hospitable, she knew they would have to reciprocate. "Should we go up front now?"

"All are in place and they can't wait to hear from you all," she said, as Coach Anna turned to instruct the team.

Walking to the front, Coach Anna could see many media personnel and noticed that all of the local radio stations had microphones on the tables, so that a wider listening audience could participate in today's most special activities. Sitting on one end of the row of tables was Reverend Norman Tadwell of Grant Baptist Church, so when Mit saw him, she ran over and hugged him so warmly.

"How are you, Mit?" he said, while holding her in his arms.

"I am fine and how are you and your family?" Mit said.

"We are doing well," he said. "My wife is somewhere in the crowd and wants to talk to you before you all go back to college.

"Thank you all so very much for inviting us to play here at Bassett High School," Mit stated.

"At first our plans were to have you all to come to the church for refreshments and fellowship, but because of church construction at Grant Baptist, we shifted this part of your program to Fort Trial Baptist Church. Because so many people in the area wanted to be a part of this glorious celebration, we decided to have all the festivities here at the beautiful high school," he related.

"I will talk to you and Mrs. Tadwell after this activity is completed," Mit said, as she turned to take her seat among the other players and her coach.

Before a standing room only crowd, the Reverend Tadwell stood and said, "Let us pray. Our most merciful Father, we pause today amidst the wonderful and special occasion when our loved one has returned to be with us, and we give thanks to You. May all we do, say and think today and all days be for Your glory, and may our deeds strengthen Your kingdom here on this special earth You created thousands of years ago. We are grateful to the school officials and the school board for allowing this program to be conducted in the beautiful facility. May Your will always be done now and forever more. Amen"

Continuing, he told the group, "I was asked to be your moderator for this part of our program today so let me begin by telling you about my acquaintance with our young lady who has returned to our neighborhood today. It was about fourteen years ago when she came to Grant Baptist Church for the first time, always seated with her parents, Dan and Pat. Ever since I have known her, she has worn her hair in a pony tail so the day she walked down the aisle to give her life to Jesus Christ, it was bouncing back and forth. What a special day that was in her life!

"Several other people want to tell their stories about Mit so now I shall call on the principal of Brown Primary School."

Walking briskly to the microphone, James Walker shook Mit's hand before he spoke to the crowd. "Mit came to our school as a kindergarten student with that pony tail just bouncing each day. Everyone loved her, and she truly was an exceptionally good young lady, extremely mannerly. But it wasn't until we had our field day in the early spring that we all saw something even more special about her. On this day she won most of the events even though she was the youngest runner. We couldn't believe it. That afternoon I called Pat, her mom, at home to tell her about what she had done, and Pat later told me that Mit never mentioned anything about it at home."

Next came Mrs. Brown, a neighbor. "Each Saturday Mit would make her rounds in the subdivision, visiting as many kitchens as time would permit. She would always come to visit us, because we were the first on her list, usually getting a muffin or some other item and go to eat it with Mr. Brown, who usually was in his shop. All of the neighbors watched her run in the fifty-yard dash with much older competitors and win handily. Obviously, it was a special feat, but she never talked about it to anyone."

Near Mit sat the wood carved statue that was so excellently done, such that those in attendance had difficulty understanding that anyone would have such artful skills. Knowing that Harris Day was from Rondon and had a story to tell, Reverend Tadwell called on him. "Mr. Day, it's your turn to tell your story about Mit."

Harris proudly rose up and nervously stood before the array of microphones, shifting from one foot to the other. "I meet my good friend, Mit, when she come to buy cotton candy at the big race. She is the best little runner in the whole wide world. She beat all them other runners every time. She come to talk to me. Nobody talk to me. I am a nobody. People don't talk to me, but Mit talked to me every time." As he talked, he would look over to where Mit was sitting with tears in her eyes holding on to every word he uttered before this quiet and spellbound audience. "I ain't got no friends but Mit is me friend always."

Mit could not stay in her seat any longer so she jumped up and ran over to Harris and hugged him so very warmly such that the people present with tears filling their eyes, also, stood and applauded for a very long time until Mit took Harris by the hand to sit with the team.

With not a dry eye in the building, a man stepped out from his seat and headed for the microphone area. "My name is John Northy and I'm from Rondon," he said. "Let me tell you first of all that Harris Day, Mit's good friend from Rondon, taught us all in our city what humility and benevolence are all about. Because of him our city now has a strong and extremely active benevolent club with Harris being honorary chairman and a very active member. But that's really not why I came today. I was the screening official years ago for our most prestigious track and field events, so when I got the application of a young lady much younger than the other participants, I called her parents and literally chastised them for wanting their daughter to participate in our fifty-yard dash.

"I know I really did embarrass the parents of this entrant, but at the time I thought I was doing the right thing. But you see, what I didn't realize was that this young lady even at that time was a most outstanding athlete who went on to win our most prestigious event by beating all competition." Calling Mit over at this time, he said, "I understand that your parents are now missionaries in Africa so I want you to ask them for forgiveness for me when I misjudged your skills and only looked at your age." Mit gave him a big hug, also.

"Mit, we all can't wait to hear your story about your adventures, but that is scheduled at the dinner this evening in your honor," Reverend Tadwell related.

At this time he said to Coach Anna, "Coach Bosley, ever since you came on the scene at Bacon College the whole atmosphere has changed. Would you mind telling us a little about yourself and how you wound up as a coach?"

This was not what Coach Anna wanted to do, but she headed to the microphone in deference to the people who had come on this day to honor Mit. Everyone gave her a standing ovation that lasted a very long time until she motioned for the people to be seated.

"It's such an honor for the Bacon College soccer team to be here as your guests today," she stated. "These are my special teams not only of soccer, but, also, of basketball wherein we face the challenges of thirty-one other teams vying for the ACUWAA national championship. The teams selected and the three-week schedule will be announced next Monday. We look forward to this tournament.

"In the meantime we have to unveil our soccer team to this date that has not played a single game. You all just witnessed our first scrimmage of any kind away from our campus. Thank you for being our spectators.

"Following college where I played soccer, took ROTC and majored in physical education and had a minor in psychology, I entered the teaching field in northern Virginia. Shortly, as a reservist in the marines, I trained on a base in eastern North Carolina, later earning the rank of major. During my eleventh year as a teacher and high school basketball coach, I saw an advertisement for a basketball coach at a small college in Virginia so I applied, not really thinking that I would be considered. To my surprise, I was invited for an interview to this mountain college, and right off I fell in love with the personnel there. So when I was offered the job, I really was a very happy camper.

"Immediately, though it dawned on me that I had no team, and in fact, did not have a single player. Realizing that the stipulation for the job was that I would have a college team competitive at the Division I level by the second year, I knew that I had a difficult job ahead. For my first day on the job I headed for the Hollow to meet this team of girls I had read so much about, thinking all the while they couldn't be as good as everyone said they were.

"For those of you who have never been to the Hollow, you will not understand my feeling as I drove up the narrow, dangerous, one lane to the end of the road where there was a quaint little church. The first person I met was Mrs. Charlene Morrow and her husband, Josh, who directed me to the top of the hill where I saw a basketball court constructed on a strip mine. The girls were playing.

"Watching them play was an awesome experience for me, because they were extremely good players. I thought I was a pretty good player until I tried to keep up with them. 'I don't know much about college players, but these girls seemed to be way beyond their youthful years in experience,' I thought standing there that day.

"As you know, they all signed a scholarship to play for Bacon College and to this date still have not lost a single game in their entire career. They are the most humble and obedient group of young people you would ever want to meet."

At this time Coach Anna asked the basketball team members from the Hollow to stand, and then she told the group about the addition of Marsha and Mit to the team. "As you all know, I am the soccer coach, also, so I want the soccer team to stand at this time. All of the girls stood as they were applauded by the large group present on this evening.

"Thank you so very much for your remarks," Reverend Tadwell said.

It was approaching time for the special banquet type dinner honoring Mit, but there were two other stories that Reverend Tadwell knew that everyone in attendance wanted to hear. Looking at the Bacon team, Reverend Tadwell said, "Would one of you mind telling about your harrowing experience several months ago in Portland, Oregon?"

The hijacking episode was one in which the girls talked little about so they just looked at one another with neither one offering to volunteer. Realizing that it was incumbent upon them to respond to the request, because it would be rude to decline, Coach Anna whispered into Esther's ear, "Would you mind telling them about this?"

"I would be happy to do that," Esther replied, always being obedient to Coach Anna's requests.

The people present had read that the girls on the team really wore very simple clothing that had been obtained through the Good Deed Industry, which salvaged used clothing for the needy. Esther's faded blouse and out of style old dark pleated skirt and well worn patent leather shoes were very typical of their dress all the while. The young people and parents were watching the best basketball player in the country walking to the microphone wearing extremely modest clothing. It was a genuine revelation to them that clothing does not a person make.

With great ease Esther began her story. "We have met many people as we have traveled around the country to play basketball, but one morning as we entered the Roanoke Airport, we began a different kind of relationship that nearly became a disaster. As we approached the ticket counter, three Mid-Eastern men got behind us. It was early so the team and the three mysterious persons were really the only ones in the airport. They traveled with us to Dallas, changed then to Tempe where we were playing, sitting each time in three different places on the airplane.

"Coach Anna was suspicious of them from the start, because she is trained in that kind of situation, but we other girls were naïve and thought nothing of their presence. The newspaper, radio and television reports warned of an impending strike by terrorists supported with credible evidence. Because of her astuteness, Coach Anna called Mrs. Maudie Graves, our good friend of the college, and Dr. Damond, our special president, for assistance. He notified the FBI who made contact with Coach Anna in Portland after the three questionable individuals had traveled with us from Tempe to Denver and on to Portland."

With all in attendance now very quiet and totally focused on Esther, holding onto every word, she continued. "Coach Anna had seen the men at our game earlier in Tempe, and when the FBI agent made contact with her as a floor sweeper before the game in Portland, he passed her a note that read, 'When you see the three Mid-Easterners, drop your towel, look at the men and yell a number that corresponds to the row in which they are located.'

"During the second half, she suddenly saw the three men on the opposite side standing together on the main floor level. She dropped her towel, yelled zero and hollered to Dorothy who was bringing the ball down the floor to take the ball to the far corner so the television cameras would follow her. Because of this action, the FBI agent and those back at

Bacon College watching on television, saw the three mysterious men.

"The afternoon before the game and following the game, Coach Anna taught us several maneuvers in case they were needed in the event the three Mid-Easterners attempted to do some evil acts. She divided us into two teams with Dorothy heading one team, and I was the leader of the second group. Getting rolls of duct tape to add to our arsenal of shoelaces, we conducted several practice session even using Coach Anna as a make-believe terrorist." When she said this, there was some laughter followed by eerie silence as each person strained to capture every word in this story that many were hearing for the first time, and the very first time that it had been related by one of the players.

"We had remained very close together during the last forty-eight hours being fearful that the individuals might do harm to us, but it never happened. Seated in the Portland Airport, we gave a sigh of relief when we looked around, and the three were absent. But that all changed when the airplane paused and returned to permit the three questionable people to board the aircraft. This was a different morning, because Coach Anna had not only trained us for various contingencies, but had our seats changed, also, so now Dorothy's team was sitting in the rear near the Mid-Easterner there, and I was with my group seated across from the one in the middle. Coach Anna was up front.

"As our aircraft made its turn to prepare for a takeoff, the three men jumped up and yelled in broken English, 'This a hijacking!' for all to hear. The two in the passenger sections brandished two knives while the one up front broke into the pilots' cabin to subdue them. It was a terrible scene, one that frightened us much more than we all expected. They physically abused some older people and held their knife to the throat of two older ladies. Up front the co-pilot was nearly killed and left in the floor, bleeding profusely, such that we all thought he was dead.

"These were mean, vicious men whose comportment had suddenly changed to animal like behavior so we girls just cowered away not wanting to be a threat of any kind to them as they were going about their hijacking scenario. We all knew that they would have some kind of demands more than just clearing the airport of additional planes, but they became very quiet, except from time to time they would show their might by hurting an older person. During the whole ordeal, we watched our coach for the signal. None came.

"Hours passed as we just sat in our seats with the other frightened passengers, not knowing what would come next from the terrorists. Much later the pilot called to the terminal with the gun of the front terrorist always to his head and his hands tied behind his back to tell them that some injured people were on the runway to be picked up. They had dumped the seriously injured co-pilot and an older lady who was kicked unmercifully down the safety chute. The atmosphere had changed. We looked for a signal. None came.

"After their additional demands were announced, they stepped up their abuse of the passengers and began to act erratically. With more frequent contacts with the terminal and not getting satisfactory answers to their demands, there came a new threat that a bomb was on board. Unless their demands were consummated immediately, the whole airplane and all on board would be blown up. We kept our eyes directly on our coach for a signal. Still none came.

"But that would change, because she was weighing the situation carefully to insure that the moment of assault would be most advantageous. Soon, she had made her decision. A fist was extended in the air, which caused our hearts to pound more rapidly and strongly in our bodies. It was time. There was no other recourse. The two groups held hands and prayed together asking God for strength and wisdom during this different kind of action on our parts, and to forgive us for what we believed we had to do to insure our safety and for that of the many other passengers. Both groups straightened up in the seats readying ourselves to attack those who had already inflicted so much harm on the passengers and the harm that was anticipated, if there truly was a bomb on board. We had gotten in the attack mode. I was more scared than I thought I would be. My group was ready just as Dorothy's. It was time. I raised by fist in the air and simultaneously Dorothy's went up, also. Time stood still. My muscles were flexed. I was ready. Coach Anna's two fists were raised. We started our attack with all our strength, using the techniques of our well-trained coach.

"All seven of us had a job to do as we jumped out of our seats on top of the surprised terrorists, and with a little difficulty in securing the knife, we soon had our assailant under control, but not before we got a few cuts and bruises. With blood splatters around the passengers panicked so there was much yelling.

"It was during our fight with our terrorist that I heard several gunshots that really alarmed me, because I knew Coach Anna was in harm's way trying to subdue the terrorist brandishing a gun by herself. As soon as we got our culprit tied and gagged, several of us headed to the front to assist our coach who had been shot in the leg, but had her terrorist in control with his face to the floor, and she held his gun.

"Because of the bomb threat, Coach Anna directed the passengers to make their way to safety, moving far from the plane itself. Rapidly, this was done such that the only ones remaining on the plane were the team and the hijackers who were securely bound by shoelaces and duct tape. After we rolled them down the chute, we came down and dragged them to safety beyond the aircraft, which suddenly exploded as you all know.

"God was so good to us on this unforgettable day as He is all days. God has given us a special leader, our coach, whom we all dearly love. If it were not for her direction and leadership, we would not have survived the evil displayed by the terrorists on this unusual day."

When Esther headed back to sit with her group, everyone stood and applauded with many not being able to hold back the tears. What an exciting story!

It was nearly time for dinner, but Reverend Tadwell knew that there was at least one more story that the group wanted to hear before the dinner meal was served. "Coach Bosley, several people have asked me to request that one of your team tell about the daring rescue several of your girls undertook with you as their leader," Reverend Tadwell stated. "Do you think one would volunteer to do that for us?"

The girls remained very quiet so Coach Anna went over to where Maggie was sitting and asked her to relate their rescue story to the group. Being very obedient, Maggie stood up and walked toward the microphones as those in attendance noticed that her clothing seemed to be very similar to that of Esther, such that they were much out of style, including her shoes that showed much wear before her father retrieved them from the Good Deed Industry. Coach Anna was so very proud of her girls as they adjusted to their environment on this day, which was such a wonderful homecoming for Mit.

"My name is Maggie Morrow," she told the group. "I am a sophomore at Bacon College, majoring in mathematics. I joined ten of my best friends from the Hollow, where we live at our college in the western part of Virginia. Not being originally from that community, my parents moved there when I was only seven years old, so essentially I grew up with these same girls on the basketball team. In fact, we did everything together ever since I can remember. I might add that we have never had a cross word in all of these special years. God has blessed me in so many ways.

"A short time ago three ladies were captured and held hostage in a foreign country. Coach Anna, who is a major in the green beret, was contacted about attempting a rescue of this group. She agreed with the stipulation that she could select the other team members so she selected our college team, but realized that she could only choose six for this rescue mission. Esther, Dorothy, Marsha, Mit, Hanna and I were selected from the group so we headed for the Mohave Desert where we trained in the desert environment much like the countryside in Abedistan, where the hostages were located.

"Our training in the desert went well, even the parachuting at night. Making sufficient progress, our learning sessions were abbreviated somewhat so off we headed for a country far away. Parachuting in at night, while the terrorists were preoccupied with our helicopter decoys, we experienced our first problem. Mit's parachute failed to open properly, so she removed the maneuverable chute and finally deployed her safety parachute that carried her straight to the ground. The enemy saw her and fired several bullets in her direction with one striking her on the leg. Hiding under the sand covered by her parachute, Mit was not discovered by the terrorists and soon found her way to reunite with her team."

Just as it was when Esther related her story, the audience was mesmerized as she spoke so articulately and with such ease. "We soon arrived at Moraba, a town near the middle of Abedistan, where it was believed the ladies were imprisoned. Stationing ourselves only several yards off the main street, we discovered all we could from that distance before we donned our full burquas to go into the street with the local women. At first it was scary to walk around in the marketplace with the Abedistany women wearing like apparel, but in a while it became much easier.

"One evening about dusk we discovered a young man hiding from others, as he stealthily walked to a spot where he dug up a Bible. Realizing that he would probably be put to death, if others knew he had the Bible in his possession, we befriended him not realizing at the time just how much valuable information he really had about the area and specifically about the missionaries. With reconnoitering completed it soon was time to plan for the rescue.

"In the still of the dark early morning hours Coach Anna led our team dressed in camouflage uniforms with lightweight shoes and face dressing wearing pistols strapped to our sides moving toward our objective. Not a sound was made as we stealthily moved across the rocky dirt street to the prison compound. Dorothy took her team of Hanna, Marsha and Mit up the steps to overcome those on the roof area. Esther and I were waiting on the bottom for Dorothy to begin her attack.

"We surprised both groups and to get the attention of one of our captors, Esther fired her pistol which helped us immensely to subdue our two. Taking the key from the bearded guard, Esther opened the door, freeing the three women who were tied together by a rope. With the captors now being tied up and taken to the middle of the street area, we discovered that Madu, the young Abedistany who had been so much help to us, now was going to lead our travels as we departed the scene. But first, he went to the roof of the prison and brought back a hand grenade from a box where many were stored to give to Coach Anna.

"Just as we left, Coach Anna threw the hand grenade atop the building where it exploded and detonated the others in storage, making a huge fireball that lit up the night sky. We traveled from cave to cave eluding the Ab Didal who were flying overhead in their helicopters. After some direct contact with the enemy, our military forces soon rescued us so that we arrived back home safely. Obviously, our success during this experience was because of the wisdom, strength and training of the special lady who leads us each day, Coach Anna. We all thank her so very much."

After lengthy applause Maggie went back to her seat, and Reverend Tadwell instructed everyone to go to the cafeteria for a banquet style dinner honoring Mit. Led into the cafeteria, the group was amazed at the several banners affixed to the walls and hanging from the ceiling, including hundreds of balloons. In addition to beautiful flowers on every table with colorful streamers, there was a soccer ball in the center of each. The head table was in an "L" shape so that all the ones from Bacon could be seated, including a place for Sarah and Harris with the group.

After the dinner, which was very delicious, Reverend Tadwell invited Mit to come to the microphone to speak to the group. Those in attendance, now seeing this strikingly dark skin blond young lady who grew up in the jungle of Costa Rica up close, realized that she was very strong, yet a beautiful person. She was dressed in very modest clothing, too, with a colorful ankle length wrap around jungle skirt and a white long sleeve blouse and shoes that appeared to be hand crafted leather. Harris stood and started the applause, yells and whistles, as Mit made her way to speak to the group. Embarrassed totally, Mit finally began her remarks, "On behalf of my team from Bacon I want to thank all of you from the bottom of my heart for this special day in the community that I call my hometown. You all have done so much work to make this celebration a highlight of our life. Thank you so very much.

"God has blessed me in thousands of ways, but in one way that I never expected was when He permitted me to join the other athletes at Bacon College to learn as well as play soccer and basketball. I certainly don't deserve this special treatment.

"My mom and dad loved Bassett as much as I did, but something happened in their lives that might happen to you some day. God called them to the mission field at a time when my dad had lost his engineering job, and I was in a coma following an accident. But during this time of total despair when we as a family were losing our worldly possessions, God was providing us with those things much more important in life.

"My parents permitted me to run in various events and play sports which made me very happy. In Rondon where I ran in track and field events I met this gentleman, Harris Day, whom I have remembered ever since, and all of my years I will continue to have him as a friend. You see, cotton candy were the first words I understood when I woke up from the coma of several weeks. During this time Harris visited me from Rondon which meant so very much to my mom and dad. With that Harris became part of our family.

"Our hospital bills mounted to so much it was impossible to pay them even though mom and dad sold our two cars and our house. But you all saw to it that they would be paid. Thank you for the thousands of dollars you gave to us for that purpose. Also, thank you Harris for your leadership in Rondon in collecting the large amount of money there which paid the remainder of the bills with several thousand dollars remaining. Please know that mom and dad used the remainder on a church project outside San Jose in Costa Rica. They were so happy to contribute the amount to construct a church building there.

"After our debts were paid we all headed to the mission field, starting in language school to learn Spanish. On the language school campus was a missionary kids' school called Challenge. I loved this little school very much, one reason being that we had a soccer team that went on to win the country's championship. It was fun.

"Soon though we were headed for the jungle area where I met many special friends, some of whom now attend college at Bacon with me. We had a soccer team, also, and our chief was especially fond of us calling us 'my team.' He scheduled many games with other villages deeper in the jungle so soon mom and dad were advancing their mission to the interior deeply into the jungle area.

"One day my dad discovered that a Junior Olympics program was being scheduled for all of Costa Rica, so with the elated approval of our village chief, he registered our jungle team to participate in this event. It was the first time that a jungle team ever played in such a tournament. Our chief was ecstatic.

"We had so much fun traveling to San Jose and winning the championship. Our chief put our winning flag on a pole near his bamboo house along with a second one we won later for all to see. I really do miss all the folks in our Corbri village, but I'm elated that God has blessed me with three now on our Bacon team. Mom and Dad were really sad when they were recently transferred to Tanzania in Africa where they have established another school there. They are very happy there spreading the Good News of Jesus Christ. You see, they have another young person with them there and his name is Galu, who recently won the Boston marathon at the age of twelve. My father was so excited about accompanying him to Boston to run in this race."

All of those present had read so much about Galu that they were surprised to hear that he was in the same village as Mit's parents. So much had been written about this young man in the newspapers and sports' magazines.

Thanking the group over and over again, Mit took her seat among the team. After closing remarks by Reverend Tadwell, everyone converged around the team of girls not before Coach Anna quietly left the others and went over to the back of the cafeteria where a poorly dressed, quiet young athlete was standing all alone. "My name is Anna Bosley," Coach Anna said, as she surprised the student.

"I am Heather Martin," the young lady said, now showing a brief smile on her face.

"What grade are you in school?" Coach Anna asked.

"I am in the eleventh grade here at Bassett," she replied.

"I noticed that you are a very good soccer player," Coach Anna stated. "Have you decided about what college you want to attend?"

"I really have not thought about college, because both my parents lost their jobs when the mill closed so we now really have a hard time at home," she noted, as she looked down to the floor.

"Are your parents here at this celebration?" Coach Anna asked.

"They wanted to come but didn't have the money to pay for their ticket," she quickly responded.

"Would you like to go to college?" Coach Anna inquired, looking the young lady in the eye.

"I would love to go," she responded

"Is your coach here today?" Coach Anna asked.

"Yes, she is right over there with your team right now," Heather indicated.

"You point her out to me," Coach Anna said, as she took Heather's hand and headed toward the group.

"This is my coach," Heather said, as she tapped her coach on the back so she would turn around.

"I am Anna Bosley," Coach Anna said, now facing a youthful athletic looking female in her mid twenties.

"My name is Thelma Overbrook," the high school coach said, as she threw her arms around Coach Anna. "I am just thrilled to death to meet you."

"You have one fine soccer player here," Coach Anna stated, as she put her arm around Heather, who now was really sporting a wide smile.

"She not only is my best player, she is my best student academically, also, and is the most mannerly of all of my girls," Thelma proudly stated.

"At visitation time next year I want to invite you and Heather to come to Bacon," Coach Anna indicated. "At that time I want to discuss college with her."

"Oh! That would be just great!" Thelma replied. "I have wanted somebody on the team to go on to college to play soccer which will boost my team here at Bassett."

"Don't forget the invitation," Coach Anna stated, as she joined the others in the front of the cafeteria.

It was late when Coach Anna left Bassett High School with her girls after they had said good-bye several times to almost all the athletes who still remained to bid them farewell. Mit had difficulty leaving her loved ones, including Harris Day, who was in the parking lot still waving as they pulled away carrying the beautiful wood carving back with her to Bacon. At the end of the driveway, Mit asked Coach Anna to stop, and she climbed over the seats to get to the front to hug Coach Anna so warmly, thanking her many times over and over again. Soon they were singing their special songs as they traveled west up the mountains.

Unintelligible Telephone Calls

Trying to juggle all that needed to be done at this time of year when there were two sports competing for time and energy, Coach Anna had a full plate as well as the girls who were practicing two sports and maintaining quality academic standards. The ACUWAA schedule included one game on their home court, two in Atlanta and the finals in New York, if they got that far in the thirty-two-team tournament. Ranked number one in Division I, Bacon was seeded number one in the South and would play the eighth seed in that region.

During the evening before their departure to Atlanta to play a first round game of the American College and University Women's Athletic Association tournament, a telephone call was received by Coach Anna that was very perplexing. The connection to the caller left much to be desired such that when the connection was finally silent the message was now a bunch of short and disjointed phrases which didn't seem to make much sense to the coach.

"I believe that was someone trying to speak to the team about our first round game," Coach Anna related to the team. "I hope the person will call back."

The group flew out of Roanoke early, arriving in Atlanta later that morning. From their hotel room they could see the arena so they just walked to their practice session that afternoon. Playing an eighth seed, all the girls played much so they were rested for their second game the next evening which was handily won just as the previous contest.

The next morning they were up early to catch the bus to the airport, but the driver indicated in an excited voice, “The airport is closed.”

“Why?” Coach Anna asked.

“There has only been one brief announcement by radio that the country was placed suddenly on red alert; thus no planes will be permitted to leave this or any other airport until the alert is lifted,” the driver said. “I will take you all to the airport so you can wait there.”

Coach Anna quickly examined the newspaper and discovered nothing that would cause the highest alert for security of our homeland. “I wonder what has happened,” she thought, as they all piled on the bus to go to the airport.

The driver of the bus elevated the volume on the radio so the passengers could hear any breaking news. Nearly to the airport, the announcer broke in and advised of a statement forthcoming from the Director of Homeland Security. “Early this morning,” he said, “we were advised of an unidentified aircraft over the Atlantic Ocean by our European neighbors so we have been tracking it ever since. At this time it’s headed directly toward our coastline and appears to be directed toward our nation’s capital. Six of our military jets have been dispatched to surround the craft and will do what is necessary to preclude injury to our citizens. The entire country has been placed on the highest alert, which will remain in effect until further notice. Another report will follow soon.”

When they arrived at the airport terminal, Coach Anna called Dr. Damond to advise him that the team would be returning to campus on a rented van, because all flights had been canceled. “There is much news about this situation on television right now,” he stated. “You know there is much speculation, and the worst scenarios don’t sound good, because many believe it’s a terrorist scheme that has been discovered.”

"It really sounds serious," Coach Anna replied. "We'll be there about lunch time."

"The students have a big homecoming planned to celebrate your first two victories in the tournament," he happily told her. "By the way we keep receiving unintelligible telephone calls, and according to Maudie, you received one before you left for Atlanta. The words are so garbled we think that someone has a wrong number and at the same time a very poor connection each time the call is made. One thing for certain, the caller is very persistent."

"I'm sorry that you all have to deal with my calls," Coach Anna said.

"On one of the calls that I received, I really thought I could make out some semblance of your name so after that I began to think who would be calling you, and would persist even with a bad connection," he indicated. "Anyway, maybe you can make something of these calls when you come."

The team always enjoyed riding in the van together as they looked out the windows at God's wonderful earth, especially as they rode through the mountains. Songs were commonplace on this morning with a different leader for each of the hymns.

Breaking into the merriment, Coach Anna turned on the radio to hear another breaking news story about the mysterious aircraft. "Our radar shows the airplane following an erratic flight path as though the pilot is trying to use deception, and to add to this mystery, it is flying at a very low altitude as though it is trying to come in under our radar system. Nothing that we have done to this point would reveal to the pilot that the aircraft has been detected so to this stage toward the objective, there has been no interruption. Our station will keep you informed regarding this strange happening taking place as we speak."

They were really making good time as they traveled to Bacon College, their very special home now. "I'll call Maudie to see how she is doing," Coach Anna said.

"This is the Bacon College athletic dormitory," Maudie said in a very businesslike manner. "How may I help you?"

"This is Anna," Coach Anna responded. "We have just turned west off I 77 near Hillsville and are on our last leg on Route 58. How are you doing?"

"I am fine," Maudie said. "We are continuing to get those mysterious telephone calls such that Dr. Damond has tried everything to trace them but to this point to no avail."

"What can you make out about the calls?" Coach Anna asked.

"There is very little except on one occasion we thought we heard your name which leads us to believe the caller has the right number but a very poor connection," Maudie advised. "Sometimes there is a long period between calls, and at other times there are two or three in a row, one right after the other. We don't believe that it's a local call or anything at this time for us to be too much concerned, but it's very aggravating not to be able to reply to the caller."

"We are sorry about the calls," Coach Anna stated, as the two disconnected.

Coach Anna never ceased to be amazed at her girls as they sang their favorite, "She'll Be Coming Around the Mountains," as she drove through the Blue Ridge Mountains. "Here they are, the nation's most outstanding women's basketball team, wearing the most modest apparel totally impervious to the worldly behaviors," Coach Anna thought.

Upon arrival at the college the campus was absolutely absent of students, which was contrary to their many other arrivals following a game. It was nearly lunch time so they quickly put their bags in the athletic dormitory and headed for the cafeteria. As they walked up the sidewalk, Esther said to Dorothy, "I wonder where everybody is."

"It's somewhat eerie now not seeing all of the activity on campus," Dorothy replied.

As they approached the cafeteria, it appeared to be abandoned with no lights and none of the workers. “It’s like a ghost town,” Diane stated, but not eliciting any laughter whatsoever.

“They have to be here somewhere,” Coach Anna indicated. “Let’s look in the coliseum.

Opening the door to the vestibule leading to the large hallway surrounding this very large and modern basketball complex, quiet filled every corner. Proceeding to the double doors to the playing surface, darkness met the group again as they peered inside. Waiting momentarily for their eyes to adjust, suddenly the lights were turned on, and on the floor were all the students and staff. What a surprise! The whole floor was covered with tables filled with delicious food donated by the benevolent person for everyone to celebrate the return of the beloved basketball team after winning the first two games of the national tournament.

It was such a marvelous homecoming with generous hugs by everyone, and the food was delicious. As they were eating, Dr. Damond slipped over to Coach Anna and whispered, “We are still receiving those telephone calls.”

“Do you even have a hint as to the caller?” Coach Anna asked.

“We just don’t know,” he replied. “Over the years we have gotten many calls from those dialing the wrong number, but nothing like this has ever happened.”

“Have you heard any more about the suspected terrorist plane?” Coach Anna asked.

“There is no additional news about the situation from that I reported to you earlier,” he indicated.

What a special celebration it was!

Back at the athletic dormitory as the students prepared to study, Coach Anna turned on the television just in time to hear a spokesperson from the office of Homeland Security. “As you know, my name is Dan Glitton, and I want to bring you up to date on this unusual activity in the airspace over the Atlantic. The mysterious aircraft, still unidentified, continues it's trek toward our mainland, and if it continues at the same direction, it's headed directly toward Washington, D. C. Earlier, one of the theories was that it was just an aberration on our radar screen, but it has been fully confirmed that it is an aircraft. To compound the problem, no one is acknowledging that it's his country's aircraft, so here we are with an unknown airplane heading our way with no identity whatsoever. I will take your questions now."

"Do the officials believe that this is a serious threat to our homeland security?" a leading reporter asked.

"The officials have weighed all aspects of this situation and are taking it very seriously," Dan responded.

"Has the president been informed?" another reporter asked.

"He has been informed and is acting as Commander-in-Chief in this matter," Dan replied.

"What has the president done thus far?" a national newscaster anchorman asked abruptly.

"He has dispatched six of our homeland security jets to intercept the mysterious aircraft," Dan responded.

Being a presidential election year, the same evening news anchorman followed, "Do you think that his actions thus far are much less than should be taken to secure our country during this crisis?"

"The president is making those decisions that best will handle the situation in which we are now confronted," Dan stated. "Unusual situations call for unique responses, so he is gathering all the data as he leads our country in this and in all situations."

The questions and answers continued for quite a while before Dan brought the session to a close. But the talk shows were gearing up to give their views on the drama taking place, but not without a heaping helping of politics. There was no way the president was going to do anything that was acceptable to his opponent so the media fanned this situation such that for a while the main story was the contrasting ways the sitting president and his opponent in the fall election would deal with the problem.

The sitting president was one who had proved himself to take whatever action was necessary to quell an enemy, and this time his opponent was taking a hawkish view of this crisis. When asked the question about the crisis, the opponent replied, "Our president seems to be waffling back and forth on this very critical matter; thus giving the enemy much too much time. This aircraft might be loaded with a nuclear bomb which could wipe out the entire east coast so this aircraft must be removed from the sky immediately."

The dichotomy of beliefs of our leaders elevated the media to great heights, as politics became the story and not the seemingly impending crisis. Coach Anna changed channels to one less involved in politics, and immediately, she heard the reporter say that he believed that our Homeland Security jets had made contact with the mysterious aircraft. Soon all channels were reporting that our jets had encircled the mysterious aircraft, but there was no communication.

There was no identification on the craft at all except a small marking on the tail which appeared to be Arabic. The news of the only identification of a faint marking on the tail really caused the discussion to change from politics to a discussion of an imminent threat to our country. "This Arabic indication, as faint as it may be, told a huge story to those trying to discover what was taking place on this day," the reporter stated. "The fact that part of the marking was painted over even adds to the mystery."

"Colonel Elliott, to base; come in base," the colonel communicated, as leader of the six jets now surrounding the aircraft.

"This is base; go ahead Colonel Elliott," the base operator replied.

"We are in position on all sides of the unidentified aircraft, but as we look into the windows, we see no movement at all," the colonel stated. "It appears that it's a deliberate attempt not to let us see them. I am very close to the aircraft and can see a faint marking on the tail that a portion appears to have been painted over. It is obviously Arabic."

"Can you describe the marking?" the base operator asked.

"It looks like a portion of an upper case 'J,'" he responded, "but it seems that the top has been painted over so only the bottom is showing."

"Can you see anybody at the windows in the passenger section?" the base operator asked.

"I am really up close to the body of the craft, and it seems that all of the windows are covered," he responded. "As I examine the cockpit section, I can see no one so I have maneuvered above and looked down into that section, and I still see no one. Let me hasten to add that from above, the shadows make it impossible to see inside the aircraft through the windshield area. Based on my recollection, it seems to be an old post-war manufactured aircraft, one of our smallest intercontinental airplanes that I believe has a passenger capacity of about one hundred twenty."

"That is very good information," the base operator indicated. "Is there anything else you can tell us?"

"While all I have told you thus far might lead one to believe that the aircraft is without a pilot," the colonel stated, "I am sure it's being piloted, because it changes its course ever so slightly when I bring my jet near. So someone is cognizant of our presence."

"How close are you to our mainland?" the base operator asked.

"Within an hour it will be entering our airspace on the eastern shore near the north of the Chesapeake Bay area. I'll keep you informed," the colonel concluded.

Dan Glitton stepped forward to address the large assembly of reporters to make a statement. "We have just received an on location report from the commander of the jet squadron who files this report. The marking on the tail of the aircraft looks like a portion of an upper case 'J' that has been painted over so only the bottom is visible. The aircraft is commercial and is one of our smallest intercontinental airplanes. With jets flying nearby, the unidentified aircraft seems to adjust its direction ever so slightly from time to time, which is the only indication that someone is on board. There is no visible sign of life in the cockpit, and the windows are covered in the passenger section. I shall take your questions now."

"What do our officials make of this aircraft behaving in such a manner?" an older man asked.

"It is believed that the suspicion is mounting such that action of some kind will be forthcoming, if there is no change," Dan answered.

"At what point will there be action to preclude this aircraft to move farther toward our homeland," a young female reporter asked. "Our new candidate for president says this is an example of the kind of leadership we had come to expect from our current White House occupant."

"Please know that our present military officials, being led by our president, are functioning in a guarded mode at this juncture," Dan said. "It's regrettable that a crisis such as this is turned into a political tug-of-war as though we are operating with two presidents who have opposite opinions on how this situation should be handled. News being so prolific on this matter unfolding today, our citizens can see what is happening and know exactly the position of the president and his rival. On the one hand, the president is moving cautiously and patiently while his counterpart is advocating shooting the aircraft down now before it enters our airspace."

After the media conference was over, Coach Anna began making plans for the next game now with a field of only eight teams left. Playing on their home court was going to be something special, because now the local folks could see the top players in the country right in their own coliseum.

The telephone rang and it was Dr. Damond's secretary requesting that Coach Anna come to the office of the president for a meeting. Dropping everything, Coach Anna jogged all the way to the administration building, and upon entering walked hastily down the hall to be greeted by the secretary who whisked her into the president's office.

The president was totally occupied trying to understand a caller, but was really experiencing a difficult situation. Seeing Coach Anna, he said, "See if you can understand what the individual wants?" now handing the telephone to her.

"Hello, hello," Coach Anna stated loudly, "I am Anna Bosley." There was still no recognition. The telephone abruptly went dead.

"Did you recognize or understand anything?" Dr. Damond asked.

"No, I didn't," Coach Anna replied. "How many calls have you received like this?"

"I believe we have received two dozen in the last several days," he replied. "This is the third one today so someone is anxious to contact us."

"Do you think someone wants to ask us for tickets to our next game that will be played here on campus?" Coach Anna inquired.

"It could be the case," Dr. Damond responded, "but the part of this total scenario that I don't understand at all is the poor transmission of the message such that we do not understand it."

"That certainly adds to the whole mystery," Coach Anna said.

Their discussion about the unusual telephone calls continued for a while, and just as Coach Anna was preparing to depart, Dr. Damond commented, "Do you think that the tournament will continue as scheduled or will there have to be a delay?"

"What is the last you have heard about the mysterious airplane?" Coach Anna asked.

"Sit down just a minute, and we'll get an up to date report on what is taking place," Dr. Damond replied.

Just as he turned on the television, Dan Glitton was making a report. "As I speak, the mysterious aircraft is under close surveillance by our six attack jets that are acting in accordance with orders from our Commander-in-Chief. Colonel Elliott advises that the aircraft is approaching our eastern shore line and will be over our soil in a few minutes. He is in position to shoot it down, if the order is given, but that does not seem likely at this juncture. I'll take your questions at this time."

Right off the very first question was one steeped in politics when the reporter asked, "The president's opponent has said again that our president is too indecisive and unwilling to match his feet with his words regarding this matter of obvious terrorism. What do you believe is causing the delay during this extremely critical time in our history?"

"As I said earlier, the president is in charge of this situation, making all the decisions, such that each minute detail is considered. It's truly not a time for politics, but one when we all should be facing this situation in unison with one strong and steadfast resolve," Dan stated.

"Some of our experts say this is a ploy well orchestrated which will be more devastating than any previous terrorist act," a reporter stated. "With this in mind why should our citizens have to risk their lives?"

"Of course, there are many opinions regarding this matter, none of which will go unnoticed by the president as he decides what is best for our country as this whole scenario unfolds."

"One expert indicated that he would not be surprised if the attack jets did turn the aircraft back to sea," a young reporter proudly stated. "First of all, how could this be done, and secondly, what would be the purpose of doing that?"

"I certainly don't want to speculate on what the experts have in mind, but it would appear to me that by causing the aircraft in question to move out to sea would put it out of harm's way for us," Dan answered. "I don't know how they would do it."

Watching until the conclusion of the press conference, Coach Anna departed the office of Dr. Damond and headed back to the athletic dormitory. When she walked into the door, Maudie yelled to her. "Come over here to watch the breaking news."

Coach Anna and Maudie watched as the newscaster told of what he believed was taking place at the moment. "We were just advised that action is being contemplated as this unknown aircraft enters our airspace, being escorted by our squadron of attack jets."

A spotter in Deltaville on the Chesapeake Bay advised that the aircraft just now flew over his area very low to the ground with six jets circling it. It appeared to be headed toward Washington, D. C.

One channel showed a video of the low flying aircraft to its viewing audience while others continued their speculation about its presence and our president's decision to take stronger action.

Suddenly there came more breaking news announcing that the president had ordered the aircraft to land at an unidentified airfield in northern Virginia, with orders to shoot it down, if it failed to respond obediently as the jet squadron led the way. Colonel Elliott made his report, "We have received the order and are now tightening the circle around the unidentified aircraft."

"Do you have your bearings regarding the landing field?" the base operator asked.

"We have all data and computations locked into the computer," Colonel Elliott replied.

"Stay in touch as you proceed toward your objective," the base operator stated.

In the remote country area near Culpeper, Virginia, local officials, including policemen, firefighters, National Guard and medical personnel, hurriedly made their way to the Hilden Airstrip. The president had made this choice, because it was far removed from any densely populated area while at the same time long enough to accommodate the landing of this aircraft that had disturbed the whole countryside during the past several hours. Also, rushing to the scene were bomb squads, SWAT Team, FBI, officials of Homeland Security and terrorist experts. The setting was taking shape but the plot was thickening.

All the girls were called from their rooms to watch the scene unfold on national television. The television camera had zoomed in on the aircraft as the six jets guided it toward the landing field in this quiet pastoral setting in a rural community. They made one pass over the field, circled to the other side before again turning it back to the landing strip, which was very narrow but long. Going all the way to the end before coming to a stop, the jets followed one after the other in what appeared to be a blocking position as they, too, came to a stop about one hundred yards from the mysterious aircraft.

The media flocked to the scene such that the local police of the area hurriedly came to keep people away from the plane that just sat at the end of the runway. No one attempted to get off, because it seemed that, if anything, those on board would be frightened with all of the attention.

The telephone rang and Maudie answered, "This is the athletic dormitory and this is Maudie speaking."

"My name is Isaac from Wasi," a man stated in a very clear voice. "I am calling for President Kantitore. He will be sending basketball girls to your country for them to see the big basketball games now being played."

"When are they coming?" Maudie excitedly asked.

"They will come soon," he said, as they were disconnected.

"Maudie, who was that?" Coach Anna asked.

"He said he was Isaac," Maudie replied, "and he indicated that President Kantitore was going to send his girls' basketball players to watch the big tournament."

"It would really be great to have them here to see our women's national tournament, but with our country being on red alert, the tournament may have to be postponed until the environment is better," Coach Anna responded.

"Do you have a telephone number of President Kantitore?" Maudie asked.

"I have it in my address book," Coach Anna answered.

Hurriedly getting the small address book from her desk, she handed it to Maudie for her to call the president. Dialing the long number, all she got was a busy signal, and this was repeated several times with the same results.

"In a way I am glad that they won't be coming at this time, because everyone is so concerned about our welfare such that we would not be able to give the basketball players our undivided attention," Coach Anna said.

"You know, I have been wondering why Isaac was making the call from Wasi and not someone else," Maudie stated, "but he does speak good English and he does know the group here."

"I am sure that is the case," Coach Anna responded. "Isaac possibly now works in the administration of the president. He is an extremely intelligent young man so I can see why they would want him on their staff."

"I wonder what he meant by soon," Maudie asked. "One thing that I remember about the Wasi culture is that what is being interpreted is sometimes much different from what is intended in the communication."

"I remember that well when we went to Wasi on the visit that sometimes we were planning to do one thing, and the hosts were planning another," Coach Anna said, as they both laughed just a little.

While this conversation was taking place in the mountains of southwest Virginia, the mysterious aircraft just sat on this out of the way country airport with hundreds of diverse personnel present, adding to the drama that was unfolding on this beautiful March afternoon. With millions of television viewers, the lead official of Homeland Security stepped to the microphone to make a statement. "For the last several hours our military jets have been closely monitoring the movement of the aircraft that you see at the end of the runway. To this point we have made no verbal contact with those on board, and as far as we can tell, they have made no effort to communicate with us. We all are aware of the erratic behavior at times of the terrorists, such that there is no objective template to throw down to anticipate their conduct. To date, this is the most bizarre situation we have had to deal. As I speak, various departments are working to effect a solution to this dilemma without bloodshed. I shall answer two or three questions at this time."

"Many believe that our president has maneuvered this aircraft to this remote area just in case our military needs to blow up this mysterious plane," a reporter dressed in clothing similar to the military personnel stated. "Can you confirm or deny this observation?"

"I can neither confirm nor deny what you have said," the official answered. "We are keeping all options open."

"Why do you think that the presidential candidate of the opposing party is so adamant in his opposite opinion to handle this crisis?" a seasoned news anchorman asked.

"That you will have to ask him," the official responded and quickly pointed to the next reporter who had a question, not wanting to be pulled into a political debate.

A young local print reporter asked, "Who do you think is on the aircraft, and why has the aircraft now found itself the center of world attention?"

"For the first part of your question," he stated, "to this point we have no hint regarding the personnel on the aircraft, but there is one theory being batted back and forth all day, and that is that the aircraft has veered off course innocently. On the other hand this theory seems to fade somewhat when we all realize that we have received no communication whatsoever. Regarding the other point of your question, we now live in perilous times, because of terrorists, and with various means of travel being available for the average person, anyone could become a terrorist. Let me add as my final statement to you at this time, there is something about this whole scenario which defies the way other crises have been handled. This one is just unique and requires our wisest decision making."

By this time at Bacon College all of the girls were hovered around the television set, watching as this strange event unfolded. "This reminds me of the hijacking in Portland several months ago," Diane said.

"It appears very similar to that dreadful day," Maudie replied. "I wonder how many passengers are on the plane, and whether or not this plane is being hijacked."

"I feel sorry for the passengers," Maggie said. "I remember how scared we were as we sat on the hijacked plane just waiting for the appropriate time to take action. But, you know, these passengers today will not have had the training we received from Coach Anna in preparation for our retaliation."

"We were so very blessed on our fateful day to have Coach Anna as our leader," Esther stated. "She seemed to know just what to do and when to do it."

"You know," Coach Anna stated, "I would not have attempted such action, if it were not for you girls." She then hugged each of the team members, as tears flowed freely during this time of reminiscing about a very dangerous situation in which the team found itself several months ago.

Meanwhile, back at the mysterious aircraft scene, a group of military personnel had been stationed around the perimeter of the aircraft about a quarter of a mile from the airstrip. About an hour later four modern army tanks were unloaded and were soon situated inside the guarded area with guns pointed directly toward the aircraft. Shortly, an army truck pulled up with ground to ground missiles, and they, too, were pointed directly toward the airplane. With considerable dispatch, five command tents were set up just off the runway to provide a work site for those making the decisions. It was becoming a military battlefield right before the eyes of those watching on television.

One young reporter, who arrived on the scene before there were limits set, made his way closer and closer to the aircraft. Being one of the lesser watched channels, few were tuned into his report, but the Bacon College group discovered this channel when Maudie was surfing the various newscasts to receive different coverage.

"This is interesting," Maudie mentioned to the girls. "It seems that this reporter is terribly close to the aircraft, which is beyond the limits that have been set for all personnel."

They all watched quietly as the camera zoomed in on the aircraft. "All the windows are covered," the reporter indicated somewhat breathlessly as they made their way through the thick underbrush. Moving even closer, he advised his viewing audience that he was within about one hundred feet of the plane so everybody could see what was causing all the mystery.

Suddenly and excitedly the cameraman said loudly, "Did you see something in the window about midway back?"

"No, I didn't," the reporter quickly responded. "Did you see something?"

"I thought I saw someone momentarily looking out the window holding something as though trying to show us something," he replied.

"Do you think they know we are here near the aircraft?" the reporter continued in a very excited tone.

"I don't believe they knew we were here, and suddenly we were seen by the one looking out the window," the cameraman indicated, as the viewing audience could see the mysterious aircraft and could hear their conversation. Soon many others had tuned in to this remote station to be kept up to date on the saga that was unfolding. At Bacon Dr. Damond and others had joined the girls in the athletic dormitory to watch the news, as it was presented by the young reporter now standing in the bushes very near the aircraft.

"I just saw something again," the cameraman loudly told the reporter. "It came from the thirteenth window."

"I saw it this time, too," the reporter indicated excitedly, as he became riveted on his objective. "It appeared to be a person holding up something for us to see."

"That was what I saw this time and earlier," the cameraman stated. "I wonder what is the meaning of this?"

"It's an unusual game of hide and seek under very harrowing conditions," the reporter noted. "Stay focused on that same window, and I believe we will receive further clues from this aircraft." The cameraman unfolded his tripod seat and focused directly on the window that had provided their only glimpse of what was taking place on the airplane.

The waiting was testing their patience, but the camera was continuously focusing on the thirteenth window. In an environment of eerie quiet with the camera pointed directly toward the window, the two observed that the cover was being opened ever so slowly this time much different from the other two openings. There appearing out the window was a young lady holding an object that looked very much like a basketball. She looked directly at the reporter and cameraman, while at the same time wanting to display the basketball for them to see.

"I know our viewing audience can see what we are seeing," the reporter related, "a young lady holding what appears to be a basketball. Our studio personnel are being asked to enlarge this picture to present a more concise view of the object being held."

At Bacon Coach Anna noted, "I believe it was a basketball being held by the young lady, and she appeared to be of African descent, don't you think?"

"I would agree with you," Dorothy stated, as the others nodded in agreement. "But I wonder what is trying to be conveyed to the cameraman and reporter?"

"I really don't know," Coach Anna replied, "but all this just adds to the mystery."

"Oh! My goodness!" Mit blurted out excitedly. "Mom and Dad often laugh when they call me to relate stories about the way the Tanzanian people set up schedules. They are always kept off balance such that a family that they perceived was scheduled to come next week would show up that day for a visit. My theory is going to be unbelievable for everybody, but I think this is the basketball girls' group from Wasi."

"That is a bizarre theory," Coach Anna said, "but if that is a basketball the young lady is holding, it could be."

Shortly, the broadcast station was showing a large close up of the young lady and the basketball. There was no doubt now that it was a basketball, and to add to the fact gathering that was mounting, the basketball was the same brand that they left with the Wasian girls when they visited several months ago.

Back at the northern Virginia mystery aircraft scene, the pressure was mounting to blow up the plane before a suspected bomb of nuclear force could be detonated, wiping out all of Washington and surrounding areas. Steeped in politics and views of the mainstream media's experts, the final outcome of most was to decide swiftly to destroy the aircraft, or if a bomb were suspected to charge the craft and defuse the bomb. The president was getting much advice from all sides as the clock continued to tick.

The story of the sighting of a basketball being held by an occupant fanned the flames of greater suspicion with the pundits agreeing that the basketball was just a ploy to give more time for the suspected culprits to do their evil deeds. With more information those in the news media were really trying to force a showdown with the present national leadership. Realizing how inflamed the citizens had gotten as time passed, the official of Homeland Security held another news conference.

Following an informative historical perspective of the event, he proceeded, "We have finally made contact, albeit so mysteriously. There appears to be at least one young lady on the aircraft who seems to want to show us a basketball she is holding. This makes no sense whatsoever to any of our team."

Suddenly, another official looking person came bursting into the tent to whisper something into his ear. "I'll be back with you in a little while," he said. "We have just received an urgent message through our 911 system."

Arriving at the command post tent, the official of Homeland Security was handed the telephone. "This is James Rafferty of Homeland Security," he stated in a businesslike voice. "How may I help you?"

"My name is Anna Bosley, the coach of Bacon College in southwest Virginia," Coach Anna clearly stated.

"You wouldn't be Major Anna Bosley?" he asked, to confirm to whom he was speaking.

"I am," she stated. "We have been watching the news about the mysterious aircraft, and we believe we know what is taking place."

"Could you tell me?" he asked.

"Yes I can," she indicated, "but I need for you to trust me in this, and immediately send a helicopter to get our team of girls so we can come to northern Virginia. I can relate the story to you or your delegated individual on the way. Obviously, time is a critical component of this situation."

"I'll have the helicopter to be dispatched from our Tennessee base so it will be there soon," he replied, now faithfully following her instructions.

Issuing orders to dispatch the helicopter, the command post personnel were busy making arrangement for something that was very mysterious to them, also. Back at Bacon the girls donned their basketball warm-up suits, gathered a few basketballs, and headed for the softball field where a large "X" marker was placed now waiting for the helicopter to arrive.

In northern Virginia the official of Homeland Security quickly returned to continue his news conference. Everyone was really quiet as he stood before the group. "Over the years I have been involved in all kinds of activities usually on the edge of danger, and this situation would fall well into that category. Our president has stood alone in these various decisions and has shown courage and patience way beyond the rest of us. Most have prejudged his demeanor and have chastised him for not taking a hawkish stance regarding this whole affair that has shocked and concerned all of us. One always hopes that some clue will be found to unlock mysteries of this kind. The interruption that caused me to return to the command tent was a most interesting telephone call that only I and the caller are aware. I believe we have solved the mystery, but not to make any premature judgments, I will let you all see the unveiling of a heart warming story in a short while. Just get into a good position behind the restraining fence and be patient, something all of us could do even more often than we do."

Not fielding any questions at this time, the reporters filed their response to the strange ending of the important media conference. Speculative behavior abounded as each station put its own spin on the statement by the official of Homeland Security. One suggested that he had received a statement from the Ab Didal that was abandoning a terrorist effort only to embarrass the president that they could fly a commercial aircraft into our airspace and even to land the same on our soil.

Another pointed out that it might be a stunt by the media to reveal how weak our coastlines really were in preventing unidentified aircraft to enter our borders. One national reporter said that he had heard a statement from a reliable source that the abrupt interruption of the news conference by the official of Homeland Security was only to delay any action a little longer. In fact, he pointed out that in truth there was no telephone call in the first place.

Back at Bacon an even larger group was in place in the athletic dormitory to hear the news, as it was being presented by the various channels trying to outdo one another. The one channel that had been reporting from the aircraft scene continued to focus on the window with the young lady. "I believe I saw a second young lady in the window just now," the cameraman blurted out to the reporter.

"I saw the second one, too," the reporter noted.

Just then overhead they could hear the whirring of helicopter props of two swiftly flying craft that were quickly making their descent to the landing site just inside the area blocked off to prevent personnel from proceeding closer to the craft.

With all cameras focused on the cargo of this chopper, out jumped the co-pilot, who watched as the Bacon team came out right behind him. "Why on earth are these girls coming to this location?" a reporter yelled loudly.

Just then the whole team was escorted hurriedly to the command post. "You made it here in a hurry," James Rafferty said, as a mild introduction. "Now could you tell us what you know about our situation here?" as he looked with great anticipation for what Coach Anna was going to say.

"Several months ago we visited Wasi, a country that had experienced a devastating famine following two serious droughts, following the parents of my girls spending many weeks feeding the people there," Coach Anna stated. "We were invited there with the parents of the girls, so in the process of the visit we demonstrated basketball to an eager group of young ladies from Wasi. The president of the country became very enamored over our demonstrations and the noticeable interest of his girls, so he asked us whether or not we would permit the young ladies from Wasi to come to our country to learn more about basketball playing. We believe that on this mysterious plane are the girls from Wasi who somehow strayed off course, and they along with the crew are frightened about the whole affair."

"But why would they not advise you of their coming?" the official asked.

"We believe they have tried during the last several days, and the messages were not intelligible, because of poor transmission on the telephone," Coach Anna said. "When we were over there, from time to time it appeared that we would totally miscommunicate on our schedule even though all of us would agree that what we were doing was what had been agreed. So, for this situation I believe they think that they are following a set plan that we have approved. I doubt very seriously that the ones on the plane really think that in some way they have misunderstood, but are adhering to directions that seem clear to them."

"Now that you are here," the official of Homeland Security stated, "how do you propose to make contact with the aircraft?"

"I have been thinking about this all the while," Coach Anna replied. "It would appear to me that there should be no deception but direct action to make contact."

"Your call to us has changed the entire complexion of the problem," the official said. "It is your show, because I have turned it all over to you. Until you contacted us, we had no definite plan how to take care of the situation, so I have full faith in you to solve this seemingly dangerous problem."

"We'll do our best," Coach Anna indicated. "My plan is for all of us on the Bacon team to walk down the airstrip directly toward the aircraft, and then get the attention of those on board."

"How will you get their attention?" the official asked.

"We will take a powerful megaphone with us, and if this doesn't work, we'll just pick up some rocks and throw against the windows."

"What kind of standby force do you want," the official asked.

"Please don't permit anyone to do anything that might cause them to distrust us," Coach Anna quickly told the official.

As the girls left the command tent while all attention was focused on them, they stopped, and Coach Anna asked them to recite with her Psalm 23:

1 *The LORD is my shepherd, I shall not want.*
2 *He makes me lie down in green pastures;*
he leads me beside still waters;
3 *he restores my soul.*
He leads me in right paths
for his name's sake.
4 *Even though I walk through the darkest valley,*
I fear no evil;

for you are with me;
your rod and your staff—
they comfort me.
5 *You prepare a table before me*
in the presence of my enemies;
you anoint my head with oil;
my cup overflows.
6 *Surely goodness and mercy shall follow me*
all the days of my life,
and I shall dwell in the house of the LORD
my whole life long.

This was followed by prayer led by Esther.

Because Esther had been so very popular with the Wasian girls, Coach Anna asked her to lead the team down the airstrip, each dribbling a basketball to the amazement of all watching on site and on television.

"I don't really know what took place in the command center," a major network reporter stated, "but it appears that this group of girls' basketball players is now headed down the airstrip, following a time for prayer, to attempt to unravel this mystery that has hamstrung our country during the last several hours. From what information I can glean from my various sources, it is believed that there is some connection between those on the aircraft and the basketball girls. All of the officials here are standing and waiting anxiously for them to solve this whole dilemma as we speak. No attack forces are making any effort to assist in any way, if the plan of the girls fails. They seem to have plenary faith in what the team is undertaking.

"Let me quickly introduce this group to you, as you and I watch them walking down the airstrip nearing the plane with each step. The coach of this Bacon College team is Anna Bosley, a major in the green beret, who trained and led her team against armed hijackers in Portland several months ago. The young lady dribbling the ball up front is Esther Minold, the most outstanding female basketball player in the country, leading her team again this year in the ACUWAA tournament. Her team has never lost a game. She and five of her teammates rescued three missionaries who were captured in Abedistan on a team led by Major Bosley. You see, if anyone can do this job, they can."

The Bacon College students and staff found themselves again watching their beloved basketball team, as they attempted to unveil the mystery now being followed by those all around the world. This was a tense time! One observer of the mysterious aircraft saga was a young man in medical school from Wasi named Mamadou, who had gone to his home country to assist the Hollow folks in distributing food during the national famine. Calling 911, he was soon connected to the command post. Being very receptive to his plan of being present to translate for the Wasian visitors, the official of Homeland Security dispatched a helicopter to get him immediately.

Meanwhile, the girls had arrived at the aircraft site, and following their yells in unison, there was no response. Coach Anna loudly spoke through the megaphone several times, but this, too, failed to get anyone's attention. Picking up rocks, they began to throw them against the windows, and when they stopped, near the middle, one of the window covers slowly was opened revealing a young Wasian lady holding a basketball. She broke into a wide smile when she saw the group of girls on the airstrip holding basketballs, too. Then several of the windows were uncovered, as a very special reunion was taking place, albeit under strange circumstances.

With all cameras focusing on the most mysterious plane, the emergency door was opened and the emergency slide was deployed providing a safe means to join their American friends on the ground. Hugs followed hugs as the two groups of basketball players met on the airstrip, and reunited as all the world watched. To make them feel at home, Esther took the Bacon girls through a set of drills in the shadows of the aircraft, inviting the Wasian girls to join the exercise. It was a joyous time for all.

After Mamadou arrived he came down the strip to meet the Wasian and Bacon girls and began to translate for the group. Expressions of love for one another consumed all his time as they made their way back toward the command tent. Before he came near the officials, Coach Anna stopped the group and asked Mamadou to ask the young pilot what caused them to veer off course, why they didn't respond to those trying to make contact, and why hadn't they called earlier to advise of their arrival?

To answer these questions, the pilot responded, "Soon after our take off in Wasi our instrument panel failed to give us appropriate readings so we knew we had only one recourse, and that was to continue, hoping that someone would send help. Regarding our communication, all of our radios went dead, leaving us with no way to make any contact whatsoever. President Kantitore told us that you all had invited us to be your guests, and that you all would take care of everything. As we approached the mainland, we knew that something was wrong so we all sat very quietly on board not wanting to cause others to be provoked by our presence."

After a period of debriefing the basketball players from two different parts of the world were transported by military helicopters to Bacon College. What a special reception they received when they arrived on campus!

Treated like royalty all the while, the girls really enjoyed their stay on the small campus in the mountains. At the tournament game at the Bacon coliseum, the Wasian girls were invited to warm up with the team so the whole nation saw this group that clogged up our national environment when confusion overwhelmed them in the aircraft.
They were a genuine group of lovely young ladies sitting behind the Bacon team as the women's team mostly from the

Hollow continued their winning ways with Esther leading the charge.

PARENTS' SEARCH

In the community around Bacon during the last several weeks, there had been much said and written about the school district after the resignation of Glenn Colson, and the employment of an experienced school superintendent from northern California who had taught at the university level. With renewed excitement now surrounding the school district, Glenn really thought his decision to step down as the school leader after fifteen years was a good one. His ideas didn't seem to fit those of the people so now with a new vision and a new leader, there would be contentment among these wonderful people who had really become his friends over the best years of his career.

The new superintendent arrived on the scene with a specific plan to involve all of the people in developing a broader plan based on the consensus of the public as they met in schools, churches and civic club buildings in different parts of the community. Attendance at these conferences was overwhelming, such that the school board now was feeling much better about the whole situation. Realizing that the people seemed to be so receptive to his leadership style of involving everyone in the process of establishing a teaching-learning environment for their children, the school board praised him and his manner in which he conducted the several meetings.

"I am so glad that we now have the kind of leadership that has brought peace and harmony among the people," the chairman said to another board member.

"He's so articulate and eloquent as he responds to inquiries of the people," the second indicated.

"Obviously, his university experience is paying off, and the fact that he has earned a doctor's degree elevates his status with the citizens," the chairman stated, continuing to heap praise on the board for its decision to employ the new school district leader.

One of those in attendance at many of these meetings was Marie Webster who had two children in the primary grades in the district. She was a current member of the site based decision making team of her children's school, and had been since her children began school. It was about this group of leaders in each school that prompted her first critical discussion at home with her husband.

"I am really twisted inside after hearing the discussions at these various meetings held by our new superintendent," she said to her husband after dinner one evening.

"What do you mean?" her husband, Ted, said. "I thought you supported the change in leadership."

"I did in a way, because what I believed would help our educational program was not effected by our previous superintendent," she said.

"In other words you believed that Superintendent Colson knew how to effect a good teaching-learning environment, but that others did not support his mission," Ted responded.

"That's correct," she quickly said. "He tried on several occasions to move the schools toward his program, but each time the citizens and teachers failed to permit such a move."

"I guess you thought that this new leadership would provide the impetus to establish a program similar to that of the previous superintendent," Ted stated. "You have now discovered that the new school leader has a different approach to present to the teachers and parents."

"Well, you are exactly right," Marie said, "but what I don't see is what kind of program the new superintendent has in mind. All that is discussed is how everyone is going to have input, but to this date I don't know what kind of plan is being considered. There is one part that will remain in place as though it's the centerpiece of any program, and in fact, it seems that in the end of all of the meetings our final outcome will be that this will be the governance for any future decisions."

"What's wrong with that?" Ted asked.

"Many people would ask me the same question, because the objective of any group in modern times is to have input," she replied, "and in education site based decision making is the best means for that. But what we tend to forget, as we become so much enamored over the conduit for input, is that there is still no direction to ensure a quality program for learning. You see, most people believe that something will emerge from these site based decision making groups greatly to enhance learning."

"Why won't that happen?" Ted asked, as he was being served his second cup of after dinner coffee.

"I will let you answer this question for yourself," Marie said. "On these site based decision making teams are teachers, lay people, a student and the principal. All kinds of issues are discussed such that there are rare opportunities to deliberate over anything dealing with curriculum or learning of students. Many meeting are bogged down with complaining about various situations dealing with discipline, and others are related to reports and lack of cooperation from parents. One time we spent the entire meeting dissecting a memorandum from the central office."

"If you were not talking about these things, what would you be talking about?" Ted asked.

"This is where we miss the boat," Marie answered. "We all get caught up in a process and totally forget about the outcome for our children in school. Right now everyone is so enamored over having someone at the helm who will listen to them that they are missing the whole point of establishing a curriculum and a way to ensure that children fulfill expectations. To this point in the transition of leadership, I have not heard one word about what children should learn, and how parents will know that their children are learning."

"From what I have heard at these meetings," Ted said, "I believe it is expected that the governance team at each school will decide what course the school will take."

"That's exactly right," Marie quickly reacted. "I don't believe that we will see any kind of improvement from what we have now, because we already have this system in place. On my team the education association teachers are too powerful to permit any kind of accountability program to be initiated at their school. The status quo begats the status quo, I believe, as I watch the days go by in preparation for change which, at this point, I believe will not be substantive, but will be more of a cosmetic dressing that everyone will cling for a while."

"You don't seem to have much confidence in the new leadership in the district," Ted noted, as he put his cup down looking Marie in the eye.

"You and I both want the same thing for our children," Marie stated, now holding her husband's hand. "I learned a lot from Glenn Colson when he spoke to us at the high school. He said that it was most important to have a curriculum that specifically shows parents what their children should learn and an electronic system to keep track with the progress. He told us that the effective school program did not permit teachers to be the only decision makers regarding education. During his last talk with us parents, he noted that the most effective way was to determine what it is children should learn, and the administration of the district would determine whether or not it was taught. The teacher's role was to decide how it should be taught."

"Does it appear that the school district now is headed in that direction?" Ted inquired.

"It seems to me that in the end we will be much farther from this concept than we ever were, as we just let whatever emerges at the school level guide our program," she responded. "Before our children started to school, I went to a meeting wherein Glenn Colson was trying to alter the school program, and instead of the teachers and parents accepting his strong accountability program, they brought up this new age school level decision making idea that they overwhelmingly supported for each school. Being very naïve at the time, I decided with the other parents, thinking that with a new way of making decisions, many good decisions would be made boosting the children's learning. Of course, as you know, this did not happen."

"Are you indicating that the final outcome of this process to provide opportunities for input is somewhat like a charade, and nothing substantive will emerge from all of these meetings?" Ted asked in a somewhat more excited tone.

"Each day I believe more and more that this is exactly what is happening," Marie stated in a voice that showed a little pride that she possessed sufficient wisdom to see through the maze, and realize that little or no substantive changes would be forthcoming.

"What should we do then?" Ted asked, realizing now how unhappy his wife was about the school situation.

"All day I have been thinking about something," she said. "I want to meet with Glenn Colson to talk to him about his program of improvement, and see whether or not I can get the new superintendent to consider it as he moves ahead with his agenda."

"I think that is the best thing you have said today," Ted stated, "and the sooner the better for me."

After dinner Marie called Glenn Colson, the former superintendent, to set up a meeting with him. He advised her that he was helping Josh Morrow, the pastor of the Hollow Church, and would be at the church the next day.

"May I come to the Hollow to speak to you?" Marie asked.

"You certainly may," he answered. "Just follow the road to the top until you get to the church."

Marie was very nervous as she drove toward the Hollow, finally making the turn up the narrow road. When she saw the first wood framed house stilted on the side of the mountain, she was reminded that the best basketball players in the country lived in this community. She remembered that some parents had really criticized Glenn Colson when the girls played for the local high school.

After stopping at the end of the Hollow, she nervously walked toward the door of the wood framed church, opened the door and saw the superintendent and another man.

"I am Marie Webster, who called you last night at your home," she said, as she walked up to Glenn.

"How are you doing today?" he asked.

"I am fine," she replied.

"This is Josh Morrow, the pastor of the church," Glenn said. "Mrs. Webster was a patron of the school district."

"Do you have time to talk to me about school?" Marie asked him.

"I always have time to talk to people about education," he replied. "Why don't we sit on this pew right here?" now leading her to a sitting area.

"During the last several weeks, I have really been frustrated about the education of my two children now in the primary grades," she related, as Josh sat nearby listening to the conversation. "While attending the meetings in which you explained what it was you planned for the school district that was rejected by the teachers and parents, I realized that what you were saying was what was needed for out children to learn satisfactorily. For whatever reason your well laid out plan was not utilized, and we continue with the same program all the while."

"What you have said is essentially how it happened," he said. "Over the years I have become more and more convinced that my plan as I presented is the best approach to educating our young people. Too many of our students seem to fall through the cracks not really by any fault of their own."

"I want to be a stronger voice in the direction of our school district so would you mind telling me again in a few brief statements just how your plan would work?" she asked, as Josh headed to his house to get Charlene to make some coffee.

"Let me tell you first of all about the current educational program," he said, as he shifted on the pew. "Our teachers who are working hard determine what to teach, how to teach and when to teach so that whatever results there are rests on the shoulders of this group. The principal considers his or her role as that of providing a comfortable teaching-learning environment for the teachers."

"Isn't that the way it's supposed to be?" Marie asked, now sitting up just a little.

"Well, everybody thinks that's the way it should be, but an effective program should look much different," Glenn responded. "A youngster in elementary school will have eight teachers from kindergarten through the seventh grade with each one having his or her own idea about what should be taught and gauges of expectation. So the primary point of a good elementary school is to have a curriculum which becomes the learning expectations of the students. And secondly, this curriculum will become expectations of the teachers as they provide instruction each day. So now with something concrete to expect from our instructional and student personnel, we are on our way in establishing an effective school. But not quite yet, as the principal will now become the student achievement manager, monitoring the progress of each student utilizing computers loaded with data during each school day. And finally, the parents will have access to the progress of their children on a continuous basis."

"But aren't we doing much of this now?" Marie asked.

"Most people think so but that's not the case at all," he said. "I believe if a school district did these things that I just mentioned, we would remove a large number of present school woes."

"Has your program ever been tried?" she inquired.

"It really hasn't, because it's been rejected each time I have tried to set it up," he answered. "One time here I came close, but in the end the 'union' won out, not wanting to cause the teachers to be accountable for the learning of the students."

"I'm sorry that they didn't support you," Marie responded.

"Of course, I only blame myself for not just going ahead and installing the program," he said. "One time I even did that until two parents who had listened to the complaint of a few teachers came to the school board to present their grievance. I never really could educate the school board on the importance of this kind of reform; thus, they wanted peace and tranquility so all complaints were generally sided with the complainer."

"I didn't realize that you had worked so hard to start your program," Marie stated.

By this time Josh had returned with Charlene, bringing coffee for everybody. It was during the time that the four were talking that Marie remembered that years ago Josh and Charlene taught the Hollow children in this same church building.

"I believe I remember that you two taught the Hollow children for a while in the Hollow," Marie stated.

"Yes, that was several years ago," Charlene responded. "They returned to the public schools in the eighth grade with the help of Mr. Colson, who was superintendent at the time."

"As your husband has heard," Marie indicated, "I have a big school dilemma regarding my two children before the start of the next school year."

"I do hope that you find a solution to your problem," Charlene said, as she hugged Marie.

Much went through Marie's mind as she left the Hollow after talking with the previous superintendent of schools. She understood exactly what the superintendent had in mind for a school to be successful, but she needed to sharpen her discernment to determine whether or not this reform program just described to her, and the one she fully ascribed was the same direction set forth by the new superintendent.

There was one thing Marie had in her favor, and that was her husband and she were in total agreement in what should be included in their school's reform program. Having a spouse of like mind elevated the family's discernment such that now the two of them could glean from the presentation what kind of changes would be made in the academic program. It was during the subsequent community meeting with the new superintendent that Marie felt she should probe for deeper meaning in what was said.

Whereas, Marie and her husband usually did not actively get involved in these kinds of meetings although they were always present, now was a different time when she heard the new superintendent expressing his chief objective in the new direction for the school district. "My main thrust in providing educational leadership will be to generate all my energies toward the further empowerment of teachers to do a better job by providing wherewithal of all kinds, academic freedom, encouragement, good salaries, and a comfortable teaching-learning environment."

This statement was followed by a standing ovation by the teachers and parents present for the evening. It was a culminating statement that pricked the consciousness of those in attendance such that for those in doubt of the quality of their new leadership, they could rest assured that he was the right person for the job. While Marie and her husband stood at the close of the meeting with the others, she believed what she heard was just the type of thing Glenn Colson had warned her about during her private meeting with him.

In a few days a meeting was conducted to answer questions of the parents, and for Marie these would be of considerable value after the powerful statement of the new superintendent a few days earlier. The media were now endorsing even the least of his suggested changes and not present any form of challenge. "Where are all the people who have unanswered questions?" Marie asked her husband. "You and I are lone wolves in seeking further answers from the highest paid official in the whole county, making considerably more than the previous superintendent was being paid."

"We should be careful not to lose track of our own agenda, that of seeking a quality learning environment for our two children," Ted pointed out, somewhat chastising her.

"I know," she said, "I am totally shocked that others are so gullible, and in the end will be a part of an educational ruse that will result in more of the same kind of education for our children. It's going to be difficult, but I'm going to let it be known that I am not in favor of the pseudo-reform being presented. Obviously, our status in the community will be sharply dampened, because the people are all excited about this very articulate and eloquent educational leader introducing an age old educational program with colorful terms. In the end nothing will be changed as the teachers will continue to handle their own classroom in a disjointed fashion."

"What are you planning to do?" Ted asked.

"We should attend the question and answer session to let our leader know how we feel," she said.

"I'm all for that," Ted quickly replied.

The session was held in the auditorium of the local school. Marie had signed up to speak on a legal pad near the rear. The chairman of the school board opened the meeting with some remarks that indicated how much the board approved of their new superintendent and the much needed progress that had been made to this point. Being far down the list, Marie and Ted listened as speaker after speaker showered the new leader with bouquets and plaudits, praising him for providing opportunities of input, thus providing diverse views which in the end would help produce a direction for now and years to come."

One could feel the pride that filled the auditorium augmented so strongly by the many speakers. Marie's courage was continuing to wane as speaker after speaker preceding her only made positive comments. As her turn neared, she wished she had made better notes, but now though, she would have to do with what she had.

"Mrs. Marie Webster, it's your turn to speak to the superintendent and school board about our proposed reform program," the chairman said. With sweaty palms, grossly over palpitating heart beating at a fast pace, and overt nervousness, Marie headed to the podium near the front.

"My background is not in education so the terms that I use may not flow as smoothly and evenly as those of others who have spoken during these several meetings in the county," she said. "First of all, thank all of you officials who have made it possible for each of us to have input along the way as we try to provide the best education possible for our children.

"For many years now I have believed that our children should learn how to read, write and compute in the elementary school, such that their wherewithal of skills will provide the necessary basis for continued learning in high school. It sounds simple enough, but when we cxamine the number of young people who are unsuccessful in grasping these basic skills, are we shocked? No, as it seems that because it always happens this way, it always should happen this way. So failure becomes commonplace or a necessary part of our educational program."

The auditorium was very quiet. Marie turned to look at her husband to get some moral support. "Is it necessary for us to be so accepting about the failing students in the basic program?" she asked. "I don't think so. Just how does this happen in our schools where professional people deal with this kind of thing each day? This is how. My husband Ted, who is sitting back there always puts his car keys on the edge of the kitchen counter, and he has been doing that for the eleven years of our marriage. He has changed key holders, added keys and other things on the chain, but he has never changed where he put them each time he comes in the house. He would not change his way of doing this, because that is just the way it's done for him.

"Our school program is handled somewhat in a parallel fashion. We don't want to change for any reason, so we talk about reform to effect improvement, but finally we find ourselves residing in our previous position. It is obvious that I am a voice of one here tonight so I appreciate your indulgence. The other evening when I heard our new educational leader say that the main thrust of his energy would be to empower the teachers, and this remark was not followed by any substantive program of change, I realized that my idea of a quality school program and that of his was much different."

Following this statement, there was low level murmuring in the group, because for the first time during this "honeymoon" period for the new school superintendent, there was a dissenter, albeit a small voice. Soon the words of those in the audience became audible such that Marie was hearing what they were saying. "I need to complete my remarks hurriedly," she thought, as she faced the restless crowd now.

"I think it is incumbent upon our educational leaders to develop a curriculum for all teacher to follow in their instruction, for the children to learn, for the parents to use to assess progress and the principal to use to evaluate individual progress. The days of the time honored report cards should no longer exist but should be replaced by continuous reporting on progress of students on broad bands of material."

With this said and with a very restless audience, the chairman indicated that she had utilized all of her time allotted. Soon the meeting was adjourned and those in attendance shunned Ted and Marie, even those who were considered close friends. It seemed that many wanted to speak to the new superintendent to reassure him that Marie's statements did not represent any kind of a consensus of community beliefs and that all stood behind him fully. Some even told him not to be discouraged by Marie's remarks, that she had always been a "lone ranger" with cockeyed views not representative of the other good people in the neighborhood.

At home finally and having tucked their children in bed, Ted and Marie discussed the remarks she said and somewhat assessed the entire evening. "It was very obvious that your remarks were very much different from the others for the evening," Ted said.

"Are you implying that they were out of place?" Marie asked.

"Oh, no!" Ted quickly replied. "I think they were very succinct, to the point and were appropriate. As you know, it did seem that those in attendance did not want to hear anything that would be construed as being substantive such that it would have to be evaluated."

"I wonder why my remarks were not considered appropriate," Marie said, probing deeper.

"I think that everyone is so captivated by our new school chief that no one is willing to examine the real issue of providing a quality education for our young people," Ted said in a reassuring manner.

"I don't want to upset the apple cart," Marie said, "but the education of our children is paramount on my mind now. I know that many of those at this meeting looked at me with a jaundiced eye and think that I am a troublemaker, but that is not the case at all."

Devin, the local newspaper owner, took a different view of what Marie Webster had said, and in his early morning edition wrote, "Marie Webster, a patron of our local elementary school, presented views contrary to all the other patrons for last evening's meeting. A discerning person could see that she was still aspiring to install the strong accountability program espoused by the previous superintendent for which he failed to garner sufficient support. Her substantive suggestion seemed to be out of place with the other comments for the evening which more than anything else supported a process and not substantive alterations to the present academic program."

During the next few days, no one called Marie on the telephone, and when she went to the grocery store it seemed that others avoided her. It was not a pleasant time for her and her family in this wonderful community of mountain folks, but she might just be one request away from the discovery of her special school.

The Request

It was obvious to Marie that the direction the school district was headed was not the way she believed would bring good results in the achievement of the children, especially hers. She was well aware by now that the employment of the new school chief was not going to bring about the kind of changes in which the community had hoped. But she was the only one who seemed to understand what was taking place, because all had gotten on the bandwagon of their newly employed leader.

"I have been thinking about something for some time now," Marie said to her husband one evening.

"What is that?" her husband asked.

"I really do believe that the educational program explained by Glenn Colson is an excellent approach to effect a good school," she replied. "But even in this situation as I believed in his plan, I have been considered an outcast just as now when I don't support the philosophy of our new educational leader."

"Are you asking whether or not your actions during the last several weeks are coincidental and not taking a very minority position just to be different?" he asked.

"I guess that is what I am trying to say," she said. "I think about this often, but there is one thing that helps me cope with my stance, and that is that my belief coincides with that of our newspaper owner who has expressed his views several times."

"Why don't you call Devin and talk to him?" her husband inquired.

"That's a good idea," Marie stated.

Not being one to harbor intended action too long, Marie called the newspaper owner to set up an appointment for the afternoon. This was her first time to be in the newspaper building so she was curious about the whole environment such that she had difficulty explaining to the receptionist why she was there. Being led to Devin's office, she was greeted cordially by a gray haired man in his late fifties.

"Please sit down," he said to Marie, as he came around his large desk to sit in a chair near her in the front. "How may I help you?" he asked in a very gentle voice.

"My husband and I have been searching for a good school for our children for the last several months," she responded.

"That is an admirable task," he stated. "All parents should do their best in discovering a place for children to live and learn, and especially during their formative years.

"Do you have children?" Marie asked.

"Yes, we have two boys who grew up here, attending the local school in the area.

"Were you satisfied with the education your children received?" Marie asked.

"Well, our children did well in school, because they learned to read well very early," he replied. "For their early years they experienced a regular type school program, and later, the superintendent introduced an exciting innovative program that I knew would provide a teaching-learning environment that would provide an opportunity of success for all children and not just those more affluent. I was really shocked that the teachers and parents refused to consider this new program for our children."

"That is why I am here today to talk to you about this," Marie excitedly stated. "My husband and I believe that what Glenn Colson presented to the people as a plan would improve the quality of our children's school immensely, but we seem to be the only ones who have this belief, as you know."

"I understand your plight," Devin stated. "I have been trying to alert the people of this for some time. As you know, I have editorialized this whole issue many times, yet the people fall prey to a process and not substantive action that would bring results. Yes, I believe the plan as presented by Glenn Colson on several different occasions would be most beneficial to our school community. Glenn foresaw the day when these kinds of AET tests would be used to evaluate our students' progress so he wanted our school district to get ahead of the learning curve. Of course, you have observed the behavior of parents when he staged his final plea for his plan."

"It is obvious that you agree, too, that Glenn's plan is sound and would bring about excellent results," Marie reacted. "It feels good to be talking to a person of like mind regarding this educational issue."

"I have no doubt at all about it," he stated emphatically.

They continued their conversation for about an hour before they bade farewell with Devin wishing Marie well in her continued search.

After bringing her husband up to date, Marie told him that she was going to get another audience with Glenn Colson the next day. Going to the Hollow the next day, Marie was surprised that Glenn was still helping Josh, but he agreed to meet with her anyway, if she were willing to come to this remote area again.

Following a cordial greeting, Marie got directly to the point for her meeting. "As you know, my husband and I have been searching for a good school for our children, and to this point we have not had any success."

"I am sorry that you have not found that special school for your children," he stated. "I'm sure it's out there somewhere, so keep on searching."

"I guess we have set our sights too high, because we now ascribe fully to your concept of a good school," Marie stated, now readying herself to ask the bombshell question. "Would you agree to set up a private school utilizing your ideas of educating children?"

Chuckling just a little, he took her hand and said, "You know, that is the best compliment I believe I have ever received. I really do believe my plan in education will correct the woes of most, if handled properly, but to set up a private school is a different kind of situation altogether."

"I would be willing to assist you in this endeavor," Marie stated quickly. "There will be many others just like me who will be looking for an educational program in the near future, and I'm sure many of the silent parents now would come to a school guided by you."

"You may see a different side of the parents from that which I have seen over the last several years," he said. "All of the parents in this area have heard of my plan, and you are the first one who has formally endorsed it."

"I believe there are others who are disillusioned and will turn to your ideas," Marie indicated. "How many children would you have to enroll to start a private school?" Marie asked, now really putting the pressure on the former school superintendent to give her a positive answer.

"You know, I have thought about trying my innovative program on a group of students, so your suggestion whets my appetite to attempt such an undertaking," he pointed out. "If I were to do this, I had rather just start with one willing parent with plenary understanding than a full classroom of students whose parents were only tepid about the learning concept."

"Then are you saying that you will do it?" Marie asked immediately.

"I would not go that far," he retorted, "but I shall think about it. Your belief in my untried educational notion gives me new life, and a heart now filled over contemplating a return to the educational arena. This time I would have parental enthusiasm. I feel like I'm filled with new energy."

"Will you really consider doing this?" Marie asked again.

"I certainly will," he said. "If I do it, your two children will be sufficient to start such a program. I do not want you to proselytize others, but to wait for them to come to you for help."

"What an exciting meeting!" Marie thought, as she drove out of the Hollow.

All afternoon one could hear Glenn whistling different tunes, showing his elation in setting up his teaching and learning techniques so there would be no reason for the program to fail. "What are you so happy about?" Josh asked, when he returned from running an errand.

"I just concluded a meeting with the lady who came here the other day, and among other things she has asked me to establish a private school in the area so I could showcase my innovative educational program," he replied. "I am not really sure that I want to do this, but the fact that she is willing to send her two children to such a program and offer to assist, it makes me feel good about such an undertaking."

"Are you contemplating establishing a private school?" Josh asked.

"Well, I have really been excited about doing that now, because of her encouragement," Glenn answered. "I have always wanted to try out my plan on real students in a school type setting so when Marie made her request, my enthusiasm was escalated to great heights."

"I know you are happy to deal with an educational issue after being away from it for a while," Josh stated. "You know we taught the Hollow children here in the church several years ago, so if you desired, you could use the church building as your school site."

"Do you think I could use the church?" Glenn asked, not really believing what he had heard.

"You certainly may use it, and Charlene and I will help you, if you wish," Josh noted.

Working the remainder of the week to effect initial plans for the new school in the Hollow, Josh advised the whole group during their Friday evening meal together about the prospect of a small private school. It was interesting that the Hollow parents volunteered their services to assist in starting this new endeavor. Although there was much discussion about the school, there was no speculation about how long it would be operated, or how many students might finally be enrolled. The clincher to the whole affair was when Josh and Charlene indicated their interest in helping Glenn on this undertaking.

By the next Friday evening much had been completed on the private school undertaking, such that a meeting was being scheduled with Marie and her husband that following Monday. A brown envelope was delivered to Glenn Colson that was found pinned to the athletic dormitory bulletin board containing a letter, as follows:

Dear Mr. Colson,

I never cease to be amazed about the good things, which come from the Hollow. Your new private school only adds to this excitement. Thank you for your willingness to provide an option for these two parents. Others will follow.

You will need much wherewithal of materials and supplies at this juncture and much, much more later. Please accept this amount of $5,000 to defray initial expenses to establish your innovative program.

An Admirer

This was the first time Glenn had been involved in any way with the benevolent person so he was overwhelmed. This act enhanced the merriment of the evening.

Needing to talk to Josh again before committing

himself to establish a private school, Glenn decided to head for the Hollow on this Sunday morning to attend church service with the good folks in this remote area of the region. Just looking around upon arrival, Glenn knew that Josh was attracting a large number of people to each worship service, which certainly caused him to think about another addition to the church building. The basketball team always came over to hug Glenn and thank him for permitting them to play basketball for the high school. It was obvious that Glenn really was proud of these lovely young ladies who had grown in number during the last year.

Following the worship service, Glenn and Josh sat on the front pew to discuss the school situation. "Josh, I couldn't wait until tomorrow to talk to you about this very important decision I need to make regarding the request by Marie Webster," Glenn stated. "For whatever reason I am interested in accepting this challenge to establish a private school utilizing my educational ideas which I could never do in the school district. When you mentioned the other day that you would let me use the church as a school building, it just seemed to open up the way to implement this innovative school."

"You certainly are welcome to use the church," Josh reiterated. "As we told you the other day, Charlene and I will be your instructional helpers in this undertaking."

"When Marie heard that you two were going to help, her eyes just lit up," Glenn stated. "It seemed that your decision cemented the whole notion for Marie."

"You have mentioned that you want to provide an electronic system of reporting so I can offer you an excellent laptop computer that we took with us to Wasi," Josh said.

"The computerization of reporting will be a big part of the total program," Glenn said. "I'll need to get a good computer programmer to help me in this part of the program. I know what I want so with the help of an electronics person, the whole plan can be put on the computer. The whole idea is to place the objectives on the computer in numerous segments and test on same, passing on to the parent continuously just how the student is doing in his work. We will want Marie to utilize her computer at home to get a full and comprehensive report of her students' progress all the while."

"It really sounds exciting," Josh stated.

"We want to have a computer here at the school that Marie can use to assess progress, also," Glenn said, continuing to show his emotion now that he was nearing the time that his idea of a sound educational program would become a reality.

"You know, Glenn," Josh indicated, "we have a young man here in the orphan home who is gifted in computers, so he may be just the one who could help in the programming."

"How good is he?" Glenn asked, showing much interest in this assistance.

"Because I don't really know what it is you want him to do, why don't you relate to him what you want and give him a specific assignment to see whether or not he can do it."

"That's a wonderful idea," Glenn responded. "May I talk with him this afternoon?"

"You certainly may," Josh replied. "Let me mention to you that the Hollow folks want to help you, also."

The afternoon was one fraught with positive decisions such that Glenn felt very good about his new undertaking. Benji, the young orphan lad, listened intently to what Glenn explained to him.

"I believe I have the program that will do everything you have mentioned," the young man maturely stated. "Several days ago a group headed by a man named Ben came here and gave to us, among other things, several programs to add to our computer. One of these programs is a powerful data base that can be used to prepare numerous reports of magnificent quality. I will develop a mock data base and prepare you some reports by tomorrow."

Early the next morning Glenn picked up several different teachers' guides for a Christian curriculum in reading, writing and mathematics from the home schooling official who was so helpful to Josh and Charlene a few years earlier. Upon arrival at the church Josh immediately handed him the reports printed out by Benji. "They are marvelous!" Glenn said. "I can't believe that young man can do that kind of work. He will do wonders for our program."

"He is very excited about doing this for you," Josh told Glenn, as they sat in the church drinking a hot cup of coffee. "He can do as many of these as you want, and I might add that he has gotten very good at data entry and has gotten some others interested in helping him."

"I think I'll see Marie Webster this afternoon to tell her that we are prepared to enroll her two children starting tomorrow morning," Glenn said. "Will that be all right?"

"That sounds good to me," Josh responded with a wide smile. "There is no need to wait."

The understatement of the year was to say that Marie wasn't excited about the private school starting the next day. "I can't believe you are going to start so soon," Marie stated. "I thought it might be the start of the new school year, but I am really happy to start now. It's been very difficult for me and my two boys during the last several days."

"What happened?" Glenn curiously asked.

"My children don't know anything about my concern over the school situation, but a couple of days ago when they were getting ready to board the bus to come home, one of the teachers approached them and said, 'I understand your mama doesn't like our new superintendent.'"

"Of course, my children didn't know what she was talking about so they came home crying," Marie related. "That was the beginning of several more comments to them indicating that what I was doing seemed to be disturbing the tranquility in the school as well as in the neighborhood. You see, I have received two anonymous telephone calls telling me how rude I was to our new school leader to insinuate in my remarks that he was not leading our schools in the proper direction. What was so hurtful, the caller asked me just how much education I had that qualified me to disagree with our experienced and educationally sound leader that we were so fortunate to have for our rural area."

"I am so sorry about your situation," Glenn said. "In life one has to commit to what he or she believes is right, and then move forward with great enthusiasm. Regarding this, you and I are doing just that."

When Marie's two children failed to be at school the next day, a rumor circulated throughout the school that she had become ashamed of what she had said at the meeting and was withdrawing her children to begin home schooling. Of course, the neighborhood developed its own spin such that one rumor indicated that the family was moving while another had them enrolling their children in a neighboring school district. Seeing her leave in the car with the children gave much strength to that rumor.

Glenn elicited the assistance of some of the retired public school personnel to get started, directing them in writing segments of objectives in various areas of reading, writing and mathematics. Adding his wife to the help list along with several others, including Charlene, Josh and other Hollow folks, the school curriculum quickly took shape. Reports of all kinds were hand prepared by Glenn such that they could be computerized by Benji, the brilliant young orphan.

Thinking ahead, Glenn wanted every part of the program developed in such a way that it could be fully replicated, if the number of students increased. Marie was required to use the computer in the Student Progress Access (SPA) Center to retrieve reports of progress of her two children. Glenn had used part of the benevolent person's gift to purchase this computer, and of course, Benji had made it possible for Marie to keep a daily and even hourly check on the progress of her two children.

"I have received more quality reports of my children in school in these few days than I have for all the other period they have been in school," Marie said to Glenn one afternoon after school. Holding letters, graphs and charts in her hand just printed, she was beginning to sense the importance of reporting on progress different from what is now being done in the public schools. The foundation for the new school in the small wood framed church was being laid much quicker than Glenn ever imagined, especially because of the excellent computerization being handled so masterfully by one considered a couple of years ago to be an outcast, not being good enough to live in some people's neighborhood.

Marie had the objectives on which her children were working pasted on her kitchen wall so that she could see the progress more vividly. She was really surprised to discover how helpful the new evaluative approach was in clearly relating the achievement of her children. Marie's husband shared her excitement.

A few more neighborhood conferences were left on the schedule for the new superintendent, and his supporters continued to grow. Input seems to be a politically correct thing to do, and input the various neighborhoods got, and all the while with strong backing from everyone it seemed, except Marie. When the last conference was held, the community folks pitched in sufficient money to buy the new superintendent a very expensive riding lawn mover to cut the grass around his beautiful home in the most affluent neighborhood. He was just loved by those who followed his "school meetings," as he called them.

At the picnic held on the athletic field of the local high school, when his gift was presented, the superintendent announced that annually he would schedule "school meetings" to gather input from all the folks. Obviously, this was received warmly by those present such that they gave him a long round of applause that included yells and whistles of endearment. Devin carried the narrative of the event in the next morning's news on the front page. The neighborhood was happy again, now having a new superintendent, who would correct their previous problems in education.

However, all was not well regarding Marie. Even many of her church members failed to speak to her, and others only coolly made small talk still harboring much malevolence toward her both covert and overt. Obviously, even for Marie's strong and committed Christian background, to select the correct biblical precepts to apply to this situation was difficult. Her natural tendency to lean toward secularism at times was a big factor in causing her relationship with others to continue to deteriorate.

Once she developed a course of action that resembled trying to do what Jesus would do, a different response to those who were once friends was about to take place. Selecting her battleground at the church, on this Sunday she hugged many and told them, " I have offended you in some way; please forgive me!"

What a difference these hugs made, and to beat it all, Marie did not use up all of her forgiveness times Jesus had advised people to use in life.

HEADWAY

It was the third meeting of the statewide group of citizens to attempt to effect change in the way many institutions were functioning in the state. While it all started with an ad hoc group of interested people, the numbers had been swelling during the last several weeks. There was one characteristic that well described the entire group and that was the participants were obviously apolitical. None had ever held any political office or had been involved before in the mainstream of politics; thus the playing field was level for the entire group.

Josh had become a genuine resource for Bob who was really an active part of this newly and loosely formed group of diverse citizens. "I don't believe any of our initial group of leaders in our first meeting several weeks ago would have dreamed of the growth and interest in their movement, albeit so simply grounded," Bob thought, as he prepared for this third meeting in this small rural setting near Hillsville, Virginia. The setting of an old barn stirred the imagination of those in attendance such that creative comments seemed to flow freely during this session.

The whole organization of new thinkers seemed to be passing under the radar of the news media to the delight of everyone. "We don't want to be shaped by our mainstream media," a middle-age man pointed out. "Thus far we have had the luxury to collect our own thoughts without new age scrutiny that we all have grown accustomed."

Bob was really amazed at the fertile suggestions by the various members, such that he believed that the group had reached a point wherein they should begin to develop a mission statement as well as presenting their beliefs in written form. "The excitement of being involved in something so monumental and above all helpful to the common man gives us great impetus to continue to expound on the subject of societal complexities precluding a greater participation of regular folks, such as we are," Bob stated. "I would like to suggest to the group that we begin to formulate our beliefs and place them in writing for all to examine and have input."

The reaction was overwhelming as the group was really applauding itself for advancing to this stage so quickly even as a neophyte organization. Bob remembered that his dad used to be much concerned when a newly elected state representative would head for Richmond to make a difference and do the will of the people. His father would say, "Son, I know our locally elected people mean well, but when they find themselves in our capital city, they become blinded to what their whole campaign included and wind up just as the others. It would be just more of the same."

Bob believed that if this very enthusiastic group of ad hoc leaders remained steadfast to the course, in the end there could be genuine reform, something that had been needed for such a long time. As production continued at a very fast pace, Bob knew that his input had been well received by his colleagues, and had become the central philosophy to develop specific and measurable objectives to be included in the body of the general statement by the members. He had advised the others that these were not his thoughts, but those of a pastor who lived in the Hollow where he was sheltered from the description of events in the world as interpreted by the present day media.

The draft of the reformation document was so intriguing that Bob could hardly wait to show it to Josh. Considerable narrative addressed various subjects in the reformation plan.

Tournament Continues

Happiness filled the mountains as the girls scurried around getting their class assignments before departing for New York to play in the semifinals against Northern State from the Midwest. The Wasian girls just tagged along enjoying every minute of their visit as a prelude for a strong and lengthy training session during the summer in the Hollow. Everything had cleared up regarding their most unusual arrival without forewarning. Mamadou and the airplane crew spent several hours in a debriefing conference with the officials of Homeland Security with the result being that everyone was satisfied.

Having been brought up in an Islamic environment with five prayers each day being expected, the Wasian girls were really curious when the Hollow girls prayed in a different manner. Coach Anna and the Bacon team were really aware of the wide chasm of difference in their religions, but Coach Anna knew that direct proselytizing would not serve a good purpose, particularly during this brief visit. The Wasian girls were very obedient and attentive as they watched every movement of the team as they prepared to play in the biggest basketball tournament of the year.

With everybody ready to depart Coach Anna met with the group in the commons area of the athletic dormitory. "We have been so blessed this day to have our Wasian friends with us at a time when we are participating in this final tournament of the year," she stated. "I would like for you all to name one blessing of God now."

Esther started by saying, "God has blessed me so much it's very difficult just to name one, but on this day one of a long list is that I am able to be with my special Wasian friends." Esther then hugged each of these African girls very hard as she walked around the room. Others followed indicating blessings of love, health, basketball skills, Bacon College, benevolent person, Maudie, parents, Pastor Josh Morrow and many more.

Following this warm session, Coach Anna asked Maudie to read Psalm 100:

1 *Make a joyful noise to the LORD, all the earth.*
2 *Worship the LORD with gladness;*
come into his presence with singing.
3 *Know that the LORD is God.*
It is he that made us, and we are his;
we are his people, and the sheep of his pasture.
4 *Enter his gates with thanksgiving,*
and his courts with praise.
Give thanks to him, bless his name.
5 *For the LORD is good;*
his steadfast love endures forever,
and his faithfulness to all generations.

Everyone noticed that Maudie recited this passage from memory just as she had done for so many others in the past.

Outside the students and staff lined the sidewalk cheering the group and holding several large banners of encouragement even though it was a very cold morning. Dr. Damond had never missed an opportunity to participate in one of these special send-offs so even being a very sick man, he was present to wish the team well. "Please take care of yourself," Coach Anna insisted, as she hugged him just before she got on the van.

"Thank you for doing such a masterful job as our coach," he responded.

"Thank you for permitting me to be a part of this most humble group of people on our campus," Coach Anna stated.

With merriment filling the two vans, the large group of girls headed out of the mountains to the Roanoke airport. Many people were waiting to speak to the team when they arrived, such that they spent considerable time talking and signing autographs. Because the Wasian girls had caused such a national stir, they, too, were popular with the crowd so they signed many autographs, also.

While Coach Anna was sitting with the girls waiting for the arrival of their plane, she began to think about something that might encourage the Wasian basketball players. One of the young ladies, whose name was Beento, was very tall, much taller than any of the Bacon team, and was very physically strong and had a high vertical leap plus possessing long arms. Not only with these favorable basketball characteristics, she spoke just a little English and was extremely affable. “She would make a good addition to our team,” Coach Anna mused. “When they return this summer for a long session of training in the Hollow, I’ll closely observe her progress. If somehow she could make our team, it would be an encouragement for the whole country’s basketball program, and they would be able to identify with Bacon College.”

New York was a huge place with many sights, but as usual the Bacon girls seemed to behave normally with no apparent change in their demeanor. Arriving at their downtown hotel, they caused quite a bit of commotion, as fans were very zealous in seeking autographs. Photographers had a field day taking many informal shots of them as they accommodated those present.

The afternoon schedule included practice time for the four teams, with Bacon and Northern State sharing the floor in the initial afternoon session. The girls went through their drills on their side of the court to the delight of the many fans who had arrived early, not wanting to miss a moment of the women’s tournament. “Have you seen the Northern State team?" one of the officials asked another near where Coach Anna was standing.

About half way through the practice session, Coach Anna let the Wasian girls participate in the drills. Being very unsure of themselves, it was awhile before they loosened up, but they seemed to be having fun. Soon the entire group was integrated into the drills with laughter abounding all the while. It was a very special time as the African girls had an opportunity to play in the most popular basketball arena in all of the U. S. A.

Following the pregame meal, the team was invited to meet the media who were stationed in the banquet room of the hotel. They wanted to speak to Coach Anna, Dorothy, Esther and Mit so the others sat in chairs provided and watched what was taking place live and on wide screen television in front of them.

With a wide array of diverse media, Coach Anna walked behind a table and sat down before several microphones. "My name is Anna Bosley, coach of the Bacon College girls' basketball team," she said. "We are very honored to be playing here in this distinguished tournament in this most treasured site and to be sitting before you at this time. I shall take your questions at this time."

"You have the longest consecutive winning streak in America so how does it feel to be playing this very powerful Northern State team in the semifinals that many say can match your team woman for woman?" a middle-age sports' writer asked.

"We have been very fortunate to have won all of our games, and regarding Northern State, I understand that they are a very good team," Coach Anna responded.

"What do you know about Northern State that has helped you prepare for this very important game?" a young lady asked.

"Actually, we have made it a practice not to study about a team that we are going to play," Coach Anna replied. "We make our assessment when we see them on the floor."

"No other Division I college coach has ever achieved at your level in all of basketball's rich history, and no one probably ever will in the future," an older man indicated sitting in the back near the other girls. "How did you get yourself to this lofty position among the many college coaches?"

"I don't consider myself in a lofty position of any kind," Coach Anna replied. "When one has players like I have, coaching is not something that is most important. I just live with my athletes and try to model after their most unusual conduct each day, living life to the fullest by loving the Lord with all my mind, heart and soul, and then loving my neighbor as myself. It seems so easy for them."

"Many of us scratch our heads each day trying to figure out how an extremely small Christian college in the mountains no less can now be our crowning team among the women's basketball programs, many of which have historically prestigious backgrounds," a national television announcer stated. "Can you put this Cinderella type scenario in some kind of perspective for us here today?"

"I have been with this team for nearly two years following five years as a high school coach in northern Virginia," Coach Anna said. "Hearing of the small college in the mountains of western Virginia, it was a dream come true for me so I applied and was offered a contract. Of course, the stipulation that the small college be competing on the Division I level in two years was a genuine challenge at first, but soon that disappeared. Being new at recruiting college basketball talent, except for my home neighborhood, I didn't know where to turn. I was astute enough to know that the major colleges and universities would have their choice of top female candidates.

"I had read about the group of girls from the Hollow, but I really didn't know anything about them. In fact, they were from such a remote area only a few of the major programs recruited them, because they thought that they would fail to meet the demands of a major program, or they would not be able to compete academically. But my first and only basketball recruiting trip was to the Hollow where I saw these girls play basketball for the first time on a strip mine outside dirt court. I thought I was a pretty good basketball player, but on this afternoon I was shown what good basketball was really like. The entire group came to Bacon and the rest is history."

"You mentioned something about academics earlier," an older woman stated. "How would you describe your team with regard to their achievement in college?"

"They are all outstanding students, entering with their SAT and ACT tests being in the top percentiles, always attending class, and excelling in their program of studies," Coach Anna proudly advised. "On our trips they spend all of their extra time keeping their college work up to date. I might add that the Bacon College professors are extremely helpful to all of the girls in providing advanced homework and adjusting test schedules."

Following several more questions, Coach Anna was replaced by Dorothy. "My name is Dorothy Buford, I am a guard on the Bacon College team. I am very happy to be here today to participate in the national women's basketball tournament."

"Let's take just a few minutes to talk about something other than basketball," a seasoned reporter near the front stated. "Your team was involved in a hijacking in Portland, Oregon, a few months ago so would you mind telling us about that ordeal from your perspective?"

"When we arrived at the Roanoke airport to travel to Arizona to play a game, three Mid-Eastern men got on our same flight, rode with us to Dallas, and as we changed airplanes to Tempe, they did likewise," Dorothy related. "We girls were not concerned about their presence even when the same three boarded the plane with us to fly to Denver and on to Portland, Oregon. This was not the case for Coach Anna who evaluated the situation from her first sighting of the men, and categorized them as being very suspicious, such that she contacted Dr. Damond, our college president.

"After Dr. Damond's second contact with the FBI, he was assured that they would provide assistance so that we would have a safe flight back home. As you know, this did not occur, but to prepare us for any contingency, Coach Anna taught us a crash course on what to do to overcome men who are bent on doing evil. On the aircraft seated with the suspicious men, it wasn't long before they hijacked the aircraft, doing all kinds of harmful acts to some of the passengers. I was the leader of one of the attack teams seated in the rear near the third hijacker, and Esther was leading the second group seated in the middle beside the second Mid-Easterner. We waited for a signal to attack but none came.

"During the next day, we could all tell that the environment on the plane was really deteriorating, such that we watched Coach Anna closely, who was sitting up at the front. We were all nervous, but our resolve was strong even when the threat of a bomb being on board was mentioned. The passengers were really frightened, and as we were nearing the time for action our own demeanor changed. Suddenly, Coach Anna raised one fist over her head. It was time! Each group prayed for God's guidance and His forgiveness for what we were getting ready to do.

"I raised my fist to indicate our readiness as we all sat up straight to get into our launching position. Esther followed with her signal. As Coach Anna's two fists were lifted above her head, we all pounced on our strong and very mean hijackers to utilize our earlier training. Soon it was all over, and we all departed the aircraft to get to safety before the bomb went off destroying the plane."

"How has this dangerous ordeal changed your life?" a young reporter asked.

"In a way it hasn't changed our behavior very much at all," Dorothy responded. "From the very beginning we have had supreme faith in Coach Anna, so this debacle only solidifies that faith in her leadership."

After several more questions Esther was asked to come to the front to face the news media. "My name is Esther Minold, a sophomore at Bacon College," she stated while looking directly at the questioners.

"You Hollow girls, as they call you, all play an unusual style of basketball, such that the other team has never defeated your team," a Sports Ramble writer indicated. "What do you attribute to your outstanding success in this sport?"

"All of our original team came from the Hollow where we all lived all our life," Esther replied. "We created our own games and used the environment in this remote area as our tools for all kinds of recreation. It was really fun! Our devotion to one activity came to us suddenly one day when we went to the church and discovered our pastor, Josh Morrow, playing an unusual game with his daughter, Maggie. We joined in the fun and have continued ever since by playing numerous games of basketball then and now. So to answer your question more directly, we concentrated on basketball, playing with each other so much that we soon could anticipate the actions of the other. It's an exhilarating experience each time we play together. They are a most humble group of teammates whom I love dearly."

"Many of us who watch you play realize that your type of playing is according to what kind of opponent you all are playing," a young lady stated. "Even with this adapting kind of participation, you have each time in every tournament been named the most outstanding player. How can you account for that?"

"We have been taught by our outstanding coach to evaluate an opponent, and then adjust our play in accordance to what we have determined," Esther answered. "We never study our opponents before a game but make our assessment during the initial minutes of the contest. Sometimes the competition calls for long range shooting, others fast breaks, while other games indicate that being a facilitator would be most appropriate. As soon as this is decided, we establish our pace and intensity to meet the challenge."

"Do you discover bickering or jealousy on the team?" another reporter asked.

"It has been only since we have been involved in press conferences such as this that this kind of question has ever been uttered," Esther responded with a smile. "I never thought there was another way to behave. I don't ever remember in all of our time together in the Hollow, at college and during games that there has ever been a remark of any kind that could be construed to be derogatory or demeaning in any way. We all are just the best of friends, and we never tire of one another. We all love the Lord with all our heart, mind and soul, and try to let our behavior send that message to all whom we come in contact. We are truly a diverse group with different family backgrounds and interest that have taken us into unique academic arenas, but the one true, succinct and everlasting bond among us is our love for Jesus Christ. That love sustains us all the while."

The media were getting an earful from the team members. They didn't seem to want to let Esther discontinue answering their numerous questions, but because of time restraints, it was now Mit's turn to face the group.

"My name is Mit Travers, and my home used to be in Bassett, Virginia, but later I lived in the jungle in south Costa Rica with my parents for a number of years where they were missionaries," she said as an introduction.

Many of the reporters had heard the rumor that Mit was not academically eligible to participate in college, because she was not adequately prepared so the first question broached that subject. "I guess you have discovered that the college curriculum is more difficult than your schooling in the jungle," a bearded reporter in the rear asked with a wry smile, feeling that he was going to expose something to his colleagues when she answered.

"I was obviously home schooled by my parents who used contemporary testing to be sure I was studying the same material as conventional students here in the United States," Mit related. "When I had fulfilled all requirements for graduation, I traveled to San Jose to take the SAT test in which I made nearly a perfect score. This was reassurance to my parents that they had satisfactorily taught me all that was required.

"Shortly before this event, Coach Anna and the Hollow girls came on a visit to the jungle, and offered me a scholarship to play soccer. You see my parents and I had talked about my attending college much during the preceding year only to put the subject aside, because my parents did not have the money to pay the tuition cost. Because of my high academic scores, Coach Anna thought about giving me an academic scholarship but decided otherwise. As the other girls, I have a full course load, and in addition I am assistant teacher in Spanish and assist some in sociology in the study of tribal behavior and languages. It's exciting to be on campus each day for additional learning."

It was almost like the shock of what she was telling them left them with their mouths wide open, because they thought they were going to hear from a backward and ignorant student raised beyond the limits of affluence. "Thank you so much for your articulate and eloquent answer to our question, which now clears up many derogatory assumptions about your past that many of us have had in our minds," a middle-age woman stated on behalf of all present to this young and strong, dark skinned blond, young lady who now fascinated the basketball and soccer world.

"You are considered to be the best college soccer player in the United States so my question to you is how did Coach Bosley discover you so far removed from what we call normal civilization?" an excited gentleman asked.

"One day the business manager of our mission came to the jungle to tell my parents and me that a group of girls from the United States was coming to Costa Rica to do evangelical work through basketball demonstrations," Mit responded. "If my parents would agree, these young ladies would come to the jungle as part of their trip. Of course, they did agree, and just as he was leaving, the business manager advised us that these girls played on the number one Division I basketball team in America. I was really excited, and in a few days we discovered another exciting part of their visit later that summer.

"You see, I have a great aunt who is the maid of the Bacon College athletic dormitory, and she was coming with the team. Their visit was overwhelming all the while. Soon after they arrived, and Coach Anna realized that I played soccer, she introduced the scholarship offer, which was an answer to our prayer. God works in such wonderful ways to give me the opportunity to be part of this wonderful family of special friends."

Several wanted to ask the next question, but the moderator called on a national reporter in a wheelchair on the left side. "Would you mind telling us about your rescue of the three missionaries?" he asked.

"Several months ago Coach Anna was contacted by our military to attempt a rescue of three missionaries who had been taken captive by a terrorist group," Mit answered. "Being a specialist in that type of military action, she agreed to undertake this mission following a clandestine meeting on the Blue Ridge Parkway with a high ranking official. One stipulation of her agreement to undertake this action was that she could select her own team. Obviously, she could have selected anyone, but she immediately determined that she wanted to take members of her athletic team at Bacon College. Of the team she could have selected any of us, but I was fortunate to become a part of this unique group headed for this covert mission.

"Training went well in the desert with long days of instruction, including parachuting both day and night until we were proficient as attested to by our most excellent drill instructors. Soon it was time to begin our rescue so we donned our camouflaged uniforms, strapped on our weapons and fastened our parachutes before boarding the aircraft to take us to Abedistan, the country where the missionaries were being held captive.

"While our training had almost been flawlessly completed, a glitch occurred immediately as we jumped out the door of the aircraft to head for a rendezvous point on the desert floor. My parachute got entangled so I had to strip it off and excite by back-up chute, but by doing same, I had no control over the direction I was falling. On the ground I was spotted by the Ab Didal who fired several shots in my direction before I escaped by hiding under the back side of a large sand dune. Soon though, I caught up with the others but not before that harrowing experience.

"Entering the town of Moraba in the still of the night, we discovered a hideout, and after a day or two of reconnoitering we headed for the streets wearing our full burquas among the other women in the marketplace. Meeting a young Christian lad was an important step in the final attempt to rescue the young missionaries, because he provided a wealth of information. In fact, his details of the prison and the captors were the most important reconnaissance we had, such that in the end he became most helpful as we made final plans.

"As you all know, our attempt was successful, and the three missionaries were rescued without getting hurt in the process. Obviously, God's hand was with us all the while."

The whole group was spellbound as they listened to this strong young lady relate the story of the rescue that truly got the world's attention. They really wanted to follow up on many other questions, because they knew that Mit had left out much of the story.

The story about Northern State was circulating rapidly among those present. A snowstorm precluded their travel by airplane from their usual departure site so the team used a rented van to travel to a nearby city only to discover that airport was closed, also. They had finally made it to an open airport, but even with no further interruptions they would not be able to arrive on time. They would be late everyone knew, but how much no one was certain.

Tournament officials were conferring about the situation in the lobby of the hotel with one stating, "If this were a snowstorm that involved more of our country, we could call the situation an emergency and alter the schedule. Because this storm only covers an isolated area, and unfortunately in the Northern State area, we could not declare a state of emergency. According to our regulations, unless a state of emergency is declared in areas involving at least two of the teams participating in the tournament, the games would be played as scheduled."

Coach Anna moved even closer to the officials further to hear what they were discussing. "It is clear that the situation surrounding Northern State only does not provide us with any avenue to change the schedule to accommodate their team. The rule is clear so the game must be played as scheduled this evening," one of the officials stated with the others agreeing.

"What is the latest time the team can arrive and not have to forfeit the game?" another official asked.

"It says here that a team of at least five members must be on the floor within fifteen minutes of the time the game was originally scheduled," the official answered.

Going to their hotel rooms, Coach Anna checked in with Maudie, and among other things told of the plight of the Northern State team that had never been to the final four tournament before, and now found themselves facing a forfeit, because of the unusual storm blanketing their area with considerable snow.

"Where is the team located now?" Maudie inquisitively asked.

"After finally getting a flight in a neighboring city, they were rerouted to Charleston, West Virginia, where they have been further delayed by a total disruption, because of security reasons," Coach Anna stated. "It seems that everything has gone wrong with the team."

Following this telephone call that was cut short, Maudie headed to her apartment to contact Thomas Miller who handled all of her benevolent work.

"This is Thomas Miller," he answered the telephone. "How may I help you?"

"Thomas, this is Maudie, and I have a unique emergency about which I want to talk to you," Maudie stated.

"How may I help?" Thomas asked again.

"A basketball team of girls is stranded in Charleston, West Virginia, and must be in New York in time to play in the semifinals of the ACUWAA tournament," Maudie excitedly related. "Could you handle all the details to get them to the arena in New York in time to play the Bacon team?"

"I'll do my best," he indicated, as they quickly discontinued their conversation.

Soon the television media were relating the story of the Northern State team that had never been involved in the finals now at risk to miss this chance, because of circumstances beyond their control. Finding the team sitting quietly in the West Virginia airport terminal, the reporter interviewed the coach. “I know that you are very much concerned that your team will not arrive at the game site in time to play,” the young sports’ reporter stated. “What is your next step to attempt to make it to your game?”

“It seems now that everything is beyond our control,” the dapperly dressed coach responded. “I have been in contact with the tournament officials who have advised me that my problems in travel do not rise to the level of an emergency covered in the ACUWAA rules so unless we arrive on time or within fifteen minutes of the scheduled game time, we will have to forfeit to Bacon College.”

“According to our records, your team has never been in the final four,” he stated. “Does this disappoint you?”

“Obviously, the whole team is devastated that after all these years we have the opportunity to play in this most prestigious tournament in our country only to be denied, because of a freak storm and a demented character running madly through the airport,” she answered. “We realize that as the clock ticks our hopes of participating fade away so we are coming to grips with our fate, albeit so very difficult.”

“Some like your chances of competing with the Bacon College team,” he stated. “What is your game plan against the best team in the country?”

“Of course, everybody knows that we had rather play one of the other teams and hopefully meet them in the finals, but that is not what is now in place,” she responded. “I will be like our team, I’m sure, as I’ll just find myself watching the Bacon players, and not concentrating on my coaching. They are a very special team of girls who have done so very much for women’s basketball. Except for television, I have never seen the team play. My very first act, when and if we do play, is to hug Coach Bosley for all she has done for basketball and for mankind in general.”

"If you don't get to play, you will really be disappointed, won't you?" he asked really knowing the answer.

"It will be the greatest disappointment in my life," she indicated. "I have been praying for help, but mainly to help me face our fate with strength and humble resolve."

The story was carried as breaking news so those around the country saw it. In the Bacon dormitory Maudie listened intently to determine the status of this team that found itself in a situation that seemed to prevent their experiencing a fulfillment of the dream of the various members of their team to play in such a prestigious tournament only reserved for the elite groups.

With the young reporter still on the scene to continue his report later regarding the plight of this group of girls, he and the girls noticed out the window two large helicopters hovering nearby, finally landing with directions from the ground crew. A young pilot stepped off the first aircraft after the engine was shut down, and headed directly toward an airport official. Following a brief meeting, the airport official moved toward the terminal, and soon found himself in the presence of the Northern State basketball team.

"I am Bob Reardon, the administrator of the terminal," he stated, introducing himself. "Who is the coach of your team?"

"My name is Emily Pearson," the coach of Northern State indicated.

"Because of your delay here and at another airport, a benevolent person has employed the services of two helicopters to take you to New York, hopefully, in time for the game," he stated. "To save time, we must hurry so I'll introduce you to the pilots outside. Right now our security personnel will clear you to leave the building."

Outside standing beside the aircraft, the administrator introduced the pilots. "This gentleman is John McCary from Raleigh, North Carolina, a retired colonel from the military, and this is Adam Tinsley from Bassett, Virginia, also a colonel who retired recently after the Iraq War. They will take you to your destination, so climb aboard, if you have no questions."

"I have many, many questions," Coach Pearson answered, "but I'll just hold them until later."

The young reporter was beside himself, so thrilled that he was the part of an exciting breaking story. Carried via television to all parts of the country, Maudie was pleased that action had been taken so swiftly. "It's going to be close," she mused, as she continued to listen to the various commentators on different channels.

"I have some breaking news regarding the Northern State women's basketball team," one television reporter indicated. "I am told that in order to save time upon arrival to meet time restraints, the team members are dressing on the helicopters. Spotters along the route tell us that the pilots are proceeding at full throttle, and now are over central Pennsylvania."

In the New York hotel the Bacon College girls were preparing to leave for the arena. Coach Anna called a meeting of the team, and stated, "I want you all to dress for the game here at the hotel."

Coach Anna turned on the television in her room to hear a sportscaster say, "This will be first forfeited game in the long and illustrious history of any major tournament, so all of us are grieving over this college team that finally made it to the final four only to be deprived of that honor they earned, because of no fault of their own. Even with no other delays whatsoever, we calculate that the Northern State University team will miss the deadline by forty-five minutes. It's such a shame!"

Even though many had given up on this major objective of getting the team to the arena on time, the two pilots were giving it their best shot. While in the war, John McCary had become a close friend of a gentleman who worked closely with the staff of the mayor of the city. Having dialed his number many times over the last several months, he remembered the number and dialed his friend on his cell phone. "This is Pete Dowdy," he stated, answering after the first ring.

"Pete, this is John McCary," he stated. "I need your help."

"What is it you need?" he asked.

"The Northern State University women's basketball team needs to get to the arena to play in the first round of the final four as quickly as possible, or they will have to forfeit the game," John stated swiftly. "Adam Tinsley and I have them on board our helicopters now flying them to New York."

"How may I help you?" Pete quickly asked.

"Could you discover a landing site as closely as possible to the arena?" John inquired.

"I can do that," Pete answered in a matter of fact manner.

"There is something else," John suddenly asked. "Could you clear a path on the streets to get them to the arena as quickly as possible?"

"That will be more difficult, but I will give it my best shot," Pete responded.

"That will be good enough," John replied. "Let me know about the landing site."

Adam Tinsley contacted John, "This is Adam; come in John."

"This is John; go ahead Adam," John replied.

"I have a very good friend in New Jersey who is a neophyte sports' reporter who has been trying to discover a good story to catapult him up the ranks," Adam related to John.

"Why don't you call him and give him first dibs on this story, if it's okay with Coach Pearson?" John indicated.

In a short while he advised John that she didn't mind, and further she stated that she would never be able to repay them for what they are doing for her and the university. "Tell her that this is not exactly free, because it will cost her tickets to a game next year," John laughingly replied.

News circulated swiftly at the hotel about the benevolent person sending the helicopters to get the Northern State University team so people were hovered around any available television set that was on. Soon the neophyte reporter released his report, indicating minute by minute, step by step, this entire bizarre situation that the basketball world was experiencing at this time. It was obvious to all concerned that the deadline was not going to be reached and that the team in the end would have to forfeit the contest, by far the most important game of their school's history.

The arena had been packed for more than two hours and now as the countdown for game time was in progress, quiet filled the arena that had been the site of the best games over the years. Everyone was aware of what was taking place.

In the meantime Coach Anna assembled her group in her room for a most important meeting. "During the last several hours we have heard progress reports of the Northern State team, as they attempt to travel to New York for their game. Regardless of their effort, the results seem to point to the outcome that they can't arrive on time for the game with us," she stated, while sitting on the side of her bed. "It is obvious that the team will not arrive on time, as indicated by the young reporter who has suddenly emerged on the scene who seems to know every detail of their travels. I have read the forfeiture portion of the ACUWAA rule book, and my interpretation is that unless a team arrives at the site of the contest within fifteen minutes after the advertised game time, that team forfeits the game to its opponent. But the rule does not indicate what the penalty is if both teams fail to meet the guideline of this particular rule.

"It is a heart wrenching situation for Northern State, and we are a part of this difficult situation. What do you girls think?" Coach Anna asked to generate a discussion among the team.

"Pastor Josh has always taught us to do two things, if we didn't do anything else: to love the Lord with all our heart, mind and soul and to love our neighbor as ourselves," Dorothy immediately stated looking directly at her coach. "Love is the key to an abundant life."

"When I was in the jungle, from time to time various situations would emerge to preclude both teams being in place for a soccer match so the other team would just wait on its opponent to get in place," Mit commented. "We just made our own rules with compassion for the team that was having difficulty."

"We have never been involved in a forfeiture, but I believe it would leave all of us with an empty feeling, if we became the victor, because another team forfeited to us because it was late for a contest," Esther pointed out. "I know the ACUWAA has to follow its own rules, but it doesn't seem that these man made rules trump those that God has passed on to us as we live on His creation."

After several of the girls made comments Esther then spoke up again. "While we prepare to leave for the arena, why don't you call the ACUWAA official at the game to indicate that we waive our rights regarding the rule regarding punctuality and will play whenever the Northern State team is ready."

"That's a good idea," Coach Anna stated, as she could observe nods from the other team members.

On her cell phone as the team headed downstairs to load the bus to travel a short distance to the arena, Coach Anna got the ACUWAA official on the line. "This is Anna Bosley of Bacon College," she indicated.

"I am Joseph Torrence," he replied. "How may I help you?"

"We are very much concerned about Northern State's travel problems," she stated. "We want to let you know that we waive any of our rights regarding this punctuality rule and will play whenever they arrive."

"I wish it were that simple," he responded. "The decision of whether or not there is a forfeiture is based only on the late arrival of a team."

Coach Anna wanted to say something else but decided to hold her comment until she talked to the girls again. Disembarking near the arena's main entrance, those standing outside were surprised when the team followed their coach to a nearby hamburger restaurant with several television sets turned to the sports' channel. The young reporter still held top billing as the channels included his report as breaking news.

"Time is the only variable the courageous helicopter pilots with the Northern State team can't overcome," the young reporter noted. "Racing through the dark sky headed for the bright lights of the 'big apple' still leaves them short of their game time goal, but they continue anyway toward a landing site not yet fully determined. After a marvelous season they wish it did not have to end this way, but they have given it their best effort with the help of a most generous benevolent act.

"One might ask, what is the rush now, because all the world knows that it's absolutely impossible to get to the game on time? The Northern State team has just acquiesced totally and are now being moved along toward their destiny by their highly respected pilot friends."

The Bacon team found a booth and pushed a table nearby, and when all were seated, they realized that everyone in the restaurant was watching what they were doing. One man turned to his wife and asked, "Isn't that the Bacon team?"

"That's the team, I'm sure," she replied.

"They should be in the arena preparing for the game," he stated.

"They don't seem to be in a hurry, because they are very relaxed and seem to be discussing something," she commented.

Meanwhile, in the corner of this short order diner, the team began its deep contemplation regarding this very bizarre situation.

"I have great empathy for the Northern State team with all it has had to overcome to get to this point only to be told, as it stands now, that it just arrived too late, and therefore, would have to forfeit its game," Coach Anna stated. "Unless any of you disapprove, I suggest that we remain in this restaurant until Northern State arrives, and the two teams will enter the arena at the same time. We'll just do what we consider the honorable thing and let the officials ponder the outcome."

The girls liked the idea, believing that it was the best position available as they utilized the precepts of the Scriptures.

Soon the television commentators were advising their viewing audience that while there was monumental concern regarding the Northern State team's arrival on time, now the Bacon team had not shown up as scheduled. One reporter had discovered that the coach of Bacon had called an official earlier to get an interpretation of the rule. "Now we have both teams that will be late," he stated. "Something must have happened to the Bacon team on the way to the arena."

Back at Bacon the students and community folks were gathered in the coliseum to watch the semifinals on the large screen. The ringing of the cell phone of Dr. Damond pierced the quiet. "This is John Damond," he answered.

"This is Anna calling from New York," the coach stated.

"Your team should be on the floor, shouldn't it?" he stated and asked.

"That's what I'm calling about," she replied. "We are much concerned about the Northern State team that has tried in vain to get to the game site on time to be thwarted at every corner, so we discussed the situation and decided to do the honorable thing."

"What is that?" he asked.

"We have decided to wait for the arrival of the Northern State team and go on the floor at the same time," she indicated. "There is no rule that applies to both teams being late for a game."

"We all here at Bacon have discussed the situation all day, and have really had much empathy for your opponent," the president stated. "Sometimes in life one has to step up to the plate, and you all are doing just that. Would you mind holding on the line while I advise everyone here in the coliseum what you all are doing?"

Walking to the front of this large group, he took the microphone to tell them what was taking place in New York. Upon completion of his report there were shouts, foot stomping, yells and just shrill sounds exuding their joy and appreciation of the Bacon team for putting honor before victory, others before selves, and love paramount in their actions. It was an enormous vote of confidence for the team and a genuine boost to its morale.

Secrets on New York streets are short lived, and it was especially true in this case, as a reporter and cameraman burst into the small short order restaurant on the corner. By this time the restaurant was very crowded now filled with curious observers. The proprietor had already made a picture of the Bacon team to put on his wall alongside several other celebrated groups over the years.

Several activities were taking place at the same time. The manager of the arena was desperately trying to calm the anxious crowd awaiting this very important semi-final game, while the ACUWAA officials were scampering to determine their next move. Suddenly, a large screen was unveiled so that the capacity crowd could view what was taking place outside the arena regarding the game.

The new focus was not on the anticipated basketball game but on the seemingly bizarre behavior of the Bacon College team that certainly was on time for the contest, but now sat in a corner of a restaurant within the shadows of the arena. "What is your team doing sitting here and not in the arena," the lanky reporter asked, still not having gotten in a good position to ask questions, because of the crowd that had become somewhat disorderly. It was a very crowded diner, the manager now witnessing the most excitement ever in his more than fifty-year history.

"We are awaiting the arrival of the Northern State team," Coach Anna responded, as the team of girls watched her.

"But you will have to forfeit the game, if you are not on time," the reporter stated.

"We think that Northern State has done everything possible to arrive on time, but just hasn't made it," Coach Anna indicated.

"All of us would agree with that assessment," he said, "but you all had no problems in your travel from Virginia to New York for the game,"

"We had an excellent trip to this beautiful city," Coach Anna replied, still not pointing out the real reason for their waiting outside the arena.

Meanwhile, much activity was evident in the arena itself as the capacity crowd viewed the wide screen, while at the same time observing what was taking place on one end of the floor. Five ACUWAA officials were engrossed in a strong conversation concerning the forfeiture rule, as they, too, now understood what the Bacon team was doing. On the brink of uncivil behavior by the up to this time very patient spectators, the officials knew that a decision had to be made quickly so that order could be maintained.

Another report from the neophyte journalist added much to the whole scenario. The Northern State team had landed on a roof several blocks away and would be escorted by the NYPD to the arena. Too much time had elapsed earlier, but all who participated in this unusual adventure continued in their efforts as though they had met the challenge. When those in attendance saw all this action on the wide screen, they began to shout in unison, "Play ball!" Cheers filled the arena as the team members disembarked the helicopters that had precariously landed on a building several streets way.

Abruptly, getting up from their seats in the restaurant to the surprise of the TV reporter, those in the crowded restaurant made way for the Bacon team to depart. From the restaurant they headed directly to the main entrance where they were escorted by a guard to their dressing room. "The time is considerably beyond the limits of a forfeit, so our presence now will not impact on the decision regarding the Northern State team," Coach Anna stated. "Hanna, you take our equipment, and the team will follow you in a couple of minutes."

Following a special prayer by Esther, the team hugged each other for a long time. In the arena Hanna received a standing ovation that was continued until the team arrived. Everyone present knew that Bacon's arrival on the floor was nearly an hour after the scheduled time of the game. It was just an eerie time for the Bacon team that had somewhat defied the rules to attempt to protect another team having difficulty meeting the demands of the schedule. The hungry fans watched in quiet repose as serenity now replaced an atmosphere of sheer bedlam.

"It's now up to the officials," Coach Anna said to Hanna.

"You know," Hanna said, "I never cease to be amazed at your leadership wherein your intuitive skills always come from the heart."

"I wish I could take credit for that," she replied, "but I have learned it from our Esther who is the powerful leader of our team."

"I pinch myself every day," Hanna said. "I can't believe that I am a part of this most outstanding team of girls."

The sound of sirens filled the air as the Northern State team was escorted by New York's finest, traversing the middle of the streets now being vacated by the courteous drivers on this night. Courtesy was not one of the characteristics of Big Apple drivers, but on this night the objective caused the occupants on the streets to succumb to their heart, as they made room for this special team to get to the arena.

In the arena the officials could be seen, as they huddled in the corner of the court near where the Bacon team was warming up. The more than one hour delay didn't seem to be an important issue for the fans, as they watched this small mountain team, now forgetting about not meeting the time restraints of the game.

Basketball fans outside the arena began to make a lane for the Northern State team, as they arrived with sirens still blowing loudly and blue police car lights flashing from several vehicles. Jogging with their belongings in backpacks, the Northern State team entered the arena to a standing ovation of everyone in attendance. Giving this beleaguered team the full respect it deserved, Coach Anna pulled her team off the floor to sit on the bench, while the Northern State team went on the court for practice.

While the Northern State team was going through its drills, an official came over and pulled the coach to the side, explaining to her what had happened and that a group of officials were now deciding on Northern State's fate. As he was talking, they both looked at the Bacon team so those in attendance could surmise what was being discussed. In a few minutes the official departed, and the Northern State coach walked directly to Coach Anna.

"My name is Emily Pearson," she said almost before shaking the hand of Coach Anna.

"I am Anna Bosley," Coach Anna responded.

"The official just told me that you just arrived for the game, also, so that now both teams were late," Emily stated. "I can't believe that anyone would do that possibly causing your team to be penalized with a forfeit, also."

"It was an easy decision, because Jesus taught us to love our neighbor as ourselves, and in this case our neighbor is the Northern State team," Coach Anna said.

"But your team has never lost a game," Emily indicated in a high pitched voice.

"That is not the important thing in this situation," Coach Anna replied.

Before the capacity crowd of serious basketball fans, Emily gave Coach Anna a strong and generous bear hug that prompted the fans to stand and applaud all over again. Following this scene of love, the entire Bacon team moved on the court and made their rounds hugging each of the Northern State girls. It was an emotional scene that unfolded on the court, as the officials continued their deliberation.

Suddenly, the warm atmosphere changed when a loud voice of a fan started a chant, "Let them play!" The chant was continued getting louder and louder and with more of a hostile tone that seemingly was directed toward the officials still trying to make a decision regarding the double forfeit or to permit them to play. One could easily discern that chaos was just around the corner, as hand clapping was joined by foot stomping. An official assessed the situation by looking around the vast arena to see the faces of those in attendance. It was not a pleasant sight.

Without warning, the pocket of officials was bombarded with all kinds of missiles tossed in their direction. Announcements pleading with the fans to refrain from throwing objects went unheeded. From the stands came several onto the floor now leading cheers as though they had been practicing for this moment for weeks. It was quickly turning into a mob scene, now almost out of control. In the midst of this total bedlam came an announcement, "The officials have decided that the game would be played, because both teams had failed to the meet the time schedule. All spectators are requested to go back to their seats."

Not only did Bacon defeat Northern State in the semifinals, but won handily the national championship two nights later with a groundswell of support from their many friends they had made over the years. It provided a time for a grand old reunion following the final game in a large dining area financed by Maudie, who delighted in sharing her wealth with others. Many got to meet the captured missionaries, the Liggons, the Northys, military personnel, Bacon friends, and so many others for the first time. And of course, Jewel Throneberry was present to write a big article for her Margone Magazine.

SOCCER TIME

Not having time to catch their breath, the soccer team headed to Pittsburgh and onto St. Louis for their initial games in this new sport. The send-off was a replication of those remembered by the basketball players, because all the students and many from the neighborhood were on hand to wish the group well. Dr. Damond was ecstatic, because now the soccer season was beginning so the benevolent person would know that Bacon College was living up to its agreement when it accepted the huge anonymous gift of money to start a soccer program. Competing on the Division I level was the second part of the stipulations for accepting the money.

Coach Anna had learned along the way not to doubt these young ladies regarding any situation, but today she knew there was much riding on the way they performed their very first intercollegiate competition in soccer. In preseason games they had looked very good, but could they live up to the high touting thrust on them by the media? There was so much pressure on Mit who was dubbed the best female soccer player in college, and she had not even played a single game.

It was just a most beautiful morning as they traveled I81 toward Roanoke. Wanting to express her love for God more, Coach Anna pulled off the road to an overlook where they all disembarked. Please hold hands, as I read this wonderful section of our Scriptures, Psalm 112:

1 Praise the LORD!
Happy are those who fear the LORD,
who greatly delight in his commandments.

2 *Their descendants will be mighty in the land;*
the generation of the upright will be blessed.
3 Wealth and riches
4 are in their houses,
and their righteousness endures forever.
4 *They rise in the darkness as a light for the upright;*
they are gracious, merciful, and righteous.
5 *It is well with those who deal generously and lend,*
who conduct their affairs with justice.
6 *For the righteous will never be moved;*
they will be remembered forever.
7 *They are not afraid of evil tidings;*
their hearts are firm, secure in the LORD.
8 *Their hearts are steady, they will not be afraid;*
in the end they will look in triumph on their foes.
9 *They have distributed freely, they have given to the poor;*
their righteousness endures forever;
their horn is exalted in honor.
10 *The wicked see it and are angry;*
they gnash their teeth and melt away;
the desire of the wicked comes to nothing.

It was a touching scene as sentence prayers were rendered, and Mit closed with a very eloquent prayer.

A small plane carried them to Pittsburgh where they landed smoothly, grabbed their luggage and headed to their motel outside the city. After a brief rest the group went directly to the field, which to the surprise of the team, the small stadium was filled to capacity. Many photographers were on hand, and there was an inordinate number of young people present.

Caroline College had a strong reputation as being a perennial powerhouse in soccer, always being in the top ten all season so little upstart Bacon would be getting a true test. Coach Anna spotted her counterpart on the opposite sideline so she ran over to shake her hand and wish her well.

"I am Anna Bosley, the coach of Bacon," Coach Anna said, just as the Caroline coach turned around.

"I'm Nancy Doones," the coach replied, only then to turn away and completely ignore Coach Anna.

Waiting to render a warmer and more lengthy greeting, Coach Anna stood only a couple of feet from the Caroline coach only to be ignored totally, as though she wasn't even present. Soon Coach Anna turned and ran back to her group on the other side of the field.

All the while she thought, "That was a very strange greeting, especially for a host coach. She must have a team problem and was preoccupied in handling a bad situation."

The darling of the media photographers on this day was Mit, who seemed to be dealing with all of the attention much like Esther had done during the past two years in basketball. The team really did look sharp as they had inserted unique maneuvers similar to the basketball team that had entertained fans each time they played.

The tri-captains of Bacon, Mit, Marsha and Esther, moved to the middle of the field upon the direction of the referee. "I can't believe that I have these three superb young ladies on my soccer team," Coach Anna mused. "Not only are they superior athletes, but they are genuine human beings, displaying extremely wholesome characteristics."

In the middle of the field Coach Anna was witnessing another setting that caused much concern. The Caroline girls turned and ran off the field just ignoring an attempt to shake hands by the Bacon girls. Several reporters noticed the rude behavior, and a couple approached Coach Anna about the situation, but she would only say that athletes sometimes concentrate so hard on contests they lose perspective.

None of the players mentioned the snubbing by the Caroline team in the huddle before the game. When the team moved to take their positions on the field, Coach Anna thought, "They never mention anything that would even remotely be construed as being negative."

Although Marsha was a slow starter, Mit, Esther, Dorothy, Maggie and the others, came off the blocks in full competitive mode. An opponent must be ready. Not having totally forgotten the behavior of the Caroline team, Coach Anna began intently to watch her team perform for the first time in college competition. Even though she had observed them in action many times on the practice field, what she was seeing today was a very fierce determination that displayed an attack seldom seen on the soccer field.

Mit was definitely in charge so the spectators who had any doubts about her ability could put them aside, because as one reporter stated within earshot of Coach Anna, "That Mit is for real, that's for sure."

For real she was, as she had scored two goals in a matter of minutes, loving every minute of the competition that had blossomed in the jungle of Costa Rica. The slight smile revealed the fun she was having playing her main sport. With a fierce illegal bump by a Caroline player, Mit was preparing to take a penalty kick from about fifty feet from the goal.

"I remember reading in the Mission Magazine about the way she addressed a penalty kick," Coach Anna thought. "I wonder whether or not she will approach this kick in similar fashion."

Surely enough, there was her foot sliding back and forth as she prepared to approach the ball. Faking one direction and kicking the other, the goalie was drawn out of place; thus the team had made its third goal.

Coach Anna played all team members liberally as the Caroline team became more frustrated all the while. When the opponent believed it was in position to mount a drive of some consequence, Marsha had warmed up and took charge with Bacon making two other goals, now leading 5 to 0. What a beginning of the soccer season!

At the conclusion of the game Coach Anna huddled with her team to praise them for their efforts and to have prayer before the team went to the middle of the field to congratulate their opponent. When she turned to go to middle of the field, Caroline had already gone to the locker room. "This is the third situation today that causes me to be concerned about our relationship with this college team," Coach Anna thought. "Some of the tactics used by the other team left much to be desired regarding sportsmanship, and now that they have failed to show their respect at the end of the game adds more to the mystery."

Headlines and articles on the sports' pages the next morning told the whole story that Bacon College lived up to its preseason billing by trouncing powerful Caroline College 5-0 before a packed stadium.

> "Most of the soccer fans came to see the giant slay the elf, but all of us should know better by now. Never underestimate the quality of play of little Bacon College who completely annihilated a perennial powerhouse in soccer year after year. For all who witnessed this drubbing of mass proportions the elf totally destroyed the giant. There was enough praise to go around to the entire team mostly made up of the country's best basketball team, but one would be remiss not to shower their mighty one with all kinds of plaudits. Mit Travers is a phenomenal player that only comes along ever so often. What a display of talent!
>
> "But wait! When I thought I had seen it all, a young lady named Marsha seemed to have gotten her second wind so she dominated the last portion of the match. It was a 'salt and pepper' afternoon under the spring's beautiful sky as Marsha took over when Mit departed the contest. But wait again! Those on the Bacon team, whom we have grown to love dearly who play on the basketball team, traded their basketball uniforms and participated as though soccer was their primary sport. I have often heard that good

athletes who play basketball can learn to play other sports well. That holds true for this group."

Tucked away on the third page of the sports' section was another article, "What about Sportsmanship?" that caught Coach Anna's eye.

"I am always amazed at the quality of sportsmanship in collegiate contests that is displayed by the teams each year. If I had the authority, I would present the most prestigious trophy of them all to the team that displays the best sportsmanship for the year. While no one else seemed to notice conduct not becoming to a collegiate team, I noticed a coolness shown toward the small Bacon College during its match with Caroline yesterday. Although I was not close enough to hear the brief greetings by the host coach, the time it consumed would lead one to believe that it was less than overly cordial.

"Watching through the remainder of the game for further hints of rude, if not crude, conduct on the field seemed to show more and more malevolence as the game proceeded. While this was obviously occurring on the one hand, a special effort was being exhibited by the small mountain college to express their love for their opponents. But it wasn't until the end of the game that the bizarre behavior of Caroline College toward the humble team from Bacon manifested itself another time, thus solidifying my belief that something was awry.

"After the Bacon College team huddled briefly to collect themselves, they turned to line up to congratulate their opponent on a good game to discover that the Caroline College players were leaving the field.

"Observing this strange behavior, I immediately headed toward Coach Anna Bosley to get her reaction. 'The Caroline team certainly behaved in an unusual fashion at the end of the game, didn't they?' I asked.

"'I believe they were just tired so they headed directly to the locker room to rest,' Coach Anna responded.

"'Your greeting with your counterpart at the beginning of the game left much to be desired, didn't it?' I inquired.

"'The Caroline Coach was working on some conflict on the team when we first greeted,' Coach Anna stated, 'I'm sure under other circumstances we would have generated a longer conversation.'"

On the outskirts of the St. Louis metropolitan area, the team made its way to the entrance of a huge soccer arena the next day. By this time the media were feverishly trying to assemble all the "moving parts" of the poor sportsmanship article; thus, there were several questions thrust at Coach Anna before they were entirely in the arena.

A general question was fired by an enthusiastic reporter who met her right in the doorway. "Why do you think you are hated so much by the other colleges and universities in basketball and soccer?"

"I really don't believe that we are hated," Coach Anna responded. Hearing numerous questions coming from the large assembly of reporters, Coach Anna advised that she would answer their interrogatories after the game with Latvary University.

The girls dressed in their blue and gold uniforms after which Coach Anna addressed the entire group. "I am so very excited to be your coach in soccer," she stated. "You know what I love the most about all of you. The most important part of your entire being is to follow the precepts and guidelines set forth by Jesus in the Bible. One of the most important, if not the most important, directions presented by Jesus is found in Matthew 22:

34 When the Pharisees heard that he had silenced the Sadducees, they gathered together,
35 and one of them, a lawyer, asked him a question to test him.
36 "Teacher, which commandment in the law is the greatest?"
37 He said to him, "'You shall love the Lord your God with all your heart, and with all your soul, and with all your mind.'
38 This is the greatest and first commandment.
39 And a second is like it: 'You shall love your neighbor as yourself.'
40 On these two commandments hang all the law and the prophets."

"Scripturally, one can find many helpful verses that will give direction to one's life," she advised. "The way one conducts herself is included in the assessment of one's own reputation that builds one block at a time over the years. When an opposing team member seems to be having difficulty meeting the scriptural guidelines, we have to be ready to forgive, something that Jesus tells us can be done over and over again. Remember that the forgiveness bucket is always full regardless of how many times you ask and receive same."

The Bacon team members were astute enough to understand what Coach Anna was trying to reveal to them, because they observed the rude behavior of their previous opponent, too. Some thought that she was advising them that similar behavior might be forthcoming in other games during the season.

But she didn't really believe similar rude conduct would be forthcoming so soon; however, here Coach Anna's extended hand was even ignored by her counterpart. Running back to her side of the field, she wondered aloud, "What has Bacon done to upset now the second team we are playing this new season?"

Changing the personnel for the midfield meeting with the referees, Coach Anna thought that this might elicit a different response from the other team. This didn't happen, because the other girls turned and headed directly to their sidelines at the termination of the meeting. Obviously, the reporters were getting a full view of the whole sorry scenario.

On the third trip down the field Mit let go a powerful kick into the corner of the net such that the fans were stunned not only that Bacon had scored so quickly, but because of the power behind the ball unleashed by Mit. It was such a rough game that the referees called time out and cautioned the Latvary players. On a toss in Mit got the ball and took it down the sideline, and seeing Esther headed toward the middle at about a forty-five-degree angle, she passed with a left-footed kick to Esther who kicked it passed the out-of-place goalie. This was a continuation of a lopsided score in favor of Bacon.

Not wanting to have a repeat of the previous game end, Coach Anna immediately instructed Bacon to go to the middle of the field for the congratulatory alignment only to see the Latvary team being called off the field by their coach. "It's going to be a difficult news conference that I have promised to the large number of media," Coach Anna thought, as she went with the team to the locker room with Hanna leading the way.

Soon she was back on the field surrounded by her girls fielding questions from the media. "How can you explain your complete dominance in your first two soccer matches ever for Bacon College?" a young reporter asked.

"Soccer is a special sport for our group just as basketball for its season, so they practice hard to succeed," she replied. "Please know that two games does not a season make."

"You will have the youngest team on the field each time you play, yet when we look at your group they participate as though they are much older," a young athletic female stated. "How is it that you can succeed with such a group when others over the years have failed?"

"Most of our players come from our basketball program," she replied. "Of course, Mit comes from the jungle of Costa Rica."

Before Coach Anna could say more, a well known reporter interrupted her answer by asking, "Do you think this is the reason why your two opponents so far are less than cordial to you all?"

What a shock! Coach Anna was getting some serious perspicacity from an unusual source, albeit shedding some light on the rude comportment of the only two opponents of this new season. "It is such a marvelous experience for us to travel to our opponent's campus to play this special game of soccer," she stated, really trying to avoid any indication that she was cognizant that the other teams had displayed poor behavior. "Competition sometimes causes us to be more anxious than at other times in our lives. Please know that we are greatly appreciative of the host schools, and look forward to their presence on our small mountain campus. Please excuse me and my girls so we can get to the airport for our flight back home this evening."

Even though they arrived very late on the Bacon campus, the students and staff were in place for a midnight greeting and celebration, including pizza purchased by the benevolent person. With the group was Dr. Damond who whispered in Coach Anna's ear that he wanted to see her early the next day.

"It was going to be a different kind of meeting with Dr. Damond," Coach Anna thought during the revelry, as all joined the merriment.

Coach Anna met Dr. Damond at his office door at seven o'clock the next morning. "Good morning, Dr. Damond," Coach Anna said, as he placed the key in the door.

"Good morning to you," he replied. "Thank you for coming in early."

In his office he placed his briefcase on the desk, pulled up a chair for Coach Anna and then moved a chair near hers in front of his huge executive desk. "Something happened yesterday that I want to talk to you about," he stated, as he was looking directly at his coach now. "I received an anonymous call yesterday from one who indicated that she was an attorney who was present at a meeting of several attorneys who are joining together to file a suit against Bacon College. The anonymous attorney indicated that she was not privy to all the details about the suit except that she was very much aware that it involved the successful sports' program of the college."

"What seems to be the matter?" Coach Anna asked, not really knowing what to say at this juncture.

"The attorney said that the group discussed several avenues to approach a suit, and to her knowledge nothing had been decided at this point," Dr. Damond indicated.

"Did she give any details of areas of concern?" Coach Anna asked.

"I didn't want to press her too much," he answered, "because I thought she might hang up. She did tell me that she would contact me again when she had some more concrete information."

"That sounds good," Coach Anna noted, "however, this still does not answer the broader question of what is wrong to justify a lawsuit."

"When we are challenged regarding our athletic program, I feel so good that you always do all things according to the rules, never dealing with any gray area," Dr. Damond said to his coach in such a praising tone.

"We have the most qualified teams one could ever assemble," Coach Anna boastfully stated.

"I know we do. Now let me show you something," he stated, as he turned to retrieve his briefcase. Pulling out the morning newspaper, he turned to the sports' page to show her the story about the previous day's soccer victory. This one is a good story, but a companion story on the second page of the paper is different, entitled, "Too Much of a Champ."

> "When does a team become too much of a champ? In recent years soccer has become a major sport in our colleges and universities throughout the land with many becoming powerhouses after years of building up their programs. Within the guidelines set forth by the ACUWAA, they press forward wanting some way to get the edge, which means more victories for their institution. In truth the name of the game any more is winning, almost winning at all costs.
>
> "But how far will teams go to become a winner which means much more money for their particular colleges or universities? At what point does jealousy play a larger role than necessary in our college athletic environment? Obviously, these are appropriate questions to be raised, particularly in today's competitive climate on the women's soccer field.
>
> "I was in Pittsburgh to watch the Bacon College contest in soccer with Caroline College. On the field was a seasoned team of girls who had played on a championship team for numerous years in the past playing a very young team of athletes from all places, the mountains where the Hollow is located. You have heard of the Hollow before, I'm sure, because that is from where the most outstanding girls' basketball team came. During the last two years. this team of young ladies has completely mesmerized the entire sports' world, winning two national championships while not losing a single game.

"To the chagrin of naysayers the college withstood a thorough investigation by the ACUWAA, yet there still more than lingers a feeling that no college could do what the small Bacon College has done by following the rules completely. Yet, they have done all that is expected of them according to the official sanctioning body for women athletics. But there is much unrest in the ranks as displayed at the two soccer matches involving Bacon College and two powerful teams from Pittsburgh and St. Louis during the past two days.

"What will be the bigger question now? Let me see if I can cast in words for you. How is it that a very small mountain school can win all of its basketball games after never having a team before last year? Now, how can this small mountain college team field a world class soccer team its very first year of competition after never having a soccer program before? These obviously are very appropriate questions to ask.

"Watching these soccer matches in two different parts of the country and witnessing a common demeanor of both opponents of Bacon College, leads me to believe there is a conspiracy of some kind underfoot. Two teams from separate areas would not display rude and demeaning behavior in the same manner, if they were not following the same script.

"No one is talking now but jealousy and pride carry one to great depts. Watch out to see what is in store next for this team from the mountains, as they do something no other team has ever done, win all games in two sports.

"Will ugliness continue on the soccer field?"

"What do you make of this article?" Dr. Damond asked, as he looked at Coach Anna.

"I have no idea whatsoever," she replied.

"Did you see, hear or feel that there is some kind of conspiracy in progress when you played the two teams?" Dr. Damond asked, trying to glean anything that would help explain the article. "Sometimes we read that reporters embellish articles such that they fail to reveal the important facts of a story."

"I hope that is the case here," Coach Anna quickly added.

"I do, too," he replied.

"Both of our teams are comprised of the most adorable young people one would ever want to meet," Coach Anna said. "They would not do anything that anyone would construe to be harmful to another person. I am so very proud of them as they represent Bacon College here and at other colleges and universities to play basketball and soccer. I hope that you can find time to go with us on an away game sometime in the near future."

"I would love to do that," he replied with a wide smile.

FRIDAY

Never being judgmental, the soccer team had not interpreted the behavior of their two opponents with any animosity whatsoever. It fact, the bizarre behavior had not been broached in any conversation among them at any time. It wasn't that they were very naïve, but that they never wanted to judge the conduct of others in any way except that of goodness.

It was Friday so they were headed for the Hollow, as usual, following practice before a large crowd in their stadium built with funds given by the anonymous donor. Watching them go through their drills with perfect precision, Coach Anna joyfully stood on the sideline observing all the while. "Esther, Marsha and Mit always remain very serious about their practice sessions, but among the others much teasing was generated," Coach Anna thought, admiring her unique team of athletes.

In the Hollow a crowded hillside caused Coach Anna to park the college van farther down the roadway than usual. "There appear to be more people here this evening," she said to Maudie, who was sporting a wide smile.

"More and more people want to be a part of this special, yet remote, group of people," Maudie responded. "It's such a thrill to come here each Friday to dine with them."

With the girls walking swiftly up ahead, Coach Anna noted, "They don't do things in the Hollow the same way as the rest of the world. I loved this place when I first visited, and each trip my adoration is increased immensely."

Maudie was an old woman, but here she was fully recovered from her illness, walking stride for stride with the most physically fit young lady anywhere. "You seem to have fully recovered from your illness," Coach Anna stated.

"Yes, I have," she indicated. "I walk each day to build myself up physically."

By the time they reached the entrance of the little church, greetings were still being given, as lengthy bear hugs were still underway as moms and dads showed their love for their children. And of course, when Maudie and Coach Anna made their appearance, the whole scene was replicated.

Josh and Charlene backed away and stood assessing the whole situation. "We have several more people than usual," Charlene said.

"Each Friday more and more show up for this affair that was begun more than ten years ago to help the Hollow folks to have fellowship with one another," Josh responded. "You know, Jesus indicated to us that we are to love our neighbor as ourselves so in doing this we have just expanded our neighborhood as we used to know it."

"I am always amazed at what you do in the Hollow," Charlene said, as she squeezed his hand. "Have you noticed that James spends more and more time with Coach Anna each Friday?"

"I have observed that, too," Josh indicated. "He is now talking with her near the window."

"Their conversation seems to be humorous, because they always laugh a lot," Charlene noted. "Do you think anything will develop from this relationship?"

"Wouldn't it be a miracle, if it did?" Josh said, as he and Charlene moved to the front of the church, speaking to everyone along the way.

The little church was bulging at the walls as more and more people joined with the Hollow folks for fellowship again on this Friday. After a delicious dinner of food from Tiger Foods and a second distribution company and covered dishes brought by many from the community, Josh advised the group that he wanted to make a few remarks. Everyone just loved his compassionate comments and scripture passages he selected.

"We have been so blessed to have this large number of folks with us this evening," he stated in his very soft voice, always presenting a very humble appearance that matched what was in his heart. "When Jesus related to us about the new covenant, he spoke boldly about love found in Matthew 22. With the augmentation of the Ten Commandments love now was at the forefront of demands on us as we relate to one another."

Expounding on the love concept several minutes, Josh concluded his remarks by reading 1 Corinthians 13:

1 *If I speak in the tongues of mortals and of angels, but do not*
have love, I am a noisy gong or a clanging cymbal.
2 *And if I have prophetic powers, and understand all*
mysteries and all knowledge, and if I have all faith, so as to
remove mountains, but do not have love, I am nothing.
3 *If I give away all my possessions, and if I hand over my*
body so that I may boast, but do not have love, I gain
nothing.
4 *Love is patient; love is kind; love is not envious or boastful*
or arrogant
5 *or rude. It does not insist on its own way; it is not irritable*
or resentful;
6 *it does not rejoice in wrongdoing, but rejoices in the truth.*
7 *It bears all things, believes all things, hopes all things,*
endures all things.
8 *Love never ends. But as for prophecies, they will come to an*
end; as for tongues, they will cease; as for knowledge, it will
come to an end.
9 *For we know only in part, and we prophesy only in part;*
10 *but when the complete comes, the partial will come to an*
end.

11 When I was a child, I spoke like a child, I thought like a child, I reasoned like a child; when I became an adult, I put an end to childish ways.
12 For now we see in a mirror, dimly, but then we will see face to face. Now I know only in part; then I will know fully, even as I have been fully known.
13 And now faith, hope, and love abide, these three; and the greatest of these is love.

After Josh would call on reports from various people in the group, more and more people wanted to be added to the group each week. On this evening Coach Anna reported on the visitation by the Wasian girls, and included in her statements information about the mysterious summer activity request by the president of Wasi involving the basketball team. "President Kantitore is going to call me during the next several days to invite us to participate in some kind of special program that he believes will improve the quality of basketball skills of their young ladies," she stated. "It seems that he wants us to train the girls here for a few weeks and then to go there for his program. I'll let you all know what transpires."

Leaving Coach Anna, James moved to the front to advise the group that he and the orphan children were making good progress in clearing a trail to the abandoned coal mine nearest the church. "We have begun to add additional supports to preclude a cave in," James told the group, many who knew that his limp was caused by the failure of mine timbers to support a mine roof that caved in on him years ago. "We are working on smoothing the area, including diverting the free flowing underground water. Of course, the orphan children are very energetic and exhibit much enthusiasm in their work."

Robert stood up and in a loud voice reported, "You will notice that our free-flowing mountain stream now has collection areas to provide points along the stream for the native trout to make beds to hatch their eggs. All that has been done thus far is to move rocks to reduce the flow down the hill so that pools were made in several places down the slope. As you all know, there are hundreds of native trout in the stream, and our effort should increase the number immensely."

"There is much interest in having a Vacation Bible School program and invite those in other neighborhoods to attend," Charlene announced. "Several of you have suggested that we extend the program for two weeks so that we can schedule all of the activities. Regarding the date, it would appear that the first two weeks of June would be most advantageous so that our college students can be a part of the activities."

Earlier Bob Waters thought of his wife and him as being guests in the Hollow, but in recent months he has felt as though he is a plenary part of the family. With that concept in mind he advised the group that he had been participating with others of like philosophy in the state to establish guidelines of government that would be more appropriate than the direction the state seems to be headed. "The group has a strong commitment to Christian values, including in its platform of making abortion illegal, limiting greatly the role of lawyers, simplifying taxation and generally empowering the individual," Bob told the group. "We are not certain how our whole approach will play out, but one thing is for sure and that is, we shall have a candidate to run for governor in the fall election."

Jim Baldwin was becoming more secure each day, having now believed he had overcome forever his alcohol addiction. His wife now living with him in the area, they had become members of the Hollow family, who were always present on Friday for the weekly celebration with the entire group. He went to the front and stated, "During the last two months, several of us have carefully examined the oldest coal mine nearest the church here to determine its fitness to use to show and tell visitors about the early coal mining experience of the community. We have used our engineering wherewithal to conjure up ways to support the roof of the mine shaft so it will be safe for people to proceed to the great depths of the entire shaft. When the plan is put to print, we shall present it to you for your approval."

The Bacon girls, Coach Anna, Maudie and others sat in amazement to hear about the wonderful things that were being done in the Hollow, but there were still other reports.

All were surprised when Dr. John Damond stood up to make a statement. "I am so proud of you Hollow folks," he said, as he looked around at the crowded church. "You all are now a model for the rest of us, and your girls have raised the bar of mannerly behavior for all of the students at Bacon College. I told Coach Anna one day something that I want to tell you this evening. Ever since your girls enrolled at the college, we have had very few discipline problems, because the other students try to emulate their lifestyle. Thank you for that.

"When we received the money for the anonymous donor with the stipulation that we participate competitively on the Division I level, I want you to know that I had my doubts. But look what we have done in basketball and now starting the same trend in soccer. I am learning that success of this kind does not come without a price. Other colleges and universities dream about having the kind of athletics we are having. Because of our great program now, we were fully investigated last year by the ACUWAA, who indicated that our program is beyond approach. We adhered to every rule and regulation; thus, we met all requirements easily.

"But that was last year. With our new sport of soccer with the same overwhelming success, I will expect a similar kind of reaction of the other higher education institutions throughout the country. Bacon has raised the bar regarding athletics, and it's difficult for the colleges who have been number one over the years to relinquish that position without a fight. We all pray that the athletic scene will be tranquil this year, but I might conclude that there appears to be some kind of discontent on the horizon now. We need to forgive those who are involved."

For several years Glenn Colson had been a strong supporter of Hollow activities, so he, too, had become an integral part of the close association of families. The Hollow girls remembered him as the strong supporter of girls' basketball when they were in high school. Now, he was fulfilling a dream of providing a teaching-learning environment that featured his own wherewithal of ideas as he launches his private school in the Hollow. "I know of no other place than the Hollow to prove an innovative plan for educating young people," he said to an attentive group. "The very small school that you all so graciously approved for me to open here is now the educational institution of two children from the same family. Over the years I have believed that educators needed to change their approach of instruction for our schools so this will give a genuine opportunity to test my ideas that are until now only theoretical at best. Thank you all for assisting in this endeavor."

All Friday evening activities of eating together with warm and rich fellowship were genuine blessings to Josh and Charlene, but this one was special. As a capstone, they both noticed James and Coach Anna holding hands again before the team departed for Bacon College.

"I believe there is a relationship being developed," Charlene said to Josh, as they turned in for the night.

THE LAWSUIT

"Hello, this is the Damonds' residence," Dr. Damond answered the telephone that had rung at three o'clock in the morning.

"I am so sorry to call you at this time of night," a female voice said, "but this is the only time I could get free."

"That's all right," Dr. Damond replied.

"I still can't give you my name," she said, "but I have more information that I want to pass on to you. I have just come from a meeting with many of the athletic directors of the ACUWAA who are extremely upset that little Bacon College is winning all its games in basketball and now in soccer, also. They are retaining several powerful attorneys to use to sue you, the board of directors of the college, the coach and really anyone who is associated with your team. To show you how far reaching this suit will expand, they will be including the anonymous benevolent person, whom they indicate, started your involvement in a program far over your heads of expertise.

"The cadre of attorneys have been charged with discovering any fallacy in your program that could at all be construed to have given you all an edge in competition. By winning all your games that no other team has ever done leads them to believe that you all are cheating in some way. The early discussions are concerned with the academic achievement of your student athletics, particularly their entrance examinations. Please know that they already have all data on your girls so they will be sifting through them to discover any discrepancies they could prove for a jury to consider. One of your students was really singled out as a primary target. Her name is Mitsie Travers.

"The various athletic departments are willing to shell out many thousands of dollars in lawyers' fees with one of their theories being that you all will discontinue sports altogether to avoid the outcome of this suit that unto itself will be damaging to the reputation of your Christian institution. In addition they didn't think that your small college would have sufficient funds to battle the strongly financed attorneys retained by the rich and prestigious athletic departments from the largest and wealthiest colleges and universities in the country.

"The suit will be filed in a few day so I'll try to give you a bit of forewarning. There may come a time soon when I can meet with you, if you would like. Please know that I believe your program is as pure as the wind blown snow of winter, but in today's world of sports it's important to win. Jealousy has clouded the minds and spirit of so many regarding your success such that their decision making leaves much to be desired. Thank you for listening. I must go now.

"By the way they have advised all coaches and others who come in contact with your team to be much less than cordial, so you should expect some rude treatment in your games ahead."

"Thank you so very much," Dr. Damond responded, realizing though that his anonymous caller had already hung up.

Failing to sleep the remainder of the night, Dr. Damond bade his wife farewell early the next morning as he headed to the office. Calling Coach Anna immediately upon his arrival, he requested that she come to the office for a meeting.

Running all the way, Coach Anna arrived panting just a little, trying to respect his sense of urgency for this conference. "Come on in," he said to her, as they both moved toward his chamber. "Please sit down."

"Thank you," Coach Anna responded.

"I received a second anonymous call from someone who seems to think that there is a strong conspiracy underway to do harm to our sports' program," he told her, while sitting near her in front of his executive desk. "At three o'clock this morning the call came, a most unusual time to say the least. The caller appeared to have been part of a meeting of athletic directors from many of our major universities who were drawing up charges to mount against us using a large cadre of attorneys. I am really shocked about the whole situation."

While Dr. Damond was trying to catch his breath, Coach Anna noted, "Obviously, something was wrong when we played our last two soccer matches. It seemed that the crude and rude conduct was not spontaneous but orchestrated such that both groups behaved in like manner."

"I think that is what this lady was saying on the telephone about the future conduct of the teams you play," he reacted. "She seemed to indicate that there was going to be an effort to engage others to join in participation of demeaning acts against our team."

"It is my wish that our opponents would not behave in this manner, but they appear to be getting their 'talking and acting points' from someone else and will only be following directions," Coach Anna noted.

"That's the way it sounds to me," he quickly replied. "You and the girls have always handled this type of adversity in such a masterful way, so I'm sure you will do the same regardless of what they do. But what about the lawsuit?"

"In recent years everywhere we turn lawyers are more and more handling our everyday decisions in matters related to any kind of conflict," Coach Anna stated. "With our present day jurisprudence, lawyers are taught the same curriculum; thus, interpretations stemming from case law can be predicted. Whereas, being a lawyer years ago was an honorable profession, more and more greed has entered the fray and has competed for their souls. Obviously, much money will be set aside for lawyers' fees."

"No doubt, you are right," Dr. Damond stated. "The anonymous caller indicated that one of the theories being batted about is that our small and poor institution will not be able to defend itself regarding the barrage of charges, and will just give up and pull our teams from ACUWAA competition. Please know that I am not one to waver when encountering an enemy yielding false charges. Recently, I read that attorneys were charging from two to five hundred dollars or more per hour to defend clients, so I guess that would be what we would expect."

"That's certainly a lot of money just to defend oneself from false claims, isn't it?" Coach Anna related, as her eyebrows were raised.

"If we employed four and paid five hundred dollars an hour, that would soon equate to a lot of money," Dr. Damond stated, reaching for his calculator. "Ten eight-hour days times four lawyers at five hundred dollars per hour would be one hundred sixty thousand dollars. That is a lot of money, but the legal charges could be elevated much more, because I'm sure they would need more time to develop a defense for us. I believe that in all it would cost more than a million dollars to defend our college."

"I have often wondered why one has to pay for legal fees for his defense, if he is found to be innocent," Coach Anna stated.

"I have often thought about our legal system and wondered what has gone wrong," he said, not really wanting to debate the legal system any more. "I just wanted you to know about my call and the hints about what you might expect when you go to the west coast to play your next three games. I know you will continue to display your strong

Christian spirit. In the meantime I'm going to convene a special session of the board of directors to discuss the matter in executive session, thus keeping what we know still as a private matter."

Early in the morning Dr. Damond had his secretary to call the board of directors for a special meeting at the college. This governing body had never been a group followed closely by media scrutiny, and everyone just thought of this meeting as being just an ordinary event. An eyebrow or two were raised when the chairman announced that the body would go into executive session, examining a legal matter.

Behind closed doors Dr. Damond advised the group of all of the information he had regarding the alleged and pending lawsuit by the athletic directors of the various colleges and universities. The eleven members just sat there dumbfounded as he related the story of the anonymous telephone calls.

Following his eloquent statement, he was bombarded with many questions from the board members. The first bunch of questions dealt with the academic background of the teams, both basketball and soccer. They knew the answers but wanted to hear them again as reassurance regarding the matter. Hearing again that the athletes met and exceeded by far all the guidelines set forth by ACUWAA, they moved on to the matter of the lawsuit itself. "If everything is in order regarding the qualifications of these young ladies, why should we be worried at all about the situation?" a local leader on the board asked.

Turning to Dr. Damond for an answer, the chairman asked, "Would you mind answering this question?"

"I'll be glad to do that," Dr. Damond said. "Let me assure all of you that our young athletes meet all the ACUWAA guidelines, so from that vantage point there is nothing about which to worry. But on the other hand, there is the matter of a legal defense for us when the suit is filed.

All of you know that our budget is austere and includes no money for matters such as this, so any legal fees would cause much damage to our program."

"What do you think our legal fees will be?" an older member asked.

"I don't really know," Dr. Damond replied, "but at three to five hundred dollars an hour a large sum could accumulate in a short while. Of course, all of us want the best for Bacon College, and it seems that in our present culture, lawsuits are inevitable and huge fees are commonplace."

The chairman led the discussion into the evening and later at the dining room table where the board ate their evening meal. The board members never ceased to be amazed at the conduct of the students on the small campus, being led by the athletes who on this evening were sitting at different tables with other students for this delicious evening meal of salad, squash, corn on cob, corn bread, fried corn, green beans, grilled chicken, roast beef, a choice of dessert, ice tea or carbonated drink.

"What has gotten into our society?" Bob Waters asked himself, as he sat with the other board members pondering what the college should do, if it really were sued.

During the night before the Bacon soccer team's departure for their three-game road trip, another anonymous telephone call was received at two-thirty in the morning. "I am sorry to call you so late," the caller stated, "but the suit day is going to be today. All the newspapers are getting an advanced copy of the charges, the Sports Ramble is contemplating printing a special issue just including the charges covered in this voluminous narrative. Radio and television channels will fill the airwaves with their own reports and interpretation of the allegations included in the suit.

"The e-mail letters are being sent to and fro to all parts of the country to tell all the host colleges and universities how to relate to your team of girls, starting during their western trip. I am not privy to the contents of these messages, but should have them today, or before Bacon plays this evening in Seattle. I will make contact with Coach Bosley at the airport and will discreetly have a copy passed to her that will give her advanced information of what she might expect to occur during this and other road trips.

"I have great empathy for your college and realize that you all have been bashed so consistently by those who want to do what you all are doing so well. That they, too, want to win all their games, but when they can't, they turn to other tactics. May God continue to bless you!"

As abruptly as she called, she departed still as an anonymous person. But the time had come to brace up for what was next.

During the early morning send-off rally, Dr. Damond took Coach Anna aside and said, "I received another anonymous call about two-thirty this morning, and the caller advised that this was suit day so I don't know what to say. I know that you all will handle any situation with grace and charm. She indicated that the host colleges and universities would be challenging you all in some way, but did not reveal how. She did say that she would pass on to you a brief of some kind while you are in the Seattle airport."

Turning to the sports' pages in the newspaper at the Roanoke airport, Coach Anna noticed an article written by a renown writer entitled, "Women's College Athletic Dilemma." It was an interesting piece.

> "Dreadfully slow in maturing, women's college athletic programs have for years taken a far backseat from that of their counterpart on the men's side of the equation. With a governmental boost a few years earlier through the provisions included in the Title IX legislation, only moderate strides were evident. It seemed that only through threats of or

actual suits against various groups would there be any noticeable progress.

"Judicial test cases seemed to side with the ACUWAA, always favoring the female programs, while many colleges struggled to finance all that was being demanded on the campuses throughout the country. The disparate incomes of athletic programs for men and women were great, so great that smaller, less fortunate colleges have almost thrown in the towel. In recent months many institutions have examined again their equal opportunity philosophy, because the money making sports of the men can no longer finance a deficit driven program of the women.

"With all of this stated in a very brief history, let me apprise you of what has taken place in the past several months in intercollegiate competition. During the last two years there has been a sudden and almost overwhelming interest in women's basketball, such that in some areas the attendance is better than its counterpart. Sellout crowds fill the arenas with enthusiasm exceeding such that anyone has ever witnessed. Obviously, a revival is taking place, and where it will stop no one knows.

"With attendance up in many areas by fifty percent one might even surmise that this phenomenon is a revolution. Isn't this what our leaders had hoped would happen with just a gentle governmental nudge? Would anyone have predicted that the Sports Ramble magazine would have carried the pictures recently of two women on its cover? How would you assess the situation? What would you attribute the good fortune of the women's world of college sports?

"Did I say good fortune? Yes. Women's sports as we know them have made a change during the last several months, being elevated to great

> heights in the media and by sports' fans throughout the country. What is the difference in the program for these past several months and that of previous years? It doesn't take a rocket scientist to figure this out that a new team not only could compete at the highest level, but to win at the Division I level.
>
> "Everyone knows this, and the fans love having a championship team while others like to compete with them. It's fun watching the women's basketball and now the soccer program improve so greatly, which provides much for the hungry fans who have waited so long for this day to come. Many believed that a female athletic program was doomed such that it would never rise to a level of respectability, but it has, and one does not have to go far to understand that the credit for such a surge of interest and enthusiasm stems from one source, small Bacon College.
>
> "But wait! Who is out there trying to kill the goose that lays the golden eggs? I hear that a killer is out there even as I write, stalking its prey."

Coach Anna just sat back in her seat having full understanding about what the author was writing. "Apparently, this author is aware that something is going to take place very soon, but at this time is not willing to divulge the full story," she thought, as she and the girls traveled for their soccer match just outside Seattle.

The members of the team accepted best wishes from the flight attendants and captain, as they departed the aircraft carrying their backpacks and wearing their very modest clothing. As usual, Mit was the darling of those in the airport, and she obliged each autograph seeker in the terminal, as did the other girls. It was always fun for them to mingle with the autograph seekers.

Just as they turned to leave a large group of young people, Coach Anna bumped into a man who was reading what appeared to be a manuscript of some kind. Papers flew in several different directions as they all tried to retrieve them. The man knelt beside Coach Anna and in all the confusion handed her a stapled set of papers, not saying a word to her as he continued to scurry around to get the remainder of his document. "What a clever way clandestinely to pass something to another," Coach Anna thought. Just as the group exited the double doors to the side to rent a van, Coach Anna turned to see the man on the other side of the terminal talking to a middle-age woman dressed in an expensive dark pants suit carrying a leather briefcase.

Soon they were on their way in their rented van, darting in and out of traffic on the busy streets, finally arriving at their motel that was only a few blocks from the large stadium. As soon as Coach Anna entered her room, she looked at the papers that were passed on to her at the terminal. Scribbled at the top was written, "Please forgive the typographical errors, etc, because I didn't have time to do anything except to get this to you as a draft, the same draft that the committee of athletic directors approved only this morning."

Carefully couched in draft like terms was a long list of suggestions in which various groups possibly could engage to show disrespect for the Bacon team. The goal seemed to be to do all that could be done to the soccer team such that it would succumb to the humiliation and just totally withdraw from competition. The initial ones that caught Coach Anna's eye were similar to the tactics used several months ago under like conditions. But one really caught her eye. "On each evening at game time a special news account will be broadcast via the sports' channel on television at the beginning of each soccer match, starting with Galton University in Washington, and will be repeated for the next two contests on the west coast."

"What does this mean?" Coach Anna thought. "There was some strong reason the anonymous caller to Dr.

Damond wanted to forewarn us about what might take place during our games so this must be it. I wonder what it really matters that is telecast on a sports' channel. We'll find out soon."

A brief rest before their evening meal, and they were off to the playing field. When they arrived to go to their dressing room, their whole world changed. It was as though cordiality disappeared with the flick of a light switch.

"We are on time, but no one seems to be available to help us so let's just walk until we find our dressing room," Coach Anna said to the group without directing it to any particular individual.

Finally, they discovered the dressing room, dressed, and Coach Anna decided that they should carry everything with them to the field. Hanna went out first with the equipment, including towels and balls. Just as she approached the field, a loud and boisterous group of students painted and dressed in all kinds of colors, surrounded her with some bumping up against her as she tried to move forward. It wasn't until the group saw the team coming out did they direct their attention into another direction. With Hanna safely onto the playing field bench area, the fans' attention was switched to the commotion near the visiting team entrance to the field. By this time the student group was vastly increased such that the team could not move. All the while they were being jostled back and forth, moving only at the discretion of those depicting now hoodlum behavior.

Some of the larger students had made their way to the center of the fray now being orchestrated with megaphones utilized by the leaders. Fearful now that harm would come to her girls, Coach Anna kneeled down holding the hands of two who in turn noticed what was happening and replicated her action. Soon all the girls bowed in prayer as the "herd" of students marched, stomped and loudly chanted all kinds of ugly remarks to the young ladies.

Meanwhile, Hanna beckoned several policemen and directed their attention to where the team was that had been so ruthlessly corralled for several minutes. At first the policemen failed to recognize the gravity of the situation, thinking that this was an ordinary college prank employed by students before big games. It was not until one of the policemen who had come to assist the girls was knocked down and stepped on by a student, did the other policemen exercise the necessary force to free the girls. As the girls were escorted to their bench, one could readily notice the mud on their clothing, tears in their uniforms and disheveled hair. It was not a pretty scene.

Having all the team members to sit on their bench, Coach Anna thought that it would be best just to sit for a while, as she talked to each girl to determine whether or not she was hurt in any way during the melee. They all appeared to be physically fit but somewhat emotionally upset that young people would behave so badly.

Many sports' reporters were on the scene with several getting a video of the entrance scene that was being viewed on several channels nationwide. Back at Bacon where many were watching the wide screen television, Maudie joined several of the students in crying as they viewed the whole scenario. Dr. Damond wondered to himself whether or not the new sports' program was worth all the humiliation to the special girls on the basketball and soccer teams.

Back at the stadium the television network carrying the game on cable showed on the wide screen what had happened at the end of the playing field. Only a few minutes before game time the Bacon team sat almost motionless on the bench still trying to put in perspective what just happened to them. Then came the bombshell. "We have breaking news," the television announcer said as all the fans turned toward the screen. "Just handed to me is a statement from the district attorney's office in our capital city as follows: 'On this date a lawsuit has been filed charging Bacon College with wrongfully enrolling certain students in their athletic program for the express purpose of participating in Division I athletics.'" He continued at length to name all persons included in the suit who would be prosecuted to the fullest extent allowable by the law. He advised that more will come later.

This announcement at this time was intended to discourage the team so that by being demoralized they would fail to perform satisfactorily. "This has really shaken them," Coach Anna thought, "much more than anything else has done. I believe they are just ashamed that other colleges would behave in such a hateful manner."

With the whole world of sports watching, Coach Anna asked the girls to hold hands while she prayed to God for safety, health and a contest played with a joyful spirit. To help them accept this terrible event, Coach Anna decided to start in the game a different group from those usually who begin a contest. "They love to encourage one another so the ones who usually start can now warm themselves up by giving encouragement to their teammates," she thought.

When the team broke its huddle, they were faced with booing that got louder and louder such that the referee asked the teams to go back to their respective benches until some semblance of quiet could be restored. After several minutes the referee beckoned for the teams to come on the field for the start of the game when two students ran onto the field and unrolled a large banner that read, "Fans, please read the second banner to our hicks from the mountains."

Taking center stage now came two more students dressed in long handle underwear carrying a lengthy banner which stated, "To help you compute the score, we will read it for you from time to time during the game." After they ran around the field with this banner, they returned and headed to the Bacon sideline to wrap the banner around Mit several times to the delight of the thousands in attendance.

The team was really upset over these actions, and Mit broke down and cried while the others hovered around her to give her support during this ugly scene. Even with the game official laughing at the student "prank," the contest was begun with a demoralized Bacon team on and off the field. Coach Anna began busily to do damage control to help her girls cope with this unusual behavior of those who were supposed to be their hosts.

Galton University was one of three very strong soccer teams Bacon would face on this western road trip. The conspirators knew this, so this was the reason the team was being bombarded by such bad behavior. Would it give support to its opponent?

The game was underway, but the spectators still were not settled, because there were some loud and unkind remarks coming from the group. The mindset of the Bacon team on the field left much to be desired, and at this juncture teammates on the bench failed to elevate their enthusiasm on the field. Even those doing the encouraging seemed to need encouraging themselves, as they, too, were lackluster in their efforts.

"The group is totally demoralized," Coach Anna thought, "I've got to do something to lift their spirits."

Calling for a huddle of the players on the sideline, just as they were assembled, Galton scored the first goal of the game to the delight of the strongly partisan crowd. A one-goal lead was all the rude students needed to boost their adrenaline, if they really needed a boost.

Out the students came and shouted near the sideline, "The score is 1 to 0. Do you understand? We will speak slower for you to understand. The score is 1 to 0." Ugliness was in vogue as the students from Galton continued their tormenting of the Bacon players near the sideline.

In a huddle Coach Anna told the girls to hold hands and stated, "Remember what Jesus taught us. We are to forgive as many times as necessary for the behavior of others against us. Always remember that God is in control. It's so hard to be a winner. You are winners not only in soccer and basketball, but you are winners in the eyes of our Lord who is looking down on us today. Thank you all for not taking any action unbecoming to our Christian backgrounds during this ordeal."

At this time there was a loud and continuous roar as Galton had scored its second goal. Now it led 2 to 0. As the second goal was recorded on the large scoreboard at the end of the field, the students again ran to the sidelines and yelled the score several times in the direction of the Bacon team. Bedlam surely was a word that could explain the environment in the stadium on this day.

The radio and television announcers were having a field day with powerful Bacon down by two goals, a wide spread for soccer.

With the tears not falling from Mit's eyes any more, Coach Anna could see a calmness come over her group on the sideline. It was time to change roles; the current players and those on the sidelines. The jubilation and celebration was so intense in the stands that not everyone observed the changing of the players. But some did. Mit was pointed out and much derogation was thrust her way. The other pony-tailed girl, Esther, also received her share of the less than complimentary remarks. Two down presented a mountain to climb in a soccer match. Yet, here they were.

The early players now were the encouragers, and the early encouragers were now on the field. There were neither gestures that would indicate any type of fierceness would now be displayed nor were there any hints as to what was about to take place. On the first play Marsha took the ball down the center of the field and passed to Esther who let go a blistering kick that struck the goalie in the head before bounding harmlessly out of bounds. Immediately, Esther went to the goalie and kneeled down to offer an apology, but she was grabbed by the arms then and dragged away by two Galton players. The fans loved the rude and unsportsmanlike conduct. They even got louder with their taunting. Some though sensed a change about to take place.

When the contest resumed the television and radio sportscasters continued their praise of the Galton team that had won three games in a row, and now were leading by a large margin against the number one soccer team. Their opponent felt very proud to be in this position of the soccer match so they had already begun to give an inordinate number of high fives to each other on the playing field. At the break with the score remaining the same, the spectators began their own celebration with congratulations being passed on to a neighbor with a comment or a pat on the back. The scene was viewed by a national audience including those at Bacon College.

"The girls have really taken a beating both physically and emotionally during this game," Dr. Damond said to Maudie.

"I really feel sorry for them," Maudie responded. "Far too many times our girls bear the brunt of bad behavior of others such that I often wonder just how much more they can take."

"It is times like this that I wonder whether or not sports are really worth all the terrible things that come along with them," Dr. Damond stated in somewhat of a defeatist attitude. "We feel their pain here watching on television, but look at what they feel. I know the team is just crushed."

Sometimes in life a good rest is strongly invigorating such that it gives those resting a new lease on priorities. This was the case on this day. "To this point this has been an unusual day for us," Coach Anna said. "You all have done a masterful job in not responding to those around you, and have applied the forgiveness principle that Jesus taught all the while. I know you remember Peter's questioning. Let me read these verses to you now found in Matthew 18:

[21]Then Peter came and said to him, "Lord, if another member of the church sins against me, how often should I forgive? As many as seven times?"
[22]Jesus said to him, "Not seven times, but, I tell you, seventy-seven times.

Back on the field on the first play Mit took the ball down the side and darted to the middle dribbling the ball with her quick feet all the while. In pursuit were several girls wearing their red jerseys, but they were too late as Mit surprisingly unleashed a most powerful kick that hit the corner of the net for Bacon's first score. A hush fell over the crowd.

On the next possession it was Marsha's turn to captivate the audience with her skill, as she kicked a sharp forty-five degree pass to Esther who just nudged the ball a little to roll it into the net with the goalie having gone for the Marsha's fake. Silence now was commonplace in the huge stadium as the Galton team was trying to gather itself to hold off the offensive minded small Bacon team. Reporter after reporter was now trying to cover his previous statements by making positive comments about the opponent of Galton. The attack by Bacon was so swift and devastating that soccer fans throughout the country knew that this was a most powerful soccer team of girls. Everyone could anticipate what would be the reaction of the fans and reporters, if this charge continued and Bacon went ahead.

The wait was shortlived, as Mit sent a high arcing kick from the sideline to the center of the net where Marsha struck a strong header into the center of the net for Bacon's third goal, which gave them the lead. The ugliness began anew with the fans almost getting out of control as Bacon marched on to an eight to two rout. The wide margin of victory whetted the appetite even more of those who were suing this small college, because it was a winning team.

The loud chant, "Cheaters! Cheaters! Cheaters!" rang out over the landscape as the Bacon team lined up to shake their opponent's hand. That would not be done on this day, because Galton had already made its way to the locker room, so the Bacon girls were left to hear the loud and vociferous demeaning yells that at times seemed to be more than the team could bear. Two state police escorted the group to the locker and advised that they would see that the team got to their van safely, and would, if necessary, escort them to their motel.

It had really been a most difficult day for the group; yet, they appeared to be composed now, showing that impervious side to the world in which they were now faced. "What a turn of events in this game!" Coach Anna thought, as she sat down alone on the bench in the locker room as the girls showered and dressed. "From an athletic standpoint I have never seen a better played soccer game at the end that totally annihilated their opponent," she thought.

The evening had been a draining experience for all the team members so they picked up some sandwiches on the way in addition to several pizzas and spent the remainder of the evening in their room. It was hard to get away from the ugliness of the world in which the team found itself. The news was replete with a multitude of stories about the game and particularly about the lawsuit, which seemed to be on everyone's mind.

"The big guns on the playing field unleashed a fierce attack in the second half in this evening's match with Galton University," a reporter stated in his nightly report. "It was beleaguered Bacon taking numerous ugly hits from fans bent on siding with the plaintiffs in this case so their march to the unusually wide margin of victory surprised even their most ardent supporters. Obviously, they are for real. But how does a team come out of no where to dominate women's sports as this team has done? The suit charges that Bacon College has broken the rules to field teams that are too powerful for other teams following the rules all the while.

"These are serious charges that, if proven to be correct, will certainly nullify the past record of this special little team that those around the country have adored for so long. But rules are rules. The playing field has to be level for all to have an equal opportunity to win. It does really seem suspicious that a team from an extremely small college can enter the ranks of Division I play and not only compete satisfactorily but to win all their games in two sports. Look at the best teams in the country that have been building up their program for many years and still do not win all their games. In fact, these same perennial winners now lose to this neophyte group from all places, a Hollow.

"This lawsuit is long overdue to get to the bottom of this swirling dilemma. Jealousy is one thing that has generated much discussion in women's sports, but there is something else. Most of us believe there is absolutely no way that a college can start a new sport and right off the blocks dominate its opponent each time out as this small Christian college has done. If that can't be done and the Bacon College group is doing it, what is this saying? Wouldn't you agree that something is not exactly right regarding this situation?

"I guess we all should have guessed that the judicial system would penetrate more and more the ranks of sports, but isn't it a shame that the college officials can't regulate their own program. One might really ask, why have our lawyers turned to this green field for their harvest? I am sorry to say that I believe that the instigators of this whole scenario are probably lawyers who see this as an unusual opportunity. The millions asked in this recovery will certainly deplete the coffers of this small institution so, if Bacon college loses this case, it will no longer exist as a college. Those associated with it will find themselves working the remainder of their lives paying their debt to what many call society. But much of this will be paying the powerful cadre of lawyers making up the team representing the athletic directors of the various colleges and universities.

"Regardless, justice must prevail. The conflict deserves an answer. All of us in any way associated with sports want to know the truth."

For all who were watching in addition to Coach Anna, this was a compelling news account which set the stakes very high. "With defeat Bacon College no longer will exist," Coach Anna thought, as she mulled over the contents of the newscast. "This lawsuit will be a huge undertaking for the college. Dr. Damond will not give in to those who are initiating these charges, because he is strongly committed to the college, and especially to the students."

Three state troopers were on hand for their next game with Orton College in southern Oregon not too far from the ocean. As they entered the parking lot for the afternoon game, the three surrounded the team to keep away those who were bent on doing some kind of harm to the team. After they dressed in the locker room Coach Anna read Psalm 23:

1 *The LORD is my shepherd, I shall not want.*
2 *He makes me lie down in green pastures;*
he leads me beside still waters
3 *he restores my soul.*
4 *He leads me in right paths*
for his name's sake.
4 *Even though I walk through the darkest valley,*
I fear no evil;
for you are with me;
your rod and your staff—
they comfort me.
5 *You prepare a table before me*
in the presence of my enemies;
you anoint my head with oil;
my cup overflows.
6 *Surely goodness and mercy shall follow me*
all the days of my life,

and I shall dwell in the house of the LORD
my whole life long.

"The waters are not still now, and it appears for several days ahead, but the Lord will comfort us," Coach Anna said. "We are the Lord's sheep and he will protect us. We are here to play a game, and not to determine the merits of the pending lawsuit, which we learn more about each day. Dr. Damond will handle this part of our athletic program with much grace and an abundance of wisdom. You have been in these truth searches before. This is no different.

"In Proverbs 3 we find these words:

5 *Trust in the LORD with all your heart,*
and do not rely on your own insight.
6 *In all your ways acknowledge him,*
and he will make straight your paths."

Joining the three dedicated state troopers, the team headed for the field with actions similar to those of the previous day in their path; however, this time the group was protected by the three men in police uniform. "Thank you so very much," Coach Anna said in almost a yelling voice for the troopers to hear over the loud and demeaning taunts coming from all corners.

"We'll be right here near your bench the entire game," one of them responded.

"This is such a relief," Coach Anna thought, as she watched her girls warm up on the field being impervious to all kinds of calls, yells and rhymes emanating from all parts of the filled stadium.

The other coach was too busy to shake Coach Anna's hand so she returned to her sideline and hugged Hanna. "Can you believe the score of the game yesterday?" Coach Anna asked.

"They really turned up the wick the last half, didn't they?" Hanna replied.

"They certainly did," Coach Anna stated. "They just seem to know where the other players are on the field all the time."

There was no coming from behind in this game with only about a third of the game completed Bacon had a commanding lead, three to zero. When they scored the fourth goal, it really became a no contest. The final score of five to one left everyone believing that something was awry, because no team could be that good and follow the rules.

In the motel Coach Anna listened intently to the newscast about the lawsuit against Bacon. A strong appeal had been presented to the judge who had been appointed to hear the case that the suit be moved forward with much haste to ensure that the soccer season would be absent a team using unqualified players on its roster. He went on to say that each day that passes the whole ACUWAA would be impacted such that it would become the organization that is punished, because of any delay. A decision on this request would be made the next day the announcer reported.

That evening after dinner she called Maudie.

"How are you and others doing?" Coach Anna asked.

"We are fine," Maudie replied quickly, "and how are you all?"

"We are doing well," Coach Anna noted. "Three state troopers escorted us at the game so our immediate environment was much better."

"We could see on television that the spectators were really ugly to you and the team," Maudie pointed out. "I know you and the team are really worn out."

"They are fine now," Coach Anna indicated. "Mit was shaken up when the students wrapped the ugly banner around her, but she soon recovered from that episode."

"The lawsuit has everybody believing that the Bacon team is not following the ACUWAA rules, but we know you are adhering to every principle down to the minute details," Maudie commented.

"How is Dr. Damond?" Coach Anna asked.

"He had a meeting with the students before the game to apprise them of all that is taking place," Maudie said. "He will meet with the board of directors again tomorrow, I'm sure, to discuss retention of a legal defense team."

The behavior of the spectators for the third game in northern California was the same as for the previous two games. A cadre of five state troopers helped ease the anxiety of the group when they faced the capacity crowd. Swirling still in Coach Anna's mind was the judge's ruling early on this day that the trial would begin on Friday, only two days away. Plangent sounds and loud voices filling the air interfered with Coach Anna's thinking, but she realized that the plaintiffs in this case had a strong hand picked cadre of seasoned trial lawyers, and to this point little Bacon had no one to present its case.

Fuel was being added to the flame for those suing little Bacon, because Bacon won its third game on this trip by shutting out its opponent and scoring four goals of its own. The girls had gotten used to the ugliness displayed toward them now so it was like old times again, one happy family. "Many strange things can happen in our present court system," Coach Anna thought, now that she was being involved personally in her first lawsuit. "Sometimes actions in the courtroom with experienced trial lawyers leave much to be desired."

It was mid afternoon when the team arrived on campus, but the students were ready with a warm reception for their beleaguered team in the coliseum. Many town's people were on hand, and all the Hollow folks were a part of the festivities. Everyone seemed to be in a jovial mood, including Dr. Damond who was shouldering the brunt of the preparation for the lawsuit. Coach Anna noticed that the board members of the college were present, and they, too, seemed to have come to grips with the whole sordid situation such that they were at peace.

For this welcome home rally the soccer girls were asked to sit in chairs on the side of the basketball court where in front of them was placed a microphone. Student after student stepped forward to speak, praising the team members for their presence on campus and being excellent role models for the rest of the students. Staff personnel added their thoughts, also, knowing what the girls had gone through the last three days, and what was ahead with the lawsuit that had captured the imagination of all media. Josh was asked by Dr. Damond to render the closing prayer.

The campus was teeming with activity the next morning as numerous subpoenas were being handed out all over campus to staff members, students, the team, Coach Anna, board of directors, Dr. Damond, his secretary, all kinds of records, many of the Hollow folks, and some neighborhood people.

"This whole situation is difficult to understand," Coach Anna told Maudie, as they sat in the commons area of the athletic dormitory. "Here the college is being sued and the attorneys for the athletic directors have been working on this for months spending thousands and thousands of dollars charging our small Christian college with wrongdoing."

"It really doesn't make sense," Maudie replied, "but I guess we here are seeing the bad side of our country today wherein lawyers and the courts are now ruling on all facets of life, even sports now. Tomorrow, there will be another part of society that will be nibbled away by our legal system."

"It doesn't seem fair," Coach Anna said. "If we were losing games, there would be no interest in our college, but because our girls are so dedicated to basketball and soccer, they are winning all their games. When any kind of dilemma emerges, lawyers nowadays will not be far behind. I believe greed has corrupted our great judicial institution."

"I believe you are right," Maudie said. "Operating on a very austere budget, I have wondered what Bacon will do to counter the legal team employed by the other colleges and universities. Bob Waters told me that his group is attempting to back a candidate for governor using a platform of serious governmental reform, and that the college was going to surprise the whole country in this lawsuit using one aspect of this reform."

"What did he mean by that?" Coach Anna quickly asked, looking straight at Maudie.

"I don't really know," Maudie responded, "but it is surprising to me about who is headed for the court site for the start of the trial."

"Who has the board of directors selected as the college's attorney?" Coach Anna asked, now becoming very intense in her interrogatories.

"I really don't know," Maudie replied. "They came out of their meeting yesterday appearing to be at peace with the whole situation. Last evening before the homecoming celebration, they met with Josh."

"Why did they meet with him?" Coach Anna inquired.

"I don't really know except that Dr. Damond's secretary purchased two tickets yesterday to Groveville, Colorado, one for the president and one for Josh," Maudie stated. "What that means, I'll leave it for you to decide."

"Josh is a most unusual man, extremely wise and at the same time very compassionate," Coach Anna said. "Dr. Damond couldn't have picked a better companion for this trip."

Groveville was a city of about two hundred thousand people, but on this opening day of the biggest trial in sports' history, it had grown considerably. Everybody seemed to have a camera, but by the time Dr. Damond and Josh were finally recognized by a national reporter, they had stepped into the courthouse. The first order of business for this day was the selection of the twelve-member jury. Dr. Damond and Josh had been directed to sit as representatives of Bacon College with Josh listed as the legal counsel for the defense.

When the judge arrived, he recognized those on the plaintiff's team, and then turned and acknowledged Dr. Damond, who had been named as the primary party in the suit and Josh, as his only legal counsel. All present were shocked when they compared the several-member team of lawyers representing the athletic directors to that of the defense. The reporters were clamoring to discover the name of the "lawyer" sitting beside the president of Bacon College.

The whole scenario regarding the jury selection was giving a glimpse of much to come later. Josh, as counsel for the college, approved of all jury candidates, even several who were in some way closely aligned with the athletic programs of nearby colleges. "What can you make of this behavior?" one reporter asked another.

"This is the biggest lawsuit in the history of sports, and the defense seems to accept whatever the strong team of lawyers of the plaintiff present without any disagreement whatsoever," the second responded.

"They just appear to be shocked by it all," the first noted.

"I don't believe that they really understand what to do," the second commented.

"By the way, who is Bacon College's attorney?" another asked.

"One reporter looked up the name, Josh Morrow, and it was not included in the list of registered attorneys in the country, so we all don't really know," he stated.

At the conclusion of the jury selection process the judge informed those in attendance that there would be a change in venue when the actual trial began on Monday. He stated that because of the unusually large amount of interest in this case, and because sports involved spectators, he was moving the court site to the large city coliseum whereby many more people could be present for the hearing proceedings.

At the close of the day's proceedings, Dr. Damond and Josh were surrounded by reporters inquiring about a long list of matters, but they graciously refused to reply to their questioning, because the whole situation would have to be resolved in the court now. Anything they said might now be damaging to their case.

At the airport a replication of media interest was encountered that was met with their same response. This did not preclude reporters making numerous pictures as they waited for their flight to Roanoke.

It was good to get back to the mountains of Virginia to be among their friends again. They had been gone only about forty-eight hours, but it seemed like an eternity. Dr. Damond was extremely pleased that Josh would be at his side during this dark period in the life of the college.

On the Monday that came too rapidly, one could readily see that there was a wide disparity between the dress of Josh and his ten counterparts decked out in their dark three-piece suits, each carrying a briefcase, on this morning in the hill country of Colorado. Josh wore an open collar faded polo shirt, blue pants and brown well worn shoes, especially worn on the heels. The coliseum was packed even this early in the morning, but Dr. Damond's attention was directed toward the cadre of lawyers of the athletic directors. "There are two women in this group so I wonder which one is the 'Benedict Arnold,'" he thought, as he looked toward the group of lawyers. At this juncture nothing was revealing that would answer his question.

At the request of the judge the plaintiff's counsel was asked to make its opening statements. Several of the attorneys made eloquent and appealing pleas to the jury in a very convincing fashion. They were very interesting, and those in attendance, including the jurors, were riveted to each speaker.

A gray-haired lawyer stood up later and faced the jury, and just as he did, one of the women lawyers turned to look directly in Dr. Damond's direction. "That must be the one who is passing information to me," Dr. Damond thought, just as the older man began to speak. "Let me tell you a story," he said to the attentive jury. "When I was little, I used to love to play games in my yard and in other yards in the neighborhood. The games were fun and with the victor came bragging rights and even more friends. I quickly learned that winning was very important in competition.

"When we chose teams, the leaders would choose those that gave their team the best probability of success, which was winning, of course. Over the years all kinds of shenanigans were attempted to boost the possibility of winning. Regardless of the rules that we had in place, someone would discover a loophole that for the moment gave his team the edge.

"I'm sure you know what I mean. You have probably played in some of these yards when you were younger. It was during this period in your life that one realizes that the most stable rules seemed not to fit the occasion all the time. In addition there were those players who always dealt with the edge of right and wrong regarding the ground rules.

"I remember one day a new kid came in the yard to play with us. The game was baseball, and he brought his own bat but would not let anyone else use it. We all noticed that he was always on the winning team often hitting a long homerun to win the game. This went on for quite sometime before the rest of us began to feel that something was different. For a new kid to burst on the scene and be an instant winner was perplexing. Later, we discovered two things about him that helped us to cope with what had happened all the while when he was participating in our yard games. We found out that he was much older than we were, and secondly, the bat he was using was filled with cork, both of which gave him a decided edge in our yard play.

"Bacon College is like this young man who used trickery to include himself in our yard games. You see, he won every time, also. We are going to prove for you without a shadow of doubt that what is happening in women's sports today would not be occurring without breaking the long standing rules of the American Colleges and Universities Women's Athletic Association (ACUWAA).

"Let me direct your attention to the fact that the Bacon College basketball team won all its games during the past two years, something that has never been done before in the rich history of women's athletics. In fact, no women's team had ever gone undefeated for a single year. But this is only part of the story as the margin of victory for this small Christian college was about thirty points per game. Keep in mind that this rise to fame came in two years whereas other colleges and universities have taken years to build up a team that can even compete satisfactorily on the Division I level. Yet, here Bacon comes on the scene to lead women's sports right off the blocks.

"Is this success only by chance, or is it because the college is not following the ACUWAA rules? That will be your question during these next several days of testimony."

The jurors and those in attendance got an earful from these several eloquent lawyers so it would be Bacon's turn after the recess for lunch that was directed by the judge. Dr. Damond was really saddened by what he had heard in these opening remarks, but Josh was trying to encourage him to boost his spirits. As Josh was holding Dr. Damond around the shoulder with everybody moving about, one of the female lawyers bumped into Josh while at the same time placing a note in his hand. It was indicated in the note that she would contact them that evening.

Walking outside for a breath of fresh air, Dr. Damond said to Josh, "I am just amazed at the wherewithal of wisdom you have, and the confidence I have in your ability to represent Bacon College in this far reaching lawsuit. Your unique plan will work, and in the end the whole college and all of its personnel will be completely exonerated. We must not tell anyone of your plan, and I have cautioned the board of directors to remain silent and not to talk to anyone about this."

"It is important for the other colleges and universities to be heard in this matter so that all the people will understand why they have a problem with Bacon College," Josh stated.

After they had a brief private time together without being the center of attention, it was now time to enter this makeshift courtroom now on the floor of the vast coliseum that housed the sports' fans from Groveville and surroundings areas. On this date there were those in attendance from all over the country.

When the judge entered to take his seat behind a large desk that was about six feet above the floor, the several thousand now present rose. "It's now the defense's turn to present its preliminary statement to the court," he said, while looking directly at Josh.

At this time Josh stood and stated, "The defense has no statement to make."

What a shock! One could have heard a pin drop, because it was very quiet. The judge was so shocked that he sat speechless for what seemed like a long period of time, and the media couldn't believe what they just heard.

A smile could be seen on the faces of the other lawyers, and even the judge after he realized that in fact the defense really did not want to make a preliminary statement, he carried a smile, also. One could almost read the minds of the lawyers, the judge and the media, because all were caught off guard. Many had been concerned that the "hick" college would not defend itself well, thereby being dubbed country louts by all concerned. You see, this was their first time to encounter other folks from the Hollow area who battled just as fiercely as the soccer and basketball teams.

News of the first day's court events shocked the whole country as they watched, as Josh indicated to the court as well as to everybody else that Bacon College had no statement to make. "What do you make of this" was asked to many so called experts of law on this evening with most laughing at Bacon's not taking this opportunity to explain its case to the world. One lawyer indicated that what happened in the court this morning was what he expected from this group from the mountains who don't seem to understand what is happening in the more affluent part of society. "As I watched the court proceedings on television today, I thought about how out of place the president and his counsel, if you can call it that, are," he stated. "It was as though the two were trying to remove themselves from the reality of the situation by just remaining quiet during the whole process."

"What would you have done differently?" the host asked, now getting more specific.

"First of all I would have employed more than one lawyer for the hapless defendant to counter the opposition that sits in this trial with no less than ten experienced legal counselors who can run down all kinds of evidence that could help their case," he noted with conviction. "Moving to the courtroom nowadays to solve conflicts is not like it was years ago. Now it's really show time for attorneys, especially in cases being decided by a jury. This is a monumental case for all the country and will be cited in similar cases for years to come, so for the defense to sit in court without a lawyer on its team seems unconscionable to say the least. And to sit with a lay person who has limited experience in world activities as one's counsel makes no sense whatsoever."

On another channel a renown trial lawyer shook his head in dismay regarding the posture of Bacon College's defense at this point in the trial. He pointed out,

"Courtrooms are made for lawyers and not lay people picked up on the street, because they have made some kind of good decisions along the way. If Bacon College loses this case, it will no longer exist as an institution of higher learning, and those named in the suit will be paying damages for the remainder of their lives. You see, there is too much of a risk not to have a good legal team on your side."

Seated in their inexpensive hotel room in Groveville, the conversation between Dr. Damond and Josh was interrupted by a quiet rap on the door. When Josh opened the door, there stood one of the female lawyers from their opponent's team. "My name is Lottie Burkhouser, the anonymous caller to you several times."

"Won't you come in?" Josh requested.

"Surely," she responded.

"This is Dr. Damond, the president of Bacon College," Josh said. "We are so glad to meet you."

"At this juncture I only have just a short time so I'll get right to the point," she stated, now taking a seat on the side of the bed. "Your opponents in this case are going to try to prove that the testing or entry records of tests of your athletes are incorrect, and that you all willfully assisted these young people providing false testing information. They are working on proving that the president of Bacon and others were so enamored over getting the large sum of money from the benevolent person, that they resorted to willful acts of wrongdoing to keep the money. To become successful competitors at the Division I level in order to keep the money, the president and others resorted to making the unqualified candidates for college entry qualified by boosting their test scores. Others contributed to these misdeeds, because of the pressure from the president. As you all know, many witnesses will be called before this court to support their theory."

"Thank you for divulging this information to us," Dr. Damond responded. "We can certainly use all the forewarnings we can get."

As she stood to go, Josh asked, "Lottie, do you think it's in your best interest to be a pretender on your team of lawyers? Would it be best for you to deal with this situation in your own heart? God has blessed you mightily with special gifts so pretending to be on both sides of an issue leads me to think that you are struggling with scriptural precepts to guide you. We love what you are doing for us, but do hope that your deception can be dealt with in the near future."

Witnesses

On the first day of presenting witnesses a most unusual event took place right before the television cameras that filled the coliseum from different vantage points. Lottie Burkhouser huddled with her nine associates for a brief meeting in which she instructed the group that she should no longer be considered a member of the plaintiff's staff of attorneys. She was joining the team from Bacon College.

A third chair was pulled up and now Bacon had its only lawyer, albeit under very strange circumstances. "I will cost you nothing," she stated to a very shocked Dr. Damond and Josh. "I shall just sit here, and if you need me in any way, just let me know."

Taking just a moment or two to collect himself after the shocking defection of a vital member of his support group bent on punishing Bacon College, the prosecutor announced his first witness, Dr. Damond.

Dr. Damond stood and walked to the witness chair and after being seated, the prosecutor stated, "Please give us your name and what you do at Bacon College."

"I am John Damond, president of the college," he replied.

"What is the enrollment and location of this college?" he asked.

"We have three hundred forty-eight students, and the college is located in the mountains of southwest Virginia," he advised.

"When did you all start competing in athletic events on the college level?" the prosecutor asked, after which he turned his back to Dr. Damond.

"We have been competing for two years," Dr. Damond answered.

"What prompted you to decide that you wanted to compete on the intercollegiate level when you had not in any way shown an interest before?" the prosecutor probed deeper.

"Our board of directors from time to time over the years had broached this subject every now and then, but there was really no serious discussion of the matter until we received a large anonymous gift of money," he answered, really wanting to continue but was cut off abruptly.

"The real reason was that the money you had received had a condition attached. Would you tell us what that stipulation was?" the prosecutor asked.

"The only stipulation in accepting the generous gift was that the college would have a women's basketball team that would be competitive on the Division I level in two years," he noted.

"Weren't you fearful that you would not be able to live up to that condition of the receipt of money?" he asked.

"I certainly was," Dr. Damond indicated.

"Almost as soon as you got the money you began to spend it on building an athletic dormitory and a new coliseum, the likes of which few in the area had ever seen before. You were spending the money, and yet you had no team and only had a coach a few weeks earlier. Did it ever bother you that your college might not be able to live up to its being competitive on the highest level of competition in two years?" he inquired.

"Of course, it did," Dr. Damond replied. "Many nights I would lie awake thinking about it."

"Would you say that you were under a lot of pressure to succeed in sports?" the prosecutor asked this time standing right in front of Dr. Damond.

"I can assure you that I felt much pressure to fulfill the requirements of the receipt of the money," Dr. Damond candidly responded. "We were about to enter a totally different arena of activity which was entirely new for me. Everybody was very excited about it."

"All were depending on you to carry the ball, so to speak, weren't they?" he continued to probe.

"I guess you could say that, because we do have a small staff, and I just took it on myself to see that we had an athletic program," he noted with some embarrassment.

The questioning continued into the morning until a break was called by the judge, and in about fifteen minutes the prosecuting attorney resumed where he left off earlier in the morning. One could readily detect the direction the interrogatories were leading, because they seemed to implicate the affable president with each of his honest answers.

"Let me see if I have this straight," the attorney said, to introduce his first question after the recess. "The media were very excited about your new program, the board of directors looked to you totally to advance this new endeavor, your staff was overjoyed, the students were beside themselves and the community suddenly was behind your college for the first time. As some would say, you were really feeling the heat, weren't you?" he asked.

"You might say it that way," Dr. Damond replied.

"You really felt you would do anything to be successful, didn't you?" he asked, now standing directly in front of the witness stand.

"Well, you know that was about the way I felt at the time," he stated while smiling, "because there was such a groundswell of interest in developing a basketball program."

"Did many coaches respond to your request for applications to coach your new team?" the prosecutor asked.

"Only a very few applied which surprised me," he answered. "We employed a young lady who had no college coaching experience."

"Did you think that naivete would be a good characteristic of your new staff member?" he asked

"One might say that would be true, because I certainly was naïve about the world of college sports," Dr. Damond responded. "She just fit right in with our staff and our team players dearly love her. She has just fit right in with our whole program."

"When did you tell her that it was absolutely necessary to win on the Division I level, and when did you tell her about the high stakes surrounding the whole athletic program?" he inquired.

"As soon as we knew we wanted her as our new coach, I told her so she would know what her challenge really was," Dr. Damond noted. "She indicated that she loved a challenge such as this one, and would face it the same way she had done with the others she had faced in her life. This is when she advised us that she was a member of the green beret, holding the rank as major."

"Was she aware of the college standards for entry to play athletics?" the prosecutor asked.

"No, she did not know," Dr. Damond said. "She told us that she would only accept those girls on her team who had met the guidelines set forth by the ACUWAA. She was very emphatic about this, and of course, this is what she has done for us."

"May I read you the scores made on the college entrance test for your athletic teams?" he asked.

Upon completing the reading of the scores, he continued. "In all colleges and universities throughout the country participating in athletics on the Division I level, only one college's athletes have scored higher than that of the other students. Do you know which college that is?"

"I really don't know," Dr. Damond replied.

"It's Bacon College," the prosecutor stated now looking squarely at the jury. "How can you explain this? Bacon College seems to find itself in a unique posture in many ways: winning all of its basketball games, winning all of its soccer games and now having an average entrance test score for athletes higher than that of the other students. Is this just a coincidence or is it just man made?"

"We just have a good group of athletes," Dr. Damond proudly responded.

"Don't you think it was unusual when your coach was helping to administer the college entrance tests to the high school students?" he asked.

"Not really," Dr. Damond replied. "We always try to be good neighbors in many ways."

"Your coach could have been in position to assist your girls on the test in some way, couldn't she?" he pointed out.

"Coach Bosley would not have done that," Dr. Damond responded emphatically.

"She really did think they were good players, and other coaches had recruited them heavily," he stated. "You did say that the pressure was on her to suit up a competitive team on the Division I level, so wouldn't it be helpful to see that the girls achieved at the acceptable level for college entry?"

"She would have not done anything like that," he pointed out again emphatically.

"Were you there when the test was administered?" he asked.

"No, I wasn't," Dr. Damond reacted with a short answer.

"Are you aware that the morning of the test one set of booklets was not sealed, which meant that it was opened prior to the testing by someone?" he indicated to the president who by now could see the direction the questioning was going.

"I was not aware of that," he answered.

"How many times over the years had someone from your college helped the high school with their college entrance examinations?" he probed further.

"I don't know of any other time," he replied.

"So now another unique situation emerges in addition to the others mentioned earlier that questions surrounding your students' college entrance test scores are introduced when your new basketball coach helps the high school administer the college entrance test to its students," he said with a smirk on his face. "I'm sure you are good at statistics so tell us the probability of all the unusual situations developing from the same college that in someway give it the edge in intercollegiate competition."

"I don't believe such a probability statement could be calculated," he answered.

The questioning had gone on through lunch time. On many of these questions the female attorney, who had switched loyalties, had requested that Josh object, but he just sat silently through the whole process. He was operating steadfastly to his plan.

"You were blinded, too, because of the huge amount of pressure to field a winning team was thrust on your shoulders, and you gave in to the pressures of greed that by your acquiescence around you, an environment was being put in place that would fulfill the desire of the benevolent person. A winning team at all cost was in the end your new philosophy driven by pride of not failing in this challenge that was thrust upon you not from your asking so you looked the other way, didn't you?" he asked.

Lottie was fit to be tied when this final question was asked such that she even stood up, but the judge commanded her to sit down. Josh still sat silently watching the proceedings unfold.

"Again I say we are so fortunate to have our female athletes on campus," he responded. "They are a precious group of outstanding students, and likewise, outstanding competitors on the Division I level of intercollegiate sports."

"I have no further questions," the prosecutor said.

After the break Josh indicated to the judge that he had no questions to ask Dr. Damond to the surprise of everyone. Following Josh's response, the judge announced that the court would reconvene the next morning at eight o'clock.

Of course, the television airwaves were filled with the report of court proceedings with five carrying a full hour on a special report. All were very surprised at the response of Bacon College, which at this point was no rebuttal at all. One reporter summed it up that Bacon was really guilty of wrongdoing; therefore it was just going to sit idly by and let the prosecutor's team prove their points. "In the end," he said, "the college will admit its failure to comply with ACUWAA rules, and use as their excuse that they were new in sports and didn't really fully understand the guidelines for athletic teams."

Several of the shows had seasoned lawyers who chastised the college for not employing a strong cadre of legal counselors to compete with the strong contingent on the prosecutor's team. A leading defense attorney on one of the early shows was asked, "What did you make of the shift of one of the counselors to the defense team?"

"I have never seen that happen before," he responded, "and for it to happen right in the courtroom before live television cameras made it even more amazing. I was so perplexed over the incident that I called one of my friends on the legal team about the situation."

"What did he say?" the host asked.

"He said that it came as a total surprise to the entire team, and because it happened just before the court proceedings began, he believed that the defecting attorney had really wrestled over this decision. She was not the type to do things dramatically, but she did in this case."

"Who was she anyway?" the host inquired.

"She was a veteran attorney with considerable background in similar popular cases and was well respected by the other team members," the lawyer noted. "She told the group that the soft spot in her heart for Bacon College led her to transfer her loyalties to the other side. It really was an amicable move."

"But wasn't she being paid well on this team?" the host pointed out.

"She was being paid very well, and as far as I know she is not earning a cent as the only attorney the college has to defend it," the lawyer indicated. "I am sure she can be a big help to the college, but from what I observed today, Josh Morrow is not responding to her advice. I know what you are going to ask next so I'll answer it now. I don't really know why Mr. Morrow is letting these special opportunities pass without inserting some kind of thoughts or expressions to prick the minds of the jury. Trials don't provide many opportunities to get one's point across, and those golden times in this case have just slid by for the defense."

"Do you have any idea who will be the witnesses called on behalf of the defense?" the host asked.

"Frankly, I have no idea," the lawyer answered. "Mr. Morrow might have a surprise witness or something, because he seems to sit very calmly listening as the prosecution team hammers away. Even after Dr. Damond so naïvely answered all of his questions with several doing much damage to their case, they both seemed to be giving the appearance that everything is fine in their camp. Yet, from what I can judge from this vantage point, the jury is getting an earful, and we have only heard from one witness so far."

Print, voice and electronic media were having a field day covering every aspect of this unusual court trial that was really changing the landscape, namely because the college was only being defended by a lay person and a Baptist preacher at that. The vociferous pundits to the person indicated that the chance that Bacon College had of winning this case only being represented by a lay person was extremely remote.

The second witness called to the stand was Coach Anna Bosley. "Please state your name," the prosecutor said.

"My name is Anna Bosley," she replied.

"What do you do at Bacon College?" he asked.

"I am the basketball and soccer coach," she indicated.

"What did you do before coming to Bacon College?" he asked.

"I was a high school teacher in northern Virginia, and I coached the basketball team," she stated.

"Did you have a winning team there?" he inquired.

"We won about one-half of our games," she noted.

"How did you get the job at Bacon College?" he asked.

"I applied after discovering that there was an opening there," she replied.

"Tell us about the whole process, if you don't mind," he asked.

"I went down for an interview with the president and board of directors, and they asked me a lot of questions about my background," she noted. "I was told that the college had never had any kind of athletic program before, but they were starting one, because of an anonymous gift of money they had received. The stipulation that the school compete on the Division I level almost immediately concerned them very much, so they spent a lot of time on this subject so that I fully understood the unusual demands on the program."

"Was this your first college interview, and didn't you think that the demands of this position were beyond one's achievement?" he pointed out.

"I was so excited about being considered for this dream job that I would have accepted any demands without hesitation," she emphatically stated. "Challenges have been a way of life for me, so when I am faced with difficult expectations, I just say bring them on. That's one reason I have been selected for several missions in the green beret, because the leaders know I love a challenge."

Her responses to the questions were really leading right in the direction the attorney wanted it to go, so he continued. "You had always met the challenges head on, but in this case you found yourself in a different environment so you didn't know where to turn," he said. "You really hadn't given much thought to the demand of competing successfully on the Division I level, yet this is what you had to do. Nothing was going to stop you to meet this demand of this position you had dreamed about for so long. You would do anything to be successful."

"I guess you could say that," she answered. "I worked almost twenty-four hours each day to obtain a team for our small college."

"You spent a lot of time in the Hollow to recruit some players, didn't you?" he inquired.

"I certainly did," she replied. "I had read about this group of girls from the mountains so that was the only group that I recruited. I was surprised that other colleges and universities were not actively recruiting this group, and they weren't really."

"Were you surprised when you discovered that none of the girls had taken the college entrance examination so really they did not qualify to participate in ACUWAA competition?" he asked, now standing very closely to her.

"Not having a background regarding the rules of participation in college athletics, I still was surprised that the girls had not been encouraged to take these tests," Coach Anna answered.

"When you discovered that not a single parent of these girls had ever completed high school, you were shocked, weren't you?" he asked.

"That really did shock me," she answered. "It gave credence for the reason the girls had not pursued the college entrance test. They were overwhelmed that they were graduating from high school, now fulfilling a dream of their parents who were so proud of them. College for them was a light year removed from their dreams."

"So you saw to it that the girls took these tests to qualify them for college entry," he pointed out. "Your zeal for assisting your prospective basketball team took an unusual twist, didn't it?"

"I don't know what you mean," Coach Anna noted.

"You decided that you would just help them on these tests, didn't you?" he inquired, now looking at the jury so they would be sure to hear the question.

"I guess you could call it assisting them," she softly responded.

"You even helped to administer the test to them, didn't you?" he asked.

"I did help the school on the day of the test," she replied. "One of the proctors was absent so the principal asked me to help on this day."

"Did you have these test booklets in your possession a day or two before the test?" he inquired.

"The principal had a work session with the helpers so I was present and had possession of the booklets," Coach Anna answered.

"You really put yourself in position to help the girls directly on the test, didn't you?" he snapped back at her.

"Oh, I would never do that," she quickly responded.

"But you did, because the pressure on you was just too great to meet the demands of the benevolent person who had given so much money to the college, and you knew without these girls your hopes were dashed, so you helped them with the answers on this college entrance test, didn't you?" he asked now bending over to look her in the eye."

"I never helped the girls with the answers," she responded.

"Do you want us to believe that your help with the testing program as a proctor was just a coincidence, the only time anyone from the college had ever helped the high school with these tests before?" he noted. "You want us to believe that these eleven girls from less than affluent families scored much above the other students without any help from you. Wouldn't that be another improbable, if not impossible, coincidence surrounding your team which seems to have an unusually large number of these so called coincidences?"

Not waiting for an answer he told the judge, "I have no further questions."

During the last phase of his questioning, Lottie Burhouser, sitting with Josh, again was fit to be tied, because of the kind of questioning presented to Coach Anna. Josh remained steadfast by not reacting to any activity in the courtroom. All observers did not understand why the college was not asking any questions to the witnesses, and its representatives were just sitting and themselves observers of the proceedings.

After a long recess the judge asked Josh whether or not he had any questions of the witness.

"I have none," Josh answered, again surprising everyone everywhere.

Surprised again, the judge asked another time, "Are you sure, Mr. Morrow, that you don't have any questions?" He knew that the questioning by the prosecution had really damaged the case of Bacon College."

"No, I don't have any questions," Josh answered albeit against the wishes of Lottie Burkhouser, who was really upset by this time.

"Let me ask some questions," Lottie pleaded with Josh in a low voice. The prosecution has painted an ugly picture of Bacon College so we must eradicate that through our own questioning."

"I really appreciate your concern for our welfare in this situation," he whispered. "Everything is going to be all right."

"How can it be when you are doing nothing to help the cause of your little college?" Lottie asked in such a way that it could be heard by the judge.

"Please have patience and trust in me as this case moves forward," Josh responded.

Soon their conversation was interrupted by the judge, who now was calling for the next witness of the prosecution. A well dressed middle-age lady moved forward to the witness stand. "Please state your name and where you are from," the prosecutor stated.

"My name is Minnie Eastridge, and I am from Bacon in southwest Virginia," she indicated in a very clear voice replete with mountain colloquialism.

"How long have you lived in the community of Bacon?" he asked.

"I have been there all my life," she answered.

"So you were there when the college suddenly received that first large sum of money from a benevolent person, weren't you?" the prosecutor asked.

"I certainly was," she proudly stated.

"How did the community respond to what was taking place?" he inquired.

"Those I knew really were excited," she said.

"Did any of you discuss what would happen, if Bacon College failed to meet the demands included when it received the large sum of money?" the prosecutor probed.

"We certainly did," she responded. "I had played a little basketball years ago and realized that only a few girls were capable of even playing on the Division I level, much less competing successfully. Many of us were very pessimistic about the whole situation so soon decided that our small college was headed for a crash for certain."

"What kind of a crash did you all talk about?" he continued to ask.

"Well, the pressure to succeed was mounting, such that we believed that if the college failed to adhere to the stipulations of the gift, it would have to close, if for no other reason the embarrassment that would come with its failure to be successful," she pointed out. "It seemed that the whole world was involved in some way. Media all the way to the renown national personalities were participating in painting a 'pressure cooker' type position of our local college. Mountain people don't ever like to be embarrassed and for my group, that is all we could see happening. Wondering how we could later ever tell someone we were from Bacon, we just decided that we would divorce ourselves from the whole ordeal."

"Then what happened," the prosecutor continued.

"Rumors began to circulate that the major universities had suddenly stopped their recruiting of the Hollow girls so we thought that possibly one or two of the girls would attend Bacon and play basketball," she said. "Then further rumors began to make their way throughout the mountains that the reason the major universities discontinued their recruiting of the Hollow girls was that they believed that coming from such a poor community and a less than an opulent high school, the girls could not meet the academic standards. One told a friend of mine that she really wanted one of the girls to play for her university, but she just knew she could not pass the entrance examination."

"Weren't you surprised when you discovered that all of the girls had passed the entrance test?" the prosecutor continued to probe deeper, now sporting a wry smile.

"I really was," Minnie answered. "While there was joy in the little community after discovering that the Hollow girls qualified for college to play basketball, our spirits were dampened when another rumor circulated that the girls had gotten help on the college entrance test. At first we didn't understand how this could have taken place, but later we learned much more about this mountain saga. Our joyful spirits were totally dashed."

"But you now are an ardent fan of Bacon College's basketball and soccer teams, aren't you?" he asked.

"I certainly am," she responded proudly.

"What made you all to change your minds?" he inquired.

"Well, when Jewel Throneberry wrote this article in the Margone Magazine about the Bacon College girls and how they were being dishonestly dealt with by all the media, we all looked at the situation differently and threw our support for the athletic program at the college."

"So, nothing was different about your concern regarding the rumors of wrongdoing on the college entrance test," he stated. "Do you ever think about it now?"

"To be truthful with you," she noted, "I still think about it often, and especially because Anna Bosley, the coach of Bacon, was curiously present when the tests were administered to the girls. The rumor that the she helped the girls succeed on the test was the biggest hurdle for me."

"I have no further questions," he told the judge.

"Mr. Morrow, do you have questions to ask this witness?" the judge asked, knowing what had been said and how powerful it was for the prosecution.

"I have no questions," Josh replied, albeit certainly not at the behest of his partner now, Lottie Burkhouser. For her this was the most unusual behavior that she had ever observed in any court proceeding, and she believed that the college was doomed, because there had been absolutely no defense at all. She knew that the whole country was observing this trial on television, and everyone was going to sympathize with the small college, because of what they believed was ignorance of the judicial system. Of course, she had been warned over the years that gaining one's sympathy in court proceedings was considered worthless, if it could not be backed up with strong supportive evidence.

While Lottie was sitting there with the defense mulling over many subjects related to the last several days, the judge stated, "Please call the next witness."

Out stepped Jewel Throneberry dressed in a dark three-piece pants suit. Confidence was exuded with each step toward the witness box. "Please state your name and what you do," the prosecutor said in a very compassionate voice.

"My name is Jewel Throneberry and I work for Margone Magazine, Inc.," she answered.

"You know the Hollow girls, as we call the Bacon College team, very well, don't you?" he asked. "Can you recall the first time you met these girls?"

"I certainly can," she answered.

"Would you tell about this initial meeting and what happened later?" he asked.

"I was trying to write a story about these young ladies who had won the hearts of those in the women's basketball world," she responded. "I set out to prove that they were not as good as all of us thought they were, so my story related that message to the world. Of course, you know by now that it was a false story in which I retracted sometime later."

"We all read your retraction," the prosecutor noted. "Something happened to cause you to have a change of heart. Would you please tell what that was?"

"Several days later I received money to make my house accessible for a make-believe handicapped mother," she answered, "so from that time forward I thought that the best course of action for me was to tell the truth about the fabricated story that had hurt the Bacon College team and all the others in any way connected with this small higher education institution."

"What did you do with the money you received?" the prosecutor asked.

"I just left it in an account in a local bank," she answered.

"Did you try to send it back to the benevolent person after having lied such that the benevolent person wanted to help this so called handicapped mother?" he asked.

"I really did," she replied, "but the bank official could not trace the source so I just left it in the bank under my name called the 'benevolent fund.'"

"But there was an even larger sum added to that fund about the same time," the prosecutor noted. "Would you please tell us about that addition to your account?"

"A first cousin with whom I grew up divided up his assets, and he included me in that division," she responded.

"Did you think it was unusual that he gave you cash money in one hundred dollar bills?" he inquired.

"Well, many would say that it was strange," she answered with a smile, "but he was very eccentric and had no faith whatsoever in our banks of today. He always kept his money in cash."

"Did you think that the amount was unusually large for a gift like that?" he probed.

"Not really," she said. "He was a very wealthy person."

"Is it true that you lied about the initial story that you wrote in your magazine about the basketball players at Bacon College?" he asked, wanting to revisit an earlier statement she made.

"That's correct," she replied. "I wish I had not done what I did."

"Let me see if I understand what took place regarding you and the Hollow girls," he ruminated aloud. "The first time you came in contact with the Bacon College girls' basketball team, you wrote a story about them that was included in the Margone Magazine, which is a most popular magazine with a very wide circulation. Several days later you were busy writing a retraction just as two sums of money were included in your bank account. The second of the large amounts was deposited in the form of one hundred-dollar bills.

"My take on this goes this way," the prosecutor stated, while at the same time Lottie Burkhouser was trying in vain to get Josh to object. "You were so enamored over the receipt of the first sum of money that when you received the second large amount from the benevolent person with the stipulation that you issue a successful retraction to the entire country, you complied without hesitation."

Jewel was really angry at the suggestions of the prosecutor, but when she began to make her verbal reaction to these allegations, she was cut off by him when he abruptly stated. "I have no further questions of this witness."

With a red face and veins noticeably popping out in her neck for all to see, Lottie Burkhouser wanted a chance to cut the prosecutor's theories to shreds, but Josh wanted no part of it.

"Mr. Morrow, it's your chance to question the witness," the judge stated.

"I have no questions for this witness," Josh replied, as Lottie gestured in despair by putting both hands over her head.

Because of the interest throughout the country in the court trial in Groveville, Colorado, many television stations carried lengthy news segments describing the scene in courtroom. Two of the major networks presented a one-hour special report at prime time in the evening covering each minute detail of the trial, especially emphasizing the unusual behavior of Bacon College who at this juncture had not done one thing to defend itself. In fact, each of the reporters pointed out that Bacon College really appeared to be guilty as charged based on the way it was handling its defense. Many continued to talk about Lottie Burkhouser changing sides, and how Bacon College could use her expertise, but continued to follow the advice of Josh Morrow. Of course, they said that this was really no noticeable counsel at all.

"I hope they know what they are doing," Maudie said to the girls, as they watched the news on television.

"I would hate to be on the witness stand," Dorothy stated. "Do you all think that Mit has arrived in Groveville to be a witness?"

"She should arrive this evening, because I understand she is to appear in court tomorrow morning," Maudie said. "Esther is traveling with her, but I don't believe Esther will have to be a witness."

The next morning was the start of a beautiful Colorado day as Mit and Esther walked into the arena. As soon as they went through the door, Mit was whisked away to the witness chamber.

Esther took a seat several rows up to observe first hand the court setting that they had been watching on television so intently back at the college. In a few minutes the judge appeared with all rising, and the first witness of the day was called.

"Would you mind stating your name and what you do?" the prosecutor asked.

"My name is Clyde Pennington and I run a hardware store," he stated in an Appalachian voice.

"Are you familiar with Bacon College?" he inquired.

"Yes, I am," Clyde responded. "I was at one time on the board of directors of the college."

"How long were you on this board?" the prosecutor asked.

"I was on the board for fifteen years before the start of this year," he answered.

"Were you excited when the college received the large sum of money from the benevolent person on two different occasions?" he inquired.

"I really didn't know what to make of the whole thing," he said. "I was much in favor of the gift at the beginning, but as time passed I soured somewhat to the idea," he replied.

"What caused you to find disfavor in this gift?" he asked.

"I never have been one who got excited over sports," he said, "and when I heard the stipulation regarding the gift, I could sense that it might be more than our small Christian college could produce. While I kept my thoughts mostly to myself, the intramural program in basketball was good enough for me."

"So, you believed that the college had bitten off more than it could chew," he stated.

"I guess you could sum up my feelings that way," he replied. "There was great pressure on all of us, and particularly our president who was carrying the brunt of the entire situation. He really wanted the college to be successful in the competition on the Division I level, and he acted as an encourager for all the board members."

"Did you ever hear rumors of wrongdoing by some to field a competitive team?" he probed deeper.

"I wish I could say no to that question, but I did hear a rumor or two regarding the entrance tests of the athletes," he responded. "Our president assured us when this was brought up to him that everything was fine so the board members put this subject aside, always trusting our president in this matter."

"What do you think?" he asked.

"I have thought about the whole sordid set of allegations for a long time," he responded. "Although my mind still swirls with all kinds of thoughts and ideas that seem to implicate our college, I still have total faith in our president."

"Didn't your president have much to lose, if the basketball team failed to succeed?" he inquired.

"He had more than any of the rest of us," Clyde answered.

"He could have done wrong in this matter to help his chances of being successful, couldn't he?" the attorney snapped.

"I have no further questions," he promptly told the judge.

It was a question of obvious conjecture that was left unanswered so with the dismissal of this witness, much was left to be pondered by the jurors who were getting an earful. The attorney had left much doubt of innocence in the minds of those who were in the end going to determine innocence or guilt. Could Josh and Lottie now get the jurors back on track by their own questioning?

"Mr. Morrow, it's your time to question the witness," the judge announced.

When Josh indicated that he had no questions, Lottie Burhouser could hardly restrain herself, because she knew the interrogatories by the prosecutor had left the Bacon College in an extremely precarious court position by each of the witnesses. Only the board of directors of Bacon College, Dr. Damond and Josh knew Josh's plan for this case.

Speculation by the experts on numerous television shows of the position Bacon found itself left much to be desired. Most believed that the little college was so backward it didn't know how to respond to the national attention it was getting. To the expert, using a lay person for its total defense was not only providing the nails for the coffin, but the hammer and all else, also. In summary, the little college that had held prominence in the national spotlight in basketball and now soccer was falling less than gracefully from its lofty perch.

After a brief recess the judge asked the prosecutor to call his next witness.

Out stepped a tall, middle-age man wearing a suit and tie. "Please state your name and what you do," the prosecutor asked.

"My name is Raymond Forrester , and I am principal of Central High School in McHone County," he said in a deep masculine voice.

"Several years ago you enrolled a group of girls from a place called the Hollow, didn't you?" he asked.

"That's correct," Raymond responded.

"These girls were considered good basketball players, but they were not enrolled in public school, were they?" he continued.

"They enrolled in the ninth grade at my school," he replied.

"Were you worried about them coming from a home schooling type situation?" he asked.

"I certainly was," he replied, "but …"

Interrupting his conclusion of the answer to the previous interrogatory, the questioner continued. "After these girls had won all your games in basketball, there were two concerns about their continuing in athletics in college. First, your school played in the lowest group in state competition of the three classifications, so there was concern that again after all these long years of waiting, you would not have a college scholarship player from your school. And secondly, you were really concerned that these young ladies, coming from the Hollow and from your school in a very poor community, would not meet the minimum academic standards of the ACUWAA, weren't you?" the prosecutor inquired and now turning to the jury to let them know that this answer was important.

"Over the years I had always wanted to have a college scholarship player from my school so this was the closest I had come to having that come to pass," he replied.

"Obviously, I was skeptical about the level of performance of these athletes on the college entrance tests."

"You had studied enough sociology dealing with heredity and demographics to realize that those students from less affluent backgrounds tend not to do as well as other students on these national tests, do they?" he asked.

"I would agree with your assessment," the principal reacted.

"From what I gather here you really wanted these students to do well on these tests, didn't you?" the prosecutor asked.

"I really did," the principal stated.

"For many days Anna Bosley was on your campus recruiting these girls for Bacon College's new basketball program, wasn't she?" the attorney asked.

"Yes, she was," he answered.

"During the earlier stages of her visits, you were not really a happy camper, were you?" the prosecutor asked.

"I was really concerned that this very small college would be able to field a team of girls to compete on the national scene, and secondly, I had hoped that a coach of a national powerhouse team would have signed one of the girls," he replied.

"But that didn't happen, so you were left with only one thread of hope to fulfill your dream, weren't you?" he indicated.

"At first I received several calls from prominent coaches I had seen on television, but suddenly they didn't call any more," he replied.

"Did you ever discover why these outstanding national coaches stopped inquiring about your girls?" he asked.

"One day I called one of them to see what had been done to cause them now to show no interest in our girls," he stated.

"What did the coach say to you?" he asked.

"The coach told me that she was afraid to take a chance on any of these girls, because of their home backgrounds, and the fact that they were attending such a rural and poor school, they would probably not be able to do two things," he said. "First, they would probably not do very well on the entrance examination, and if they squeaked by this requirement, they would probably not successfully fulfill the requirements of the classroom. So it would be best to recruit those students with stronger academic backgrounds."

"This left you with only little Bacon College to recruit your girls, and you didn't want to fail in this situation, because you then would not have any hope of having any student sign a letter of intent from your school from the group of girls, would you?" he continued.

"That's exactly right," he answered. "This was the best chance the school had ever had to have a college scholarship player of this kind."

"You were determined not to fail, weren't you?" he said.

"I was going to give it my best shot," he said.

"So now Coach Bosley's presence on campus was more important for you," he stated. "In fact you and other members of your staff invited her for lunch many days that spring."

"She really in a way became an extension of the faculty," he said. "Everybody liked her very much."

"She even sat in on your training session for the college entrance testing, didn't she?" he asked.

"One of the proctors was absent so I asked her to assist us on the testing day," he replied.

"Did the Bacon College coach come to your office from time to time?" he inquired.

"Yes, she did," he responded.

At any time did you ever leave the office while she was present?" the prosecutor asked.

"I surely did several times when someone would need to see me about a problem," he answered.

"Where did you store the college entrance tests you received from the testing service?" he probed.

"I kept them in my office," he noted.

"On the morning of the test were you surprised that both the verbal and nonverbal portions of the test were opened?" the prosecutor asked.

"Not really, because the head proctor knew that I had them," he responded.

"What if I told you the head proctor denied opening the packages before the administration of the test?" he asked.

"I don't know of anyone else who would have wanted to open them," the principal responded.

"Would it have been possible that Coach Bosley could have opened the packages of tests?" he continued.

"She could have, but I don't think she did," the principal noted in support of Coach Anna.

"Looking back, do you think it was a wise decision that she helped on this testing, because of the inordinate amount of pressure she had to be sure the girls qualified for college to meet the standards of the ACUWAA?" he asked, again turning to the jury to get their attention.

"There were many rumors circulating in the area regarding the tests," the principal noted. "Some indicated that it was a conflict of interest for her or for me to have been involved, because of our vested interest in the outcome. For me it was a fulfillment of a dream that the girls do well on the test, and for her it was the fulfillment of a budding career. The stakes were high with everything riding on the success of this group of Hollow girls."

"I could have not said it better," the prosecutor stated. "I have no further questions.

Witness after witness had been questioned with not a single one being cross examined by Josh, so the talk show world and special programming teams spent much time trying to theorize what kind of plan the defense had, or if it had a plan at all. Following the principal's heartfelt candid answers to his interrogatories, much was discussed about how the truth was being presented by each of the witnesses. "Albeit very damaging to the defense, each of the witnesses seems to go overboard to tell the truth with many adding embellishment that certainly paints a bad picture of Bacon College," one television reporter noted with mixed emotions.

Later, the judge stated, "Would you call your next witness?"

Through the door of the witness chamber came a very physically fit dark skinned blond young lady with a pony tail, wearing very modest clothing. "Please state your name," the prosecutor indicated.

"My name is Mitsie Travers," she replied. "Everyone calls me Mit." All eyes were on this young lady that everyone knew as the best female college soccer player in the country.

"Would you tell us a little about yourself?" the prosecutor asked.

"I was born in Bassett, Virginia, but my parents moved to Costa Rica when I was very young to begin missionary work," she stated. "After my parents completed language school in San Jose, they were assigned to the jungle in the south zone of this Central American country. In the jungle we became a member of the Corbri tribe where I lived for nearly nine years among the natives of that area."

"During this period in the jungle, where did you go to school?" he asked.

"My mom taught me most of my subjects, but my dad helped teach me mathematics," she replied.

"I guess you could say that you were the best in your class," he stated, followed by some laughter.

"My mom taught some Corbri students who were very good students," she quickly replied.

"According to the Sports Ramble, you led your school team in San Jose to a junior national championship, and later were the star of your jungle team that won two more junior national championships in soccer," he stated. "Is that correct?"

"I played on these teams that were composed of excellent soccer players," Mit answered.

"Did you ever think about college?" the prosecutor inquired.

"I wanted to go to college, because both of my parents had gone," she replied, "but my parents and I realized that we did not have sufficient money for college."

"But you are now in college at Bacon, aren't you?" he indicated.

"We are certain that my enrolling in college was because of God's intervention," she noted. "One day Coach Anna and the Bacon girls arrived on a mission trip to our small village. During this visit she offered me an athletic scholarship to Bacon."

"Had you ever been approached by another college coach?" he asked.

"No, I had not," she answered.

"But something else happened later that concerned your soccer coach, didn't it?" he inquired.

"Some time later the business manager of our mission came to the village to talk to my parents and me about the scholarship offer," she replied.

"Why didn't he telephone you about his inquiry?" he asked.

"We had no utilities at all in the village, so to communicate we had to travel back and forth," she indicated.

"Was he excited when he arrived?" the prosecutor asked.

"He was really excited, because he had been so very much enamored about my getting the scholarship to play soccer in the United States," she replied.

"Your business manager knew that many more people might become involved in missionary work, if he could use you as a model, one who now was being offered a free education at Bacon College," he stated. "Were you aware of how important you had become in the whole scheme of things?"

"I was elated over getting the scholarship, because my college would not cost my parents anything, but I was not aware that more importance was riding on my going to college," she answered.

"What did he have to tell you and your parents on this exciting visit?" he asked.

"He advised us that Coach Anna had called and was really concerned that I had not taken the college entrance examination," Mit answered. "To take care of this situation, Mom and I traveled back to San Jose with the business manager who said that he had ordered the test that should be delivered immediately to his office."

"What happened in San Jose?" he asked.

"Mom and the business manager helped me prepare for the test," she answered.

"How many days did they work with you to prepare you for this test?" he asked.

"I believe we worked four days on this test," she replied.

"What did you make on this examination?" he inquired.

"I really don't know, but it was satisfactory to meet Coach Anna's requirements," Mit replied.

"Was the help you received important for your success on the test?" he asked.

"I really believe it was," Mit answered.

"I have no further questions to ask this witness," the prosecutor stated to the judge.

The whole picture had been painted well by the legal team of the prosecution that the pressure on Bacon College to be successful at the Division I level was so great that personnel resorted to wrongdoing to meet the entrance requirements of the ACUWAA. The legal experts on the talk shows said that the team of prosecutors had pulled off a slam dunk, but they indicated that there would be additional witnesses to ensure an obvious verdict in favor of the athletic directors.

One retired and very successful prosecuting attorney on one of the talk shows made an interesting statement to a large television audience. "During the last several days I have been studying the background of this lay gentleman representing the defense," he said. "I have talked with Lottie Burkhouser, also, who told me that Josh Morrow was the most unusual person she had ever met. She went on to say that sitting by his side in the courtroom each day, she had begun to sense an unusual amount of confidence even though to this point, he was saying nothing in court and out of court nothing of any significance. She said that many believed he was just a country lout, but as the days have passed his confidence of the situation bleeds off on all those around him.

"His past is one of obscurity in the Hollow among his flock. It dawned on me as I researched his past that he was the one who led so successfully the feeding of the people in Wasi when the president of that country threatened harm to any who tried to help. Not only did this group of Hollow folks feed these people, but now the president has the girls' basketball team training his girls in Wasi. What a turn of events! By the way for the first time this country has a good relationship with our government now after all these years.

"While this has nothing to do with the entrance tests for the college students, remember that Coach Anna Bosley led the team against the hijackers to prevent harm to the passengers. Later, she led her group of girls to rescue the three missionaries held captive in Abedistan by the terrorists. These are unusual people who have done much for society even as we consider them outside the affluent society, as we know it. I say all this to say to you that when one puts all this history together of Josh Morrow, we probably don't understand his kind of wisdom. He seems to be outside the lines in his decision making. Don't count the college out yet."

Interest in the televised case was still at a high level as days passed with the flood of witnesses responding to inquiries by the seasoned and experienced legal veterans heading the assault on Bacon College. It was not over yet as the judge advised the plaintiff to call his next witness to the stand before a capacity crowd in this huge coliseum in Groveville.

Out came a dapperly dressed middle-age woman whom most present recognized. "Please state your name and what you do," the prosecutor stated.

"My name is Tamatha Milller, the head basketball coach of Darden University," she replied.

"How long has your university had a women's basketball team?" he asked.

"This marks our fifty-fifth year," she stated.

"Over the years your school has had a powerful basketball program, such that other institutions of higher learning are very envious," he said. "How long did it take to build up such a rich program of competing at the highest level in intercollegiate sports and doing it year after year very successfully?"

"For many, many years we struggled to have a successful team of girls," she said. "With continued building we finally began to come to the top about a dozen years ago."

"Were you surprised that the very small college in the mountains of Virginia could come on the scene at the Division I level and win immediately?" the prosecutor asked.

"Obviously, I was shocked," she responded. "We had worked for years and years to have a winning program, and here this small unknown college enters the field and wins all its games. One has to remember that during the first year of competition these girls on the Bacon College team were only freshmen. This made the situation even more shocking."

"Did you recruit any of the Hollow girls when they were in high school?" he asked.

"Yes, I did," Coach Miller replied.

"Did you try to sign any of the girls?" he asked.

"No, I didn't," she replied. "I visited the school and later went into the Hollow for a home visit, and after my discoveries there, I didn't believe that these young people would score enough on their college entrance test to qualify to play in the ACUWAA. Secondly, even if these students passed the entrance test, I didn't believe they could pass the courses on the university level. I really hate to say this, but I was really embarrassed to be around the girls, because they seemed so backward about modern things."

"In summary, you didn't believe these girls were sound enough academically to perform in the classroom of your university," he reiterated.

"That is a reasonable description of my reasoning for not recruiting the girls further," Coach Miller said.

"I have no additional questions," the prosecutor stated.

Declining to ask any questions to the coach by the defense, the judge called a recess.

With the resumption of the proceedings a man very informally dressed with a long pony-tail headed toward the witness stand. "Please state your name and tell us what you do," the prosecutor indicated.

"My name is Albert Gastine, and I am a professor of sociology with major emphasis in probability and statistics at McGrane University."

"Have you ever done studies regarding test results of college entrance tests?" the prosecutor immediately asked.

"I have done numerous studies on this subject," he replied.

"What are some important factors that contribute to the success or lack of same of students taking the college entrance tests?" he asked.

"The most significant variable in every instance is the socio-economic level of the students," he said. "When controlling this variable, the students appear to be more like each other with less significant factors contributing to the kind of scores that they make."

"Could you describe in more detail what kind of college entrance test scores you would expect from a group of students from a poor neighborhood environment whose parents never completed high school?" he asked.

"For a group in which you just described, they would probably fall one standard deviation from the mean when compared to all those tested," he stated. "This means that these students would be expected to fall below the average of the entire sample of students."

"Is this usually the case?" he continued.

"It's almost always the case," the professor related immediately.

Having no further questions, the witness stepped down after being informed that the defense had no questions.

It was late in the day but the judge asked the prosecutor to call his next witness. Once this witness was seated, he stated. "Please tell us your name and what you do."

"I am Mildred Cardoner, and I work with the ABC Testing Service in Atlanta," she responded.

"Does your group handle the college entrance examination?" he asked.

"It does," she replied, "but let me add that there are more than one test utilized by our institutions of higher learning. Our college entrance test is the most commonly one recognized by the colleges and universities."

"Would you walk through for me how your testing service administers its test to high school students?" the prosecutor asked.

"I would be glad to do this," Mildred replied. "Usually a principal of a high school will contact us requesting that his or her school be a testing center for the area. Upon approval we employ the principal and two or three proctors to administer and oversee the session of testing, and forward the test booklets with answers back to us."

"Who receives these tests?" he asked.

"The person designated by ABC Testing is responsible for this," she stated. "That person and the others working as proctors agree to follow the strict guidelines to maintain the integrity of the tests."

"Has any school ever mishandled the tests?" he asked.

"We have had a few instances where an overzealous individual involved in the testing has acted inappropriately," she answered. "One individual gave parts of the test to the teaching staff and instructed them to help the students prepare for the test."

"What did your company do to correct the obvious misdeed?" he asked.

"What we did was to retest all of the students," she quickly replied.

"But wouldn't that give them an advantage of having been tested twice?" he inquired.

"We have several versions of the test so one could take this test many times, and the integrity of the results would remain in tact," Mildred stated.

"If you discovered what you believe was wrongdoing regarding your testing program, what would you do?" he asked.

"Without hesitation we would require that the students take the test over," she responded.

"I have no further questions," the prosecutor stated.

With none coming from the defense the judge adjourned the court proceedings until eight-thirty the next morning. "Be prepared to call your witnesses tomorrow morning," he advised Josh, as he arose and left the courtroom at the end of this long day.

The anchorman on one of the major television channels led off with this story. "Serenity and calmness surround the defense team in the most watched and listened to trial in the history of our country," he stated, while showing scenes from the courtroom set up in the municipal coliseum in Groveville, Colorado. "Not a single question has been asked by the defense made up of Josh Morrow, a young Baptist preacher, who now has the burden of responding to the large arsenal of attorneys on the other side of the courtroom. The 'Benedict Arnold' attorney, who sits with him now after defecting in the presence of live television, struggles to maintain silence as she observes the ruthless tactics of the other team.

"We have talked about this unusual defense all day while watching the proceedings ourselves with some interesting comments emerging. One more observant of our group commented on what was taking place. He said, 'I know that the college has no chance whatsoever against this extremely powerful cadre of lawyers, so the defense team is going just to sit back and hope in the end that Bacon College can just ask for forgiveness and move on with their program.'

"Sympathy goes a long way when contrition seems to come from the heart," the popular reporter stated to his large number of viewers. "But this kind of feeling does not apply to court proceedings, because facts in a case override one's feelings so to this point this jury has only heard one side of the story. Some have even surmised that all the facts are in, and the jury could start immediately to deliberate on what they have heard. The question now comes in two prongs.

First, will there be witnesses for the defense, and secondly, if there are, who will they be?" The athletic directors have pulled out all stops so there is little left for Josh Morrow. To this point, all we see is nothing or as one candidly described the main player charged to save the name and reputation of this little college as a 'country bumkin,' who is drowning by the minute in the real world far from the shadows and protection of the Hollow. This evening we shall continue our report on this monumental trial being conducted in Colorado."

During the evening, there were several stations carrying lengthy reports about the court events of the day. The programs were replete with derogatory comments about Josh, so demeaning that Maudie and the girls just cut off the television, not before Maggie broke down and began to sob. Soon she was joined by the entire group. Realizing the gravity of their emotions, Coach Anna got her Bible and read the scripture dealing with forgiveness, advising them that even Peter had a hard time with this concept as noted in Matthew 18:

23 *"For this reason the kingdom of heaven may be compared to a king who wished to settle accounts with his slaves.*
24 *When he began the reckoning, one who owed him ten thousand talents was brought to him;*
25 *and, as he could not pay, his lord ordered him to be sold, together with his wife and children and all his possessions, and payment to be made.*
26 *So the slave fell on his knees before him, saying, 'Have patience with me, and I will pay you everything.'*
27 *And out of pity for him, the lord of that slave released him and forgave him the debt.*
28 *But that same slave, as he went out, came upon one of his fellow slaves who owed him a hundred denarii; and seizing him by the throat, he said, 'Pay what you owe.'*
29 *Then his fellow slave fell down and pleaded with him, 'Have patience with me, and I will pay you.'*

*[30]But he refused; then he went and threw him into prison
until he would pay the debt.*
*[31]When his fellow slaves saw what had happened, they were
greatly distressed, and they went and reported to their lord
all that had taken place.*
*[32]Then his lord summoned him and said to him, 'You wicked
slave! I forgave you all that debt because you pleaded with
me.*
*[33]Should you not have had mercy on your fellow slave, as I
had mercy on you?'*
*[34]And in anger his lord handed him over to be tortured until
he would pay his entire debt.*
*[35]So my heavenly Father will also do to every one of you, if
you do not forgive your brother or sister from your heart."*

Promptly at eight-thirty the next morning, the judge gaveled the court in session. Immediately, he looked over at the defense team about which the entire country was talking, and said, "Mr. Morrow, you may call your first witness."

"I have no witnesses to present," he stated, shocking the judge such that he was speechless for a long time. To compose himself, he called a recess after only being in session not more than sixty seconds. The media were aghast, the plaintiff's super team was confounded and the viewing audience everywhere sat in disbelief.

About fifteen minutes later, the judge reappeared. After he was seated he advised the court that at eight-thirty the next morning, each party would be given time to present its final comments to the jury.

Regular programming was being interrupted during this day to advise the viewing audience that all testimony in the trial of University Athletic Directors v. Bacon College, et al, had been presented to the jury. It was announced that the close came suddenly and without warning, because the defense presented no witnesses. This was only one more bizarre incident in what some called a comedy of errors by Bacon College.

Meanwhile, the soccer team prepared to host Steeleman College in an afternoon game. Because the girls had learned to cope with the rude behavior of its opponent, they continued to be their warm and courteous selves and were just impervious, when they were snubbed by the Steeleman team.

The college really needed this game to get their minds off the court case in which it was involved. The cheering and playfulness provided an environment like old times, and the score of five to one reminded the capacity crowd that they had a special team. Some though were ruminating about the whole issue of alleged cheating on the college entrance tests. "Would this make the whole team ineligible if they are found guilty, and that is what appears will happen?" many thought, as they emptied the soccer stadium after the game.

During the previous evening, the judge sought the advice of many of his judicial friends, several of whom that had been enrolled in the same jurisprudence as he, but none could relate to him a similar situation in their experience. This was new ground for him.

The next morning the judge said, "The plaintiff will now make its final comments to the jury."

"Standing with legal pad in hand, the prosecutor began a talk that lasted far into the morning, theorizing how Bacon College had cheated to get these poor country girls eligible to participate in collegiate basketball. "Without a shadow of doubt," he loudly stated, "the pressure was on the president of Bacon College, the board of directors of Bacon College and certainly on the newly employed coach who was to have a winning team. They were well into their program before they realized that high school students just couldn't enroll in college and begin to play sports. They were really shocked to discover that their recruits for sports had to do something else—pass a college entrance test.

"It was the eleventh hour so the coach resorted to other tactics, because she knew enough about testing to realize that the demographics were not in her favor. At this point one might say that the deck was stacked against her. Along the way she had become alarmed that all other colleges and universities had abruptly stopped recruiting the girls from the Hollow. She knew why, but because she had not recruited other students and had put all of her eggs in one basket, getting these girls was all that mattered now.

"With the constant and continuous pressure made to bear on the coach by the college officials, the coach looked in another direction to solve her problem. In the office of the principal often, she discovered the college entrance test booklets, and used them to tutor her new recruits in her athletic program. As you know, the girls defied all laws of probability and statistics in their college entrance scoring. Their scores were far superior from those of other students, and when compared to other athletes around the country in other colleges and universities, their scores were at least one standard deviation above them.

"You have heard witness after witness relate their stories about this situation such that guilt is the only verdict one could ever imagine in this case."

The prosecutor continued for considerable time rehashing the comments by the various witnesses, and from time to time alluding to the bizarre behavior of the defense. At one point he told the jury that the defense failed to call its witnesses, because it did not want any self-incriminating evidence to add to the scorching evidence presented by his team.

After a very long and eloquent discourse he finally brought closure to his remarks. At this juncture the judge called a recess, so Josh, Dr. Damond and Lottie Burkhouser sat in an area removed from anyone else.

"Shall we pray," Josh said, as the three held hands with heads bowed. "Lord, we ask for your divine guidance as we make comments not only heard here but around our country. Please forgive those who have transgressed against us, and help us to continue to show our special love to our fellow man. Your words on the cross are just as applicable today in this huge courtroom. Thank you for your Holy Spirit that hovers over us all the while. Amen."

"Thank you for your prayer," Dr. Damond said.

"Are you ready, Josh?" Lottie asked, as though she knew that whatever was going to be stated would be pure as wind blown snow. "Thank you for letting me sit on your team. Regardless of the outcome of this case, Bacon College will be the big winner."

Bringing the court back in session, it was Josh's turn to make comments to the jury. "We are ready for you to make your final comments to the jury," the judge said, not really knowing what to expect.

Without a single note or legal pad Josh stood in the center of the courtroom, and said, "Thank you so much for permitting me to speak to the court," he stated, with the entire coliseum so quiet one could hear a pin drop. "Before I make my comments, would you please bow with me for prayer?" Bowing and with all others following his lead including the judge, he said, "May the precepts taught by our Lord and Savior, Jesus Christ, guide our thinking and our actions as He commanded that we love the Lord with all our heart, mind and soul and our neighbor as ourselves. Amen."

The television rating for this part of the court proceedings was the highest ever recorded. Josh continued, but the tears had begun to roll down the cheeks of many as this poorly dressed preacher from the mountains began his comments. "I am so happy to be here with you to say a few words that might help you formulate your decision regarding this conflict that has emerged. Bacon College and its girls are most apologetic for whatever difficulties they have caused others in the sports' world.

"I have always been interested in sports so I know how you feel. Teams should do their best to win, because that's the reason for having contests of all kinds in the first place. Bacon always strives to do its best.

"You all have a difficult job here now," he said looking right at the jury with a little smile on his face, "but I want to help you in that matter. I know what you are thinking as I stand before you that there is no way Bacon College is innocent of these charges, because of all the evidence so professionally presented by the outstanding group of attorneys. I know you have had sympathy for Bacon College, because it first had only me and later added a second to the team. Then when there was not even a shred of cross examining, you almost washed your hands of the whole defense team.

"It is your job to examine the evidence presented in this court and decide accordingly. But let me look at the huge dilemma with which the whole country and you are dealing. If you find Bacon College guilty of the charges of the athletic directors based on the evidence, most people will agree with your verdict. But suppose you declared that Bacon College is innocent of all charges, what would that mean?

"Of course, some would agree with this verdict. but most would not. What I am saying to you is that any verdict in the minds of many, even in the best of court proceedings, is somewhat absent of truth. Some will assess your verdict as being true and others will see it otherwise. Life is somewhat like this, and we have learned to make decisions that are not purely true. How can truth be discovered in our daily lives is a broader issue not to be examined further today? I want to help you all determine truth in this case that has been conducted by this court over the last several days.

"I realize that your minds are made up regarding Bacon College's guilt or innocence which might reveal to us that searching deeper for truth, which only comes from our

Lord, will take us far in relating with heavenly love for our neighbors. Because we at Bacon College want truth to prevail in this case so badly, we are asking you, the court, to set aside a time to do something possibly in this courtroom.

"The defense, Bacon College and its board of directors, request that to remove even a shadow of doubt of wrongdoing of this group that all the athletes of Bacon College be retested utilizing whatever college entrance test the court selects. And further, it recommends that the testing be done publicly so under the scrutiny of the whole country."

Objections from the athletic directors' team of lawyers were loud and for a brief period the judge had difficulty maintaining order. Soon though, having added another bizarre twist to an already unique trial, the judge finally got the lawyers to stop hollering their objection to the most unusual request.

Not knowing how to respond, the judge adjourned the court until the next morning when he would rule on the request. It was truly a night to remember. The evening television programs dealing with the strange turn of events in Groveville filled the screens in most of the households around the country. Most were applauding the defense for offering this solution to the dilemma that had spellbound the viewers over the past several days. "How could the judge refuse this unusual request which would bring an end to speculation of wrongdoing by Bacon College?" a seasoned trial lawyer added on a major television network. "For me, admission is good for the soul, as I have observed over the past several years how our courtroom proceedings have become more circus like and so much less civil. Just think about this case which all of us in the legal community would applaud mightily. It's an example of what is happening to our system of justice.

"I hate to say it but greed has overwhelmed all of us, and with my peers and me continuing to badger society's guidelines, our behavior is going to get much worse. Every part of our society is becoming a green field ready for harvest by our attorneys. Let's take a brief trip down memory lane regarding lawsuits. Do you remember the tobacco lawsuits? Do you remember the hot coffee suit? Do you remember the restaurant service lawsuit? Do you remember the numerous school lawsuits? Do you remember the university enrollment policy lawsuits? Do you remember the malpractice lawsuits against doctors? Do you remember employee lawsuits against employers? Do you remember discrimination lawsuits?

"Lawyers are just waiting to be a part of some lucrative lawsuit. In this case Athletic Directors v. Bacon College, et al, our so called best lawyers in the country joined the prosecution team to outshine in court over this small Christian college that was defended by a country preacher with no law training whatsoever. Josh Morrow just changed the landscape of the judicial system. Now instead of speculation and theories presented in Hollywood style in our courts, we might consider discovering the truth without so much acting and distortion.

"Does the judge have an option regarding the request by Mr. Morrow that the girls retake the college entrance examination? He certainly has none. But look what is happening on many of our television networks as the legal team of the athletic directors is trying to convince in trial lawyer fashion that the jury should decide guilt or innocence. But look what the little defense preacher said, 'In conflicts of this kind, the most important thing is to discover the truth, whenever possible.' In this case he has presented a way to discover truth without leaving any doubt whatsoever.

"If our athletic directors and their legal team believed that what they presented to the court that the Bacon girls cheated, they should be pleased that the tests would be given to them again. They should be happy, because now they would have their point proved, and there would not ever be any doubt."

Promptly, at eight-thirty the next morning the judge entered the courtroom, sat down and looked over the capacity crowd before gaveling the court in session for this historic day. With the athletic directors' legal team almost yelling "Your honor" many times, the judge called a sheriff's deputy who immediately left the courtroom. In less than a minute he returned escorting an older man with gray hair wearing a dark three-piece suit.

After he was sworn in he took a seat in the witness box. "Please state your name and your profession," the judge stated.

"My name is Edgar Gabriel and I am the chief executive officer of ABC Testing Service," he answered.

"Thank you for coming to Groveville with such a short notice," the judge said. "I know you have been keeping up with the trial here regarding allegations of wrongdoing concerning one of the Division I athletic teams. The defense has requested that with the cloud of doubt surrounding the whole situation regarding the college entrance examination that all of Bacon College's scholarship athletes be retested. Would you please give us your opinion on this matter?"

"I would be glad to do this," he responded. "I can say without any hesitation that the administration of a second test to the athletes would remove all doubt. And to assist all who are judging this situation and don't understand how our testing service protects the integrity of its test, let me say that we have just developed the most recent version of the college entrance examination that has not been used before. This one includes a writing section, something we have not ever used before?"

"Are you saying to us that the administration of this new version of the test to these athletes will prove without a shadow of a doubt the truth in this matter?" the judge asked.

"It will prove guilt or innocence absolutely," he emphatically stated. "If the athletes got no help on the previous college entrance examination, their scores will be almost the same as on the previous test. If they wrongfully received assistance on the previous test, their scores will reflect that, also."

"You may step down," the judge said. Ignoring the loud pleas from the athletic directors' contingent of trial lawyers, he advised the court. "Two days from this date at eight-thirty in the morning all the scholarship athletes from Bacon College will appear in this courtroom to be administered the college entrance examination under the direction of officials of the ABC Testing Service. The court is now adjourned until then."

Because the soccer team was traveling for a two-game road trip, they did not hear of the judge's decision until they arrived at Talleytown University in southern Louisiana. As soon as they arrived at their motel, Coach Anna met with the group. "Following our second game in Texas, we are going to travel to Groveville, Colorado to retake the college entrance examination," she advised. "I know you all will be glad to put this dark situation behind so that everyone will know that we didn't cheat on anything. At the game this evening be prepared to take a lot of abuse, because I'm sure there will be those wanting to taunt you, because you are winning."

Because the environment was so loud and ugly, Coach Anna walked directly to the bench with the assistance of a state trooper. The officials didn't seem to be concerned that several student groups came near the Bacon bench to display something very derisive or to unroll a large banner with demeaning messages. One group came out holding plastic milk jugs painted like cookie jars with a cardboard hand sticking in the jar, yelling, "This is what you look like when you get your hand caught in a cookie jar."

Another group with painted faces carried a banner that read, "Which one of the following best describes your team? a. You are liars; b. You are thieves; c. You are cheaters; d. All of the above."

Given a cold shoulder by Talleytown, the team huddled for prayer, rendered so compassionately by Esther. On the field they went to get in place for the start of the game when several students ran on the field and handed each Bacon girl a sheet that was described as cheat notes. Coach Anna and Hanna ran onto the field to collect the papers.

In spite of the efforts of the spectators Bacon handily won the game six to one. Their second game on this road trip was very similar to the first with the Bacon team of girls winning this one seven to two before a rude and raucous crowd of spectators.

All of the Bacon girls met in the crowded, huge parking lot of the coliseum the next morning with Josh, Dr. Damond, Bob Waters and the other board of directors, parents of the girls, and Maudie. Arrangements had been made and expenses paid by the benevolent person. It was a touching scene as the parents stood hugging their daughters. James was standing near Josh, Charlene and Maggie holding Esther with one hand and Coach Anna with the other. With cameras and media encircling the group of country folks from the mountains of southwest Virginia, Josh spoke, "God has blessed us all mightily and gives us all windows of opportunity to express truth in our daily lives. Our system of justice provides this opportunity for us to clear up this misunderstanding.

"Please bow with me as I pray. Our God who made the heavens and the earth including the beautiful mountains here in a state we all would have not seen had it not been for your special blessings. We thank you for giving all of us the wherewithal of wisdom to solve our conflicts in a way pleasing in your sight. We ask for Your divine guidance over our athletes as they retake this college entrance examination. Amen."

The contingent of media had increased immensely such that the number of state troopers on hand was beefed up to protect the Bacon group, as they moved through the parking lot followed by that huge number of folks. Overhead two helicopters and a blimp provided shots from above to those watching on every major channel.

The double doors of the main entrance of the municipal coliseum were opened, and Dr. John Damond came walking in with pride shown all over his face leading his Bacon group. A few steps in the building, the parents separated from their children, and Josh led the girls to the main floor where there were student desks placed in the center. Simultaneously, the judge came to take his seat on the bench to oversee this historical moment that would change jurisprudence after this day. The jury was already seated not really knowing their status in the proceedings from this point.

"I now call this court in session," the judge stated. "At this time Mr. Gabriel will begin the administration of the college entrance examination to all the scholarship athletes of Bacon College."

The testing continued until lunch when food was brought in for the girls, testing service officials, jury and the judge's staff. The testing was completed at three when all the answer sheets were passed to the proctors.

"The court will adjourn until eighth-thirty tomorrow morning, at which time the results of the test will be reported," the judge announced.

During that evening Maudie took everyone out to eat in a secluded place so they could have privacy away from the court proceedings. She said that she had been saving her money over the last several months just for a special occasion such as this.

In the courtroom the next morning with the girls sitting with their parents, the judge announced that the court was in session. A deputy sheriff brought Edgar Gabriel with his brief case of testing data. "Do you have the results of the administration of the college entrance test by the Bacon College students?"

"Yes, I do," he answered.

"Would you tell the court your results?" the judge asked.

"Two of the girls scored in the ninety-ninth percentile, seven in the top ninetieth percentile, and all except three scored at or above the seventieth percentile," he replied. "These three were at the sixtieth percentile level. For the writing all did outstanding except four, and they fell in the 'good' category. By the way one of the girls did an exceptional job on the writing assignment."

"Did they meet the requirements of the ACUWAA?" the judge asked.

"They all far exceeded the standards set forth by the American Colleges and Universities Women's Athletic Association," he answered. "I might add that based on my long experience in testing, these young ladies are very exceptional student athletes."

With this new information the jury was asked to meet to render its verdict. Having the shortest jury deliberation one could ever remember, the jury foreman announced, "Not guilty."